The Priority Unit

Center Point
Large Print

The PRIORITY UNIT

MAINE JUSTICE
• BOOK 1 •

SUSAN PAGE DAVIS

CENTER POINT LARGE PRINT
THORNDIKE, MAINE

This Center Point Large Print edition
is published in the year 2017 by arrangement with
the author.

The text of this Large Print edition is unabridged.
In other aspects, this book may vary
from the original edition.
Printed in the United States of America
on permanent paper.
Set in 16-point Times New Roman type.

ISBN: 978-1-68324-478-3

Library of Congress Cataloging-in-Publication Data

Names: Davis, Susan Page, author.
Title: The priority unit / Susan Page Davis.
Description: Center Point Large Print edition. | Thorndike, Maine :
Center Point Large Print, 2017. | Series: Maine justice series ; book 1
Identifiers: LCCN 2017019185 | ISBN 9781683244783
(hardcover : alk. paper)
Subjects: LCSH: Large type books. | GSAFD: Mystery fiction.
Classification: LCC PS3604.A976 P75 2017 | DDC 813/.6—dc23
LC record available at https://lccn.loc.gov/2017019185

The Priority Unit

Prologue

"Chris? Talk to me." Detective Harvey Larson edged along the brick wall of the rundown ranch house, toward the back door. He had sudden misgivings about going in to bring in a small-time drug dealer. Getting the warrant and backup had taken too long. What if the dealer had gotten word that an informant had tipped them off?

"Yeah?" came Chris's quiet voice over the shoulder mic.

Harvey tried the doorknob. The door opened at his touch. He shot a glance at Jim Haines, the tactical officer behind him.

"The back door's unlocked," he said for Chris's benefit.

"Go," Chris said.

Too late now to back out. Harvey nudged the door open a few inches. Why wasn't Chris Towne ringing the front doorbell?

Bad vibes came as Harvey and Jim stepped inside a cramped utility room, pistols ready.

Light streaked in from the kitchen beyond. The doorbell rang, and footsteps sounded.

He'd only taken one stride toward the kitchen when a burst of gunfire exploded. Harvey flattened himself against the wall by the clothes dryer and listened. Jim crouched behind it.

Harvey stifled his cry to Chris. Was he okay?

Silence. Then something moved in the next room, and footsteps retreated.

Jim nodded to him. Harvey whipped around the corner. The kitchen was clear. He dashed to the next doorway.

Chris lay sprawled in the front entry. The door behind him stood wide open. The second backup man huddled on the steps, holding his stomach.

Harvey reached for his mic. "Officers down. Send an ambulance." The dispatcher tracking them already knew their location.

He scanned the front walk and driveway. Whoever had been in the house was gone. He checked the other rooms. Nothing. Not more than thirty seconds had passed when he knelt by his partner, but he knew it was too late.

Jim Haines was at his partner's side on the steps, and Harvey heard the other man's voice. That guy would make it.

Harvey sat down on the floor against the wall and hauled Chris's head and shoulders onto his lap, waiting for the ambulance that was already too late. What would he tell Chris's wife, Marcia?

Only that morning, Chris had given him a pep talk. Harvey's marriage was falling apart. He and Carrie fought constantly. When his shift ended yesterday, all Harvey wanted to do was go home and unwind. Instead, his wife gave him grief about the crummy apartment that was all they could afford on his salary and then ranted about the number of times he pulled night duty.

"Things are going pretty good at work, though, right?" Chris had said. "In January you'll get a raise. That will keep Carrie happy for a while."

Harvey leaned back against the wall. There would be no more pep talks. He'd thought they could handle this, but they should have waited, insisted on more backup. This couldn't have gone worse.

A siren sounded in the distance, reminding him this was all his fault. How could he tell that to Marcia?

Harvey didn't leave the police station until 2 a.m. He drove home under orders to get some rest and report to the chief at nine o'clock. He trudged up the stairs, dreading going into their apartment. Carrie would either be waiting up to scream at him for being late again, or she would be out with her friends partying. He almost preferred the latter, if that would mean he could take a shower, wash Chris's blood off him, and try to sleep.

Fighting with Carrie was the last thing he wanted to do. Maybe the sight of his bloody clothes would shock her into silence.

Carrie had long since decided her husband was not a social asset. When he did have weekend nights off, Harvey was too exhausted to socialize with people he didn't like. Carrie's friends didn't like him, either. They made snide comments about hanging out with a cop, about his presence putting a damper on their fun.

He took out his keys and braced himself as he turned the lock. It was a Friday night. Chances were that if Carrie was home, she would be three parts drunk.

The door opened upon silence and darkness. He flipped the kitchen light switch and shut the door. After one step, he stopped. The kitchen table was gone. A burglary? Or just Carrie rearranging furniture? He scanned the room.

Aside from a few dirty dishes in the sink, the kitchen counter was bare. That was odd. No coffeemaker. No toaster. The only thing left was the stupid Irish cop cookie jar that Carrie's aunt had thought made a quaint shower gift eight years ago.

But Carrie wasn't one to clean the kitchen that thoroughly. He opened a cupboard. The dishes were gone.

A strange feeling radiated from his chest. Not the adrenaline rush he'd had when he realized that he and Chris had been set up tonight. It was a sick, achy certainty that the inevitable had happened.

He walked to the living room doorway and flipped another light switch. The room was bare except for the scarred maple coffee table and several piles of books, his books. She had dumped out on the carpet.

"Great. Just great." He felt like driving his fist through the wall.

One more room, but he knew what was coming. The bedroom looked bigger with only the queen-sized bed in it. No dressers. No lamps. He threw open the closet doors. His dress uniform and civilian clothes hung neatly on his third of the closet rod. Carrie's two thirds was empty.

He studied the closet for a long moment, then pulled off his jacket and started to hang it up. He stared at the blotches on it. Could the cleaners get the blood out? He hung it on Carrie's side, where it wouldn't touch anything else and closed the door.

He unbuckled his shoulder holster and stood for a moment with it in his hands. He always put it on his dresser, but the dresser was gone. Wasn't one dresser enough for her?

He swore and laid the holster down on the carpet.

Chapter 1

Ten years later

"So, your computer programmer went missing yesterday . . . what time?" Harvey stood near the office doorway, looking around carefully. His partner, Eddie Thibodeau, stood to one side, waiting patiently, his gaze darting about the office.

"I saw him around nine or so yesterday morning." Bart Owen sat down behind his gleaming walnut desk. "I asked him to come in here to discuss the project he was working on. Then I went looking for him after lunch, but he wasn't at his desk."

"And no one here at Coastal saw him for the rest of the day?" Harvey asked, fishing a small notebook and a ballpoint pen from his shirt pocket.

"That's right. I asked a few people right away—my partners, of course, and the employees who work near him, but . . ." Owen let it trail off with a shrug. "Seems no one saw him after noon."

"His car wasn't in the parking lot?"

"I didn't check. I just assumed he'd left in his car for lunch."

Harvey glanced at his notebook. "You called it in last night."

Owen cleared his throat. "Yes. At first I figured he must have had a call from home and left early. You know, kid fell off his bike or something."

Harvey nodded.

Owen sank back in his chair. "His wife called me at home about seven-thirty. Wanted to know where Nick was. Shocked me, I'll tell you. I came back here just to be sure he hadn't come back to the office, but there was no sign of him."

"Eddie, check Dunham's voice mail."

"We have access to his company-issued phone and laptop," Owen said. "He had left the laptop on his desk, and we couldn't get a location on his phone."

"Did he have a personal phone as well?"

"Probably. Most people do."

"Eddie, get the laptop."

Detective Thibodeau nodded and left the room.

"And you called the police station from here last night?" Harvey asked.

Owen ran a nervous hand through the fringe of brown hair at the back of his head. "I called Lisa Dunham back first. Tried not to panic her, but I suggested we ought to call the cops, just get it on record, in case something had happened. But they told me they couldn't do anything until Nick had been missing twenty-four hours."

Harvey nodded. "That's standard with adults, unless there's reason to think it's an emergency."

Owen straightened, a belligerent set to his jaw.

"Well, I figured this morning was time enough. Lisa's frantic. No sign of Nick all night, and that's not normal. So I called again as soon as I got here."

"You're right, sir, it's not normal for an adult to disappear like that. We'll take a look around. How many employees do you have?"

"We have twenty people working on software. Designers, programmers, editors. The three of us partners. There's an in-house accountant. Oh, and a couple of security guards. It's a very competitive business."

Harvey scribbled furiously in his notebook.

Owen raised one eyebrow. "So, you think something's happened to Nick?"

"Can't say yet, sir. When you returned to the office last night, was there anyone else here?"

"No. The parking lot was empty."

"No custodians?"

"Not last night. They come in Tuesdays and Fridays."

Harvey wrote it down. "We'll be taking a close look at Mr. Dunham's work station. Could you please send the employee who saw him last to me there?"

"Certainly." Owen headed for the hallway, his step more confident now that he'd been given something to do.

Harvey went out to the large workroom where the Coastal Technology employees worked, typing on keyboards, or talking on the phone or texting. The large room was open, and a gourmet coffee bar drew his eye. A couple of comfortable seating areas included sofas and recliners. A young man was tapping away on his smartphone while walking on a treadmill in one corner. Not like any office Harvey had ever worked in.

Several people glanced up at him uneasily as he walked past them. Eddie was bent over a desk in the far corner of the room. A choice spot, Harvey guessed. He'd fought for the corner position in the Priority Unit's office at the police station, so he'd be out of traffic, in a quiet, inconspicuous place where he could work undisturbed.

"Eddie, treat this room like a crime scene. Tape off this work station and get a couple of techs in to go over it. Find out if they have the employees' fingerprints on record. I'll get a list of clients and other people who've worked with Dunham this week."

Eddie warily eyed the computer equipment. Everything was spanking new. "Right. We don't generally pull missing persons, Harv."

Harvey took a pair of latex gloves from a pocket, pulled them on, and opened the top drawer of the desk. "Ace programmer disappears from an up-and-coming computer company. His car's missing, too. The captain thought it was significant."

"Dunham's not the first white collar worker who decided to bail on his family." Eddie pulled out his cell phone as Harvey surveyed the contents of the desk drawer.

He counted at least six flash drives among the office supplies and lifted a black zippered case from the drawer. "Without his blood test kit?"

Eddie's eyes flared. "This guy's diabetic?"

Harvey opened the case and checked inside to be sure. "I'd say so."

Eddie whistled.

Harvey walked around the desk, scrutinizing the floor and electronic equipment. "Ask Mike to have someone check all the hospitals for diabetic emergencies. And I think we'd better get over and see Nick Dunham's wife right away. Get Pete and Arnie over here to question employees. Set up the techs for fingerprinting, then we'll go see Mrs. Dunham."

Eddie nodded, his dark eyes gleaming with interest now, and began making his calls as Harvey went to the men's washroom. It was spotless, and he opened the cabinet under the sink, then the one above. He went back out into the workroom.

"Techs will be here in ten minutes," Eddie said.

"Great. I'll bag the laptop, but Mr. Owen gave me the impression I'll only see what they want me to see. He did tell me what Dunham was working on yesterday."

"They can keep you out of a computer?" Eddie asked.

"Apparently. At least, they think they can."

"Excuse me."

Harvey turned around. A young woman was standing near the corner of Dunham's desk.

"May I help you?" Harvey smiled involuntarily. Her long golden braid gave her a wholesome, unspoiled appearance. She wore no makeup to distract from her flawless complexion, and her gray eyes held a mixture of apprehension and curiosity. She was the sort of girl he'd expect to sell him a dozen ears of corn at a farm stand.

"Mr. Owen told me to see you. I'm Jennifer Wainthrop." She stepped cautiously forward, darting a swift glance toward Eddie, then looking back to Harvey.

She wore a deep blue skirt and a lighter blue blouse—silk, if he wasn't mistaken. Most women wore pants to the office these days, and her choice of a skirt surprised him. The executive image had changed a lot over the years, and apparently Coastal Technology of Maine favored business casual—upscale, but casual. Harvey took in the simple neatness of her hair, pulled back from her temples into the thick braid.

He squelched a flash of annoyance. Her appearance was irrelevant to the case, and he didn't want the distraction. He was known in the unit and the entire police department as a man who stuck to a case doggedly until it was closed, but never got involved. It had become almost a matter of pride that he never let his work intrude in his personal life. Not that he had much of a personal life anymore.

"It's best if you don't touch anything here, ma'am," he said easily, but he found the intensity in her eyes drawing him a step closer. "Is there another room where we could talk?"

"The conference room, down the hall." She turned toward the door, and her braid swung below her waist, against the back of her shirt.

"Eddie, come find me in the conference room when you're done here."

"Right." Eddie stared after the girl, his eyes reflecting his appreciation.

Harvey scowled at him but said nothing. He'd noticed her understated beauty himself, and he'd sworn off women years ago.

Her skirt swished about her calves as she led him down the hallway, and he made himself look away from her trim ankles. He had no business looking at a witness as a woman.

And she was definitely a woman, he decided as she turned to face him in the software firm's conference room, not the girl his brain had registered as a first impression.

Now that he'd passed forty, they all looked so young. She was probably a computer whiz the company had hired fresh out of college. He wondered how old she was, and caught himself up short. What did it matter, anyway? She was too young for him, even if he were looking for companionship, which he wasn't.

"Ms. Winthrop. I'm Detective Larson." He extended his hand, hoping his tone conveyed nothing but proficiency.

"Wainthrop," she corrected gently.

He swallowed. He rarely made mistakes with names, and instantly he felt less competent.

"Ms. Wainthrop. I'm sorry."

She shrugged slightly and clasped his hand for an instant. The warmth of her palm startled him. He glanced around at the functional room trying to quickly subdue the adrenaline and the slight guilt that eroded his confidence. A long oak table was flanked by a dozen matching, leather-covered swivel chairs. The carpet was thicker than his mattress, and the colorful abstracts on the walls probably cost a bundle. Definitely high end. He pictured the stark interview room in his unit's office at the police station on Middle Street. Its low-budget, Early Municipal decor compared unfavorably to this.

He took a deep breath and turned back to face the witness.

"Would you like to sit down?" Jennifer asked. She felt a quiet authority radiating from the detective. He wore it as easily as he did his comfortably shabby jacket. His outdated brown-and-navy striped tie was loosened at the neck of his pale blue cotton shirt. His vivid blue eyes didn't miss a thing, she was certain.

"Yes, thank you."

He sat at the end of the long table where the partners and software designers presented new concepts to their clients. Jennifer pulled out a chair and sat at the side of the table.

She had expected a barrage of questions, but he didn't seem in a hurry to interview her. As the seconds ticked by, her apprehension grew.

"Ms. Wainthrop."

She nodded, a tiny acknowledgment that he'd gotten her name right. His face softened then, the fine lines at the corners of his eyes deepening into creases that suggested he smiled a lot. She felt suddenly that she could trust him.

The gleaming badge clipped to his breast pocket drew her eye, and she sensed that, for Larson, upholding the law was a lifelong passion. She wasn't so sure about his handsome young partner, with the snapping dark eyes and black jeans. He was too good looking for a cop, but this one she could feel comfortable with. Detective Larson had a solid steadiness that was calming. She would do anything she could to help him find Nick Dunham.

• • •

Harvey opened his pocket notebook. "Mr. Owen told us that, as far as he knows, you were the last one to see Mr. Dunham yesterday."

Her eyes widened in dismay. "Oh, I hope not. He's been gone that long?"

"It's all right, Ms. Wainthrop. We don't know yet that anything is wrong. Just tell me how he was when you saw him yesterday."

She swallowed and took a deep breath, her eyes focusing somewhere over his right shoulder. "Nick was fine when I saw him. My desk is next to his. We usually say hello in the morning." She glanced at him as though suddenly remembering something different about yesterday. "He told me before lunch that he was working on a special assignment."

Harvey nodded. "I believe Mr. Owen was supervising Nick Dunham's project."

"Probably."

"Where did you see Mr. Dunham?"

"Near my desk. I'd been in to Jack—um, Mr. Rainey's office for a minute, to check on something about the retailing program I was assigned to, and when I came out, Nick was getting ready to go out for lunch. He stopped and talked to me, just for a minute."

The detective said nothing. It was his usual ploy to keep witnesses talking without steering their account of events, but he could well imagine

Nick Dunham stopping to have a word with this beauty.

"He asked if I had plans for lunch," she said uncertainly. "Is this what you want to hear?"

"Yes. Please continue."

"Well, he said he would bring back something for me if I wanted, and I said thanks, but Jane Morrow and I were going out to eat together." She looked at him expectantly.

"You and Nick Dunham are friends?"

"Yes. Well, sort of. We've worked together for a year or so. He's very bright. Friendly, but not outgoing."

"Pardon my asking, but is there anything personal between you?"

"You mean—no. He's—Nick is married."

Harvey was used to offending people with his questions, but he was sorry it was necessary. She seemed like a decent, conservative girl, but he needed to hear it in her own words.

"So, you didn't want the relationship to become closer?"

She looked down again. "I'm not sure what you're getting at. We're friends, but not close friends. The nature of our work doesn't let us socialize much. All of us speak to each other, but it's very superficial, I'm afraid."

Harvey studied her face. Her anxiety seemed to be rising. Maybe there was more to it. Maybe Dunham had made a pass at her, and she was uncomfortable with that. Or maybe she really liked the guy, but didn't want to cause problems in his home life or at work. "So what happened then?"

"He went out for lunch, and I kept working until quarter past twelve. When Jane was ready, we left together. I didn't see Nick after lunch. I don't think he was even here when we came back, but I'm not positive. I wasn't looking for him. I'm sorry."

"No need to apologize. We just need to know what he was doing up until the time he disappeared."

She winced at that. "Do you think he's in trouble? An accident, maybe?"

"Was Mr. Dunham in good health?" Harvey asked, skipping over her questions without compunction. It was his job to gain information, not give it, and he'd learned over the years to inspire trust while keeping his own counsel.

"Well, he was diabetic. It came up at the Christmas party, I think. He took his coffee black, and I don't remember him eating many sweets. Other than the diabetes, though, I'd say he was in pretty good shape."

Harvey nodded. "Is there anything else you can tell me about yesterday? Anything unusual?"

"I . . . don't think so."

He cast about for another question he could ask her. He knew he should be at Dunham's house now, questioning his wife, but for some reason he didn't want to bring this interview to an end. A rogue thought entered his mind. He could ask to see her driver's license and check her birth date. She would believe him if he told her it was standard procedure to check her ID.

No, Eddie might do that, but Harvey wasn't given to bending the rules so he could check out women. Just realizing he had thought of it appalled him. He glanced down at his left hand. The gold circle on his ring finger taunted him.

He stuck with procedure. She had made it clear that she didn't date married men. The strong conviction that she was sincere buttressed his resolve to keep his own vow, even though no one else in the world would care. It also heightened his admiration for her.

He did take her phone number, in case the police department needed to contact her again outside office hours and forced himself not to think about the way the morning sun streaming through the window illuminated her deep gold hair where it was pulled back sleekly at her temple.

"How are the partners, as bosses go?" He watched her eyes.

There was no sign of uneasiness as she answered. "They're all right. They like to maintain a little distance, and they don't mix with the rest of us outside work, but they usually treat us fairly."

"Is there a union?"

"No, we negotiate our contracts individually."

"Are you satisfied with yours?"

"Yes."

Harvey nodded. He was stalling, and he knew it. Time to end this before he made a fool of himself. She was smart enough to figure it out if he stepped over the line of propriety. And if she knew what he was trying not to think at this moment, her trust and cooperation would evaporate in a hurry.

"I guess that's about it, Ms. Wainthrop. If we need to contact you again, I'll give you a call."

Eddie breezed in from the hallway, and Harvey resolutely pushed his chair back and stood.

"Thanks for your help."

"I hope you find him soon," she said.

Eddie's brilliant smile was instantaneous. "That's what we're here for."

She nodded at Harvey and left the room briskly, avoiding Eddie's gaze.

"What did I say?" Eddie asked, looking after her.

"Nothing. She's just taking this very seriously. He's her friend, and she was the last one to see him."

"She can't be a day over twenty." Eddie

watched her out of sight and turned back to find Harvey scowling. "What?"

"Twenty-three," Harvey muttered. "At least."

"No way."

"Come on. Are Pete and Arnie on the way?" Harvey shoved his notebook into his pocket and headed for the exit.

"They'll meet us in the parking lot." As they walked down the hallway, Eddie gave him a summary of his findings at Dunham's desk. They stepped out into the cool March sunlight, and Eddie pulled on his worn leather jacket. "And, Harv, I found a vial of insulin in one of the drawers."

"So, he left his insulin, too."

Eddie shrugged. "Might of had more that he took with him." He waited, and Harvey knew he was watching him. "What's eating you, Harv?"

"Nothing." Harvey walked toward his fifteen-year-old green Ford sedan and leaned on the hood, watching the street for Arnie Fowler's SUV or Pete Bearse's car.

"Hey, she's a pretty girl," Eddie persisted.

"Woman."

"Yeah, woman."

Eddie was smiling, and Harvey turned away, his feelings all askew. He knew Eddie had never seen him unnerved by a female before. What was it about Jennifer Wainthrop that had thrown him such a curve?

"I wonder if she's single." Eddie stared innocently toward the street.

Harvey said nothing.

"We might need to go back and question her again, after we see the wife."

"This is business, Ed." Harvey berated himself for even responding to Eddie's baiting. He glanced at him. As he'd suspected, Eddie found this extremely amusing.

As if she'd like anything about me, Harvey thought. Eddie, with his charm and his Gallic good looks, was the one the girls always threw themselves at. Besides, he was *not* in the market.

"There's Pete's car." Eddie nodded toward the street, and Harvey was glad to put the subject of Jennifer Wainthrop behind him.

Jennifer kept at her work all afternoon, but was aware each time a stranger passed through the office. In the large room, more than a dozen programmers and designers sat at their computer stations, working or taking a break when they pleased. The bosses were big on freedom and creativity. The editors worked at the far end of the room, closer to the hallway that led to the partners' offices.

Two new detectives came around, questioning each worker. She told them she had already been interviewed by Detective Larson, but repeated her story for the benefit of the newcomers, Bearse and Fowler. Fowler was older, and she guessed he was near retirement. He had an engaging manner and seemed to be the one questioning most of the female employees.

Bearse, prematurely balding and somber, seemed more efficient, asking a few brisk questions, scribbling his notes, and moving on to the next worker, but she had to wonder if Fowler didn't glean more information.

One of the program designers, Audra, laughed at a remark from Detective Fowler, and Jennifer caught a startled glance from Jane, at the next desk. Audra was not known for her good nature and could cut a man down to size in seconds if he called her a "gal," but after Arnie Fowler left, she kept the distracted air he'd inspired for some time.

It was nearly three o'clock before one of the partners, Ron Channing, came into the workroom and addressed them all in a strained voice, striving to reassure them that the investigation into Nick's absence was progressing, and that Coastal Technology would carry on business as usual. Channing was stern-featured and broody. The company morale might have benefited more if Mr. Owen had been the one to speak to them.

Dylan Pressey, one of the software designers, asked if the police had any leads.

"We haven't heard anything from the investigating officer yet," Channing admitted, "but I'm confident we'll learn soon that Nick is fine. I'm inclined to think he was called away suddenly and forgot to inform us, that's all."

Right. Jennifer wasn't usually cynical, but Nick Dunham was a family man in good standing. He had two young children, and his wife, Lisa, adored him. She showed up once a month or so for a lunch date with her husband, and all the women at Coastal knew the Dunhams' marriage was solid.

At the end of the day, Jennifer was surprised when Mr. Owen called her, Tessa Comeau, and John Macomber into his office. Channing was there, too, sitting in the comfortable wing chair at one side, and Jack Rainey, the third partner, entered the room right behind John and Jennifer.

"Jennifer, Tessa, John." Owen was always a bit more formal than the other partners, but usually he was affable. Today he seemed absolutely stiff. Jennifer watched him, sensing that he was affected deeply by Nick's abrupt disappearance.

Owen cleared his throat and nodded deferentially toward Channing and Rainey. "My partners and I have decided to go ahead with a new project. Before this unfortunate occurrence, we had planned to put Nick Dunham in charge of it. But it would be poor business for us to delay beginning the project."

Jennifer glanced at Tessa, but she was watching Owen with interest.

“We’ve been commissioned by a private client to create a rather extensive program,” Owen went on. “It’s very ambitious, and will absorb all the energy the three of you can give it for several weeks. It’s an extremely important account for us. We’ll start you on separate sections of the program tomorrow morning. Later, we’ll have the translators and editors help you. We will reassign any unfinished projects you have on hand. Any questions?”

“Residuals?” John asked timidly. The programmers were normally entitled to a percentage royalty of programs they initiated or contributed to extensively.

“I’m afraid not,” Owen said. “This program will be marketed overseas, and it’s a one-time fee for us, but it will be significant, and I expect you to receive a hefty bonus when the work is done to the client’s satisfaction.”

John and Tessa nodded, and Owen looked expectantly at Jennifer. She was disappointed but felt she had no choice. The work-for-hire contract would eat up time she might have spent on programs she designed, which were her best chance to build a nest egg.

“You three are our best designers. This will be worthwhile for you.” Channing had been silent until then, and Jennifer looked at him. His melancholy face held its customary guarded expression. Was he trying to make them feel special because they'd been selected for a difficult job? Probably he hoped he could mollify them into doing an arduous task that would be very profitable for the firm. She knew she and John Macomber were better at programming than any of the three partners, and Tessa was known for her creativity.

The firm's partners were business minded, and they knew computers. Rainey, especially, was detail oriented and could pound out a workable technical program quickly, if all the protocols were standard. The youngest of the three, he was an intuitive troubleshooter. Owen was a born marketer and courted clients assiduously. Channing was somewhat creative and studied the software market with a quick eye for the customers' needs. But none of them was truly an innovative thinker. When they needed a complicated program without glitches, they turned to John and Jennifer. Or Nick Dunham.

"So, Jennifer," Owen said smoothly, "will you be ready for this new assignment in the morning? Things are in a bit of a muddle just now, but I'm sure this question of Dunham's whereabouts will be cleared up soon, and the client insists that we begin this project immediately."

"Certainly." She hoped her confusion didn't show. Normally, Rainey or one of the other partners handed her an assignment without questioning her readiness. This job must be different somehow. Or was it just the unsettled feeling in the office, with Nick missing? Everything seemed tentative, as though all the people at Coastal held their breath, waiting for the detectives' permission to exhale.

As she prepared to go home, her thoughts focused once more on Detective Larson. He was in charge of the investigation, she was sure, although she hadn't seen him since their interview. She'd heard Bearse's end of a conversation with him, when Larson had apparently called for an update. She hadn't meant to listen. Bearse had spoken quietly but had stood quite close to her work station when he took the call on his phone.

"No, Harv, nothing solid. He closed out the program he was working on just before noon and hasn't logged on since. Still no activity on his company phone. And one guy's pretty sure Dunham's car was in the parking lot when he came back from lunch."

Jennifer thought about that off and on all evening. She tried to remember if she had seen Nick's car, but she and Jane had gone out the front door and down Market Street for sandwiches at a deli they frequented. She'd paid no attention to the parking lot. Too bad. If only someone had sensed sooner that something was wrong!

She thought of Lisa Dunham waiting at home

for her husband to return, struggling to be strong for the children. If she knew Lisa better, she might have called her.

She'd have to leave it up to Detective Larson and his squad to solve the puzzle and bring comfort to the Dunham family. If ever she'd seen a man capable of bringing order out of chaos, it was Harvey Larson. Dependable. Competent.

Jennifer puzzled over the favorable impression the detective had left. Why did Larson inspire calm and hope in her, when Owen and Channing's speeches to the employees only fueled speculation and dread where Nick's fate was concerned?

Chapter 2

"Time to move on to something else," Captain Mike Browning counseled six weeks later. He sat with his elbows on his desk, leaning on his clasped hands.

Harvey sighed. "I hate to leave a case unsolved."

"I know. But on this one, we're past the point of diminishing returns."

"You've put everyone else on other cases." Harvey tried not to let discontent creep into his voice. For weeks he had immersed himself in the life of Nick Dunham, with no success. The man had vanished, leaving no trail to follow.

Apology darkened Mike's blue eyes. "We won't close the case, of course, but I need you and Eddie. We've got a backlog of cases waiting for attention. I feel sorry for the guy's wife and kids, but we've got to let this one go, Harv."

Eddie sat back, watching them uneasily. He was the youngest man in the unit and lacked the maturity and experience of Mike's other detectives. Eddie was smart, but his third-generation Franco-American status—his grand-parents had come down from Quebec to work in the mills—gave him a scrappiness that was sometimes misplaced. The KKK no longer harassed the French in Maine, but some of the old tensions from local prejudice lingered. Eddie usually exuded charm, but he was up for a fight on short notice.

"I don't say it's a kidnapping," Harvey admitted. "No ransom demand. We're way past the time for that."

"No, if it started as a kidnapping, something went wrong," Mike said.

"Yeah. The company says the last location registered on the car's GPS was in the mall parking lot, but the car wasn't there."

"You think someone disabled the computer and then took the car elsewhere?"

"Looks like it."

"Nick Dunham could have done that," Mike said.

"So could a lot of other people he worked with. What do you think, Eddie?" Harvey asked. He seldom disagreed with Mike's decisions, but, then, he seldom had to put a case in mothballs. He'd gotten used to success, and the elite detective unit was a formidable team, known for cracking tough cases. But this one had stymied them.

"Well, his car disappeared with him," Eddie offered. "The captain's right about that. Somebody drove it away."

Mike nodded. "Don't discount the possibility that Dunham doesn't want to be found."

"I don't buy it." Harvey plunked his coffee mug on the desk. "Pete found a witness who said the car was in the company parking lot after lunchtime."

"One out of two dozen." Mike shook his head. "Harv, you know how hard it is to get consistent testimony from a group that big."

"All right, what about the insulin? The man's diabetic. His wife says he's got to have insulin twice a day, minimum."

"He took it with him," said Mike.

"How big a supply? Come on, Mike. He hasn't contacted his doctor, and he hasn't filled his prescription. Lisa Dunham thinks he'd need to do that within a week."

Mike's jaw hardened. "The plain truth is, you don't know how big a supply he had on hand. Maybe he built it up inconspicuously over a period of time, planning for this. Or maybe he's getting it off the internet, from some borderline legal supplier."

"Or maybe he went into a diabetic coma and died somewhere," Eddie put in.

"That couldn't happen," Harvey protested. "I've kept after all the law enforcement agencies and hospitals in the state and alerted all the morticians. Dunham wore a medical alert dog tag. If he wound up in an emergency room or a morgue, we'd know it."

"You alerted New Hampshire." Mike rose with

his empty coffee mug in his hand and headed for the coffee maker.

"All of New England. And there's been nothing. No diabetic John Does. I put the word out to pharmacies and hospitals all down the coast. I've been working this thing, Mike."

"I know you have." Mike came back to the desk and sat down with a sigh. "The thing is, you've done everything, Harv. You've covered all the bases." Mike sipped his coffee. His sympathy showed, but Harvey could see that he wouldn't give in.

"Everyone at the office says he was a good father and husband," Eddie said.

Harvey nodded. "I've looked for anything that would show otherwise, and it's not there. No out-of-town business trips without his wife in the past year. No pretty women at the office who left the job recently. No beautiful client he spent time with."

"There's got to be something," Mike said.

"Dunham's thirty-five and happily married." Harvey could be stubborn when he wanted to. "He loves his kids, and he's not the workaholic type who lets the family down. He was there for every birthday dinner."

"We didn't just talk to his coworkers," Eddie agreed. "We questioned his friends, and even his in-laws. He was a good guy."

"Was." Harvey looked morosely into his coffee.

"Come on, Harv, we don't know he's dead." Mike was trying to cheer him up, and Harvey smiled wryly. After so many years together, the captain was used to his melancholy temperament. Harvey couldn't help it. If he wasn't working at full steam, he was depressed. But it was his bleak personal life that got him down, not his job. He didn't usually get caught up emotionally in his cases. That was one of several factors that made him a good detective; he could separate the job from his feelings.

"Why *don't* we know he's dead, Mike?" Harvey's eyes locked the captain's. "Because if he's dead, we ought to know it by now."

Mike sipped his coffee. "Remember that guy who jumped off the city pier last summer? Took us a while to find him."

"Maybe Dunham's living someplace under another name," Eddie said.

"He loves his family," Harvey reminded him.

"So, maybe he's got amnesia."

They all laughed.

"There are documented cases," Eddie said, but with a smile.

"Maybe," Harvey conceded, "but you know that is so rare. And the diabetes thing. I still think, if he's alive, that will lead us to him."

"Put it aside," Mike said. "It's still open, and if anything at all comes in, you'll be the first to know, but I've got an urgent case that I need you two to handle."

Harvey made himself unclench his teeth. It wouldn't do Nick Dunham any good to let this wear him down. But he still had a ray of hope—why, he couldn't say. Maybe it was the girl. Jennifer Wainthrop, the one bright spot in this case. Something about her had touched him.

But the case was going inactive. His only connection to Jennifer was being all but severed, and that made him feel even more depressed.

He leaned back, defeated. "All right. What's the new case?"

Jennifer was tired. She'd worked steadily on the new program for weeks, and she still didn't know what it was for.

Channing kept her mostly on the security features, while John handled the body of the program. Tessa worked on sections that would mesh with hers and John's when it was finished, but the bosses made sure each part was compartmentalized, and no one but them saw the whole thing. And the programmers were all sworn to secrecy.

Jennifer's convoluted creations would deter the most persistent hacker—at least she hoped they would. As to the rest of it, she hadn't a clue what the system would do. She had a vague idea it might be military; either that or industrial. But a program for use in the public sector wouldn't be this hush-hush, and even the one military-commissioned program she'd worked on hadn't had security this tight.

It was wearing her down, and she went home every night exhausted.

That weekend she drove to her parents' farmhouse in Skowhegan, two hours to the north. Time with her family lifted her spirits, but she faced Monday and the return to work with dread.

She and her sisters, Abby and Leeanne, stayed up late Saturday night. They watched *National Velvet* together for the umpteenth time, then lingered over hot chocolate, catching up on each other's lives. Jennifer missed them terribly when she was in Portland and wished she could stay at home longer.

"It's so dreary around the office since Nick Dunham vanished," she confessed.

Abby popped a cheese curl into her mouth. "You need a social life." She had graduated from nursing school the previous spring and was working at a hospital in Waterville.

Jennifer smiled. "I suppose your coworkers have ideas about what constitutes a fun weekend."

"Sure," Abby said. "Get your friends together and have a party."

"What friends?" Jennifer asked, more acidly than she'd intended. Abby winced, and Jennifer said quickly, "Sorry. I just haven't had a chance to get to know many people outside the office."

Abby stared at her. "You won't meet anyone if you don't go out. Haven't you dated *anyone* since you moved down there?"

"A few guys have asked me out, but I haven't found one I really like. There was this one double date with Jane, from work. She set it up, and we went to a Sea Dogs game. What a disaster. The guy I was with was kind of loud—not my type. And then he fell on Jane's date."

"Fell on him?" Leeanne fished a melting marshmallow from her cocoa with her spoon.

"A pop fly came into the stands, and he jumped for it and landed on Brent. We had to send him to the hospital for x-rays."

It would take a very special man to tempt Jennifer to go out again. The ill-fated outing with Jane was her only date since her senior year of college. Her breakup with her last boyfriend during graduation week had left her cautious. She'd graciously turned down Jane and Brent's friend when he called her with another invitation.

The prospect of starting over, getting to know someone from scratch, and laying herself open to disappointment again was more formidable than her loneliness.

"What about your roommate?" asked Leeanne. She was in her sophomore year of college, and she took her studies seriously. "Don't you do things together? She must know some guys."

Jennifer sighed. "Donna-jean is impossible. I don't think we'll ever be friends. And the guys she hangs around with scare me."

"Too bad." Abby leaned back on Jennifer's bed and punched up the pillow. Her hair, long and golden like Jennifer's and their mother's, splayed out on the white cotton pillowcase. "Isn't she a hairdresser? You should let her give you a new cut. That would help you get to know each other."

"I don't think I want to know Donna-jean that well," Jennifer said, "and I know I don't want her messing with my hair."

"Don't cut it," Leeanne said. "You've grown it out forever."

Jennifer smiled. "I won't, at least not without a lot of thought first."

"Why don't you just stay home with us?" Leeanne's logic was innocently endearing, but Jennifer knew her days at home were over.

"It's called earning a living. There are no computer jobs up here that pay as well, and I can't mooch off Mom and Dad, after everything they've done for me."

"I know you send Mom and Dad money," Abby said.

Jennifer shrugged, but didn't meet her eyes. "It was really hard for them last year, with you both in school. Jeff and I agreed we both had to get out on our own, and we tried to help. After all,

Mom and Dad financed us through college for the most part."

"As if Jeff helps much," Abby muttered. "He's barely making ends meet."

"At least he's supporting himself." Jennifer empathized with Jeff's career struggles. He'd ground through four years of college as an education major, then decided he hated it during his practice teaching stint. He'd moved home and pumped gas for a few months, then decided to apply for a vacancy on the fire department. He'd found his passion at last and gone on to take advanced EMT classes.

"Well, I appreciate what you and Jeff have done." Leeanne turned to hug Jennifer. "But we miss you."

"I miss you, too. If I could find a roommate half as great as you . . ." She shuddered, remembering Donna-jean's raunchy rap music and the odor of smoke that permeated their tiny rental house, even though she had specified non-smokers when she advertised for a roommate. "I never should have taken Donna-jean on as a roommate. I wish she'd move out."

"Maybe I could get a job in Portland," Abby said eagerly. "Then you could tell her that your sister was going to use her room, and she'd have to leave."

Jennifer smiled. "Mom and Dad would have fits if another daughter defected to the biggest city in Maine. Besides, you haven't been on your job all that long. Let's get the school loans paid off, then we'll think about the rest of our lives."

Abby nodded ruefully. "Guess you're right. It won't be long before Travis is ready for college. I just get the feeling you have a grim existence down there. We could have so much fun together!"

Abby was so outgoing, she would turn Jennifer's placid life upside down if she had the chance. Jennifer wasn't ready for that, either.

"Aren't there any eligible men at the office?" Abby asked.

"No, they're all either married or total techies. You have to have a certain personality to want to spend all day—" Jennifer broke off, staring at her sisters. "What am I saying? I'm a tech nerd, too."

"You are not," Leeanne protested. "You're sweet and fun and—and beautiful!"

Tears sprang into Jennifer's eyes. She smiled at Leeanne.

"Isn't there anyone?" Abby asked plaintively.

The quiet, efficient detective came to mind, but Jennifer pushed that thought away. He was too old. Probably married. She was sure he'd worn a wedding ring on the hand that held his notebook. And she would never see him again, anyway.

But if there ever was someone, she hoped he'd be like that—a man who knew his job and could command respect. And most of all, someone she could feel safe with. That was critical. She tried to picture his face. The bright blue eyes were easy; the rest was hazy, but she knew she'd recognize him again in an instant.

"Well?" Leeanne eyed her speculatively.

"No, there's no one."

Harvey sank into his desk chair late Thursday afternoon, exhausted. He and Eddie had chased a pair of car thieves all week. A late vigil the night before had brought success, and they'd made the arrests. Today was a blur of interrogation, phone calls, paperwork, and conferences with the assistant district attorney. When his report was done, he could go home.

To what? It was almost better when the job kept him busy day and night. He opened a computer file and began the report.

He was nearly finished when Eddie called across the room, "You all set, Harv?"

"Five minutes."

Eddie had driven that day and would drop him off at his apartment. The other two detectives headed for the stairway calling a general good-night, and Mike was packing his briefcase. Harvey scowled at his monitor in concentration as his phone trilled. He quickly banged out the last few words and reached for it.

"Harvey? It's Tim Lewis."

The voice took him back a long, long time, and he sat immobile. Carrie's brother wouldn't call him without a compelling reason.

"Tim. What is it?"

"It's Carrie." He sounded strained, and a heavy feeling settled on Harvey's chest.

"What's happened?"

"She's gone, Harvey."

Heavier. He took a slow breath, trying to read a less final meaning into the simple words, but he couldn't. "You mean, she's dead?"

"Yes."

"Oh, no." Harvey slumped back in his chair. "When?"

"Yesterday morning. I thought you'd want to know."

"Yes. Thanks, Tim." He closed his eyes for a moment then opened them quickly. The images of Carrie were too vivid. "What happened?"

"They're saying an overdose."

That didn't process easily. Even in college, when she was at her wildest, Carrie had veered away from drugs. She'd maintained she was too smart for that. Alcohol, maybe; not drugs.

"An overdose of what?"

"Sleeping pills. There was a note."

"You mean it was deliberate?"

"I guess so."

At least it wasn't illicit drugs. But suicide! She'd been unhappy much of the time Harvey knew her, but she dealt with it in her own way. When she was angry, she threw things. When she was depressed, she went out and partied. And when she was bored, she opted for a change of scene and company.

He sighed. "I don't know what to say. Why did she do it?"

"She was depressed. Worse than usual, I mean. You knew she got married last year?"

"No, I didn't know."

"Well, she did. He walked out on her last month."

Harvey felt as if a big chunk of his life had been stolen. He'd held out against a divorce, but she rejected all his overtures. After he'd been alone three long, empty years, Carrie had filed anyway.

The papers had come in an innocuous white envelope with the return address of a lawyer's office in Lexington, Massachusetts. Still, he hadn't been able to bury the hope for reconciliation. Someday she would get her life together and come back. Wouldn't she? He believed it was possible, and had tried to live accordingly. She'd been gone ten years, but he still considered himself married.

Now he realized that, for Carrie, reconciliation had never been a possibility. She had said as much, loudly and often, but he'd managed to cling to a shred of hope.

It hit home now. He'd been ostracized from the Lewis family so completely that she had been married for a year, and no one had breathed a word. True, her family was two hours away, near Boston, but it seemed odd that he hadn't heard. You would think some mutual friend would have spilled it to him. Of course, that was assuming they had any mutual friends. Carrie's friends were too snobbish for Harvey, and she had openly despised his police buddies.

For now, Harvey wouldn't allow himself to think about her being married to someone else, but he felt a vague ache that began somewhere near his heart. Their marriage may have been a mistake, but it still mattered.

And he'd been part of the family once. Not the best-liked member of the family, perhaps. He grimaced as he remembered his mother-in-law's bitter words the last time he had seen her. It wouldn't surprise him if she'd cut him out of all the wedding pictures and whited out his name from the genealogy charts that were so dear to her. But he and Tim had a good rapport at one time, and Carrie's feisty grandmother had a soft spot for him.

Still, no one had called him or dropped him a line when the woman he'd pledged his life to had made such a momentous decision. It took her death to make someone say, *Hey, shouldn't somebody call Harvey?*

"Tim, I'm sorry. I know you loved your sister. When is the funeral?"

"Tomorrow. We should have called you sooner, Harvey. It's been rough. Mother is distraught."

"I don't doubt it." Harvey hesitated. "What did the note say, if I may ask?"

"That she couldn't take it that he'd left her. And that she didn't want to cause us pain, but she couldn't go on anymore. It was kind of rambling."

A lot of things went through Harvey's mind, dominated by images from suicides he'd responded to as a patrolman. At last he said, "Tim, this doesn't have anything to do with me, does it?"

"I don't think so. She didn't mention you in the note. She would never tell us what happened between you two."

Harvey took a deep breath. Too late to plead his case now, but something inside him wanted Tim not to hate him. "It wasn't my choice—the divorce."

"I kind of figured that. But you two went eight years, and no kids. I thought maybe that had something to do with it."

"That was part of it." Memories gushed in. Carrie's audacious pursuit of him, a social nobody, in college. Her parents' disdain. Their grudging consent to the marriage. The wedding in a splendid Gothic chapel none of them had ever set foot in before.

Their wedding vows had seemed so full of promise. He had meant every word, and at the time he'd been sure Carrie did, too. Then came Carrie's hurt incredulity and the Lewises' anger when he'd announced that he was leaving law school in favor of the police academy; Carrie's discontent and gradual alienation; sharp words and long, lonely nights. Better not to get into any of that with her brother.

"How's your father doing?"

"Taking it stoically," Tim said.

"How about you? Are you okay?"

"No, not really, but my wife is great."

"Your wife?" Harvey was startled. "How long have you been married?"

"Four years. We have a little boy."

"That's great, Tim. I'm glad for you."

"Thanks. You never—you're not married, are you, Harvey?"

"No. I'll be down tomorrow for the service. Hang in there."

He sat for a few minutes without moving, waiting for the weight to lift. It didn't.

Eddie came in from the break room whistling, his jacket slung over his shoulder.

"Where's Mike?" Harvey asked.

"Locker room."

Harvey got up and walked the length of the office, sorting his thoughts as he went. His brain was adapting to the change in his life, putting new data into compartments where he could retrieve it later and reprocess it.

"Mike, I need tomorrow off."

"What's up?" Mike was taking his suit jacket off and hanging it in his locker.

"Carrie's . . . passed away."

Mike turned quickly. "I'm sorry. What happened?"

"Sleeping pills."

"Oh, Harv. Of course you can go. When is the service?"

"Tomorrow afternoon."

"Boston?" Mike asked.

"Yeah."

Mike had known Carrie during Harvey's marriage, and that he wasn't on good terms with her family. He also knew Harvey was a loner and didn't like to be fussed over.

"Do you need someone to go with you?"

"I'll be okay."

Mike nodded. "Is there anything Sharon and I can do?"

"No. Thanks. I'll see you Monday." Harvey quit trying to fight the fatigue and let his shoulders slump as he left the locker room.

Chapter 3

Pete and Arnie were gone, and Eddie was sitting on the corner of his desk.

"You ready?"

Harvey nodded.

They went down the stairs. The elevator was always slower than the stairs, and the men seldom used it unless they were escorting prisoners or visitors. After Eddie started his truck and headed out of the parking garage, Harvey decided it was time to tell him.

"My ex-brother-in-law called me a few minutes ago."

"That can't be good." Eddie glanced at him, then ahead as the light changed on Franklin Street.

"Carrie's dead."

"Oh, man."

Harvey opened his mouth then closed it.

"I'm sorry, Harv."

Eddie had never met Carrie, but his eyes were liquid anyway. He'd been a brash, tough French kid out to prove himself when he joined the unit five years ago, but that had changed. He was like a younger brother to Harvey now. Any event that upset Harvey's world affected him, too. There was some comfort in that.

Eddie would have called me a year ago, Harvey thought.

"Are you okay?"

Harvey didn't answer right away, reaching for the honest response. "Maybe."

"You want to come over and eat supper with me?"

"No."

Eddie stopped in front of Harvey's building. "Call me if you want company."

"Thanks."

He got slowly out of Eddie's truck and went up to his apartment. He sat down in the living room. It looked the same way it had the day after Carrie left, except that he had more books now, and it was dusty. He'd never gotten around to replacing most of the furniture she took with her. Bleakly, he surveyed the one overflowing bookcase, the stacks of books on the floor against the walls, the three chairs, one of which held his portable TV, and the coffee table so ugly she hadn't wanted it. He should have bought more furniture. Any normal man would have.

He hated the knowledge that he couldn't stand to make the smallest change in either his apartment or his life, because every tiny movement distanced him farther from Carrie and made the separation more final. Well, now it was really final.

He picked up an empty mug from the coffee

table and threw it across the room. It shattered against the woodwork with a loud, splintering crash. It didn't make him feel any better. He'd always told Carrie it wouldn't. He sank back into the chair and stared at the fragments. He wasn't sure he wanted to pick them up.

The phone in his jacket pocket rang. He sat still, and after eight rings it stopped. He realized his face was wet with tears, and for the first time doubted he'd be able to maintain his famous iron control.

Could he drive to Boston in the morning with his insides churning? And what would he say when he faced Carrie's parents? *I loved her. Really, I did. And I tried to make things right. Whatever she told you, I wasn't the bad guy.*

No, he could never say those things to them. Maybe not to anyone.

He went into the bedroom and took off his jacket and hung it in the closet, then unstrapped his holster. He laid the cell phone down beside the holster on the unfinished pine dresser from the thrift shop, then his wallet and keys and the rest of his gear.

He opened the top drawer and slowly pushed aside the regulation black socks and white handkerchiefs. The envelope was still there. He opened it and took the divorce decree out.

Carrie M. Lewis, of Boston, Massachusetts,

plaintiff, from Harvey A. Larson, of Portland, Maine. It was all there. The wedding date and place, the court and date of decree. The spaces for children to be argued over were blank. The bitterness hit him with a shocking intensity. Irreconcilable marital differences. That was all anybody got divorced for anymore. But who decided the differences were irreconcilable, anyway? Shouldn't he have had a chance to refute that?

He sat on the edge of the bed, then stood up again. He turned around and faced it as he would an enemy. He hated that modern maple bed. Carrie had picked it out. Why hadn't she taken it with her? Eight years with her, then ten without her. He'd slept in it long enough. He tore the blanket and sheets and pillow off into a pile on the floor.

The doorbell rang, and he stood there breathing fast, staring at the bedding and the divorce decree he'd let fall to the floor.

He turned abruptly, went out to the kitchen, and looked through the peephole. Eddie stood on the landing with a McDonald's bag in his hand. Harvey opened the door in resignation.

"Hi, Harv, how you doing?"

"Okay."

"You eat anything?"

"No."

"I got Big Macs here."

"Come on in. Thanks, buddy. I'm really not hungry."

Eddie set the bag on the counter and took the food out: Big Macs, french fries, and a chocolate shake for himself and Coke for Harvey. He hoisted himself up on the counter.

Harvey smiled a little. "Have a seat, Ed."

"Don't mind if I do. Here, take this." He held out a container of french fries.

Harvey pulled himself up on the counter on the other side of the sink, and they ate the food.

"You want to shoot some hoops?" Eddie asked.

"Maybe."

"Or would you rather go down to Clark's?"

"What, kick back a few beers?" Harvey asked.

"Well . . . that's what we used to do when you were blue."

Harvey looked at him. "I'm thinking that makes about as much sense as throwing things."

Eddie shrugged. "When you used to get really depressed, we'd go out and get a twelve-pack."

"Not anymore." It was a sudden decision, but he knew it was one he would honor. Drinking wouldn't take away the pain. He had long since proven that. He wasn't sure he wanted the pain to go away, anyway. He needed to feel the grief and hurt for Carrie, and then let it be over.

"I should have been smarter than that. And I shouldn't have taught you to do it."

Eddie shrugged. "Well, do something physical, then. Don't sit here and think about it. Let's play some ball, or go running."

"Okay, let's run. But you gotta help me do something first."

"What?"

"Take a bed apart."

"Why?"

"I'm getting rid of it."

"Your bed?"

"Yes."

"Harvey, I've seen your apartment dozens of times. Man, you've got no chairs. We're sitting on the counter. Do you think this is a good time to divest yourself of furniture?"

"Yes." Harvey took a sip of Coke. "I can't sleep in it any more, Eddie. It's part of the old life."

"Whatever you say."

"I want it out of here. Tonight."

"Okay. Help me load it in my truck. I'll drop it at the junk shop on Brighton Avenue in the morning."

They went into the bedroom and wrestled the mattress and box spring off the bed and leaned them up against the wall, then pulled the frame apart.

Eddie sneezed. "You haven't had this thing apart to clean it in years, have you?"

"Was I supposed to?"

"Spring cleaning, at least."

"Oh, tell me you spring clean your apartment and take all the furniture apart and dust it."

"No, my mother comes over and does it."

They carried all the pieces down to the street, where a cool breeze wandered in off the bay. They went back up for the unwieldy mattress and stopped for breath halfway down the steps.

Mrs. Jenkins downstairs poked her head out of her doorway. "What are you doing, Harvey? You boys are awfully noisy tonight."

"I'm sorry, Mrs. Jenkins. We're just getting rid of this bed."

"You don't want it?"

"No, my pal Ed is going to take it to the used furniture guy for me."

"I'll take it," she said. "Unless you want a lot for it. Is it all good?"

"It's fine. It's just old, and I don't like it. I'll give it to you, Mrs. Jenkins."

They carried the mattress into her living room. Her husband and son came out and helped carry the rest in.

Harvey and Eddie ran the three miles they usually ran on Friday mornings, and then they ran their Monday route. It was dark when they got back to the building, walking the last half mile.

Harvey leaned on the hood of Eddie's truck, gasping. "Remind me never to try to run that far again."

Eddie was breathing almost normally by then.

"You gonna be okay tonight, Harv?"

"Yeah. Thanks. Thanks for coming over."

"No problem. Think you can sleep on the floor? Because you can come over and sleep on my couch."

"No, I'll be fine. But I don't think I'll run in the morning."

"That's okay."

"Good night." He held out his hand, and Eddie gripped it and got in the truck.

Harvey went inside and dragged up the stairs. He got in the shower and stood there for a while, letting the hot water ease his aching muscles. Then he put on boxers and a T-shirt, spread the mattress pad out on the rug in the almost-empty bedroom and lay down with his pillow. It seemed his lifestyle was getting simpler and simpler with each item he removed from the apartment, but his life got more and more complicated.

Harvey arrived at the funeral home on the dot of one, signed the guest book, and slipped into a chair toward the back just as the service began. His badge was pinned to his vest under the suit jacket, so it wouldn't show, a concession to Carrie and her parents.

He looked around and saw a few people he recognized, but most of the family was up front where he couldn't see them clearly. The service was short and subdued, even for a funeral. No one got up and told poignant stories about Carrie.

At the end, he got in line and braced himself for his view of the casket. It was open, and a blanket of pink roses lay over the half of the lid that covered her from the waist down, and a ribbon with "Daughter" in glittered script hung down over the edge. He hadn't sent flowers, and he felt suddenly that he should have.

Don't stare too long, he warned himself. She didn't look the way he remembered her. Older, of course, but puffier. Her eyelashes didn't look right somehow, and her hair was in a style he'd never seen her wear. Maybe the mortician had just done a bad makeup job. It wasn't really Carrie, at least not his Carrie from more than a decade before.

He moved on, uneasy, following the herd into the next room. Tim Lewis clapped him on the shoulder and said quietly, "Harvey, good to see you."

"Hello, Tim." Carrie's kid brother was strangely mature. He was carrying a sober-faced toddler and introduced his wife, Anne. He didn't use the ex-word, just said, "Anne, this is Harvey Larson," and Harvey knew he had already filled her in on his status.

Carrie's parents ignored Harvey, but he didn't blame them, really. He was just another piece of Carrie's unhappy life. Mrs. Lewis sobbed uncontrollably, and her husband stood beside her, shaking hands mechanically with the people who murmured their condolences.

Carrie's cousin Rachel accosted him with a tentative smile and made some banal remarks: How've you been; it's been a long time.

Across the room, a tall, fortyish, dark-haired man with a mustache leaned against the wall, hands in his pants pockets, shoulders sagging.

"That's Carrie's husband, Jason," Rachel said. "Isn't he pathetic? I told Aunt Cora he shouldn't be here."

Harvey immediately felt empathy for the man, and wondered what Rachel had told Aunt Cora about himself.

"Harvey! It's really you!"

He turned toward the warm voice and smiled for the first time in days. Carrie's grandmother approached slowly, a glint in her eyes. He moved toward her, and without hesitation she put her arms around him and kissed him soundly on the cheek.

"I've missed you!"

"Thanks, Gram." The two had always gotten along well when Carrie and Harvey were together. He had visited Grandma Lewis often, and had always found good conversation with tea and cookies at her house. His own grand-parents were long gone, and he had gladly taken Carrie's grandmother into his heart.

"You look just the same," she said.

"I do not. But you do." Her white hair curled softly around her forehead above her glasses, and her back was still straight.

"Well I guess neither of us is any younger. Why don't you take me home after the graveside service?"

"Sure, I'd like to," he replied. "You don't want to go to the house?"

"Too morbid. They'll all be squished into a hot, crowded parlor, talking about poor Carrie. You come with me, and we'll catch up."

"I'll do that."

She moved on to speak to out-of-town relatives, and Harvey braced himself to face Glenn and Cora Lewis. His father-in-law shook his hand and murmured, "Larson. Didn't expect you."

"I'm sorry, sir," Harvey said, sorry both that Carrie was dead and that he had come. He wondered if he had made a mistake and should have stayed in Maine.

Cora turned away from him, leaning against her husband's arm. "I need to sit down, Glenn."

Mr. Lewis threw Harvey an apologetic glance and steered his wife to a chair.

The funeral director came to them, to send them out to the lead car of the cortege. Harvey went out to his car and waited for the procession to form. He pulled into line behind the Lincolns and Cadillacs, and they crept to the cemetery.

Carrie's mother was nearly prostrate by the time the interment service ended. Harvey kept an eye on Grandma Lewis, and he placed himself beside her when the family turned away from the grave.

"You dear boy." She took his arm. "Where's your car?"

Tim appeared on her other side. "Want to ride back to the house with us, Grandma?"

"No, I don't," she said tartly. "Harvey is taking me home."

Harvey smiled at Tim. "I'll take care of her." He led Grandma to his car.

"You've still got the old Ford!" Her eyes sparkled.

"Are you sure you want to be seen in it?"

"Of course."

He helped her climb into the front seat and find the seat belt. When he got in, she eyed him. "What cases are you working on now, Harvey?"

"Hm. Well, there's one I wish I was still working on. I can't seem to let go of this case I couldn't solve. A man disappeared from his office, and we couldn't find him."

"Ever?"

"Well, it's only been six weeks or so, but it does bother me. No leads."

He drove to her snug white house, confronting the past at every turn. She held his arm as they walked into her unchanged kitchen. Grandma walked slowly to the sideboard and opened a tin of gingersnaps.

"Homemade cookies," Harvey breathed. The smell brought back a wave of memories. He took off his driving glasses and folded them into his breast pocket, bringing out his handkerchief for the tears that had stayed at bay during the funeral. Odd how something as simple as home-baked cookies could trigger them.

"It's all right to cry." Grandma patted his arm. "You sit down." She put the teakettle on and got two bone china cups and saucers with violets on them from a cupboard.

"I've really missed you," he said. "I didn't know how much."

"We can still be family, Harvey." She smiled at him and brought out teabags, sugar, and cream, not milk. She took two silver-plated spoons from a pressed glass spoon holder on the sideboard and sat down with him at the table.

"I wish you were here just on a social call. Poor Carrie."

"She got married again," said Harvey.

"Yes. She didn't tell you?"

"She never told me anything."

"I'm sorry, Harvey. It's been distressing. I'm glad you came."

"How could I not?"

She looked at him keenly. "I wish the two of you could have worked things out."

"Some things just didn't seem to be workable."

"I thought at one time you hoped for a family."

He said slowly, "I wanted it more than anything, maybe too much." The old woman watched him intently, and he knew suddenly that she would believe him. "We could have had a family, Gram. She just didn't want to."

Grandma was silent a moment. "I'm sorry. I can't understand why she didn't want children. She was my granddaughter, and I loved her, but I didn't understand her. Or like some of the choices she made."

The teakettle whistled, and she started to rise.

"I'll get it." Harvey poured the two cups full. She handed him a linen napkin and passed the cookie tin. He swished his tea bag around in the cup and took it out, squeezing it a little on the spoon. He didn't really want to talk about Carrie.

Grandma said, "I've prayed for you a lot over the years, you know."

"Have you?"

"Oh, yes. I always ask God to take care of you and to bring you to Himself."

He poured a little cream into his tea and stirred it. God was something he had ignored for the most part, except for an occasional bout of curiosity. The concept didn't fit very well into his life. "Do you think God actually does that?"

"Land, yes. It's the only way to get to God."

Harvey shook his head, uncomprehending. "I don't follow you."

"It's in the Gospel of John." She got up and moved stiffly to the sideboard where a worn, leather-covered Bible lay on a doily. She brought the book to the table and opened it in front of him, turning the pages.

"Here, you read it. Verse 44." Her finger rested on an underlined sentence.

He could tell it was important to her, so he read it. "No man can come to me except the Father, who hath sent me, draw him." Of course, she would use the old translation she'd grown up with, but the meaning was straightforward.

"It's Jesus talking, of course," she said.

"I've wondered about God," he admitted. "Not a lot, but sometimes. I mean, can we know that He's real? Or does faith just leap past that? Some people seem to have no trouble believing He's out there, but . . . I don't know, Gram."

"Don't you want to believe there's a higher power? That someone who knows what He's doing is in control of things?"

"Well, sure."

She smiled. "You must read what it says in Hebrews." She turned a few pages. "There. Hebrews 11:6. 'But without faith, it is impossible to please him, for he that cometh to God must believe that he is, and that he is a rewarder of them that diligently seek him.' It sounds like you,

Harvey Larson. Without faith. It's right there, boy. If you reached out, you could touch it."

Harvey smiled up at her. "You keep praying for me, Grandma."

"I won't stop. Maybe one of these days you'll come to the end of your own strength, considerable though it may be. And when you do, you'd better latch on to that faith."

"Believe that he *is,* huh?"

"Seek him diligently, Harvey."

She pushed the Bible gently aside and sat down. They ate cookies and drank tea, and Harvey began to relax and tell her about some of his cases. Grandma listened avidly.

"I always knew you were a good policeman. It's what God made you for. But I hoped you would find someone, Harvey. I'd like to see you happy."

He unbuttoned his jacket and leaned back in the chair. "I've just never considered that, Gram. Carrie was it for me."

"But now?"

He shrugged. "Who knows?"

"Isn't there anyone special?"

Harvey hesitated. "Not really, but . . ."

"Tell me about her."

He couldn't help smiling. "She's just a woman I met through work. I don't know her at all. I only saw her once, but she made a real impression on me."

"Be patient, Harvey. Maybe you'll have a chance to further the acquaintance."

He nodded, then picked up his cup and looked into it. "I didn't really think about it before. I just felt like it wasn't appropriate for me to look at another woman."

Grandma pulled a sheet of paper from between the leaves of the Bible and said, "What's her name?"

"Jennifer."

She wrote on the paper.

"What's this?" he asked.

"My prayer list. Now you and Jennifer are on it together."

"That's nice." He wondered how Jennifer Wainthrop would feel if she knew about this development.

"You must write and tell me if your suit is successful."

He smiled. "I may never see her again, Gram."

"Something tells me you will."

He laughed then, for the first time in ages. "I think Jennifer would love you, Grandma. She seems like a traditional kind of girl."

"That's the kind of girl you should have married in the first place."

Harvey shrugged. "Well, like I said, I don't really know her."

Grandma leaned toward him and grasped his wrist. "Harvey, don't throw away the opportunity."

"What if there isn't an opportunity?"
"Then make one."

Traffic was worse than ever on the northbound interstate. Plugging along at fifteen miles an hour approaching the river that separated Maine and New Hampshire, Harvey felt his restlessness mount. He knew road crews were working on the highway north of the bridge. Irritated, he consulted his watch. He had hoped to get back in time to check in at the office for an hour or so. Overhead, gray clouds formed a low ceiling. No doubt it would rain before dark.

At the apex of the crowned bridge, the van in front of him stopped abruptly, and Harvey hit the brake. He rolled down the window and peered out, trying to see if there was any movement at the far end of the bridge. All three lanes of northbound vehicles sat still, while the southbound travelers whizzed past them. He sighed and flipped on the radio.

Five minutes later, he was able to inch forward a few yards, then the line of cars halted again. Frustrated, he threw the transmission into park, climbed out of the car, and leaned against one of the girders on the side of the bridge, gazing out toward the Atlantic.

I'm not married anymore. It hit him hard. He'd refused to acknowledge the end of his marriage, but now there was no denying it. He thought of gentle Grandma Lewis and smiled ruefully. *Well, Grandma, if there's a God, he's probably laughing at me right now. You think he's trying to get my attention?*

Slowly he raised his left hand and studied the plain gold band he'd worn for almost twenty years. He wondered where Carrie's was. Suddenly he grasped the ring with the thumb and index finger of his right hand and twisted it, wrenching it off over his knuckle. Before he could talk himself out of it, he raised it over his head and threw it overhand, hard, as far out away from the bridge as he could make it go.

He couldn't follow its path down to the dark water.

Car horns blasted behind him, and large raindrops pelted him as he hurried back to the car. The traffic moved slowly. Another hour to Portland, at least.

Chapter 4

Jennifer's brain whirled with the never-ending loops she devised to keep hackers out of the special program. Yesterday Jack Rainey had told her to mesh her segment with John's and then try to break into the program. It had been all too easy. She was trying to correct the flaws, grimly ignoring the irony of trying to make her program so good she couldn't crack it.

After she had been at it three hours without a break, the lights in the office flickered and went out. The uninterruptible power supply for the computers beeped until the generators came on with auxiliary power. Her concentration was broken. A cup of tea, she decided, pushing away from her desk.

Jane Morrow was pouring a mugful of coffee as Jennifer approached the coffee station.

"What's with the power outage?" Jennifer asked, poking through the basket of wrapped tea bags for peppermint.

Jane eyed her in surprise. "It's a howling thunderstorm. Where have you been?"

"I guess I was concentrating so hard I didn't notice."

"Well, you don't have a window," Jane conceded.

Her quick intake of breath made Jennifer look up sharply. "What?" she whispered.

Jane lowered her gaze and murmured, "That Arabic guy is here again. He just went past the door."

Jennifer strode to the doorway and looked out. Sure enough, a tall, thin man with black hair was disappearing in the direction of the partners' offices.

"He's not bad looking," Jane said.

"Do you think he's a client?"

"I don't know. He was in there all morning a couple of weeks ago. I thought maybe he was interviewing for a job."

Jennifer shook her head. "No, I've seen him a couple of times. I think he's either consulting or buying."

"You're probably right."

"So, what are you working on?" Jennifer selected a tea bag and reached for a cup.

"Translating your retailing program into German."

"Really? They're going to market it in Europe?"

"Apparently." Jane smiled with a hint of sensuality. "I get to meet with Herr Enberg next week. He'll test the program, and we'll make revisions in the script."

Jennifer made a face. "Better you than me. He makes me nervous. Besides, what about Brett?"

"Brent. He's still hanging around, but that

doesn't mean I can't enjoy working with a nice-looking guy once in a blue moon. Don't you like to meet new people?"

"Well, sure, but . . ."

"But what? It livens things up a little."

Jennifer filled her cup with water. "I'd find it distracting, I think."

Jane laughed. "That's the general idea. I spend all day staring at a computer screen. But on Monday I get to stare at Herr Enberg."

"Is he married?"

Jane's blank expression told Jennifer her friend hadn't given it deep thought. "I met him once before, and he wasn't wearing a wedding ring."

"Do men wear wedding rings in Germany?"

Jane frowned. "I don't know, but what does it matter? He's probably only over here for a week or so. It's not like we're going to form a lifelong attachment."

Jennifer sighed.

"That's it, isn't it?" Jane asked. "You won't settle for anything less than a lifetime commitment. I tried to set you up with Brent's friend Aiden, and you practically ignored him. He wasn't marriage material, so you couldn't just relax and have a fun afternoon."

"Jane, I wasn't the one who ended the date. He injured Brent severely."

"But you brushed him off when he called you later."

Jennifer felt a pang of regret. "I didn't mean to upset you. And I don't think I hurt his feelings too badly."

"He didn't have enough time to find out whether he liked you or not." Jane pursed her cherry red lips in a pronounced pout.

Jennifer shrugged. "Aiden wasn't right for me, and it's just too much trouble to start something and then be disillusioned."

Jane picked up her coffee mug and headed for the doorway. "Some guy really did a number on you, huh?"

Jennifer stood staring after her for a moment. How did Jane know? Was it that obvious? Sometimes she wished she could be more like Jane, seize an opportunity to have a good time with a nice guy and not let it carry any weight. But she knew she would never give even a tiny piece of her heart again, until she met a man who was absolutely, irreproachably rock solid.

Harvey methodically laid out his plans to his squad late Wednesday afternoon. Mike had given him complete rein on the latest investigation, and the four detectives of the unit would work together on a new drug case. He wondered why Mike was handing him more and more responsibility, instead of giving it to Arnie, who was the senior detective and Mike's best friend.

They were finalizing their strategy when Mike

approached his desk. Harvey glanced up then looked again, his eyes drawn by an urgency in Mike's face.

"Harv, I know it's quitting time, but . . . you remember the computer guy who did the vanishing act a couple of months ago?"

A rush of adrenaline surged through him. Of course he remembered.

"Nick Dunham."

Mike nodded. "They're pulling his car out of the Presumpscot River, behind the dam up in Pleasant Hill."

Harvey swallowed. "Is he in it?"

"Don't know for sure, but the diver who hooked on the chain read the license plate, and they called me. Haven't brought it up yet."

Harvey bit his lip. "How'd they find it? The GPS in the computer wasn't working."

"The river's getting low. A kid climbing around on the dam saw the roof of the car under the water." Mike handed him a slip of paper. "Here's the number of the trooper in charge."

Harvey snatched the paper and growled at Eddie, Pete, and Arnie, "All right, you guys get out of here, but be ready first thing in the morning. We leave at 7:30 sharp."

"You want me to go with you, Harv?" Eddie asked, his dark eyes large and wistful.

"Naw, I could be up all night with this. Go home and unwind. Get some sleep."

"It's out of our jurisdiction." Eddie's regret was plain.

Mike turned back, halfway to his desk in the middle of the open room that housed the five men of the Priority Unit. "You get up there stat, Harvey. You might make it before they tow the car. If there's a body in it, you make your case for him being killed in Portland. You've put too much time in on this. I don't want the State Police to get it."

"The car's in Falmouth," began Pete Bearse, the unit's legal student. He'd been taking night classes at the USM law school for years, and Harvey was afraid they'd lose him to the bar someday. "If the autopsy says he drowned . . ."

Mike glared at Pete. "Until we hear that from the M.E., it's our case."

When he stepped into the general office at Coastal Technology, Harvey automatically searched for Jennifer Wainthrop. He'd avoided going back to the building during the first phase of the investigation, sending the other men instead, while he questioned Dunham's wife and coordinated a massive search.

Her chair was empty. He scanned the large room and spotted her, sitting in an armchair and clicking keys on her smartphone. The sight of her set his pulse hammering.

She looked casual and yet sophisticated today,

in gray pants and a knit pink top. His earlier take was reinforced—functional and conservative, but intriguing.

Her hair was different. The wealth of tresses was knotted demurely on the back of her head. How could that cascade of shimmering gold be tamed by one flimsy clasp? One deft movement would release it, and—

She looked up and saw him across the room, freezing for an instant, her lips slightly parted. He couldn't help smiling as her gray eyes flared momentarily. She recognized him.

She didn't smile, but she nodded ever so slightly and looked back at her phone. Harvey stood still for another moment, breathing slowly. From this distance, in the soft artificial lighting, he wasn't positive, but it seemed a flush had crept up her face. She shifted in the chair, turning a little away from him, and he watched the back of her neck. Her shoulders were stiff, as if she knew he was watching her, but the curve of her neck was at the same time alluring and vulnerable.

She looked older in the Grace Kelly getup. Maybe she wasn't out of reach on principle, after all. Immediately he gave himself a mental kick. Grace Kelly wasn't even in his generation, let alone Jennifer's. Why did he think of her? Okay, he was an old movie buff, and Jennifer did bear a resemblance to the actress in her prime.

Still, she was in Eddie's peer group, not his.

But something told him Eddie, who was every girl's type, would not be Jennifer's type.

The partners knew he was coming, and he had brushed past the security guard at the door, saying he'd find his own way back to their offices. With a guilty start, he realized his intent. He'd hoped to see Jennifer again, to somehow manage a private word with her.

The admission brought on confusion that he wasn't used to and didn't like. It had been years since he'd felt the desire to cultivate a woman's acquaintance. But he wasn't married any more. Why not go at it directly, just call her some evening?

There was the age factor, of course, and then there were the regulations. But she wasn't a major player in the case, and when it went inactive, what difference did it make? But he'd made himself stay away from her.

Until today. The intervening weeks had given him time to think about his turbulent feelings after their first meeting, and he'd thought about them a lot. He had a legitimate excuse to see her again, but had avoided it.

In the back of his mind, Carrie was still a deterrent when he'd met Jennifer, he could see that now. He'd told himself he didn't want to plunge into the treacherous social whirl again. He was settled, and while he might not be exactly content with his life the way it was, he didn't want to repeat the emotional havoc he'd been through before. And so he'd sent Arnie or Eddie to deal with the Coastal Technology partners and employees after that first day.

But now, whether consciously or not, he had decided that he wanted to follow through on the acquaintance. Was this what Grandma Lewis had meant? Jennifer had haunted his sleepless nights for weeks, and now that he'd seen her again, he knew he couldn't walk away without some sort of personal contact. He had to know if it was just him, or if she felt it, too—the illogical, unexpected attraction.

Slowly, deliberately, he walked around the edge of the room and stopped next to her chair.

She stopped texting.

Jennifer sat motionless for an instant. From the corner of her eye she saw him, but before his approach her inner radar had been screaming. If he had left the room, she would have known it immediately without looking.

"Ms. Wainthrop."

She lifted her head slowly. "Hello."

She hadn't thought of him as handsome before, but that was her new first impression. *Safe* had been her initial thought eight weeks ago, but now she wondered if that assessment was accurate. Could he actually be dangerous in ways she hadn't foreseen? Her ragged pulse warned her. Something beneath his ordinariness startled her.

His trendless clothes were rumpled, and he had a hint of stubble on his chin. He smiled again, and the crow's feet deepened, pulling her attention back to his eyes, rimmed below with the cast of fatigue, as if he'd been short on sleep for days.

He glanced over her head, and she looked around quickly, catching Jane staring openly. The brunette quickly resumed her typing, but with a smile on her Cherry Mist lips.

"I wondered if you'd be so kind as to take me back to the private offices." The detective's tone was calming, but his nearness counteracted the effect.

"Of course." Jennifer rose, determined not to show a scrap of the elation she'd felt when she'd seen him. That resolution was destroyed when she almost dropped her phone and fumbled to catch it.

"Good save," he said.

She swallowed hard. "This way."

When she moved past him she would swear she felt warmth radiating from him, but that was silly. She quickened her pace. By the time they were out of the workroom, in the hall, she knew her face was scarlet.

"Which of the partners did you wish to see?" she asked woodenly, without looking back at him.

"I'll need to speak to all of them," Harvey replied, "but first—is it all right if I ask you a few more questions?"

Jennifer's step faltered, and she glanced sideways at him as he came alongside her. "Certainly." She tried to sound as calm as he did, hoping desperately that she would give away no hint of the countless times she'd thought of him in recent weeks. Mr. Owen's door, far down the hall, was closed. "They may be busy at the moment, anyway, but it looks like the conference room is free."

She led the way then turned to face him, extremely aware of his proximity.

Harvey took the same chair he'd used before and tried to rationalize his decision to update one of the firm's programmers before breaking the news to the bosses. "Ms. Wainthrop—Jennifer."

He could read her confusion, although she hid it quickly.

"We've had a breakthrough in the Dunham case, and I came to see if anyone here has remembered anything that might help us continue the investigation."

She nodded gravely, her eyes never leaving his. It sped his heart up, and he took out his notebook as a diversion.

"I heard about Nick's car on the late news

last night," she said. "The reporters said there was no trace of him, though."

"That's right. The keys were in the ignition, but . . . no driver."

"Poor Mrs. Dunham." Her stricken look and gentle tones told him her compassion was genuine. "Mr. Owen thinks it was an accident."

"That's unlikely. All the doors were firmly closed. The car went in the water not far above the dam. A sober person wouldn't be likely to have an accident there, and a drunk wouldn't have gotten out."

"Strange, his disappearing in the middle of the day like that," she said.

"We don't know the car went in the water at night," Harvey told her, "but the last known location we have for it was in the afternoon, and several miles away."

She nodded. "As you say, if it was at night, or if he was drunk . . ."

"I take it he was sober when you spoke to him that morning."

"Absolutely. He wouldn't drink on the job."

"How about off the job?"

"I don't know. We didn't see each other outside the office."

He studied her for a moment. "So, what about the other partners? What's Ron Channing's theory?"

She cocked her head slightly. "Mr. Channing

isn't given to voicing his opinions in public. All I've heard him say is, this is an unfortunate occurrence, and we must carry on, that sort of thing."

"And Rainey?"

She shrugged. "He's funny."

"How?" She hesitated, and Harvey scanned the notes he'd made earlier. "Let's see, he's divorced. And he's quite good looking. Does he have a social life?"

"I don't know," she said.

"Don't the girls in the office speculate?"

"Well, there aren't that many unattached women here. Jane used to drool over him, but I think even she gave up."

"Why?"

"I think he's compulsive or something. He never looks at you when he talks to you, and he always wears a necktie to the office, but I don't think I've ever seen him wear the same tie twice. That's kind of weird these days. He's intelligent, but . . . well, he's odd."

"It's been two months. Is Dunham's desk still empty?"

There was a speck of surprise in her eyes. "No. They let John Macomber move into Nick's spot a couple of weeks ago."

"Did Macomber ask for it?"

"I don't know. But we all expected Nick to come back, you know? Nobody wanted to clean out his desk and say that he wouldn't. But that seems less likely every day, doesn't it?"

"Yes."

"John was packing Nick's things into a carton one day, and he said Mr. Owen had told him he could have that spot if he wanted it."

Harvey reached inside his jacket and held out a business card. "Look, my office and cell phone numbers are on here. Will you call me if you think of anything that might help us?"

"Of course."

The rumble of deep voices reached them through the open doorway.

"Sounds like the meeting's over." Jennifer glanced toward the door and slipped the card into her pocket. "Do you want me to take you to the partners now?"

"In a minute." He sat still until she met his eyes again, returning the look placidly for a moment, then looking away suddenly with a slight intake of breath.

"Was there something else, Mr. Larson?"

"Yes. I'd like to talk to you some more. Would it be possible for you to eat lunch with me?"

Her surprise came closer to shock now, almost panic. It was a surprise to him, too. His reticent side had been betting he wouldn't have the nerve.

"You mean about Nick? Because I really don't know anything I haven't already told you."

"No." He swallowed. "I mean I'd like to get to know you. Personally."

There. It couldn't get any plainer.

As she surveyed him speculatively, he wished that he'd sent Arnie Fowler over to speak to the Coastal partners and gone to chase the drug dealers in his place. Arnie was in charge of that case now, and Mike had authorized two uniformed officers to help him, freeing Harvey to make the rounds to Lisa Dunham and her husband's employers.

But asking a young woman for a date wasn't part of the plan. The silence hung between them too long, and he knew it was a mistake. How could he be so foolish as to imagine a gorgeous woman half his age would go out with him? Time to apologize and retreat, if he could figure out how to phrase it.

"I can't today," she said.

His heart skipped a beat. Was she trying to turn him down without insulting him? Some pert graduate student in psychology had probably written a book on how to turn down middle-aged men without permanently damaging their egos, but obviously Jennifer Wainthrop hadn't read it yet.

"It's okay. I understand."

Something like regret crossed her face. "I promised my friend, Jane—"

Why couldn't she just leave it at that? He

forced himself to smile. “It’s all right, really. I shouldn’t have—”

“Tomorrow?” It was tiny, almost inaudible, and she looked terrified.

“Did you—did you say *tomorrow?* You mean, lunch tomorrow?”

“I’d love to.”

The relief was overwhelming. He laughed, and she smiled, too. Her gray eyes were clear, and the struggle was gone.

Chapter 5

"I don't understand why they took his car clear to Augusta." Bart Owen fidgeted as Harvey doled out the basic facts on the recovery of Nick Dunham's car. Ron Channing sat still, watching Harvey without blinking, his dark eyes narrowed. Jack Rainey fiddled constantly with his key ring, never meeting Harvey's eyes.

"The car was found outside the city limits, so the State Police took over." Harvey tried to be patient, but he was still simmering from his confrontation on the riverbank with the trooper in charge.

"But you're the investigating officer," Owen said uncertainly.

"In the missing persons case, yes," Harvey agreed. "But since we can't prove a crime was committed, they don't have a compelling reason to hand us the car. Oh, they'll share information with us," he said hastily.

Channing's eyes darkened. "But you wish you had that Toyota."

Harvey didn't bother to reply.

"So, what does this mean?" Owen sputtered. "Is Nick Dunham dead or alive?"

Channing leaned forward, his lips tight. "It means it wasn't accidental, Bart. Either Nick's skipped on us and Lisa, or someone's gone to a lot of trouble to get him out of the way."

Bart Owen looked at Channing, then back at Harvey. "You've been to see Lisa?"

"Yes," Harvey said. "I went last night, as soon as we knew for sure the car was empty."

"Is she all right?" Owen's forehead creased as he leaned back in his padded chair.

"She took it quite hard." No sense telling these two that Mrs. Dunham had gone hysterical on him, and Harvey had comforted her as best he could while her ten-year-old son telephoned his grandmother.

He'd been there nearly an hour with her, until Nick Dunham's parents arrived. It was the little girl's wracking sobs and the boy's stoicism that had gotten to him, more than Lisa Dunham's weeping. Young Justin had stared at him with unspoken accusations, as if it were Detective Larson's fault his father's car had been found abandoned in the river, and his father was still missing. Detectives were supposed to find clues, weren't they? Then why wasn't he out there finding some, instead of bringing them news that was worse than nothing at all?

"We'll have to call on her tonight." Owen turned wearily to Channing. "Can you go over with me, Ron, when we close?"

"Can't see the need."

"Come now, it's a matter of courtesy." Owen seemed mildly scandalized that his partner could not see his duty, but Harvey knew from Channing's unyielding demeanor that he had no intention of going.

"I'll go with you, Bart," Rainey said. He shoved the key ring into his pocket. "We'll have to do something for her if Nick doesn't turn up soon."

"We've let her draw Nick's paycheck the last eight weeks," Owen said uneasily. "I'm not sure how long we can continue that."

"It's gone on long enough." Channing stood up. "You two can go see her if you want, but don't promise her any settlement. It's not our fault he decided to abandon his family."

"You don't think—" Owen broke off and rubbed his temple.

"You're certain the company isn't missing any assets?" Harvey had asked that question the first day of the investigation, but they'd had more time to take stock now.

"No, nothing's missing." Rainey turned and looked out the window.

"Well, I'll leave you gentlemen." Harvey slipped into the hallway and glanced at his watch. It was past noon. He paused in the doorway to the workroom, but most of the stations were vacant, including Jennifer's. He was slightly disappointed, but nothing could dull the elation he'd banked carefully before meeting with the partners.

Tomorrow. It was almost within reach.

The Priority Unit office was empty when he reached it. Harvey turned on his computer and went looking for information. He kept the flickers of guilt at bay by reasoning that he needed to know what he'd gotten himself into.

Facebook first. Okay, she had a profile with a stunning photo at the top, but her last posting was three weeks ago, mentioning a younger brother's birthday. A friend had tagged her in an old picture where Jennifer was wearing a softball uniform. She didn't seem to be on Twitter, but Instagram gave him better results. She wasn't really active on it, but more so than on Facebook. Her last post was two days ago.

Jennifer's birth record was easy to locate, with the access his official software gave him. It told him she was born in Skowhegan, the county seat of Somerset County, north of Portland. She was the daughter of George and Marilyn Wainthrop. He'd been sixteen when she was born. He almost gave up when he'd done the calculation, but Grandma Lewis's words echoed through his mind. *She's the kind of girl you should have married in the first place.*

He did a quick check on her father and found he was solvent, a 55-year-old executive for an agricultural products company. Harvey found birth records for five other children of the same parents, a larger family than most these days.

He tried to imagine Jennifer as a little blonde girl with pigtails, surrounded by her siblings. Jeffrey was the oldest, then came Jennifer, Abigail, Leeanne, Travis and Randall. The youngest was only fifteen, a sophomore in high school. Harvey felt ancient.

Mike breezed in from the stairway, swinging his briefcase. "Whatcha doing, Harv?"

"Background check."

"Anything new on the Dunham case?"

"Not really. I saw Mrs. Dunham and the business partners. I'm just waiting on word on the car from Augusta."

Mike frowned. "We shoulda had that car."

Harvey shrugged. He'd fought that battle yesterday and lost. "You need me now?"

"No, but when the boys get back from lunch, they might need your help on their case."

"I'll be here."

Harvey moved on to her credit record. She'd had a car loan on a six-year-old Ford Escort, a reliable, inexpensive car with no character. She'd finished the payments on time a year ago. Her father probably picked it out for her when she was in college. She had two credit cards, and she always paid them off at the end of the month.

Coastal Technology's personnel records were

his next target. The firm had a state-of-the-art electronic security system, but with a password-breaking program and some finesse, he had access within minutes. The records were a gold mine. Jennifer had a contract for five percent of the profits from any software she created there, and so far she had created or worked extensively on seven programs. Her performance reviews were cautiously positive—the best one could expect, he figured.

She was a University of Maine graduate, and he went after her transcript. Good grades, computer major, philosophy minor. That surprised him. And she played varsity softball in college, hence the uniform picture he'd seen earlier. Yeah, he could see her swinging a bat. She also appeared in a student production of Shakespeare's *A Midsummer Night's Dream* her junior year.

He glanced around the room. No sign of Eddie and the others yet. He checked his stocks. They were holding steady. The pharmaceutical company he was watching as a potential investment was up two points.

The stairway door opened.

"Harv! Am I glad to see you." Eddie dragged his chair over near Harvey's desk and peeled off his jacket. "We've got interviews scheduled for most of the afternoon. Can you help us out?"

"Sure. What have you got?"

Eddie's jacket landed in a heap on the floor.

"Well, that girl who was caught with the cocaine isn't in school today."

"What do you mean, she isn't in school? Is she sick?"

"I dunno. She just wasn't there."

Harvey scowled, and Eddie's eyes widened.

"Guess I should have checked, huh?"

"Let's go." Harvey stood and reached for his jacket. "Where are Pete and Arnie?"

"They're checking out some leads. Two patrolmen went with them. Nate Miller and Jimmy Cook."

"Ride with me and fill me in," Harvey growled as they headed for the stairway.

"Opposites attract." Jane Morrow smiled at Jennifer over the rim of her cup. They were eating lunch together at a sandwich shop two blocks from Coastal.

Jennifer considered ignoring the cryptic remark, but she knew exactly where Jane was headed. "As in you and Brent?"

Jane laughed. "Brent and I are very much alike. You and the dashing detective, however . . ."

"I wouldn't call him dashing."

"What would you call him?"

Jane's eagerness made Jennifer wary. Her instinct was to keep quiet about the lunch date she had made for tomorrow. She didn't want all the women in the office discussing it before she had a chance to decide whether she liked Harvey Larson. She chewed a bite of her sandwich slowly then leaned across the table with a question of her own. "Are you still working with Herr Enberg?"

Jane frowned. "No, he's gone back to Berlin. And you were right. He's married."

"I never said he was married. I just asked."

"Well, I asked him if he had a family in Germany, and he does." Jane shrugged. "I'm not complaining. Brent and I are getting very cozy."

Jennifer nodded. She didn't really want to hear the details, but at least she had thrown Jane off the track of Detective Larson.

Ron Channing clicked open the electronic folio he would present to several executives of a company in Singapore in twenty minutes. Everything was ready. He was ninety percent sure he could sell the client on the program prototype.

The door to his office whooshed open, sending a surge of wind across the room.

"Jack, what's up?" Channing closed his iPad with one hand as Rainey closed the door and faced him, his brow creased in annoyance.

"We've had a security breach."

"Really?" Channing was mildly surprised. They spent a great deal of time and money putting tight security measures in place at Coastal.

"Someone's tapped into our company files."

"What, online?"

"That's right. Henderson told me. I'm working on it personally."

Channing opened a desk drawer and picked out a notepad and pen. "Have you traced it back?"

"We're working on it. I figured you'd want to know right away."

Channing swore. Rainey strode to the window and looked out at the traffic. "I've got a hunch it was Myer Digital. They've been selling knock-offs of our most popular programs for two years."

"But we've never caught them actually stealing the ideas," Channing said. "They usually wait until the program's on the market, then come out with a cheaper, no-frills version."

"We'll get them this time. I had Nick Dunham insert new cross checks into the system three months ago."

"I remember."

Rainey turned to face him. "Unless I'm mistaken, we'll be able to tell where this breach originated."

Channing nodded. "Too bad we've lost Dunham. He was the best we had."

Rainey shrugged. "Jennifer Wainthrop's just as good, although she's not as aggressive."

"She's clever."

Rainey smiled faintly. "Yes, she is that. We'll have to make sure nothing happens to her."

Channing picked up the iPad and stood. "Have you told Bart about this latest development?"

"No. Guess I'd better."

"Could be it's some kid just trying to see if he can access private data for kicks."

Rainey frowned. "I don't think so."

"Well, we'll wait and see what the tracer shows. Better not let Henderson know too much. Loose lips and all that."

Rainey spread his hands. "That's why I'm working on it personally, Ron."

Harvey was nervous as his date with Jennifer drew closer. He made himself concentrate on the drug case at the high school, but it was hard keeping his mind on it. A guidance counselor's tiny office had been loaned to them for interviews. He finished questioning a student and let her go back to class. Half an hour to go.

"Harv, you got a date or something?"

Eddie peered at him, and Harvey realized he had checked his watch about twenty times in the last hour. He took a deep breath. "Actually, yes."

"*Bien*." None of the shock Harvey had expected showed in his partner's face.

"I need to speak to that girl whose mother found the coke in her room. Tonya Breton."

"She's not here."

"Again?"

Eddie winced. “I tried to call her house, and nobody answered.”

“But we spoke to the mother yesterday and told her to send the girl back to school.”

“I know.”

“This beats all.”

“You want me to get her mother’s work number?” Eddie obviously didn’t want to make that call.

Harvey sighed. “I’ll go down to the principal’s office and get it. You stay here and interview the next kid on the list.”

The principal, Arthur Bonney, was pacing when Harvey arrived at the office.

“How much longer are you and your men going to be here, Detective?”

“As long as it takes, sir. You wanted us to stop the drugs from coming into the school, and that takes time.”

Bonney sighed. “What can I do for you?”

“Could you please call Tonya Breton’s mother? It seems Tonya is absent again today, and we need to talk to her.”

Harvey waited impatiently in the outer office while Bonney made the call. The principal appeared in the doorway, concern lining his face. “Her mother says she left for school this morning.”

“We’ll check on her.” Harvey went back to the guidance office.

“Eddie, get over to the Bretons’ house. If Tonya’s home, request female backup and take her to the station. If she’s not there, call me immediately.”

“Right.” Eddie headed for the door then turned back. “Harv, you drove today.”

Harvey stared at him blankly. “Oh, right.” He reached in his pocket for his car keys. “Here you go.”

“What about your lunch date?”

“I’ll take a cab.” He hated the idea even as he said it.

Arnie Fowler raised his eyebrows. “You got a date? That’s unprecedented.”

“No big deal,” Harvey said, but he couldn’t meet Arnie’s penetrating look.

“So take my car.”

“Really?”

“Really.”

“Thanks, Arnie.”

Arnie shrugged. “Pete and I will grab something to eat and meet you back here at—say, 1:30?”

Harvey had expected ridicule, or at least some good-natured teasing from the other men in his unit, but instead they were coming through for him, and they hadn’t pressed him for details, or even for the identity of the woman he was meeting.

“Thanks a lot. And, Eddie, call me on my cell

phone the minute you know something about Tonya."

He parked in front of Catassi's Restaurant and looked around the parking lot. He didn't see Jennifer's blue Escort. He got out of Arnie's car and walked slowly toward the door. What if she didn't show? No, she wouldn't do that to him.

He had chosen the restaurant deliberately. It had an intimate dining room and great Italian food, but was off the beaten track for police department employees, and not too close to Coastal Technology. The last thing he wanted was to eat lunch with Jennifer in the same room with half a dozen cops. He didn't think she wanted her gossipy friend Jane to spot them, either.

He was nearly to the entrance when he saw the little blue car enter the lot. He waved, and when her hand fluttered in a return greeting, he smiled. A breeze off the bay ruffled his hair as he waited for her to park.

"Hi." She smiled then went all sober.

Harvey reached for her hand and squeezed it gently, then released it. "Hi. I'm glad you came." He knew he was smiling like a deranged clown, but he couldn't help it.

They stepped into the dim interior of the restaurant, its private atmosphere enveloping them. He was glad he had picked this place. The tables were far enough apart to give the illusion of privacy. They had tablecloths at noon, soft music, linen napkins, and flowers on the tables. It fit Jennifer somehow.

They ate salad and lasagna and breadsticks, but mostly they talked. After the first awkward moments, Harvey began to relax. He drew on the information he had gotten from his computer search and eased her around to talking about her work and her college days.

She held up her end of the conversation. They talked some about computers, and she asked him about police work and what kinds of software would make his job easier.

He couldn't keep his eyes off her, yet he found it difficult to meet her gaze for long. Her eyes were intent, perhaps a little cautious.

He wasn't used to being watched while he ate, and he thought she was nervous, too. She held her fork delicately, slicing her lasagna into small bites. She wore a silver and turquoise ring on her right hand, but nothing on the left.

Finally he couldn't stand it any longer. "So, you're single."

"Right." She took a sip from her coffee cup and put it down carefully on the saucer. "How about you?"

He hesitated. "I—my wife passed away . . ."

Her lips parted, but she didn't look away the

way most people did when you threw that little tidbit into the conversation. "I'm sorry."

"It's okay. It's been a long time."

"How long?"

He gulped. "Well, actually, not that long. Since she died, I mean, but . . . we were separated." He picked up the last bread stick and broke it into little pieces. "I mean, she left me. We, uh—we were divorced." He grimaced and shook his head. "I'm not very good at talking about this."

She blinked twice and nodded. "I shouldn't have asked."

"No, you should. It's all right. I just . . . well, it wasn't my idea, and when she insisted, I . . ." He let it trail off.

"Maybe you're not ready for this," she said gently.

"Ms.—Jennifer—I—" He swallowed. "Can I tell you something?"

She nodded, but she was terribly somber, and her gray eyes were huge. Some first date this was turning out to be.

Well, he'd started. He had to finish.

"Ten years ago, we separated. I tried to work things out, but she didn't want that. So, I've waited all this time, hoping . . ."

"What?"

"Well, I guess I was hoping she'd change her mind. But she never did. And now she's dead."

Jennifer sat back and studied him. “I’m sorry you went through all that.”

“Thanks.” It seemed inadequate, but he couldn’t think of anything else to say. This whole thing was harder than he’d expected. It was as if the specter of Carrie was standing just behind his right shoulder.

He sipped his coffee. Things weren’t going well. Maybe Jennifer was having regrets already. He put the cup down. “Look, it’s part of my life, but it’s over. If there’s anything you want to know, you can ask me.”

“Same here,” she said.

He smiled. If she only knew how much he knew already!

The waitress came to the table and asked brightly, “Would you like dessert?”

“No, thank you,” Jennifer said, and Harvey shook his head.

The waitress left the check facedown on the tablecloth, and Harvey moved it toward himself slightly.

There was another silence then Jennifer said, “Well, if you really don’t mind, there is something I’d like to ask.”

“Go ahead.”

“Do you have any children?” Her eyes were painfully serious.

“No.” He looked everywhere but at her, not sure how to respond. The longing for children was an old wound, one he'd forced himself to ignore for years. But he supposed it was natural for her to wonder. "I wish I did. You know, sometimes things just don't turn out the way you planned. But there aren't any kids."

"I'm sorry," she said softly.

He could see that she was sincere, but he wasn't sure if she meant she was sorry that he had no children, or that he hurt because of that. He hadn't intended to reveal so much. This was getting more depressing every minute. "How about you?" he asked, striving for a lighter tone. "Do you like kids?"

"Oh, sure." She sat back with a relieved smile. "I come from a big family."

"Six kids," he nodded.

"How do you know that?"

She was obviously startled, and Harvey knew he had unintentionally tipped his hand. He never did that when interrogating people, but this beautiful young woman and her sensitive questions had thrown him off balance. He eyed her cautiously. "Didn't you say something earlier about brothers and sisters?"

"No, I didn't."

"Oh. Well, hey, I'm a cop." It was Eddie's standard excuse for when people thought he had crossed the line, but somehow it felt a little flat.

"You mean you're like Sherlock Holmes, and you can tell things about people just by looking at them?" Her direct gaze unsettled him even further.

"Not exactly." He grabbed for his water glass.

"This seems like a little more than checking Facebook—which I don't use that much. You did a background check on me, didn't you?"

Harvey sat very still. He could feel his face reddening. What could he say to undo this? He sneaked a glance at her, and her stare was boring into him. *Great. Ten years after my divorce, I finally get my nerve up to ask for a date, and this happens.*

His only hope was to come clean. Avoiding her accusing eyes, he said, "I'm sorry. It's been a long time since I've asked a woman out, and I was a little nervous. I thought it would help if I knew something about you. I could ask you to go to the theater with me because I knew you liked drama, or we could go to a ball game because you played softball. I'm really sorry. I shouldn't have done it. We're not supposed to use the equipment at work for personal reasons, but—"

"What else do you know?" She sounded like she was strangling, and Harvey felt doomed.

"Uh, well, you were a straight A student, you pay your bills on time, and your company values you highly . . ."

Was she laughing? Her eyebrows were up and she was shaking a little.

"I looked for you on social media, too, but I didn't find much."

"I, uh, I don't use it much."

She looked around and signaled to the waitress. "We'd like some more coffee." There was authority in her voice now. When the waitress turned away, Jennifer looked straight at him, and he made himself meet her gaze. Just because she'd looked for a profile didn't mean he was off the hook.

Very slowly, she said, "You'd better start talking. There's a lot I need to know about you, if you want to even the score."

Jennifer had never suspected this from him, but perhaps to Harvey it was second nature. Here was a man who could access all kinds of private records because he had official clout for the police department, and he had used that to find out what her hobbies were and how many brothers and sisters she had. Her initial outrage gave way to amusement.

She took a deep breath and tried to put confidence in her voice. "So tell me about yourself, Detective Larson."

"You mean you're not mad?" He still looked guilty. "I'm surprised you haven't stormed out of here yet."

"Yes, I'm mad," she said, but her tone belied it. "I'm a good enough hacker that I'll bet I could have gotten at your credit record and your college transcript, too."

"The Meeting of the Computer Nerds," he said. "This could be hazardous."

Jennifer weighed her options. She really liked him, she couldn't deny that. "Okay, let's call a truce. No more electronic spying, all right?"

He nodded, looking down at his hands on the tablecloth.

He definitely was uneasy now, facing her across the small table, and she felt sorry for him, getting caught like that. It was out of character for her to treat anyone severely, and she knew that she didn't really want to be too harsh with him. She had been on edge since the day she'd first seen him, the day after Nick Dunham disappeared, but it was important to remain calm now. True, she liked him enormously, but she wasn't sure yet that she ought to.

She smiled. "Talk."

His eyes snapped up to hers, wide and a little startled. His irises were cornflower blue. That couldn't be natural. Would a cop wear tinted lenses?

"What do you want to know?" he asked.

"Do you always run background checks on women you meet?"

"Never. You're the first. Except for suspects, of course."

His look was so artless she believed him.

"Are you wearing contacts?"

"Uh, no. But I have driving glasses." He squinted at her as though unable to believe she had asked that. "What else?"

"Tons of things. How old are you? Why did ou become a cop? Do you like it? Do you like me? Do you think I'm *too* computer-nerdy? Do you like pizza? What do you do on weekends?" She stopped for breath. "And am I talking too fast?"

He sat with his chin resting on his hands, his elbows on the table, watching her. "I listen fast." His eyes crinkled at the corners. "What should I answer first?"

Jennifer felt suddenly very adolescent. "Age, please."

"Forty-one."

She sipped her coffee and thought about that. The gulf between them seemed to have widened.

"Is that okay," he said at last, "or did I flunk the test?"

She didn't know what to say, but she knew she had lost control of the conversation.

"Because I'd really like to pass it, and I think I already blew the essay." He looked earnestly into her eyes, and her heart did a sudden flip.

It was a moment before she could trust her voice. "You pass."

He smiled, and the crow's feet deepened. The

look held for a few seconds, and Jennifer sat still, willing her heart to slow down.

A soft whir came suddenly, and he apologetically reached in his jacket pocket and brought out a phone. "I'm sorry. I'm in the middle of a case, and I asked my partner to call me."

"It's all right." She sat back and watched him. He averted his eyes and turned slightly toward the window.

"Yeah, Ed. She's not? No, you'd better go over there. Make Mrs. Breton understand that if she doesn't cooperate she's an accessory. Yeah, meet me back at the school in thirty minutes."

His ring was gone, she noticed. The skin on his fourth finger was pale where a wedding band had been, not so long ago.

He put the phone away, frowning, but when he looked at her, his expression softened. "I've got to be back by 1:30, but I really want to continue this. Can I see you again? Will you have dinner with me?"

Don't look eager. Aloud she said, "Tonight?"

"Yes, tonight."

Jennifer hesitated. There were still one or two points that bothered her. And what would her parents say about her dating someone so old? But she wanted to see him again. She looked all around, but there weren't any cue cards.

"Can I think about it?"

"Okay, but I really need to head back."

They got up, and after he paid the check they went out into the brilliant sunlight. It was warmer than when they went in, and everything seemed too bright. They walked across the parking lot in silence. She clicked her remote to unlock her car, and when they came to it he opened the door for her.

"Thanks. I enjoyed lunch." She looked up at him. He wasn't all that tall. Her brother Jeff would tower over him. But she liked the way he looked, the way it felt to be with him.

He stood facing her, watching her closely, as if her next words would seal his fate forever. She wasn't sure she liked this new feeling of power.

"So, what do you think?" he asked.

"How tall are you?"

He broke the stare then and laughed. "Five-eleven."

She nodded, thinking rapidly about the consequences of accepting another date with him. A detective sixteen years older than she was, who had been married and divorced and widowed, sort of. A man who made his living looking at murder victims, no doubt, and had endured his own private agony. She wasn't sure she could deal with all that.

"I'm five-four."

"I know."

"Oh, right." She smiled. He had wanted her

to like him. That was why he'd checked her out so thoroughly. It amazed her, given her own insecurities. He cared about how she perceived him, and he wanted to continue the relationship. If he was willing to take a chance, why couldn't she? She caught her breath, and made the decision. "Okay, I guess, but not tonight. It's too soon."

His blue eyes widened, as if he hardly believed it. "Tomorrow?"

"If you swear you won't do any more checking between now and then."

"I promise." He looked down at the pavement, but she thought he was smiling. "And I do apologize."

She nodded. "It's all right. In fact, it's a little flattering. Sneaky, but flattering."

He shrugged sheepishly. Looking at her, he sobered. "I'll pick you up at seven."

"Do you know where I live? Oh, stupid question."

He just smiled.

Harvey hurried back to the high school. Arnie Fowler and one of the uniformed officers, Nate Miller, met him in the foyer.

"We think we've got a break," Arnie said in a low voice, as they walked toward the guidance office. "One of the girls on the list asked for her mother, so I let her call home. She's definitely feeling guilty about something, and I think when the mom gets here she might tell us something."

"Where is she now?"

"Pete's with her, and Jimmy's talking to one of the boys."

Harvey nodded. "Eddie called in. Tonya Breton's mother told him her daughter phoned her from the Maine Mall. Said she skipped school because she couldn't face her friends or us. She's supposedly headed to her mother's office. I sent Eddie over there."

He opened the door to the room they were using. Jimmy Cook sat opposite a thin boy who wore a slightly defiant expression, but twisted his class ring nervously.

Harvey raised his eyebrows, but Jimmy shook his head slightly, his lips tightly compressed.

"All right, Jim, when you're done here—"

The sound of an explosion jarred the school.

Chapter 6

The four officers stared at each other.

"What was that?" The boy looked toward Harvey, and his voice rose and cracked as he spoke.

"Jimmy, stay here." Nate, Arnie, and Harvey ran down the hallway and out the front door.

Eddie was picking himself up off the walkway just outside. The police car sat where Nate had parked it earlier, and five yards behind it was a fireball.

"Move the squad car!" Harvey yelled.

Nate ran around to the driver's side and gingerly hopped in. He turned the key, threw it in gear, and roared down the driveway thirty yards, parked and got out. He walked back to where Harvey, Eddie, and Arnie stood outside the entrance. All along that side of the school, students hung out of windows and stared at the fire.

"That's my car, isn't it, Ed?" Harvey said.

"Yup."

"Man!"

"Well, look at it this way: you needed a new car."

Harvey made a face at Eddie and pulled out his cell phone.

"This is Detective Larson. I'm at the high school, and I need the bomb squad."

"Bomb threat?" the patrol sergeant asked. "Because if it is, you'll need to evacuate immediately."

Harvey sighed. "I wish it were a bomb threat. My car just blew up."

There was a moment's silence then the sergeant said, "Copy that. The bomb squad will be there in fifteen minutes. Any p.i.?"

"No, we're fine, but send a few extra guys if you can, for crowd control," Harvey said.

They stood watching. The flames roared, and smoke billowed high. A charred half-page of Harvey's Maine atlas came fluttering down.

Nate picked it up. "Huh. Ashland."

Harvey frowned. "My winter jacket was in there."

"You should clean your car more often, Harv," said Eddie.

Harvey turned on him. "What happened? Are you okay?"

"I think so."

"Your hand is bleeding."

Eddie took out his handkerchief and swabbed at the cut. Harvey looked closer.

"Not too bad. Glass, probably. You want it checked?"

"Nah."

"Anything else hurt?"

"No. I was lucky, I guess. I got out, and I was almost to the school door when it blew."

"Where's Tonya?"

"She was ready to talk, so I sent her and her mother to the station with Cheryl Yeaton."

Arnie whistled. "Good thing."

Harvey nodded. It was a very good thing.

"The back window in the squad car's cracked," Nate offered.

"Terrific," Harvey said. "Make sure you file the damage report when you get back."

Nate nodded.

"Go in and see if Jimmy's got things under control. Tell the principal to get the kids settled down if he can. Keep them in their rooms."

"Shouldn't we evacuate?"

"I don't think so. The bomb was out here, and they're not. They're probably safer inside."

Nate went into the school, and Arnie said, "You think someone in the school did this?"

"I don't see how, unless they planted the bomb before Eddie left here." Harvey scowled, thinking of all the possibilities.

"So, who did it, and when?" Eddie asked.

"Someone could have done it while you were at the Bretons' house, or Mrs. Breton's office. How long were you there?"

He shrugged. "Twenty minutes max."

"Right. As soon as Yeaton got there, you left. Five seconds after you got back here, kaboom."

"A pro could do this in thirty seconds," Arnie said. "It was probably while you were at Mrs. Breton's office."

"It's not your fault, Ed," Harvey said. "Don't look so depressed. I'm just glad you made it back here okay."

"How could I get in a car with a bomb and not know it?"

"It depends on where they put it. It must have had a timer."

"Do you think Tonya did it?" Eddie's eyes darkened.

Harvey gritted his teeth and shrugged. "She's only sixteen. It's more likely her cocaine supplier did it or had it done. When the metal cools off, the bomb squad might be able to tell us what kind of device it was."

The fire was burning itself out. Eddie leaned on a pillar at the entryway and watched it, frowning.

"You'd better take the rest of the day off," Harvey said.

Eddie grimaced. "Forget it. This isn't a day to sit around."

Arnie laughed. "No, it's a day to check your life insurance policy and tell your mother you love her."

Two police cars rolled into the school yard, and a fire truck approached with its siren wailing.

"Talk to these guys, Arnie," Harvey told him. "There's something I need to do."

• • •

"Did you hear?" Jane Morrow asked Jennifer when she returned to the office from lunch.

"Hear what?"

"Nick Dunham was seen in Florida."

Jennifer stared at her. "I don't believe it."

"Tom Henderson just told me."

Jennifer shook her head. "Detective Larson was here yesterday, and he didn't say anything like that."

Jane frowned. "As if the police would tell us. Tom told me some friend of his e-mailed him that the FBI has a lead in Florida."

"Oh, come on. The FBI telling Tom's mythical friend is more believable than the local police telling us?"

There was affront in Jane's arched eyebrows. "Well, I believe it. He ran off and left Lisa and the kids, and is working at a nightclub in Orlando."

"Don't tell me. He's a bouncer."

"No," Jane said stiffly. "He's a singer."

Jennifer tried to hold back her laughter, but she couldn't help it. The tension of the last two days boiled over. It started as a low chortle, and quickly escalated.

Jane stared at her. "What? You think that's—" She winced. "I guess you're right. It is pretty funny."

Jennifer gasped and touched her friend's sleeve. "Jane, does it make sense to you that a man who wants to disappear would take a high-profile job as a singer?"

Jane began to laugh. "Remember the Christmas party, when we were all singing 'Jingle Bells'?"

"Do I ever. Nick can't sing."

"Okay, I get it. Tom was pulling my leg. But that's a pretty nasty joke, if you think about it. What if I'd seen Lisa and said something to her?"

"Yes," Jennifer said. "It's not at all nice."

Jane went back to her desk, and Jennifer turned to her computer. She wished she hadn't put Harvey off. All afternoon she regretted it. But tomorrow would be better. Maybe by then she could sort out the apprehension that had grabbed her when Jane mentioned Nick Dunham. And maybe by then her pulse would quit racing every time she thought of the fine lines that formed at the corners of Harvey's vivid blue eyes when he smiled at her.

But tomorrow was so far away.

It was after five o'clock when Jimmy took Harvey and Eddie back to the police station in the squad car. Harvey was glad on one level that he didn't have to rush home to get ready for a date, but part of him wished he was seeing Jennifer tonight. Maybe then he could forget about how close his best friend had come to annihilation.

Mike stood up as they came out of the stairway into the office.

“Are you guys all right?”

“I’m okay,” Eddie said. He looked ruefully at the Band-Aid on his hand. “I feel bad about Harvey’s car.”

“You can use one from the motor pool until you get something else,” Mike said. “I already called our insurance guy to come see you tomorrow, Harv. You should get a check right away. So, where are you on the case?”

Harvey sat down wearily at his desk. “I’m actually more optimistic than I was this morning. A girl Arnie questioned gave us a tip that may lead to some arrests.”

“Great,” Mike said. “I told the detective sergeant to put one of his men on this car bomb thing.”

“Not us?” Eddie asked, openly disappointed.

“You’re too close to it. Let them handle it.”

“If we solve the drug case, we’ll solve the bombing,” Eddie predicted. He headed for the locker room.

When they were alone, Mike looked keenly at Harvey. “You sure you’re okay?”

“I was nowhere near it when it went off. Eddie’s the one who had the close shave.”

“I know.” Mike stroked his chin. “Something’s been bothering you lately. Is it Carrie?”

Harvey smiled grimly. “I’m good, Mike.”

His captain nodded. “All right, I’ll leave you alone. Just keep me posted. This car bomb might not have anything to do with the school case."

"I know. I keep trying not to think it, but it's possible someone wanted Eddie out of the way."

"More likely it was aimed at you." Mike took his blazer from the back of his chair. "Could be someone with a grudge against you from a case you handled years ago. Be careful, Harv. You and Eddie both need to check your vehicles before you start the engine."

"Right." Mike left by the stairway, and Harvey sat for a moment, staring at his computer screen. It was late. He would come back for an hour or two Saturday morning and catch up on his reports. He ran a hand through his hair. This had to be the craziest day of his life.

Jennifer unlocked the door and let herself into the little rental house. She was relieved that her roommate wasn't home yet. Donna-jean had a way of making her feel ill at ease in her own home. She had advertised for a roommate when she got the job in Portland, knowing it would be hard to pay the rent alone, and Donna-jean was what she got. How many times had she wished she'd taken longer to decide and interviewed more candidates?

She took her portfolio and jacket to her bedroom, then went to the tiny kitchen. As she scanned the contents of the refrigerator, the doorbell rang.

She looked out the kitchen window. A beige van sat in the driveway, a commercial logo clearly visible on the side panel. She went quickly through the living room and opened the door cautiously, keeping the security chain on it. A young woman about her age stood waiting.

"Flowers for Jennifer Winthrop."

"Wainthrop," she said automatically. "Did you say flowers?"

"Yes, ma'am. Someone is thinking of you today."

Jennifer smiled, still not quite believing it, but the woman held a rectangular box and a clipboard. She unfastened the chain and took the package.

She locked the door again and carried the box to the kitchen table, her breath coming in shallow gulps. Her stomach fluttered as she carefully lifted the lid.

Roses. Velvety yellow roses. Their fragrance surrounded her, giving rise to a wild, riotous hope.

She pried the tiny card out of the envelope. *Jennifer, the hours are dragging. Until tomorrow. Harvey*

Her pulse galloped as she pictured him telling the florist, "A dozen roses. Perfect yellow roses."

She strode quickly to her bedroom and opened the leather portfolio she carried to work. After ransacking the pockets inside, she extracted his business card.

Should she, or shouldn't she?

She went back to the kitchen with her phone in her hand. She punched in the first three digits of Harvey's cell phone number, then hit "End." She found she was as nervous as she had been when she drove to the restaurant to meet him for lunch.

The scent of the roses washed over her, and she went to look at them again. It was years since a man had sent her flowers. More than three years now, and they hadn't been as nice as these. These were serious flowers.

She clicked on her phone, took a deep breath, and called. It rang three times. She nearly hung up, but then his voice came, confident and sure.

"Detective Larson." There was just a hint of fatigue.

"I—Hello—I—it's Jennifer." She gulped.

"Well, hello. This is a nice surprise."

"I—is it all right for me to call you like this?"

"Sure. I told you to."

"That was if I had information. I don't really, but—well, there is something, but I really called about the flowers."

"Aha."

There was silence, and for a panicky moment she thought, *Oh, no! This is a mistake!*

"You seemed like a rose person," he said, and her relief was so sharp she sat down on the floor and leaned back against the cupboard.

"Thank you," she breathed. "They're wonderful."

"I'm glad you like them."

Jennifer closed her eyes and tipped her head back against the hard cabinet door. His voice alone was enough to set her adrenaline flowing.

"You said there was something else?" he asked, and she jerked upright.

"Well, yes, sort of. I—" She made herself inhale and exhale quietly. "Do you think Nick Dunham is still alive?"

"Honestly? My instincts say he's not, but we have to keep going as if he is, keep hoping he is. I keep checking with the hospitals and watching the law enforcement updates, but so far there's nothing solid."

Jennifer sighed. "There's a silly rumor going around the office that he's trying to make it as a singer down in Florida."

"Interesting."

"Have you heard anything like that?"

"No. We've followed up on all the tips that were called in after his disappearance, but this is the first I've heard of Florida."

"Orlando," Jennifer said quickly. "My friend Jane told me. Some guy in the office told her he'd heard it by e-mail. But Nick doesn't sing. It struck me funny at the time, and I told her it was a joke. Is it?"

Harvey was quiet for a moment. "I don't know.

Probably, but I'll check it out. Do you have this guy's name and phone number?"

"Tom Henderson. I don't have his home number."

"But he works at Coastal?"

"Yes. He works on the infrastructure."

"He's not a programmer?"

"Well, sort of. He's not a designer, but he takes care of the company's network."

"I see."

Jennifer had the comforting feeling that he did see.

"I'll have a little chat with Mr. Henderson this evening."

She winced. "I didn't mean to make extra work for you."

"Don't worry about it. We want to find Nick Dunham. A little overtime is incidental."

She heard a car in the driveway again and stood to look out the window.

"Detective—Harvey? My roommate just came home."

"Okay, I'll see you tomorrow night."

"Right. Thank you."

Reluctantly she hung up. She went to the table and stuffed the card back into its envelope, then tucked it in her pocket. But there was no hiding the gorgeous roses. She opened the cabinets, searching for a vase. She was lifting the roses carefully from the green tissue paper when Donna-jean poked her head into the kitchen.

“Wow! Excellent! What’s the occasion?”

Jennifer took a deep breath. She’d had two minutes to plan what she would tell her roommate about Harvey.

“A friend of mine sent them.” She smiled as mundanely as she could manage, but her heart still pounded.

Donna-jean smiled knowingly. “Some friend. He must be filthy rich.”

“Well, no, I don’t think so.”

“Then he’s in love. Congratulations.”

Jennifer swallowed. “I—Thanks.”

But Donna-jean had already retreated into the living room, and Jennifer heard her bedroom door close. The stale smell of tobacco that perpetually wafted around Donna-jean was, for once, overpowered by the scent of roses.

Eddie sat at his desk, banging out a report with two fingers on the keyboard. At last he finished and swiveled toward Harvey. “So, you ready to go home?”

“Actually, I just got a tip in the Dunham case. I’m going to stay for a while and follow it up.”

“Need some help?”

Harvey considered that. “I’m not sure yet. It’s an office rumor. I’m trying to get to the source.”

“I’ll stay,” Eddie said.

"No date tonight?"

Eddie shrugged.

"You don't usually lack for a date on Friday night," Harvey said.

"I'm seeing Nicci later. You know, the waitress from Clark's? She doesn't get off 'til ten."

"You're reduced to picking up cocktail waitresses now?"

Eddie bristled. "Hey, she's smart. She's a student at the university, and that's how she earns her tuition money. I don't suppose you want to double?"

"Not."

"She's a physics major."

"Really," Harvey said dryly, searching online for Thomas Hendersons in Portland. He found three. One was a dentist. He dialed the second one and got a busy signal. He tried the third number, and a woman answered.

"Hey, is Tom in?" Harvey said brightly.

"Who's calling, please?"

"This is Harvey. I know him from Coastal Technology." Harvey cringed inwardly, and glanced up at Eddie, but his minor fiction hadn't even registered with his partner. Eddie had peeled the Band-Aid from his hand and was examining his wound. When Eddie had joined the unit, it had been up to Harvey to instruct him on how to lie glibly. Why was he suddenly developing a conscience?

"He's not home yet," the woman said. "He had to run an errand, but he should be here in a half hour. Try his cell."

"I'll catch up with him later." Harvey hung up. "Come on, let's get a ride home. We can get your truck and grab a bite to eat, then we'll swing by this guy's house."

At 6:45 they left the Burger King and headed for Tom Henderson's house.

"You'll have to drive Monday," Harvey said. He and Eddie had carpooled to work for almost three years. They lived only a couple of blocks apart and rode around together all day, anyway.

"No problem." Eddie turned onto Forest Avenue.

"Strange day," Harvey said. At noon he'd almost destroyed his embryonic relationship with Jennifer, but somehow they'd gotten past his blunder and moved to firmer ground. The roses had helped. Maybe he hadn't forgotten everything about women after all.

"Not every day your car blows up."

Harvey jerked back to reality. He'd almost forgotten about the car. "Right."

"*Je le regrette*."

"Forget it, Eddie. It wasn't your fault."

Eddie shrugged, and Harvey knew it would be a long time before he would forget it.

"If you see my folks, don't say anything, okay?"

Harvey smiled. "You think your parents don't read the paper?"

"Did you see any reporters?" Eddie asked anxiously.

"That hotshot from the *Press Herald* was there before the fire was out, and the Channel 13 truck came in while the bomb squad was working."

"Guess I'll have to explain things to Maman, then." Eddie sighed. "You sure you're not mad at me, Harv?"

"No, Eddie, I'm not mad." How many times had Eddie asked him that in five years? He guessed he ought to expect it; there were plenty of times when he'd yelled at Eddie or dressed him down for carelessness.

Eddie had come into the unit green and awkward. It had taken Harvey a while to accept the reality of working with a new and inexperienced man, but it hadn't taken him long to like Eddie. He was rather pleased with the way his protégé was turning out.

"So, do you like her?" Eddie asked.

"Who?"

"The girl you ate lunch with. It was that computer girl from Coastal, wasn't it?"

"I taught you well, didn't I?"

"I didn't have to shadow you or anything. It wasn't that hard to figure out."

Harvey smiled, but wasn't sure how much to tell him. "Yes, I like her."

"*Elle est belle.*"

"If you said what I think you did, then *oui.*"

"How old is she?"

Harvey pretended not to hear.

"Oh, come on, Harv—"

"Twenty-five, all right?"

"Man, you are robbing the cradle!"

Harvey refrained from comment.

"You going to see her again?"

"Mind your own business." Harvey looked out the window, feeling guilty. "Okay, okay," he relented as Eddie pulled up in front of Henderson's house. "We're going out tomorrow night."

"Wow! You didn't waste any time."

Harvey inspected his fingernails. "Can't at my age."

They were sitting in front of a well-kept, two-story house in an upper-middle class neighborhood. They got out and walked up onto the porch. Harvey punched the bell, and a woman opened the front door to him, full of curiosity and expectation.

"I'm Detective Larson, with the Portland P.D. I'd like to speak to Thomas Henderson."

Harvey always regretted the way their eyes clouded when they realized the police were on their doorstep. She stepped back uncertainly.

"Sure . . . I guess. Wait here."

She turned away but didn't close the door.

Sometimes they did, and his danger radar would scream. But it was a warm evening, and Mrs. Henderson apparently had no immediate reason to want to shut the police out.

Her husband came from the kitchen, with his wife hanging back a few steps. Harvey did a quick appraisal as he approached. Late thirties, well dressed, tired but wary.

"Mr. Henderson?"

"Yes."

"I'd like to ask you a few questions about Nick Dunham."

Henderson's eyes flickered. "Nick's been missing for two months."

"I know. I'm heading the investigation. May I come in?"

There was a little confusion, a touch of uneasiness, but Harvey expected that.

Henderson stepped back, and Harvey followed him into the living room, glancing quickly back toward the truck. Where had Eddie wandered off to? Harvey hoped he wouldn't get into trouble for snooping around.

Henderson sat down on the sofa, and Harvey took a chair opposite him. Mrs. Henderson hovered in the kitchen doorway.

Harvey opened the interview with a smile. "When did you last see Nick Dunham, Mr. Henderson?"

He shrugged. "The day he disappeared, I

suppose. I told the detectives when they were at the office. They questioned all of us."

Harvey nodded. "Have you heard from Nick since then?"

Henderson's eyes widened. "Of course not. I mean . . . nobody has, have they?"

He seemed genuinely baffled by the question, and Harvey moved along smoothly. "Have you heard anything *about* Nick since he's been missing?"

"What do you mean?"

Harvey shrugged slightly. "Rumors, speculation . . ."

"Well, sure, maybe. I mean, there are stories going around the office."

"What kind of stories?"

"I don't know. Everybody has their theory on what happened to Nick."

Harvey waited a moment, until Henderson met his eyes. "What's your theory?"

Henderson held his hands up defensively. "I thought it was up to the cops to have theories. You're asking *me* where he is?"

Harvey smiled. "Have you heard the one about Orlando?"

"Orlando? As in Florida? Yeah, I guess I've heard that. It's stupid."

Harvey nodded. "How did you hear that story?"

"I don't know. Must have been from one of the

women in the office. Some of them stand around and gab by the hour, you know? You go to get coffee, and you hear snatches of conversation."

"One of your coworkers told me they got that story from you."

Henderson stood up. "Like I said, Nick's disappearance is a topic that won't go away at Coastal. When he was there, nobody noticed him. But now that he's gone . . ."

"So, you're certain you didn't get that item from an outside source."

Henderson's eyes narrowed. "What did you say your name was?"

"Larson. Detective Larson."

"So, you work at the police station on Middle Street."

"That's right."

There was something in Henderson's eyes now that Harvey didn't like.

"Well, I don't know if you understand the computer business, Detective. It's very competitive."

"Yes, I realize that."

"Nick Dunham is very good at what he does."

"So I've been told."

Henderson nodded. "You want my theory? Nick's gone to another company. Far away. He's not singing in bars. He's in Los Angeles, or Paris, or Tokyo, writing software."

"And left his family behind?"

"Well, it happens sometimes, doesn't it?"

Harvey stood up. "If you hear anything concrete, let us know."

"Absolutely." Henderson was almost jovial as he showed Harvey to the door.

Eddie was in the truck. As he buckled his seat belt, Harvey said, "Take me back to the station, quick."

Eddie's eyebrows arched. He threw the transmission into reverse and backed out of the driveway.

"You got something?"

"Nothing definite."

"You think he knows something?"

"Maybe. I'm pretty sure he deliberately planted the rumor with the woman he knew was most likely to spread it around the office."

"Not Jennifer."

Harvey frowned. "No, not Jennifer. Her friend Jane."

"Oh, yeah, I remember her. Brunette. Not bad looking. Talks a blue streak."

"I'm surprised you haven't taken her out by now."

"Harvey, this is business." His injured tone made Harvey feel guilty.

"I suppose you think I'm breaking the rules?"

"No. I didn't mean that. The case was inactive 'til Wednesday, right?"

Harvey took a deep, slow breath. "That's right."

Eddie stared straight ahead as he drove. "That

Henderson's got a boat, two snowmobiles, and a pop-up camper. I wonder how much he makes?"

"His wife probably works, too," Harvey said.

Eddie shrugged. "Probably. Hey, you want me to take you car shopping tomorrow?"

"Maybe. I haven't had a chance to look at the ads yet."

"You want a new car?"

Harvey scowled at him. "Never buy anything new, that's my motto."

"You ought to look in *Uncle Henry's*."

The weekly shopper booklet was a Maine institution.

"Yeah, maybe. But I don't want to have to drive two hundred miles to look at something."

"I can take you to a dealer."

"I never buy from dealers."

"You never buy from anybody. Harvey, you are out of the consumer loop."

"You're right."

"You should get a sports car."

"I don't think so."

"New girlfriend." Eddie smiled at him.

"She's not my girlfriend. We ate lunch together once."

"All right, a truck, then."

"I don't want a truck."

Eddie drove into the parking garage. "So, what are we here for?"

"I need to check Tommy's e-mail."

"You're going to crack into his private e-mail files? I don't know, Harv. Don't you need a warrant or something?"

"E-mail's not secure. Everybody knows that."

"Yeah, especially with you around."

They climbed the stairs swiftly, and Harvey turned on his computer. It took him less than two minutes to get into Coastal's files this time. He skimmed Henderson's personnel record then tried to access the company's e-mail system. That took a little longer.

"Want me to make some coffee?" Eddie asked.

Harvey barely heard him. "Sure." When Eddie placed a steaming cup at his elbow five minutes later, he sat back and sighed.

"What?"

"He's cleaned it out recently. No way to tell if he heard the Nick Dunham rumor from outside, like he told Jane."

"Did you talk to her?" Eddie asked.

"No, I was hoping to skip that step, but I guess I've got to." He sipped the coffee and made a face. "This is awful."

"Sorry."

"I think your punishment is to interview Jane Morrow. Make sure Jennifer got this straight."

"Oh, come on, Harv."

Harvey pulled out his pocket notebook and thumbed through it. "Here's her phone number. Remember, she's not bad looking."

Chapter 7

Jennifer spent much of Saturday reviewing her limited wardrobe and trying to classify her feelings for Harvey Larson. A strong attraction, for sure, and she was certain he reciprocated. He was funny, he was intelligent, but there was a trace of insecurity, too. And he'd been divorced before his wife died. She wasn't sure she could get past that.

A dinner date was rare for her, and nothing in her closet seemed suitable. She had the afternoon free and decided to go shopping. She drifted in and out of a few stores and gave up. Her four-year-old print dress would have to do.

Harvey arrived punctually, wearing a suit and glasses. He could pass himself off as a professor or a stock broker, she thought. Maybe he did, on undercover cases. The sun was getting low, and his blue eyes gleamed behind the glasses as he smiled at her on the doorstep.

Immediately, Jennifer wished she'd bought a new dress. Her floral print seemed fussy and out of date.

Donna-jean, as usual, was gone for the evening. Jennifer was glad she hadn't been on hand when Harvey arrived, as a wave of shyness swept over her.

She stopped in surprise on the steps. A red Subaru was parked in the driveway. “This is your car?”

He hesitated. “No, it’s a loaner.”

Part of her was satisfied. The little red car didn’t go with his personality. She had sensed that he would have a nondescript sedan that would blend in and keep him from being noticed. But another part of her was alarmed. Loaners meant trouble.

“Your car’s in the shop?”

“No, it blew up yesterday.”

He opened the car door for her. She stared at him. She could tell he was serious, and it frightened her.

Harvey smiled. “It’s okay. You can get in.”

She climbed in and arranged her skirt while he went around to the driver’s side. Maybe she should have worn dressy pants.

“You weren’t kidding, were you?” she asked.

“It’s one of the hazards of the job.” He started to buckle his seat belt. “Oh, I almost forgot.” He pulled a piece of paper from his inside breast pocket. When he did it, she glimpsed the badge pinned inside his jacket and the butt of his gun. A shiver went through her, and she took a deep breath.

“What’s this?” She took the paper gingerly.

“It’s my make-up test. I didn’t answer all your questions yesterday.”

She unfolded it, glancing at him, trying to read his mood. It said:

1. Because I always wanted to be one.
2. Yes.
3. Very much.
4. Not really.
5. Yes, pepperoni.
6. If I'm not working, I read, go to the shooting range, read, check my stocks, read, play basketball with my partner, and read.

She smiled and folded it up again. "Now I just have to remember what the questions were." She put it in her purse, and he started the car.

"Don't I get a report card?" He seemed relaxed, contented almost, and Jennifer felt the tension dissipating.

"A-plus."

"Really?"

"Sure. You love your job, and you like pizza. What more could I ask?"

"Do you want pizza tonight? I mean, I was thinking something classier, but if you really crave pizza . . ."

"No, take me wherever you were thinking of."

"There's a place on Monument Square that specializes in seafood. Is that okay?"

"Sure."

He headed into town. It struck her suddenly that he had done a very good job of distracting her from the fact that his car had been sabotaged. She watched him furtively as he drove, until he turned a dazzling smile on her. She didn't care then, about the car. She was just glad to be with him, and if he didn't want to talk about it, that was all right.

He was witty and charming that evening. They ate sea scallops and talked for hours. He told her about his older sisters and how they looked out for him after their parents died, hoarding the money that was left to supplement his college scholarships. When both parents were killed in a car wreck, Harvey had been eighteen, about to enter pre-law at Harvard.

Ivy League, Jennifer thought with dismay. He must have had huge scholarships. Her parents had struggled with the bills to UMaine. Jeff had been a senior her freshman year, and they had both worked. Her junior year, Abby had entered nursing school. There was never enough money. Her job at Coastal Technology had allowed her to help out a little with Abby and Leeanne's education.

"I was going to go to law school, but I decided I'd rather enforce the law than argue it." He smiled a bit apologetically.

They were from different universes, she could

see that now. She took a deep breath. "And where do your sisters live?"

"Near Concord, New Hampshire. It's where I grew up. They're both married and have children."

He asked Jennifer about her childhood, and she described the farmhouse in Skowhegan and her sister Leeanne's herd of goats. Harvey had a repertoire of funny cop stories that kept her in stitches. Then he bemoaned his partner Eddie, and how he'd had to baby-sit him through his first year on the job.

"You really like Eddie, don't you?" she asked.

"He's immature in some ways, but he's my best friend now. Not to mention he's saved my life several times."

"I guess you look out for him, too."

He nodded deferentially.

They talked about music. Harvey liked jazz.

"I'm more into classical," she said cautiously.

Harvey shrugged. "I can live with it. Would you like to go to the symphony sometime?"

"Well, sure, I guess." Jennifer tried to keep her hands from shaking as she poured tea into the tiny cups.

"You minored in philosophy."

She nodded. "Seems useless now."

"I'm sure it wasn't wasted."

She shrugged.

"No, really," Harvey said earnestly. "It tells

me that you like to think about ideas. That's important."

"But not very practical."

"And underneath the dreamy exterior, you're a pragmatist."

She smiled and sipped her tea.

"So, what are you reading now?" he asked.

She had to laugh. "A biography of Pascal."

"Aha! See, you still like philosophy."

"I didn't say I didn't like it."

"So, he's the guy who invented the computer, right?"

She sat back a little and tried to decide if he was teasing her. "Yes. It was a mechanical thing. But you knew that."

"Sure. The computer language is named after him. All nerds know that."

"Do you know about the wager?" she asked.

"Hmm, Pascal's wager. It's been a long time." His brow furrowed. "Something like, if you take the bet you win, and if you don't, you lose big?"

"Right. He told his friend the gambler he believed God was real, and the friend should bet on it. If he did and Pascal was right, he'd win, and if Pascal was wrong, he'd lose nothing. But if he didn't take the wager and Pascal was right, he'd lose everything."

"I don't know about that metaphor," said Harvey. "I think faith is more than just covering your bases."

"Oh, me too. But it's thought provoking. Can we ever know for sure that God is real, or is believing more important than the reality? That's something I'd like to know."

"You think a lot about God?" he asked.

"Some. Don't you?"

"As a matter of fact, I've been thinking about him a lot lately."

Jennifer felt a slow-burning excitement. She'd half expected him to brush off her comments. She leaned forward. "So . . . what do you think? Is God real?"

He seemed to weigh his answer carefully. "I don't know, but . . . I kind of hope he is."

She nodded. "Me too." But she wasn't at all sure she would ever know.

The discussion on books broadened. Harvey was an eclectic reader, and she had a mental picture of his apartment, lined with bookshelves and comfortable chairs. He seemed to read everything, from best sellers to obscure authors.

"I like mysteries," she said, feeling just a little silly.

Harvey grinned. "Mysteries are great! I like legal thrillers. What do you like?"

"I like detectives."

He nodded expectantly, and she flushed.

"Oh, well, you know. Lord Peter Wimsey, Hercule Poirot . . ."

"The classic detectives."

"Yes, because the writing is so good. But I like spy stories, too. Escapist literature, my father calls it."

The waitress came to refill their glasses, and Jennifer wondered if the uniformed girl thought Harvey was her father. She was enjoying his company. Every woman should have the chance to go out with a smart, attentive man once in a while. She would be very disappointed if he never called her again.

When they left the restaurant, she wished the evening wasn't over. The house was dark when they walked up the steps.

"I guess Donna-jean isn't home yet," she said.

"She's the bad-news roommate?"

Jennifer smiled. She had told him a little about Donna-jean. She fished her key ring from her pocket and gulped as he reached for it. Did he expect her to ask him in? The only men who had been inside the little house were her father and brothers and Donna-jean's boyfriends.

She glanced up at Harvey warily, and he looked a little nervous himself.

"I enjoyed the evening," she said.

Harvey smiled. "So did I. Do you think—"

He broke off as a car drove up, and Donna-jean bounced out, shouting noisy goodbyes to the occupants over the blaring music that pulsed from within.

"The infamous Donna-jean, I presume?" Harvey asked.

"The very same."

She trudged up the walk as the car pulled away and stopped in surprise when she saw them.

"Well, Jennifer, a date at last?"

"Donna-jean, this is Harvey. Harvey, this is my roommate, Donna-jean."

"The guy with the roses? Pleased to meet you, I'm sure." She was tipsy and loud, fumbling with her key ring.

"The door's unlocked," Jennifer said.

"Oh, did I interrupt the good-night kiss?"

Donna-jean stumbled through the door and slammed it.

Harvey looked down at the ground with a tight little smile. "Well, I guess I'd better go." His eyes met hers, and Jennifer caught her breath as the intimacy returned. "Can I see you next weekend?"

She hesitated. "What did you have in mind?"

"I checked the paper this afternoon. There's a jazz concert in the Old Port, or we could go early to the art museum. Unless you'd prefer Shakespeare? *As You Like It*, at the university on Saturday."

Jennifer stood still, savoring the feelings that washed over her. His confidence was back, and he'd gone to some trouble to search out something she would like. "I like that play."

"Let's do it, then. And I'll check out the symphony's schedule for another time."

Another time. Already he was planning their future together. It made her feel wanted and pampered, and a little shy of his direct masculinity.

"What do I wear to the play? I mean, is it a student production?"

"No, I think it's a professional group from out of state. They have a big production at graduation time every year. It should be good."

"So, slightly formal?"

"If you want. I think it's up to us what we want it to be."

Inside her, the excitement warred with a nagging caution. But he was so different from any of the men she had ever liked before. He wasn't impulsive or arrogant. Despite the slight nervousness she had detected earlier, he had remained gracious and thoughtful. From the moment she'd opened the door to him tonight, she'd known she wouldn't refuse another invitation. And she would definitely buy a new dress.

Harvey looked down at her, a smile playing at his lips. "What part did you play in *A Midsummer Night's Dream*?"

She laughed. "You don't want to know."

"Yes I do. I'm guessing Hermia. Tell me it wasn't the donkey."

"No, it was Snug."

"*You* played a man?"

"Yeah, it was fun."

"Wasn't Snug the guy who got to be the lion?"

"Yup."

"That's a funny part. I'll bet you were cute."

"No, I was very fierce," Jennifer said with dignity.

"Right." He was shivering a little.

She reached for the doorknob. "I'd better go in."

He nodded, his eyes very serious. "Good night, Jenny." He squeezed her hand for an instant and stepped back.

Jennifer swallowed hard. "No one ever calls me Jenny."

"I'm sorry."

"No, it's all right. I mean, if you want to . . ." He smiled, and she felt very young and inept. She made herself open the door.

"More trouble?" Channing asked. He leaned back in his leather-covered swivel chair and eyed his partner coolly. "I guess our electronic security isn't as tight as I thought it was."

Jack Rainey sat down opposite him and locked his hands across his stomach. "I've got Henderson on it, but I'm not sure he should be the one handling this."

"Why is that?" Channing asked. "We agreed we can trust him."

"We're pretty sure this breach originated from the same place as the last one."

Channing swore. "Not that cop again?"

"Portland police station," Rainey agreed. "It's got to be Detective Larson."

"Why do you say that?"

"Because he's smart."

Channing sighed and picked up his telephone receiver. "Bart, are you free at the moment? Jack's in my office, and we'd like you to step in here if you can." He hung up and stared gloomily at the painting on the wall near the door until Bart Owen's quick tap came on the oak panel.

"What's up, Ron?" Owen asked cheerfully as he entered.

Channing scowled. Bart Owen was the oldest of the partners, and by far the most optimistic. When things were looking shaky, he found Bart's upbeat outlook irritating.

"A hacker got into our company records again Friday night."

Owen shrugged. "We don't keep anything sensitive in there. Confidential, yes, but not top secret. All of that is secure, and we're very careful."

Rainey turned from the window. "The police are looking at us again, Bart."

Owen frowned. "I see. Well, I don't like it, but I suppose it's inevitable. Unfortunate, this whole business with Dunham. It comes at a bad time for us. They found his car, and he was last seen here. We can't do anything about that."

"We need to tighten the security features on our company databases and our cloud storage," Channing said.

"Well, yes." Owen smiled. "Put Jennifer Wainthrop on it. She's capable."

"I'm not sure that's a good idea." Owen's eyes widened in surprise, and Channing looked away. He knew Owen had always liked Jennifer and encouraged him and Jack to put her on the most important projects. But Channing wasn't sure she had the temperament for the stress involved, or that her loyalty to Coastal was unshakable, even if she was a better designer than the rest of them put together.

Jack Rainey stepped forward. "Bart, this cop who's looking at us . . . the first time, he looked at Jennifer Wainthrop's personnel file. This time he went after Tom Henderson's."

Owen's brow furrowed as he considered that. "You think that's significant."

"Of course it's significant," Channing snapped. Sometimes he wondered why he and Jack had teamed up with Bart. He could charm the clients, but he was definitely a step behind when it came to shrewdness.

Rainey said, "Detective Larson went to Henderson's house Friday night and asked him about Dunham. Then someone at the police station broke into Henderson's personnel file and e-mail."

"You think they believe Henderson had something to do with Dunham disappearing?"

"Who knows?" Rainey shook his head.

Owen looked from him to Channing. "But Jennifer?"

"I'm not sure we can trust her," Rainey said. "He looked at her file last Thursday."

"Why do you think he's investigating our employees so minutely?" Channing asked the older man, watching his face carefully.

"I don't know." Owen was clearly baffled, and Channing felt the same way. "Are you sure it's the detective?"

"Who else could it be?" Channing rubbed his forehead.

"But he's not trying to access the new program," Owen said.

Channing said slowly, "He doesn't know about that program, Bart. And we've got to make sure it stays that way."

Rainey sighed. "I don't know if we've got anyone besides Jennifer who can build a program that will keep this detective out."

"Now that Dunham's gone," Channing agreed.

Rainey shook his head. "She's even better than him, Ron. I'm just not sure . . ."

Owen looked from Rainey to Channing.

"Surely the police couldn't get into any files that would cause suspicion."

Rainey went back to the window. His silence told Channing that Jack was uneasy. He looked at Owen. "If Larson starts monkeying around with our databases during business hours, when the designers are online and working on projects, some of our programs could be compromised."

"And if someone were working on the special project," Rainey said ominously, "that would be very bad."

"Do you think Henderson is safe?" Owen asked.

Rainey nodded with the slightest reservation.

"But he's not as smart as this cop," Channing said.

"Oh, surely the city doesn't hire people the caliber of our staff," Owen began, but Channing interrupted him.

"That cop went to Harvard. I did some checking on my own. He's not someone you want to mess with."

Rainey said slowly, "If he's that clever, and he knows computers . . ."

"What? You're thinking we should hire him?" Owen asked. "Maybe that's not a bad idea."

Channing shook his head. "His record's clean as a whistle. His captain can't praise him enough."

"Nobody's untouchable," Rainey said, fingering the knot in his silver and burgundy tie.

"No, I think the original plan is best."

Owen's eyes narrowed. "What plan is that?"

"Just business as usual," Channing said.

Owen stepped forward and leaned on the edge of his desk. "You know I don't like this contract we've taken on."

"Yeah, I know, Bart."

Rainey stepped closer to Owen and put his hand on his partner's shoulder. "We had this discussion months ago. We're in it now, and we're in it together."

"It was just a simple program then, a harmless program for a foreign client."

"Well, things got a little complicated," Rainey said.

Owen stared at him for a moment, then turned abruptly and left the office.

"What do you think?" Rainey murmured.

Channing sighed. "I think we'd better be careful."

"I'll take care of this."

Channing pushed his chair back and stood up. "Make sure you do, Jack."

Rainey nodded. "We'll have to keep Henderson out of it. He's useful, but the less he knows, the better. And right now he thinks the cop is just looking at him because he didn't give him a pat answer the other night."

"All right. We'll get someone else to beef up the security."

"It may have to be Jennifer. There's no one else, Ron."

Channing scowled. "Keep Henderson at his usual mundane routine, and try to find something to distract Bart."

"He's going to Concord tomorrow to meet with the hospital executives there and push the administrative programs."

"Perfect."

Chapter 8

On Monday evening, Harvey made himself do laundry and buy a few groceries. He hadn't been home enough lately to make the apartment messy, but it was dusty, and he decided to do a little cleaning up. He didn't know why he had kept the place so long. After Carrie had left him, it was easier to do nothing. But now the memories were kicking in, and he wished he had moved out long ago.

As he hung up the clean shirts he'd pulled from the dryer in the basement utility room, his thoughts strayed to Jennifer. All through the previous evening, he had tried to decide whether she made him feel really young or really old.

He'd suspected a woman her age could shred his ego in seconds, but he'd ignored his instincts and asked her out again. He hadn't really cared whether she chose Shakespeare or the concert, as long as she would see him again. He would have taken her anywhere. Well, not bungee jumping.

He opened the day's newspaper and was circling ads for used cars when the doorbell rang. Eddie entered the kitchen and thrust a bright orange *Uncle Henry's* booklet into his hands.

"Page fifty-three."

"Well, hello to you, too." Harvey opened the

book and saw an ad Eddie had circled. A six-year-old Ford Explorer. "I don't know, Eddie. That's a lot of money."

"How much was the check from the insurance company?"

"Two thousand."

"Figures. That old car was ready for the scrap yard. Well, it's not like you don't have it. You're a tightwad."

"How about this '67 Mustang for four grand?"

"No, Harvey," Eddie said deliberately. "Do not get an older car. Women like new cars."

"Jennifer's not like that."

"Do you think she wants to ride in a car older than she is? Besides, it would be too easy to spot on a stakeout."

Harvey sighed and called the number for the SUV in Scarborough. "We can look at it tomorrow at 6:30," he told Eddie. "Will you take me after work?"

"*Oui, monsieur.*" Eddie flashed his bright smile.

"Can I take Jennifer?"

The smile dimmed. "I guess."

The closer Jennifer got to home after work on Tuesday, the faster her pulse raced. She was glad the driveway was empty when she reached it. She hurried into her bedroom and changed her clothes.

Harvey's invitation had come as a surprise. He'd called at 9:30 the evening before, just as she was preparing for bed.

Car shopping with his buddy wasn't the most romantic outing she could imagine, but Jennifer didn't care. It seemed safe. She could watch him interact with Eddie, and there would be no question of will-he-or-won't-he-kiss-me with his partner along.

She heard a vehicle in the driveway and glanced out the window. Eddie and Harvey got out of a black pickup. Her heart leaped, but there was an ache there, too. She remembered the car bomb, and the reason for this outing. She swallowed hard, picked up her key ring, and went outside.

"Hey, kiddo," Harvey said as she came down the steps. "You ready to roll?"

She nodded. "Hi, Eddie."

"Hi, Jennifer." Eddie's smile was brilliant.

"Did you guys have a good day? No bombs or anything?"

"We're fine, and we've wrapped up the drug case," Harvey said.

"Great! So, we're going to look at a car."

"A sport utility vehicle," Eddie corrected her.

"Really? That surprises me." She sat between them in the pickup. While Eddie drove, he described their work day. It was a convoluted story, ending with the arrest of a drug dealer who had been pushing his wares to high school students.

"Did you find out who put the bomb in your car?" She couldn't keep the edge from her voice.

"Not yet," Harvey said quietly. "Don't worry. We will." He put his arm up around the back of the seat, barely touching her shoulders. She felt a little comforted, and tried not to let herself blush.

Harvey seemed to like the forest green Explorer. He walked around it several times and lifted the hood while the owner rattled off the vehicle's history.

At last he smiled at Jennifer. "Want to go on a test drive, kiddo?"

She climbed in, wondering if the nickname would be permanent. She didn't like it. It emphasized the age difference, and it made her wonder if she looked childish in her jeans and sweater. She had put her hair up for their dinner date, but had it in her usual long braid tonight. Maybe it was time to think about cutting it. She didn't want him thinking of her as his little sister.

"I could really like this thing," Harvey said, adjusting the side view mirror. He tried out all the lights and the air conditioner, the parking brake, the power windows and locks, the radio, the CD player, and the heater. They drove a few blocks, then headed out away from town. After a couple of miles, he turned back.

"So, you like it?" she asked, and wished she hadn't. He'd already said he liked it.

He nodded. "I like it."

Eddie was waiting in the owner's driveway, lounging against the fender of his truck. Harvey parked the Explorer, and he and Eddie kicked the tires and talked to the owner about police work for twenty minutes. Harvey asked what the gas mileage was. They settled on a price, and he wrote a check. The owner said Harvey could drive it home with his license plates. Jennifer rode with him, and Eddie tailed them in his pickup.

They stopped at McDonald's for supper. Eddie told funny stories about his French grandmother, who always called him Édouard and expected him to come at least once a month for a tête-à-tête and bring her bonbons. He said "*les bonbons*," the French way, and Jennifer laughed. Harvey smiled indulgently. He'd probably heard all Eddie's stories before.

"Hey, Jennifer," Eddie said, "I was saying to Harvey that we ought to have a double date sometime."

"That might be fun." She looked at Harvey.

"Sure, Eddie. We'll let you know." He sounded tired.

Back in the Explorer, he pulled out onto the highway and watched to make sure Eddie got out behind him. He reached over in silence for

Jennifer's hand. Her heart lurched, and she curled her fingers around his. When they got back to her house, Eddie drove on past it and honked his horn. Harvey went around and opened the door of the Explorer for her, then took her up the steps and unlocked the house door.

"So, Saturday night?"

His blue eyes glittered in the dusk, and again Jennifer had the feeling he was struggling with insecurity.

"I'm looking forward to it."

He smiled then. "Me, too. I hope tonight wasn't too boring."

"No. I think . . ." She looked up at him, wondering how honest they could be at this point. "I think we need time like this."

He nodded. "Just normal time together."

"Yes."

He shoved his hands into his pockets and stood looking out toward the street. "It's been a long time since I did this. Spent normal time with anyone, I mean."

Jennifer swallowed. She wanted to be the normal part of his life, but it still felt scary, as if a huge, unknown risk lay ahead. If she allowed herself to care deeply for him, how badly would she be disappointed later?

Harvey was staring at the Explorer.

"So, you like the car."

He laughed. "Don't let Eddie hear you call it a car. But, yes, I like it."

"Would you . . ." She took a deep breath and began again. "I've been working on a program that might interest you. It's early, and I thought . . ."

He watched her, smiling but silent, and Jennifer could see he wasn't going to give her any help.

"It's just a simple flagging program, but it might help you at work. I mean, if it doesn't duplicate something you already have at the police department. I made something similar for a . . ." She stopped, willing herself to stop babbling. Harvey's expression was unreadable, and her hopes plummeted. He would think she was too aggressive. She ought to have waited until the program was perfect and their feelings for each other were defined.

"You mean you designed a computer program just for me?"

"Well . . . yeah. Other people could use it, but I meant it for you. If you want it. To help you . . ." She was doing it again. She stopped.

His smile turned into a huge grin. "I'd love to see it."

Jennifer exhaled in relief. "Then, would you mind coming in for a minute? It's . . ." She gestured vaguely toward the door.

"I didn't think you'd bring the computer out here."

"Right." She turned hastily to open the door.

• • •

Harvey followed Jennifer into the little house and stood just inside the door. Her nerves were so bad he could almost hear them jangle. She crossed the living room quickly and turned on her computer. He walked slowly toward her, looking around. Bright, cheerful drapes and throw pillows, family photos, and a poster-sized Van Gogh reproduction over the computer desk. The room was as big as his living room but had twice as much furniture. A bookcase, a rocking chair, crocheted afghans, a TV set and stereo. It smelled like roses, but he didn't see the bouquet he'd sent her. It must be in another room.

She turned part way and looked at him over her shoulder. "I really don't know much about police work, so maybe I've oversimplified things. Please don't laugh if it's not something you can use."

"I won't."

"Okay. I could install this on the computer you use at work, to flag items you want to stay updated on. It's better than a simple search program."

"In what way?" he asked.

"Say there's someone you've put in jail. You flag his name, and when he has a parole hearing, or is released, or—or—escapes, or anything, you would get an update."

Harvey chuckled involuntarily.

She winced.

"Sorry. I know I promised not to laugh, but if he escaped, I think they'd tell me."

"Right. Well, you know what I mean. If something was added to his record—"

He nodded. "For instance, if the patrol sergeant downstairs made a notation in his file?"

"Precisely!" Her gratitude was evident, and he smiled.

"It sounds useful."

"Do you really think so? Or would you get that information anyway?"

"Not necessarily. It sounds great."

"Does your department download records from a network regularly?"

"Yes, they've tried to get all the state, county, and municipal records standardized, and we get updates every day, but it's a chore to wade through them."

"Well, this would take away the headache and save you a lot of time. It would show an icon on your screen after each download, if any of the items you'd flagged had new input. Sort of like telling you that you have e-mail."

Her earnestness stirred him, and he wanted to reassure her. "Okay, take this man we arrested today, for example. If he makes bail or has a probable cause hearing, the computer will alert me?"

"That's the idea. And if he got a traffic ticket

in Fort Kent a month from now, it would tell you. Look, it's easy." She guided him rapidly through the steps of entering data into her program, and he was deeply impressed, both with her professionalism and the capabilities of the software. The confidence she'd shown at their first lunch date was back, and he liked it.

He moved closer and put his hand lightly on the back of her chair, peering at the monitor. "What if I wanted to find crimes with a certain M.O.?" He was thinking of the bomb under his car, but he didn't want to tell her that. "Say, murders by cyanide poisoning."

"Sure. Just enter a few words describing the crime. It would comb past records for matches and then send you an update whenever another murder was committed with cyanide. Until you disabled that flag."

"Terrific. You worked all this out yourself in a couple of days?"

She flushed and kept her eyes on the screen. "Well, a couple of months back, after you first came to the office, I started thinking about how the police keep track of things. I heard somewhere that a lot of old records aren't computerized yet."

"That's true."

"So I started thinking about how to make it easier, and I came up with this."

"Do you have it copyrighted or anything?"

"Not yet, but I will once it's finished. I've put my icon in it for security."

"What's that? Like a signature?"

"Yeah. It's a little group of characters in the program for no reason. It *is* a lot like a signature, or a copyright notice. So I can tell it's my work."

"Like an artist signing a painting?"

"Sort of. If someone copies the program, they'll copy that, too. No one will recognize it unless I tell them what it is."

"I usually get updates directly on my open cases from other officers within the department, but I can see this being really useful on input from older cases and new crimes in other areas."

"Exactly. Over time, I think it would help you a lot. That is, if you keep updating what you need and the cases you want to follow."

He nodded. "So, when can I test the program?"

"I'd have to install it on your computer, after I work out the details. If the department would let me, that is. I'm sure they're picky about who changes the programs on their computers."

"Yes, but I'm sort of high up in the chain of computer-approval people. It would only affect my computer, not the whole network, right?"

"Absolutely."

He nodded. The program wouldn't help him on his personal computer, since he couldn't access restricted law enforcement files with that. "Could you come to the police station after work one evening and do that?"

"Sure. I'll let you know when I'm ready."

"I'll mention it to my captain. I think he'll be impressed."

She swiveled the chair around and looked directly at him. They were very close. Her eyes widened in surprise, and she pushed the chair back a couple of inches on its wheels. "So, would you like something to drink?"

It was almost a squeak, and Harvey smiled, stepping back to avoid making her more nervous. "Sure, what have you got?"

"Coffee, milk, iced tea . . ."

"Iced tea is fine."

She went to the kitchen. Harvey's eyes strayed to the family photos displayed on top of the television. He picked up a framed photograph of six smiling youngsters. The Wainthrop siblings, he assumed. Jennifer, in a Skowhegan Indians sweatshirt, had her arm around one of her sisters and was grinning widely. Four blonds, two brunettes. They all seemed to have perfect teeth. He wondered how many of them had needed braces, and how George Wainthrop had paid for it.

He was putting the frame back when Jennifer appeared in the kitchen doorway. Her face was pale, and she was holding a white, plastic-wrapped bundle.

Chapter 9

Harvey stared at the bundle, his heart sinking. He'd seen packages like that all too often. "Where did you get that?"

"In the freezer. I was getting the ice cubes, and it was in there, between the broccoli and a box of ice cream."

"Just great." He took it from her by the edges and held the packet up to the lamp.

"What is it?" Her voice quavered.

"Probably heroin."

"That's what I was afraid of."

He carefully undid a strip of tape and examined the powder more closely. His first instinct was right. "Donna-jean's, I take it," he said.

"It's got to be hers, unless her boyfriend or somebody . . ."

"Well, she must know about it." He tried not to let his anger show, but Donna-jean would have to face his wrath for putting Jennifer in this situation.

"Is she in trouble?" Jennifer asked in a small voice.

"Of course. We've got to make sure *you're* not."

Her eyes were huge, and she swallowed hard.

Harvey touched the sleeve of her sweater

lightly. "Sit down, Jenny. Let me explain something to you."

She sat on the very edge of the sofa, staring up at him. He sat next to her, placed the bundle on the coffee table, and reached for her hands. "If for some reason the cops searched this house, you and Donna-jean could both be arrested. You both live here."

"But I didn't know anything about it."

"I realize that. But it's her word against yours, and your prints are on it now."

She looked sick. "You're not serious?"

"I'm not trying to scare you. I'm just trying to make you see that if you continue to live with that woman, you could end up in serious trouble, through no fault of your own. Who holds the lease on the house?"

"I do."

"Okay. We've got to get her out of here."

"I don't know how to make her go." Jennifer sank back, defeated. "Maybe I should just move out and leave her the house. I don't want to live with her anymore, that's for sure."

"Jenny, I know confrontation is hard, but she's the one who's broken the law. Why should you be punished?"

Tears filled her eyes, and he sighed.

"You had the house first, right?"

She nodded.

"Do I have your permission to search the place?"

"You can do that?" Her tear-filled eyes were hopeful.

"As long as you say I can. I can't search her bedroom, but I can search yours and all the common areas."

"Go ahead."

He squeezed her hands. "Relax. It's going to be okay."

He knew she couldn't relax. She stood and watched, arms folded tightly, as he methodically searched the living room. The bathroom was next, with no results. When he stepped into Jennifer's bedroom, her anxiety seemed to peak.

"You don't expect to find anything in here, do you?"

"Not really, but you never know. The nightmare roommate might plant something."

She stood in the doorway, her hands nervously rubbing the sleeves of her sweater. Harvey felt a little self-conscious as he lifted the edge of the mattress and shook the pillows out of shams that matched her blue quilt. When he got to the dresser, he asked her if she would take a look in the drawers and underneath them, to see if there was anything she didn't recognize. She seemed relieved to do that herself while he checked the closet, the night stand, the bookshelf, and under the bed.

He didn't find anything in Jennifer's room, the living room, bathroom or kitchen. He carried the trash can into the driveway and emptied it onto newspapers, and by flashlight found some marijuana butts in the leavings of an ashtray. He put them into a sandwich bag, in case for some reason he needed to check the DNA. The amount of weed was too small for a legal charge nowadays, but the heroine stash was plenty.

He cleaned up the trash and went back inside.

"It's nearly nine o'clock. When will she be home?"

"Hard to say, but she has to work tomorrow. She ought to be in soon."

"This druggie holds a job?"

"Yes, she's a hair stylist."

"Don't ever let her get her claws on your hair."

Jennifer laughed. "Believe me, I don't."

"Did you tell her what I do for a living?"

Her eyes widened. "No, I don't think I did. Are you going to arrest her?"

He reached out and touched her shoulder. "I think I have to. I'm sorry."

She gulped. "You couldn't just threaten her and tell her she has to move out?"

It was tempting, but he knew he couldn't do it. "Jenny, this amount of drugs is a major violation. There's at least eight ounces here, probably more. That implies that she's furnishing. I can't let her go. If anyone found out I knew about it and didn't do anything, it would mean my badge."

Jennifer drew a deep breath. "So, what do we do?"

"I'll call for an on-duty unit to come and get her. You might feel better if I'm not the one who makes the arrest."

She nodded, her eyes glistening with unshed tears.

He took out his phone and called the station. Jennifer leaned against the doorjamb, her arms crossed, listening. He knew the night sergeant.

"Brad, this is Harvey Larson. I've got a situation where a female friend of mine has found her roommate's heroin stash. Can you send a unit out here to pick up the roommate when she gets home? I'm off duty, and I'd really prefer someone else handle this."

"What's your 20?"

He gave Jennifer's address and told Brad he would wait until the officers arrived. "You might want to get a warrant for her bedroom," he added. "I've searched the rest of the house."

"On the way," said Brad.

"I'll stay until it's over," Harvey told Jennifer when he had hung up.

"You're tired," she said.

"This is important."

She turned and went into the kitchen, and he followed, standing in the doorway, unsure of where her volatile emotions were taking her. The yellow roses filled a vase on the small table, and the fragrance was much stronger in here. She opened a cabinet and took down two glasses.

He stepped to the counter and leaned on it, watching her closely as she took the pitcher of iced tea from the refrigerator and poured it. "This is for the best."

"I know," she said.

He wished he dared to put his arms around her, but she maintained an aloofness. The trust factor between them was still fragile, and the drugs seemed to test it to the breaking point.

"They'll be here soon."

Jennifer put one glass in his hand. "Let's sit in there."

He followed her back to the living room and sat beside her on the couch, on her left. That way his gun was on the side away from her and nearer the front door. He hoped the other officers would arrive before Donna-jean did, but he was prepared if they didn't. His badge was in his pocket. The open plaid shirt he wore over his dark T-shirt hid his shoulder holster.

He sipped his tea and set the glass down. Jennifer avoided his gaze. That hurt. Would she end up hating the way he earned his living, like Carrie had? When she flicked a glance his way, he said softly, "Jenny, please don't hold this against me."

"I won't." She bit her bottom lip.

“You don’t want to live with a drug user. For a lot of reasons.”

“You’re right. I know you’re right.” After a moment she said, “Let’s talk about something else.”

“Like what?”

“I don’t know. You like the new computer program?”

“It’s fantastic. Really. I think it will save me a lot of time and help me do my job better.”

She nodded. “Good. That’s what I wanted.”

But you don’t want me to do this part of my job, he thought. It hung unspoken between them.

Lights flashed on the ceiling. Apprehension crossed Jennifer’s face, and she went to the window and peeked out under the bottom of the shade. “There’s a car out there.”

“Is it the unit?”

“No, it’s Donna-jean.”

“Oh, boy. Is she alone?”

“Yes.”

“Good. Just be casual. Let her get all the way in and close the door. Then ask her about the drugs.” Harvey moved to the chair at the computer desk. He wished the patrolmen had arrived, for Jennifer’s sake. A key turned in the lock.

Jennifer stood near the sofa.

“Hi, Jennifer.” Donna-jean’s eyes were heavily

lined and shadowed. "Whose SUV outside?" Her eyes flicked over to Harvey, then back to Jennifer. "Oh, it's Howie."

"Harvey," Jennifer said.

"Whatever. I thought maybe you had a new boyfriend." Donna-jean nodded in Harvey's direction. "Hi."

"I want to talk to you about something." Jennifer pointed to the plastic package on the coffee table. "I found this in the freezer. Is it yours?"

Donna-jean's eyes narrowed and her lips went pouty. "Well, I do have kitchen privileges, don't I?"

Jennifer straightened her spine. "Yes, but I don't want your drugs in my kitchen, or anywhere in my house." Harvey was proud of her, but he sat still, saying nothing. Donna-jean was the type who would incriminate herself, given the opportunity. He'd seen it before.

"It's not *your* house."

"No, but I live here," Jennifer said firmly, "and I don't like it."

"Oh, Jennifer, you're so boring! Give it to me and I'll keep it where it won't offend you." She reached for the bundle, but Jennifer turned and handed it to Harvey.

Donna-jean stood stock-still, looking back and forth between the two. "I don't get it. Does Howie want it? He'll have to pay for it."

"How much for all of it?" Harvey asked.

She smiled and named a price.

He stood, placing the package on the computer desk. "Donna-jean, I'm a cop." He showed his badge and stepped closer to her. "You're under arrest. You have the right to remain—"

"I have no idea where that stuff came from. It must be Jennifer's."

"No good, Donna-jean. It's yours. You're the one who tried to sell it to me. There's a patrol unit on the way to take you down to the station." He brought out his handcuffs.

"The squad car is here." Jennifer moved to open the front door, and Harvey recited the Miranda rule. When the two officers walked in, he had snapped the cuffs shut, and was saying, "Do you understand these rights?"

He didn't know the two men Brad had sent over, but the sergeant had apprised them of the situation, and they took over from Harvey. He kept Donna-jean where she was while they searched her room, turning up a small amount of marijuana, two nickel bags of heroin, and some paraphernalia. They treated Jennifer respectfully when they took her statement and then said a cordial good-night to the detective as they left with the prisoner and the evidence.

Jennifer sat down abruptly on the couch. Harvey went over and stood in front of her.

"Are you okay?"

"Yes."

"You sure?"

"No."

Harvey grimaced. "Jenny, I'm sorry. I don't see what else I could have done." He started to turn away, but she put her hand out and grasped his wrist.

"Thanks."

"Just doing my job."

"No, it was more than that."

"You're right. I want to keep you safe. As long as she was here, you wouldn't be safe."

"You think she was using me."

He did. Innocent Jennifer was the perfect cover for someone like Donna-jean, and the perfect scapegoat if need be.

"You're very intelligent, but you're also very tenderhearted. I think she knew that and took advantage of you."

Jennifer nodded but didn't look at him. Donna-jean's presence seemed to hang over them. Harvey ached inside. He wanted to comfort her and reassure her, but she didn't seem inclined to let him at the moment.

"What do I do with all her things?" she asked.

"Does she have family around here?"

"I could get hold of her mother, I think."

"Call her tomorrow and ask her to come pack the stuff up. Make sure you're here when she comes, so she doesn't pack anything of yours by mistake."

"Could I just box it up myself and ask her mother to come get it?"

"If she's comfortable with that." He hesitated, not wanting to leave her alone. "Are you going to be all right here tonight?"

"I think so."

Her sadness tore at him.

"Well, lock up tight when I leave. And give me a call in the morning, before you take off for work, okay?"

"Okay." She got up and walked with him to the door. "You take care, too. I don't like people putting bombs where they think you're going to be."

He touched her gleaming hair with his fingertips, to confirm that there wasn't really a barrier between them. He wanted to warn her further and instruct her on what to do if Donna-jean's boyfriend showed up at the door, but that might alarm her to the point where she would back off and never let him reach out to her again.

"Good night." She didn't respond, but he couldn't just walk out the door. He leaned toward her and kissed her cheek, just forward of her right ear. She caught her breath and stepped away from him.

He went out, closing the door gently, and stood listening until he heard her put the security chain in place. Wearily, he walked toward the Explorer. His satisfaction with the new vehicle was gone. He took a penlight from his pocket and got down on his knees to look under it on the driver's side, then walked around to the back, then the passenger side. When he rose and dusted off the knees of his jeans, he glanced toward the house. Jennifer was watching him from the living room window.

Great. The one time he wished she wouldn't look at him.

The idea of the boyfriend or a drug customer showing up worried him. Before backing into the street, he called the station to ask that patrol units in the area drive by the house now and then.

Jennifer dressed slowly for bed after Harvey left. She was glad he had stayed. She wouldn't have had the nerve to confront Donna-jean alone. In her blue terrycloth robe, she loosened her long hair and brushed it, her mind running off in all directions. The computer program, the car bomb, drugs in the freezer, and Harvey in danger every day.

He checked his new vehicle for bombs. He'd only had it a couple of hours, but he believed someone could have sabotaged it during the time he was inside her house. Stark terror washed over her, and her fingers clenched around the handle of her hairbrush.

She padded to the back door and checked the lock, then checked the front door again. What was she getting into by dating a detective? His best friend had almost been killed by getting into his car. How could she ever feel safe with him?

She went into Donna-jean's bedroom and checked the lock on the window. An acrid smell lingered faintly. She wrinkled her nose. Secondhand tobacco smoke was bad enough. Was her brain addled by Donna-jean's second-hand marijuana? Harvey had done the right thing.

At last she went to her own room and sat on her bed. Still she hesitated to turn out the light. It was silly, and it bothered her, but it was there. This fear wasn't just because of Donna-jean's escapades. It went deeper than that, and she didn't want to live in fear the rest of her life.

She had broken up with one man because she'd felt he was a threat to her. It was different with Harvey. He wasn't the menace. His unknown enemies were, and she might be hurt because she associated with him.

Somehow that frightened her less than the thought that she might lose him.

She crawled under the quilt and turned off the lamp. In the darkness, she felt for her flashlight. It was within easy reach. She groped for her phone. It was right where she always put it at night, on the stand with the lamp.

She was very tired, but sleep eluded her. It didn't seem fair for her to drift off to sleep when Donna-jean was in a cell in the city police station. An enormous load of guilt pressed down on her. Somehow, she ought to have prevented Donna-jean's arrest. But in order to do that, she would have had to prevent her from using drugs, either that or ignored the whole mess. But then she would be culpable herself.

If I believed in God, I wouldn't be confused. And I wouldn't be afraid, ever. I could ask him to protect me. And to protect Harvey.

Chapter 10

She called, as he had requested, at 7:15 the next morning, slowly pressing the buttons.

"Jenny. I'm glad you called. How are you?" He sounded calm and rested. For some reason, that bothered her.

"Harvey, where is Donna-jean now?"

"Probably in the county jail until the arraignment."

She sighed. "I shouldn't have told you."

"Don't ever say that." His voice was stern, but the next moment it melted into tenderness. "I'm sorry it had to be this way."

She knew his contrition was genuine, but she also knew he couldn't have acted differently. She grabbed a tissue and wiped her eyes. "Her mother called me this morning. Donna-jean called her in the middle of the night from the police station. Mrs. Jacobs is not very happy with me."

"She knows her daughter was the one who made the decision to use and distribute drugs. You had nothing to do with that. I'm just sorry you got caught in the middle."

"It's not your fault. She wanted to come get Donna-jean's stuff today, but I told her she'd have to wait until I get home tonight."

"Good. Does the name William Cassidy sound familiar?"

"No, I don't think so."

"How about Donna-jean's boyfriend?"

"Oh! Billy?"

"His prints were on the wrapping. Jenny, he's a known drug dealer."

She couldn't breathe for an instant. "Harvey, he was in the house lots of times."

"You'd better have the locks changed as soon as possible. Call your landlord today."

"Okay. Can you find out how Donna-jean is doing?" She hated to ask it of him, but the thought of Donna-jean in jail was still a heavy weight on her heart.

"I'll get an update on her status and call you at noon if I can."

"Thanks. Her mother was going to get a lawyer for her."

"That's good." He paused. "Jenny, you're not going to . . . resent me for doing this, are you?"

"You had to do it. And I guess I'm just trying not to think about the danger she put me in." She shuddered. *A drug dealer in my house.* Knowing it for certain was a million times worse than the discomfort she'd felt when Billy was just Donna-jean's scruffy boyfriend in the next room.

"All right." Harvey was silent for a moment, and she hated herself for doubting his judgment, even for an instant. He sounded wary when he asked, “Are we still on for Saturday? The play, I mean?”

“If you still want to.”

“Of course I still want to.”

His ready answer bolstered her, and she realized she’d been afraid he thought less of her now, because of her empathy for Donna-jean. “I want to go with you,” she said firmly.

Harvey picked Eddie up a few minutes early. He’d told him about Donna-jean when they met to run at dawn. There was no way to keep something like that from Eddie.

“I knew I should have stuck with you after that trip to Scarborough,” Eddie said.

“Too bad you missed it. Will you get the schedule of arraignments from the district court? I told Jennifer I’d check on her roommate this morning.”

As soon as they entered the office, he pulled up the report on Donna-jean’s arrest. Everything was by the book, and he sighed with relief. He closed the file and accessed the electronic data on closed cases. With any luck, he’d be able to find reports of past bombing cases on the computer.

Mike came in at eight and walked straight to Harvey’s desk in the corner.

“What’s this about you making a drug bust while you were off duty last night?”

Harvey sighed and tore his gaze away from the

monitor. "It just happened. I was there, and it happened."

Mike waited, frowning slightly. Harvey told himself that after all these years he shouldn't be surprised anymore. Mike was always on top of things.

"There's no problem, Mike. My friend stumbled on her roommate's supply, is all, and it was too big to ignore."

"Your friend."

"Yes." Harvey moved the computer mouse, not looking at Mike. "Look, I know this is unusual, but I called for a unit, and everything's fine. You can take that to the bank."

"I saw the report. I'm not worried about procedure. I'm concerned about you."

"I'm fine, Mike."

"You met her eight weeks ago."

Startled, Harvey glanced up at him.

"Jennifer Winthrop," Mike prompted. "I told you, I saw the report, and I know how to use a computer."

"It's Wainthrop."

"Huh. Anyway, you met her on the job."

"Is that a problem?"

Mike sighed. "I guess not. That missing persons case is a dead end, anyway."

"Maybe."

The captain eyed him closely. "You all right, Harvey?"

"I told you, I'm fine."

"Fine enough to bring her to my house for dinner?"

Harvey ran a hand through his hair. "Well, I don't know. It's early for stuff like that."

"Have you met her family?"

"Not yet."

Mike nodded. "Let me know when she's ready to meet yours." He turned toward his desk, and Harvey smiled.

"Mike!"

Browning turned, swinging his briefcase. "What is it, Harv?"

"The M.O. on the car bomb is too much like Bobby Nason's for me to like it."

"I thought Bobby was in jail, thanks to you."

"He got out in February."

Mike set his briefcase on his desk and came back to Harvey's station. Harvey gestured toward the computer screen. "It was a pipe bomb with a timer, stuck to my gas tank."

"Ouch. Eddie was lucky to get out alive."

"Yeah. If he drove any slower, he'd be dead."

Mike sat on the corner of Harvey's desk. "Can you get a line on Bobby?"

"I'll try. We're done with the school case. I may have to go to the DA's office this morning."

"You think the bomb is related to the school business?"

Harvey shook his head. "Not really. It's possible

the dealer rousted Bobby Nason out for the job, but I don't see it that way."

"It happened too fast," Mike agreed. "You'd only been on the case a day, and you hadn't done anything but question kids."

"Way too soon for the supplier to try to kill me."

"So who did it?"

Harvey grimaced. "If I knew that . . . but whoever hates me hired Bobby Nason, I'm pretty sure."

"Maybe Bobby's working on his own. You're not his favorite person."

"When I have time, I'll see if I can pick up any information on his whereabouts."

Mike nodded thoughtfully, then smiled. "So, you got a new vehicle. I saw it in the garage. Nice choice."

Harvey said grudgingly, "Eddie talked me into it. He thought I needed to update my image."

Mike stood up. "Be careful, Harv. And take care of that girl. Eddie tells me she's a knockout."

Jennifer rapped on the door of Bart Owen's private office.

"Come in."

She advanced toward his large walnut desk. "I looked over the program you asked me to. It seems like a pretty good security program, Mr. Owen, and the firewall is state of the art."

"We thought so, too. Dunham did an excellent job. The tracers work fine, and until recently the system seemed resistant to outsiders. But the hackers are getting smarter and smarter, and we've had a couple of minor breaches recently. Can you fix it?"

Jennifer had thought about the problem as she viewed the program Nick had made for the company. "I don't think a simple patch would do much. Do you want me to make a new program? Not a new system, but a program that will work with this one. I think I can add a couple layers of new safety features."

"Will that keep outsiders from getting at our data?"

Jennifer shrugged. "They say nothing's tamper-proof, and I would have thought Nick's program would do the job. But I can at least make it harder for anyone to break in. It might be enough to discourage them. It would slow them down, anyway."

Owen nodded. "Well, these industrial spies are determined nowadays. Companies are hiring kids that think of nothing else but computers."

"It will mean putting aside the special project for a while," she said.

Owen sighed. "Yes, well, to be frank, we have no one else who can do this job. My partners are quite anxious about security, and they want this taken care of immediately. We'll keep Tessa and John working on the other project, and when you've attended to this little matter, you can get back to your portion."

"All right, sir. I'll do my best."

She left his office with mixed feelings. It was good to know you were needed. It was also unsettling. If she failed to meet her bosses' expectations, where would that leave her? They would think she was incompetent if she couldn't keep a high school kid out of their company's payroll data and personnel files.

On another level, she was glad to be free of the top secret project for a few days. She hated working on it, not knowing what it was for. It was going to be marketed overseas, and she wondered if the designers weren't just a little out of their depth. At least with her current assignment, she could picture an opponent. Some bright but misguided teenager was out there, intent on cracking into the posh software company's databases. She could foil him, she was sure.

And the intense work would keep her mind off Donna-jean and the car bomb.

She looked around the bullpen where they all worked. It was noon, and Jane wasn't at her desk. Jennifer took her purse from her desk drawer and stepped out the side door, into the parking lot.

She hesitated, then turned quickly toward the sidewalk. The Arabic client was standing near her car, talking earnestly with a dark-featured young man she had never seen before. She felt the teeniest apprehension and decided not to approach her car near them, but to walk to the deli for a quick sandwich.

A smidgen of guilt struck her. Was it reasonable caution, or was she prejudiced? She hadn't been careful enough lately, and look where that had gotten her with Donna-jean. She straightened her shoulders.

As she waited for a break in the traffic, she took another quick glance over her shoulder. The younger man was standing at the car next to hers, with his driver's door open, and Massal seemed to be lecturing him. As she turned away, Jennifer saw the young man glance toward her. There was no recognition in his gaze, but there was something. Maybe he was just searching for anything but Massal to focus on, and she was there. Not for long. There was a gap in traffic, and she hurried across the street.

Chapter 11

Harvey rang Jennifer's doorbell on the dot of six Saturday night. It had been a long week. Far too long since he'd seen her on Tuesday. He'd nerved himself to call her Thursday evening, and he was glad he did, but talking on the phone was never satisfactory. She was still shy with him, and he couldn't tell how much of her reticence was natural and how much was caused by the traumatic events of the week.

He heard the security chain rattle, and anticipation coursed through him. Jennifer opened the door and stood looking at him, breathing fast. "I'm sorry. I was—" She glanced over her shoulder.

"No problem. You look terrific." She had on a green, shiny dress that was definitely expensive. It looked custom made for her, and the asymmetrical front with frog closures gave it a subtly oriental flavor. Her hair was up, in the Grace Kelly look again. Would she know who Grace Kelly was?

He put out one finger and just touched the high collar of the dress. "Silk?" Immediately he wondered if he was being too familiar, but the fabric screamed to be touched.

"Y-yes. Do I pass the dress code?"

"You bet." He wanted to shower her with lavish compliments, but she would squirm if he did. Somehow she had achieved glamour, and it was a far cry from the timid girl-next-door impression she'd given him and Eddie when they'd gone car shopping. He wished he'd bought her more flowers, dozens of showy, expensive flowers, and he wished he'd taken more trouble with his own appearance.

He was wearing the same suit he'd worn the week before. He'd bought it ten years ago for his partner Chris's funeral and kept it for best afterward. In the old days, all the detectives had to wear suits and ties to work, but not so much now. Putting it on had made him feel over-dressed—until he saw Jennifer in that dress.

She gave him a tremulous smile, and he reached for the sweater she held. It was a light, shimmery gold cardigan that rivaled her glinting hair. He held it as she slipped her arms into the sleeves. A faint whiff of—was it lilacs?—something good—wafted up to him.

"So, how'd it go with Donna-jean's mother?"

"Okay. She got most of the stuff Wednesday night, and I shipped the rest this morning."

He nodded. "No hassles?"

"No. She was upset with me at first. I felt really bad, but . . ."

"They let her go yesterday."

Jennifer's eyebrows arched. "They did?"

“Yes. She had a hearing, and she’ll appear in court in a few weeks. Her record’s clean except for a couple of traffic tickets, so she’ll probably get a suspended sentence.”

“She hasn’t contacted me.”

“No, the judge told her not to.”

“Were you there?”

“Yes.”

She looked at him for a long moment, and he expected her to pepper him with more questions, but she didn’t.

“I feel so bad, Harvey.”

“I know.” He squeezed her shoulder. “It’s all right. I just don’t want you thinking you’re the bad guy here.”

“Well, *you’re* certainly not.”

“Hey, if you want to blame me, go ahead.”

“No. I won’t do that. You were right.” Her chin came up defiantly, and he had to smile.

“You know Donna-jean brought this on herself.”

Jennifer nodded. “I keep reminding myself of that. And she needs to face the consequences, but I—” She broke off and shrugged. “I’ve got to quit analyzing it. Let’s go.”

He walked with her to the Explorer and opened the door for her. She smiled up at him, then looked away quickly. “Thanks.”

The shyness was still there, and it gave him more confidence. It didn’t seem logical, but he accepted it, along with all the other jumbled feelings Jennifer brought him.

When they entered the restaurant, he looked around in surprise. He hadn't been there in years, and he knew without actually remembering it that his last visit there had been with Carrie. He should have chosen another spot.

Jennifer seemed somewhat intimidated by the atmosphere, and he thought the prices on the menu shocked her a little. He smiled to reassure her, and her anxious expression melted into a bright smile. Her mood seemed to have changed, and they talked easily while they waited for their food. He realized suddenly that he was very happy. He hadn't expected it, ever again, but there it was.

The play at the university was funny, and well acted. Rosalind had the right touch, and good chemistry with Orlando. Phebe, the shepherdess, was an accomplished comic. Harvey tucked away her line, "Who ever loved, that loved not at first sight?" for future contemplation. He wondered if he could hold Jennifer's hand, and he decided that was not in the script. But her eyes shone as she watched the actors.

It was chilly when they emerged from the theater at ten-thirty.

"I don't want to take you home yet," Harvey said as they walked toward the SUV. In the old days, he would have suggested a drink, but he'd kept his promise to himself since Carrie's death and stayed away from alcohol. He didn't want to relapse, and besides, the thought didn't fit with Jennifer.

"How about we stop for a soda?" he asked.

"That's great."

Harvey smiled. His chronic depression seemed to have lifted.

He hesitated as they approached his Explorer. "I hate to mention it, but I have to check the vehicle. I guess you know that."

She nodded gravely.

"All right, it will only take a second. Just wait here."

She stood in silence, watching him from several yards away. Part of him wanted to hurry, making it seem unimportant, so she wouldn't be worried. Another part wanted to be extra careful, so he'd be certain they weren't in danger.

It was late, and there wasn't much of a crowd at the Burger King. Harvey managed to get a table near the window where he could watch his Explorer, so he wouldn't have to check under it again when they left. They sat across from each other, sipping Pepsi through plastic straws.

"I had fun tonight," he told her.

"Really?" She looked up through her eyelashes. They were so long, he wished he had a caliper to measure them.

"Really. So, do I still owe you on conversation?"

She smiled ruefully. "I wish you'd forget about that."

"I deserved it." He stirred the ice in his cup with his straw, smiling. "So, any more questions?"

"No."

"No?"

"Well, maybe." The mile-long lashes swept her cheek. "Do you wear that gun everywhere?"

He chuckled. "Not in the shower." She smiled, too. He would have made more jokes about wearing his gun on a date, but the incident with Donna-jean was too unfunny. "You just never know."

She nodded. "Harvey, do you—" she hesitated, bouncing between assurance and insecurity again.

"Ask me anything," he said in a low voice, and her eyes flickered.

"Do you think I'm too young for you, or you're too old for me?"

He smiled a little and shook his head. "Maybe it's the same thing. But, no, I don't think you're too young. As for me being too old, I guess if you think I am, then I am."

"I don't."

"Well, neither do I." They sat in silence for a moment, and he added, "I've always thought that the older you got, the less age mattered."

She creased her paper napkin as she pondered that. "Is it immature to question my maturity?"

He laughed. "You got me. You know, some people claim there are advantages to a May-December romance."

"You haven't hit December yet! More like a May-August romance, don't you think?"

Her gray eyes had a fire in them that ignited something in him, something he hadn't felt for a long, long time. He reached for her hand.

"Jenny, you're beautiful."

A flush crept upward from the collar of her dress. She caught her breath and looked away.

"I'm sorry. I mean . . . not that I said it, but if I made you uncomfortable . . ."

Her gaze came back to his, and the blush deepened. "Doesn't it bother you a little that I don't remember the same things you do? It must be exasperating when you mention something, and I have no idea what you're talking about. Like the Howdy Doody Show or something."

He smiled. He couldn't remember Howdy Doody, either.

"You mean like JFK being shot, or the first moon landing? I don't remember those things, either. But we all latch on to different events that make an impact on us, especially when we're young."

"Like 9-11?"

"Yeah, like that. To answer your question, no. It doesn't bother me a bit. Something I might remember well is just a paragraph in a history book to you. So what? It still happened. You've got other things you feel as strongly about."

"I guess so. But those things shape us."

"Spoken as a philosopher?"

"Maybe."

Harvey smiled. "I've been thinking about a person from the past lately. Someone you probably don't remember. I don't actually remember her, either, but I've seen a lot of her movies."

"Who?"

"Grace Kelly. Do you know who Grace Kelly was?"

"Wasn't she the one who married the prince of Monaco and died in a car wreck?"

"That's right. She was before my time, too, but see, if it's far enough in the past, we can both like what she did and enjoy her work without it being weird."

"Why Grace Kelly?"

He shrugged and tried to sound casual. "I thought you looked like her tonight. She wore her hair that way sometimes, and she had the same natural grace you have."

Jennifer seemed at a loss for a moment. "You're talking about me?"

"Yeah. I hope that doesn't offend you."

"I don't think so. She was . . ."

He smiled. "Yeah, she was. But we can make real memories of our own. Mutual memories. Can't we?"

"I like that thought."

Intense feeling ambushed him. He was seeing a potential future for them. Was she seeing that, too, or was she looking back over the meager memories they had made together so far, all bittersweet and fragile?

"Jenny, this can work. I know it can."

She said softly, "You make it sound easy."

Harvey watched her quizzically. She was young, and still a little wary of him. Maybe she wasn't as ready as he was. "It just takes trust."

Her face clouded. "That's the hard part, isn't it?" She reached for her purse. "We should probably get going."

"All right." He rose, slightly confused. He wanted her to feel safe with him, to trust him with her most private thoughts. But most of all, in that moment, he wanted to see her smile again.

He put her in the front seat of the Explorer, got in, buckled, and started the engine. Then he looked over at her.

"Are you okay?"

She nodded. A tear hung on her long eyelashes, but she didn't wipe it away, and he thought she didn't want him to know she was crying.

"You sure?"

"Yes. It's just . . ." She turned her face toward the side window. "I'm sorry."

"Jennifer, I thought things were going well. If

I said something that upset you, please tell me."

She was silent. Her expression had been so open and soft one moment, so guarded the next. He reached into the pocket of his suit jacket for his handkerchief and held it out to her. She took it and held it to her eyes.

"I'm sorry. You said a relationship takes trust."

"It's crucial. Do you think you could trust me?"

"I think I do, but . . ."

She didn't offer an explanation. After waiting half a minute, he put the gearshift into drive and pulled out of the parking lot, heading for her house.

He felt helpless. This wasn't just because of Donna-jean, or even the unseen threat of the bomber. She was dealing with something else, something that ran deep. He went over in his mind all of their conversations, especially tonight's, looking for a gaffe on his part. Had he blown it by comparing her to someone dead and gone for decades? Or had he somehow stepped in it talking about memories and disasters?

He drove without speaking again until they reached her house. Her car sat in the drive-way, and the house was dark.

He turned to her in the dimness.

"Jenny, I don't understand, but I want to."

She pulled in a deep breath. "Let's just say I had a bad experience."

"I'm sorry."

She dabbed at her eyes. "I haven't dated much lately because of it."

"Well, it's been a while for me, too. If I did something out of line, I wish you'd tell me."

"No. No, you've been great." She struggled to control her voice. "I know it's not fair to you, but . . . the thing is, someone told me once to trust him." She looked at him cautiously. He let the silence hang between them. Finally she said, "I found out I couldn't."

He nodded slowly. He was more than a little gun shy himself, but this was more than that. He wanted to go after the man who had hurt her. To take the memory out of her heart, the way he'd removed Donna-jean from her house.

He opened his door and got out, went around to her side, and walked her up to the door. She got her keys out, and he took them from her and opened the lock.

"Look, I—" She looked up at him and swallowed, then said in a rush, "Do you want to come in for a minute? I just—I don't want to leave it this way."

"Are you sure?"

She hesitated, looking into his eyes. "Yes."

He touched the sleeve of her glittery sweater gently. "Only if you promise to tell me when you want me to leave. You say the word, and I'm gone."

She nodded, and her gray eyes were huge.

He followed her in, feeling a bit displaced. What was it about her that made him willing to muddle through this emotional swamp? Deep inside him burned a conviction that he could make her happy given the chance, and that he would do everything in his power to make sure he never caused her to cry again.

They sat in silence on the sofa for a long minute. Jennifer's breath came in shaky gulps. He wondered if she was still leery of being alone with him. The thought raised his protective streak. He wanted her to love him, but first he wanted her to feel safe.

"Jenny." He reached over and took her hand.

"What?"

"If there's something about me that makes you uncomfortable, let's talk about it now. Don't let it simmer."

"No, there's nothing."

"Yes, there's something."

She bowed her head, and he took that as tacit agreement.

"Is it the fact that I'm a cop?"

"No." She looked up at him quickly. "That's a little scary in some ways. I keep trying not to think about how much danger you're in, but . . . I think I can handle it."

"Are you sure? Because for some women it's just too hard."

She looked directly into his eyes. "Was your wife that way?"

He nodded. "She never wanted me in this business. When we got married, I was planning to be a lawyer. But it wasn't what I really wanted." He sighed. He'd always felt a little guilty about it, but he couldn't make himself want to be an attorney.

"You're a good detective."

He smiled. "You don't know that."

"Yes, I do."

"Been checking up on me?" She laughed, and he squeezed her hand. "Something happened to you. Maybe a long time ago. It's made you cautious with men."

She gave a little nod. "You're right, Mr. Holmes."

"Can you tell me about it?"

"It's not your fault. It just hit me when you said it, and I heard him so clearly, saying 'trust me.' I shouldn't have let it bother me when you said that, but I did."

He sat back. "It seems to me we both have some baggage from the past. If we're going to make this work, we need to start from here, and just go on."

"I'll try."

"Good. And if there's anything else you want to know about me, I'll tell you. Anything at all."

"If you're sure, there's something that's been bothering me."

"Just ask, Jenny."

He waited for the blow, and it came, as direct and piercing as he'd feared.

"Your wife. Did she leave, or did you? What happened?"

He sat silent for a minute, preparing himself. "She left me. Our marriage seemed like a good idea at the time, but things deteriorated fast. She was never happy with me. Even the first year, she wasn't satisfied. I think she was hoping I'd change my mind and go back to law school. She didn't like me going into the Academy. She didn't like living in Maine. She didn't like being married to a cop. She didn't want children, and she ended up not wanting me. She left me after eight years, and three years later, she divorced me."

"Was she unfaithful?"

"I think she was. I never looked for proof."

"How about you?" Her voice was very small.

The weight on his spirit lightened. This was what she really wanted to know, and he could answer this question without regrets. He looked deep into her eyes. "No. Not during the whole time we were married, and even after that. I tried to patch things up with her, but I guess I wasn't very good at it. And she had already made up her mind."

He waited. A tear rolled down her cheek, and remorse hit him. He'd done it again.

She wiped her eyes with his crumpled handkerchief. "I'm sorry you had to go through that, Harvey."

"Me, too. It wasn't fun."

"Do you still . . . think about her?"

"Of course I do."

"You told me she died not long ago."

He nodded. "Suicide."

She winced, and he wished he'd cushioned it a little. "We didn't have any contact for the last ten years. Then her brother called me and told me she was dead. It was a shock, but . . ." He stood up, unable to face her for the moment. He walked over to her computer and stared at the Van Gogh print above it. *Starry Night.* It was full of bright, swirling balls of color that no one would really mistake for stars. Sort of like the churning, colliding memories that came back in a rush. That awful night, watching Chris die . . . the long hours at the police station . . . going home to find Carrie had left him. The worst night of his life.

He turned to face her. "It was almost a relief," he confessed. "Not that I wanted her dead. Of course I didn't want that. But it was a definite, unchangeable ending to that part of my life."

She nodded. "Sometimes it's better just to know when it's really over."

He felt his tension ebb and walked slowly back to the couch and sat down beside her. “You sound like you know what you’re talking about.”

She shifted a little and put one hand up to her hair. “It seems almost trivial, compared to what you’ve had to deal with.”

He didn’t believe that for a second. Anything that had affected her this deeply was far from trivial.

“Jenny, if there’s somebody else in your life . . .”

“Not now,” she said quickly. “During college. It ended in a hurry, and it was painful, but mostly because I’d been foolish.”

He studied her serious gray eyes. He would never believe she was a fool. But her heart was so soft, she might have had misplaced affections in her not-so-distant youth. He sorted the pieces she had given him and put together the border of a picture puzzle. “You were too trusting.”

She nodded soberly. “But it’s over. Completely.”

“How long ago?”

“Three years now. When I graduated. I’m past it. Really.”

He smiled at her earnestness and reached for her hand. “I’m glad.”

“Sometime maybe I’ll tell you the details, if you want me to, but . . . let’s just say it cured me of wanting to date for a while.”

"I understand." He decided that was enough for now.

Jennifer's smile was a bit regretful. "My friend Jane—you've met her—she was getting after me for being a social misfit. I'd only had one date in the two years she's known me, and to her that was unthinkable. But I don't think I was ready until . . ." She looked down at their clasped hands, and her voice dropped. "Until I met you."

He pulled in a deep breath. "Don't sell yourself short. It's been nearly twenty years since my last date."

She looked up at him through her incredible lashes, and Harvey knew he was committed. It was too soon. It was senseless. His sisters would be horrified. He didn't care.

He stood up. "Time for me to head out."

She stood, too, a little flustered. "All right. Thanks for everything. It was a great evening, and I'm glad we could talk things out."

Still he lingered, not wanting to end his time with her, but knowing he should.

"I have tomorrow off. Can I see you again?"

Her slow, melting smile was worth all the jitters and misgivings he'd felt since he'd met her.

"What do you want to do?"

"You choose. I'll take you anywhere." Maybe he should mention the bungee jumping caveat.

She stepped closer, and he could almost feel

her intensity as she stared up at him. “There is something I’ve been wanting to do, but I haven’t dared to do it alone.”

“Now I’m intrigued. Whatever it is, we’ll do it.”

“Just like that?”

“Yes.”

Still she hesitated, and a tiny frown settled between her eyebrows. “I’d like to go to church.”

He almost laughed, it was so unexpected. “Great. Where?”

Jennifer blinked. “I don’t know. I never go to church.”

“Me either,” he said. “So what are you, Catholic, Protestant . . .”

“My mother used to go to a Methodist Church, I think.”

“My folks were Congregational. There was Sunday School when I was really little. Bible stories and Kool-Aid. But we quit going. I don’t think I’ve been in a church in thirty years, except for weddings.”

“But you’ll go?”

“Sure.” A great tenderness filled him.

Her smile was full of wonder. “So, where should we go?”

“I dunno. Sounds like we’re both token Protestants. Why don’t we look online?” He took out his phone and clicked for a search. He put in her address and asked for churches within two miles. He was surprised at how many there were.

He sat on the couch. Jennifer sat down beside him and ran a hand over her hair. He wished she would pull out the hairpins and let it fall free around her shoulders. He looked back at the screen.

"Okay, there's a church just down on the corner of School Street."

"I know where that is," she said.

"Me, too. I drive past it every time I come over here." He looked at the ad again. "It's, uh, Baptist. Do you want something else?"

"No, that's okay, and it's close."

He nodded. "We'll try it, then. It says, *Sunday School for infants through adults, 9:45 a.m.; Morning Worship, 11 a.m.*"

"Do we do Sunday School?" she asked.

"I don't know. I thought that was for kids, but it says 'through adults.' "

"Well, I'm certainly ignorant enough about God that I could stand to hear some Bible stories." She brushed a tendril of hair back behind her ear, and he itched to touch it.

He put the phone away. "We'll try it, then. I'll pick you up at nine-thirty in the morning. If we hate it, we can leave."

She smiled and whispered, "Thank you. I didn't really think you'd want to go."

"Have you been thinking about God a lot lately?"

"Quite a bit."

"Pascal?"

"Maybe that started it. Some of the things I read about his commitment to God . . ."

"I've been thinking about it, too," Harvey said, and she looked up in surprise. "Grandma Lewis was talking to me about God. She's . . . my wife's grandmother. She and God are good friends."

Jennifer's eyebrows went up. "How do you mean?"

"She talks about him all the time. Talks to him, too, I guess. We were drinking tea after the funeral, and she showed me something in her Bible that I haven't been able to forget. It said something like, 'Whoever comes to God must believe that he exists.' I can't remember the exact words. But it won't go out of my head."

Jennifer said slowly, "So you can look for God, but you can't find him unless you believe he's real?"

"Something like that. I don't know. I wish I'd written it down. Do you have a Bible?"

"No," she said.

"Me either."

They were both silent for a moment. Harvey thought of all the books in his apartment, and the thousands he had read.

"So what do we do?" she asked.

"Launch an investigation together."

"Okay. What are we looking for exactly?"

"If God is real?" he asked tentatively.

She nodded. "And if there is a God, can we be sure? It's supposed to be unprovable, isn't it?"

"That's what the agnostics say."

"So how does anyone ever really know? Or do they just believe it and hope for the best?"

"Some people are like that, I guess, but not Grandma Lewis. She seems to know she's going to heaven, and she's sure she'll be on good terms with God when she gets there."

"Did she say anything else?"

He thought hard about that conversation. "Yes, she said that God draws people to himself, and that's the only way to find him."

"You mean it won't do us any good to investigate unless he wants us to find him?" Her eyes darkened with disappointment.

"I don't know. This is not my area of expertise."

"Well, I want to know if God is real, and I guess if he wants me to find him, I will."

Harvey nodded. "All right. We'll go to this church tomorrow and see if they give us any clues. If there's no evidence there, we can try a different church next week."

Jennifer looked up at him with a frank wistfulness. More than ever he wanted to take her in his arms. He moved toward her slightly, leaning toward her on the couch, and brought his hand very gently to rest on her hair. It was as soft as he'd imagined.

"Jenny—"

She jumped up. "I think—" She glanced at her watch. "It's time for you to go, Harvey."

He stood up slowly. Her face was flushed, and her breathing shallow. He'd asked for it. *Say the word, and I'm gone.*

"Okay, kiddo."

She grimaced slightly, and he nearly apologized, but thought better of it.

"Nine-thirty," she said.

"I'll be here."

She smiled, and her gray eyes were luminous. He decided she wasn't mad at him. Far from it. The joy surged through him again. Couldn't she see that he loved her? Apparently not. And if he blurted it out now, she'd retreat again. He walked slowly to the door and opened it, then turned back with his hand on the knob.

"Don't watch me out the window if you don't want to see me get my suit dirty." He winked at her.

She laughed, and he was glad he'd been able to leave her in a cheerful frame of mind. He checked under the Explorer. Nothing. It seemed almost pointless. The whole bomb business seemed unreal, except for the memory of his burning car. That was not an illusion. Eddie had the small scar on the back of his hand to prove it.

He looked up at the sky. The stars were pale over the city. How long would it take him and Jennifer to decide whether or not God was really up there? *If he's real, I guess I should be thanking him that I'm still alive.*

Again he remembered Grandma Lewis, and wondered if God really did draw people to himself, like a relentless magnet.

He thought he might be ready for that. He'd spent too many years trying to figure out his own life. Time to let someone else take over. But he didn't really want to be pulled in unless Jennifer was pulled in, too.

Chapter 12

Jennifer watched him, in spite of his warning, but furtively, from behind the curtain. When his Explorer left the driveway and rolled down the street, she sighed. She wasn't afraid in the empty house tonight, but she wanted to talk to someone. She was ready to share her happiness. She took out her phone and called the familiar number for home.

"Mom? It's me, Jennifer. I'm sorry to call so late. I just wanted to say hi."

"That's okay, honey," her mother said. "We weren't asleep yet. Your father is trying to set the new alarm clock." She laughed. "They haven't made friends yet. How are you doing?"

"Okay. Pretty good actually. I've met someone." There. It was out.

"Really? How exciting! What's he like?"

"Oh, Mom, he's great! You'd really like him. He's very considerate and polite." She sat down on the couch.

"Sounds like a nice boy. What's his name?"

"Harvey."

"That's an old-fashioned name. What does he look like?"

"Nice looking. Blue eyes, brown hair, kind of wavy. Medium height, crinkly lines at the corners of his eyes."

"That's quite a description," her mother said. "I take it he's special."

"Very." Jennifer sank back against the couch cushions, wondering how special she was to Harvey. She had never felt so strong a pull toward a man. The nervous tension between them that evening had been so thick it nearly choked her. It was exciting, but at the same time terrifying.

"Honey, that's wonderful. When can we meet him?" Before Jennifer could answer, her mother said, "Just a minute. Your father wants to talk to you."

"Hi, Jenn."

"Hi, Daddy. Did you give up on the clock?"

"No, I think I have it cowed. What's this about a man in your life? Should I be jealous?"

"Oh, no, Daddy. He's the kind you've always wanted me to wait for."

"Well, it's about time. What does he do?"

"He's a policeman."

"Really? Well, that's not so bad. Probably doesn't earn much. State trooper?"

"Portland P.D."

"How old is he?"

She hesitated. "He's older than me."

"What kind of an answer is that?"

"Well, he's younger than you."

"Older than you and younger than me," her father said. "Shall we just split the difference?"

"Just about."

There was a pause. "Are you telling me he's forty?"

She sighed. "Actually, forty-one."

"I don't like it."

"But, Daddy, you'd like *him,*" Jennifer said. "It's the man that matters, not some number."

"You've never won an argument with me yet, young lady."

"Come on, Dad, he's really nice. He takes care of me."

"Be more specific."

"Well, can I tell you something and you won't get upset?"

"That depends. What is it?"

"My roommate Donna-jean is gone."

"Good. I never liked her."

"Well, it turns out you had good reason. She was keeping drugs here, or at least letting her boyfriend keep them here. I found some in the freezer."

"Good grief, Jennifer, you can't have that!"

"I know. And Harvey had her arrested."

"Who's Harvey?"

"This guy we're talking about."

"Oh, the boyfriend."

"Don't call him that."

"All right, the cop."

"Exactly. He's a cop, and he knows how to handle crises like this. So Donna-jean is gone."

"She moved out?"

"Well . . . yes. Tuesday night."

"Just don't tell me Harvey's moving in."

"Daddy!"

"Well, what's the part I won't like?"

"The part about the drugs."

"Oh. All right. When do we get to meet him?"

"I don't know. We haven't talked about that yet."

"How long have you known him?"

"I met him a couple of months ago. He came to the office on business."

"When that man disappeared?"

"Yes." The familiar unease returned, the way it did every time she thought about Nick.

"Well, you be careful. I still don't like that situation. I don't think you're safe down there."

Her mother came back on the line. "What's your father so upset about, Jennifer? Is it something about Harvey?"

"Oh, he's just being Daddy. Make him tell you about Donna-jean."

"All right, honey. You should have come home for the weekend."

"Well, I'm glad I was here, Mom."

"Oh, you and Harvey had a date. What did you do?"

"We went to a Shakespeare play tonight, at the university. It was really good. And we went to Burger King after, and . . . and we talked." She definitely couldn't mention the part about

Harvey coming in unchaperoned. Her parents were the most conservative people she knew.

"That sounds like a very nice date. Does Harvey have any brothers for Abby and Leeanne?"

"Oh, Mom."

"Bring the boy home to meet us, honey."

"He's not a boy, Mom. He's a man."

She heard her father say in background, "That so-called boy is forty-one, Marilyn!"

Her mother started protesting, and Jennifer said, "Look, Mom, I've got to go to bed now because Harvey and I are going to church in the morning. I'll talk to you again soon."

The sky was overcast Sunday morning, and the temperature was cooler than it had been all week. Jennifer wore a long-sleeved navy dress and pinned her hair up. Harvey arrived a few minutes early.

He took her hand when she came out the door. "You look great. All set to begin the investigation?"

"All set."

In the vehicle, he said, "Sometime soon, we ought to make a trip to Skowhegan."

Jennifer stared at him. "Did you have my phone tapped?"

He laughed. "I told you, no more spying."

"I guess that would be too bizarre. It's just that I talked to my parents last night, after you left."

"Oh yeah?"

"Yeah, I told them about you, and they want to meet you."

"I've never been to Skowhegan. Should make an interesting outing."

Jennifer eyed him cautiously. "Dad nearly hit the ceiling when I told him how old you are."

"Maybe we'd better wait awhile on the trip."

"Oh, I don't know. The sooner they get to know you, the sooner they'll realize how good you are for me." He smiled broadly at that, and she dared to say, "My mom says you sound like a nice boy."

"Oh, great! How am I supposed to deal with that?"

"Just be you. They'll love you."

His smile was a bit smug, and Jennifer found herself blushing for no reason.

He drove into the church parking lot. There were twenty or so cars already parked, and people were walking toward the front door of the church. Harvey shut off the engine, went around and opened her door. In the row across the driveway, a family got out of a mini-wagon. The husband took a baby out of its car seat while the wife smoothed a little girl's pink dress. Jennifer looked at Harvey anxiously. He gazed up at the steeple, then at her. He winked and took her hand, and they started toward the building.

"Good morning!" The father had the baby up on his left shoulder and stuck his right hand out to Harvey. They shook hands, and the man said, "I'm Rick Bradley."

"Harvey Larson."

"Glad to meet you. This is my wife, Ruthann."

Mrs. Bradley smiled. "Hi. Are you visiting today?"

"Yes," said Harvey. "This is Jennifer—"

Rick's hand went out to Jennifer, and he interrupted Harvey with, "Welcome, Mrs. Larson."

Jennifer shook Rick's hand, looking helplessly at Harvey.

"Uh, it's Jennifer Wainthrop," Harvey said. "We're not married."

"Oh, sorry." Rick didn't seem too flustered. They all walked toward the church together.

"How old are the children?" Jennifer asked Ruthann.

"Clarissa is two, and Ethan is three weeks."

"Only three weeks? So tiny!" She tried to glimpse the baby's face, but Rick had him covered with a receiving blanket.

When they got inside the foyer, Rick said to Harvey, "There's an adult class in the auditorium, and a singles class in the fellowship hall. Take your pick."

"Uh—" the ultra-blue eyes semaphored Jennifer for help.

"Mrs.—Ruthann," she stumbled, unable to remember the last name. The woman looked eagerly toward her. "Could you make a recommendation for us?"

"Well, the adult class is for any adults. The singles class, I think, is mostly college students and career people in that age group."

Jennifer concluded that, while she might fit in there, Harvey would feel ancient. "I guess we'll stick with the auditorium," she said, and Harvey looked as if he'd had a reprieve.

"We'll be in there," Ruthann said with a smile. "We just have to take the baby to the nursery and Clarissa to her class." They moved off down a hallway, and Harvey and Jennifer faced the auditorium door. He looked like he was bracing himself.

"Are we okay?" she whispered.

"So far, so good." Harvey kept her hand in his, and they walked about halfway down the aisle. He stopped by a pew and raised his eyebrows. She glanced around and nodded. They sat down and waited.

After a minute, Harvey leaned toward her. "Are we allowed to hold hands in church?"

The idea that it might not be acceptable startled Jennifer, and she pulled her hand away and looked quickly around to see if anyone had noticed. He elbowed her, and nodded ahead. She looked, and saw a couple about three rows ahead, and the man had his arm across the back of the pew behind the woman. Harvey took her hand back. Her cheeks grew warm, but she was happy.

"How do you do, folks?" A graying man in his sixties stood at the end of the pew. Harvey jumped up, releasing Jennifer's hand, said hello, and shook the man's hand.

"I'm Pastor Rowland. Welcome. I don't believe I've met you before."

Harvey gave the introduction, saying "Jennifer Wainthrop" quickly this time, so that her names didn't get separated. The pastor smiled. He had a pleasant face, and Jennifer noted crow's feet like Harvey's behind his wire-rimmed glasses. "Do you live in the area, or just passing through?"

Harvey said, "Jennifer lives a few blocks from here, and I live over on Arden."

The pastor nodded. "I hope you enjoy our class this morning. Perhaps we'll have a chance to chat later." He went on down the aisle.

Harvey sat down and looked at Jennifer with a flick of his left eye, sort of a half-wink. "No sweat."

Ruthann and Rick came in the far end of the pew without the babies and sat down a couple of feet beyond Jennifer. Ruthann smiled at her, and she smiled back.

Turning to Harvey, she whispered, "What's their last name again?"

"Starts with a B."

"Booker?"

"Bradley."

She felt as if they had passed an examination. Harvey took out the pocket notebook that he used for witness statements and wrote, "Rick and Ruthann Bradley. Pastor Rowland." He raised his eyebrows with a smile at Jennifer and slipped the notebook back in his pocket.

"Is that how you remember everything?"

"It's a habit. Have to write everything down on my job."

A middle-aged man stood at the front of the auditorium, at a lectern set on the floor below the platform.

"Good morning. Turn to Colossians chapter one."

Jennifer looked at Harvey in dismay. He was checking out the books in the rack in front of them. The two blue ones turned out to be hymnbooks. The black one was a Bible. Harvey smiled.

"Where did he say?"

"Colossians?" It was an odd word.

Harvey flipped through the Bible. He turned to the front and found a table of contents and ran his finger down the row of titles, searching for something that looked like what the teacher had said.

"Here." Ruthann was close beside Jennifer,

and she was holding out a Bible, opened to the right place. Jennifer accepted it gratefully and handed it to Harvey, noticing with surprise that there was writing in the margin in several spots, and some sentences were highlighted in yellow.

The teacher introduced himself as Dick Williams. "Last week we began studying this book, and we learned that it is a letter written by the Apostle Paul to Christians in the city of Colosse. Today we'll learn about the attributes and deity of Jesus Christ."

Jennifer hadn't really thought about Jesus Christ in connection to the quest for God. In her mind was a nebulous idea that Jesus was supposed to be God on earth, or God's son, she wasn't sure which.

Their eyes raced over the page, trying to catch up with Dick. Harvey located the place and tapped it with his finger. Dick was reading, "In whom we have redemption through his blood, even the forgiveness of sins, who is the image of the invisible God, the first-born of every creature; For by him were all things created, that are in heaven, and that are in earth, visible and invisible . . ."

He read on, and Jennifer stared at the Bible, trying to keep up with the foreign ideas she was hearing. If it was really talking about Jesus Christ, then Jesus had created everything, and he existed before anything else. It didn't make sense to her.

When Dick stopped reading, she looked at Harvey, feeling overwhelmed. Jesus could not be the same as God; it said he was God's image. She felt very confused. Harvey stroked her hand, then let go of it and started writing in his notebook.

To her relief, Dick jumped back to the beginning of the passage he had read and began explaining it slowly, phrase by phrase. Jennifer had never heard anything like it. Harvey scribbled notes furiously, and she wished she had brought a notebook.

Dick reached a portion that talked about Jesus on the cross, and how that reconciled people to God. She had never understood how the cross could help people, and she wasn't sure she did when the class was over, but she felt that she was close to a breakthrough and wished she had a recording of the class and could play it back a few times.

Harvey sighed deeply and looked at her. "I got most of it. We can go over it later. Some of it's too deep for me."

She nodded and passed the leather-bound Bible back to Ruthann. "Thank you." She felt shy and slightly stupid. "We don't know much about the Bible yet."

Ruthann smiled. "You can use it for the worship

service if you like, or I can help you find the place in a pew Bible."

"Thank you, we can use this." Jennifer touched the pew Bible. She hesitated, then leaned toward Ruthann. "May I ask you something?"

"Certainly."

"I noticed that you write in your Bible. Is that okay?"

"Yes, it helps me remember and understand things, and to find verses again later."

"Sort of like in a textbook?"

"Yes." Ruthann had a pointed chin, curly light brown hair, and nice hazel eyes. She wore a floral print dress and black flats. No makeup, except maybe lip gloss. She hadn't laughed at Jennifer's question, and Jennifer liked her.

"Where do you live?" Ruthann asked.

Jennifer told her.

"That's right near here, isn't it?"

"Yes, it's not far."

"Are you two—" she broke off, and Jennifer realized she was looking at her left hand for an engagement ring.

"No, we're just friends. Well, more than friends, but . . ."

Ruthann smiled. "Sorry. I shouldn't be so nosy."

She's seen us holding hands, Jennifer thought.

"How do you know where to find the place in the Bible so fast?"

Ruthann smiled. "I guess you just have to memorize the books of the Bible. I learned them when I was a kid, so it comes easily now. But you just take a list and memorize them in order, sort of like learning the alphabet."

Jennifer thought about that. "How many books are there?"

"Sixty-six."

Learning sixty-six strange words like "Colossians," for which you had no associations, all in order, seemed a huge undertaking. She turned to Harvey. "Did you hear what she said?"

He nodded.

"You could do it," she said. "You remember names and numbers all the time."

"Not without my notebook."

Another man approached Harvey from the aisle, shook hands, and gave him a folded paper program with a color landscape on the front. Harvey opened it. Inside were the church address, telephone number, pastor's name and service times. Then there was an agenda for the worship service, listing hymns, prayer, offering, announcements, and special music. The hymn numbers were listed, and the title of the sermon was near the bottom—"Come unto Me, text: John 6."

"This is helpful." Harvey took the pew Bible and turned to the table of contents so he could locate John chapter six before the service began.

He tore a scrap from his notebook and used it to mark the place.

The choir filed into the seats on the platform, and Pastor Rowland and another man sat in chairs behind the pulpit. The pianist played softly, and the auditorium grew quiet. The man with Rowland stood and began the service.

The first half hour was full of music and inspirational comments from the song leader. They stood for the first hymn, a song that was strange to Jennifer. She found it in the hymn-book, and the words were also projected on the wall above the platform. After a few measures, Harvey began picking out the melody. As his baritone grew stronger with each line, she felt a pleasant shock wave. He could sing! How could she not know that? She tried to follow along and listen to him at the same time.

When the offering was taken, Harvey whipped out his wallet and extracted a five-dollar bill. The choir was in tune, and the music washed over them. Whether God was really there, or it was a psychological effect, Jennifer thought\ she would like to go to church every Sunday. She felt virtuous for being there, and happy for being there with Harvey.

The pastor stood up and prayed, then began his sermon. When he read through the scripture, Harvey had it ready, thanks to his bookmark.

A few verses into the text, Harvey stiffened

and peered intently at the Bible. “It’s Grandma’s verse,” he whispered, and out came the note-book. He kept up his marathon notes all through the sermon. Jennifer listened intently, trying to get beyond the atmosphere and find the faith her studies in philosophy hadn’t given.

“All that the Father gives me will come to me, and whoever comes to me I will never cast out,” read the pastor. Jennifer touched Harvey’s left hand. If that part was true, God would let them find him. He gave her the half-wink, and she knew he’d caught that, too.

Suddenly it was over, and the pastor offered a short prayer. People got up and started walking out, talking in the aisle. Jennifer looked toward the Bradleys. Rick had left the pew.

Ruthann smiled. “Rick’s getting the children. It was nice to meet you, Jennifer.” She held out her hand, and Jennifer took it.

“You, too.”

Harvey leaned toward her. “Thank you, Mrs. Bradley.”

“I hope to see you again,” she said.

Rick came back with the baby against his shoulder and Clarissa holding his other hand. A diaper bag hung behind him. When he was close, Ruthann began to move toward him.

On impulse, Jennifer said, “Mrs. Bradley!”

Ruthann turned around with a smile. Jennifer stepped closer. “May I see the baby?”

"Of course." Ruthann took Ethan from Rick and brought him over to Jennifer. He was sleeping, and his eyelids were lined with blue veins. Fuzzy, light brown hair covered his head, and his miniature fingers curled delicately in repose. "Would you like to hold him?"

"Oh, yes!" Jennifer held out her arms, and Ruthann laid the baby tenderly in them. He stirred a little, then settled back into sleep. Jennifer caught her breath. She couldn't remember holding a baby so young.

"He's beautiful," Harvey said in her ear, his voice husky. She turned around just a little so he could see better. As he reached out one finger and stroked the baby's cheek, she watched Harvey's large, soft eyes.

She brought Ethan's head up to her cheek for a moment, the silky hair tickling her skin, then handed him back to Ruthann. "Thank you so much."

"Anytime."

Rick leaned toward them. "Are you folks going to be here tonight?"

"What's tonight?" Jennifer asked.

"Evening service," said Rick.

"Not sure," Harvey said. "What time?"

"Seven."

They looked at each other. "Maybe," Harvey said to Rick.

The Bradleys gathered up their children and belongings and moved toward the door.

"Ready?" said Harvey.

"Ready." Jennifer hung her purse on her shoulder, and they stepped into the aisle. The auditorium was nearly empty.

"I couldn't understand it all," she said.

Harvey nodded. "There was so much to try to put together."

She said softly, "If I get my own Bible, I'm going to write notes in it like Ruthann does. And if we come back here, I'm definitely bringing a notebook."

Harvey gave her the crinkly smile and held her hand again. They moved into the foyer, and the pastor stood there with a woman beside him, shaking hands with each person who passed. When they reached him, Jennifer dropped Harvey's hand and shook the pastor's.

"Miss Wainthrop and Mr. Larson," he said with a smile. She wondered if he had a pocket notebook, too. "So glad you could be here." He shook Harvey's hand. "This is my wife, Mary." She had a sweet, peaceful expression. Her hair had less gray than her husband's, curling softly around her face.

"We're happy to have you here," she said, and Jennifer believed her.

"Is there anything we can help you with?" asked the pastor.

Harvey hesitated. "This is all new to Jennifer and me. There are some things you said this morning that I just couldn't take in."

"I'd be happy to talk about it."

"We're not very quick at following you around from place to place in the Bible. I tried to write it all down so we could look at it later, but I think I missed a few things."

Mr. Rowland smiled. "Would you like to stay for a few minutes now, or perhaps come back another time?"

Harvey looked at Jennifer. "Now okay?" She nodded. He said sheepishly to the pastor, "This is sort of an exploratory trip for us. We don't have much of a religious background, but we both thought we'd like to look into it."

Mrs. Rowland said, "Why don't you eat dinner with us? Then you can talk things over with my husband."

Harvey said, "Oh, we couldn't put you out."

"Nonsense," said Rowland. "It would be our pleasure."

Jennifer wasn't used to spur-of-the-moment dinner invitations from strangers, but they followed the Rowlands to their house, across the parking lot from the church.

Jennifer offered to help Mrs. Rowland set the table. She would have liked to hear all the pastor was saying to Harvey in the next room, but her mother's training in guest behavior took over.

The pastor's wife removed potato salad and sliced ham from the refrigerator, followed by applesauce, pickles, and bread.

"I try to plan a cold dinner on Sunday," Mary said, "so we don't have to worry about cooking. We usually invite someone over, and today was supposed to be the Penneys, but Mr. Penney was ill. I guess the Lord wanted you here."

Jennifer eyed her cautiously. Did God really want them there? How could he care about two people who didn't even know if he existed?

Harvey came to the doorway. "Jenny, come here! You've got to hear this!"

She went into the living room. "What?"

"I told the pastor about Grandma Lewis showing me that verse after the funeral, and he says it's not a coincidence that he talked about it today."

Jennifer looked at Mr. Rowland. "You have an explanation?"

He smiled. "The Bible teaches that there are no coincidences. God is in control of everything. He uses different circumstances and people to bring about various events."

"So God made Grandma Lewis read that verse to Harvey?"

"Well, I wouldn't say he *made* her, but he guided her."

Jennifer sat down beside Harvey on the couch and gave the pastor her full attention.

"When a believer, such as Mrs. Lewis, is in fellowship with God and seeks to do his will, he will lay things on her heart," Mr. Rowland said. "God prompted her to give Harvey that particular scripture verse. And then he guided me this week to prepare a sermon on the same passage. I have no doubt he wanted you to get a double dose of John 6:44."

Jennifer looked at Harvey. The implications were enormous. Harvey's face was intent, but a little skeptical.

"How do you know what to write your sermon about?" he asked. "How does God tell you?"

"I pray and ask him to guide me," said the pastor. "Usually as I read the scripture, I feel a burden to speak on a particular topic or passage. I expect your grandmother is a praying person."

"Oh, yes, she prays all the time," said Harvey. "She's praying for Jennifer and me. I saw her write our names on her prayer list." Jennifer was startled. Harvey went on, "She told me she's been praying for me for twenty years."

"And God has honored that today," said Pastor Rowland. "He brought you here to learn about him."

"But we picked this church off a computer map," Jennifer said.

"And who do you think caused you to pick this one out of the scores of churches in the area?"

Jennifer shook her head. "Those things don't happen in real life."

The pastor smiled. "They happen all the time."

They moved to the dining room and sat down to eat, and the conversation went on. Mr. Rowland patiently answered their questions. Jennifer helped Mrs. Rowland load the dishwasher while Harvey and the pastor sat at the table over coffee, continuing to talk.

At last Harvey said, "We've taken so much of your time, pastor. We should go now, but I can't tell you how much this means to Jennifer and me. We started out last night wondering how we could learn if God is real. You've given us a lot to think about."

"I'm very glad you came," Mr. Rowland said.

Harvey threw Jennifer a quick glance. "I haven't asked Jennifer about this, but I'd like to come back tonight."

"Definitely," she said. "You're not coming without me." Harvey laughed at that.

The pastor handed Harvey the Bible he had been using. "Take this with you. You can use it until you get one of your own."

They left the house and walked across to the Explorer.

"Thanks, Jenny."

"For what?"

"For wanting to come back, and, well, everything today."

"Do you believe all that stuff he was saying? That God knew we were curious and brought us here?"

"It's an awful lot to swallow." Harvey looked toward the church. "Do you think you'd like coming back here every week? I never in my life thought I would like going to church, but this is totally different from the mental picture I had."

"If we decide we believe it, I think we would be very happy coming here." She watched his face.

"And if we don't believe it, it's a moot point." Harvey handed her the Bible, and she felt a bit disappointed. Had she really expected him to believe it all at once? And did she believe it herself?

He pulled out his handkerchief and laid it on the pavement, then knelt on it to look under the Explorer at the gas tank.

"Get back, Jenny!" He jumped up and grabbed her around the waist and ran with her fifty yards away from the vehicle.

Chapter 13

"There's really a bomb?"

"Afraid so. Pipe bomb with a timer."

"Oh, no." The amazement in Jennifer's eyes turned to fear.

Harvey took his cell phone from his pocket and called the police station. "I need the bomb squad pronto."

"You have a 10-71 at the church?" the sergeant asked.

"No, it's not a bomb threat, it's a bomb, on a vehicle outside the church."

"Can you start evacuation?"

"The church is empty. The vehicle is the only one in the parking lot. I think it's got a timer, and the device could detonate any second." The man was wasting precious time. Harvey described the bomb to him in detail. Finally the sergeant said he would send a squad ASAP. Harvey broke the connection and called Mike at home.

"Mike, it's Harvey. There's a bomb under my car, and I'm afraid it could detonate before the bomb squad gets here."

Jennifer stood by him, white-lipped, and he reached for her hand.

"Hold tight," Mike said. "I'll light a fire under those guys."

"Bad analogy, Mike."

"Where are you?"

Harvey told him.

"I'll be there in ten minutes," Mike said.

Harvey put his phone away. "My captain's coming. He'll be here before the squad can get their gear on."

"What good will that do?"

"Maybe none, but Mike has had demolition and incendiary training."

"Harvey, is the Explorer going to blow up?"

"I hope not. But it could." *Wouldn't the insurance company love that?* He looked down at Jennifer. "You'd better get back to the Rowlands' and tell them what's going on, so they won't have heart attacks if it blows."

She headed for the pastor's house. Harvey stood watching his vehicle and feeling helpless. A couple of minutes later, Jennifer and Mr. and Mrs. Rowland came out of the house and stood looking toward him, and beyond him at the Explorer. He walked over to them.

"Better not go any closer. These things can throw shrapnel a long way."

"Who would do this?" asked the pastor.

"We're not sure, but my other car was blown up ten days ago. It looks like the same M.O. to me."

"Jennifer says you're a police officer," Mr. Rowland said.

"Yes, sir." The topic hadn't come up before. He took his badge out and clipped it to his jacket so the bomb squad would know he was a cop.

"But you never found out who planted the first bomb, did you?" asked Jennifer.

"We have an idea, but we haven't caught him."

"Someone with a grudge against you?" asked the pastor.

"We think it might be a guy I put in the state prison. But we were never sure the bomb was even meant for me. It could have been meant for my partner. He was driving my car that day. Someone could have hired this man to do it. We don't know what the motive is."

Mrs. Rowland looked warily across the parking lot. "Is there danger to the church building?"

"There's always danger from these things, ma'am. Unpredictable. But I think it's far enough from the building that the windows won't break." He measured the distance with his eye. "I think," he said again, doubtfully. "Be thankful the place is empty."

Mike's car came tearing in seven minutes later. He drove up close and hit the brake, then jumped out.

"Brief me, Harv." The two stepped away from Jennifer and the Rowlands.

"Pipe bomb with a box on the gas tank," said Harvey.

"Same as before. You eye-balled it?"

"In person. It had a couple of wires attached."
"So you think it's a timer, no remote detonator?"
"I don't know for sure."
"Probably safe unless you start the engine." Mike started walking toward the Explorer, and Harvey hurried after him.
"Mike!" Harvey grabbed his arm. "It's a machine. It's not worth the chance."
Mike stopped and eyed Harvey, then the Explorer, then Harvey. At 55, Mike had a wife who loved him, three grown children, and assorted grandchildren.
"You're right." He ran his hand through his hair and looked at his watch. "Where's that unit?"
A siren wailed in the distance.
"They're coming," said Harvey.
They stepped back nearer Jennifer and the Rowlands.
"How long you been here?" Mike asked.
"We got here at 9:40. The church emptied at twelve. We didn't go back to the vehicle then. Instead we went to this house for lunch," Harvey gestured behind him to the Rowlands', "and we came out about five minutes before I called you. I did my standard check underneath, and there it was."
"So they could have put it there at any time between 9:40 and 2:30."
"That's right."

The sirens were loud now.

"Probably a delay timer like the last one."

"I don't know, Mike, but they've got to be watching me."

Harvey glanced behind him. Jennifer was staring anxiously at him. Mr. and Mrs. Rowland seemed to be looking at the ground, and he realized they were praying. He felt better.

A patrol car, followed by two fire trucks, roared into the far end of the parking lot and cut their sirens. Mike and Harvey walked toward them. The fire trucks parked near the road, and the patrol car stopped halfway to the Explorer. Two men in protective gear hopped out, and Harvey and Mike went to them.

"Hey, Reynolds. You guys are slow," Mike said.

"It's on the other side, eight inches from the front of the gas tank," said Harvey.

Reynolds went on his back, and his head and shoulders disappeared under the SUV. Two firemen started getting a hose out, and the rest stood back in their gear, watching from a distance.

Harvey held his breath as he realized what Reynolds was risking.

Reynolds wriggled out from under the Explorer and stood up. He had a piece of galvanized pipe in one hand, and two colored wires dangled from the other.

"Nasty little thing." He grinned and pulled off his helmet and face mask. "Looks like something Bobby Nason would make. He was the last bomber we had in town, wasn't he?"

Mike said, "Could be his. But, then, could be anybody's. You investigated that car bomb last week, didn't you?"

"Sure did."

"Well, that was Detective Larson's old car." Mike nodded at Harvey.

Reynolds said, "Same M.O. Pipe full of black powder. Buy it at any gun shop. Mechanical timer as a delay mechanism. A wire hooked to the ignition circuit with an alligator clip, and another wire clipped to ground."

He showed them the timer, a battery powered alarm clock set at five minutes to twelve. "You turn the key, and five minutes later, when the hands come together, *boom!*" He shook his head. "We don't get many bomb cases. Lots of bomb threats, not many bombs. This will be great for my men—a chance to see one that didn't go off."

Mike said, "You guys go over that vehicle with a fine-toothed comb. I want a report on my desk by 8 a.m., including fingerprints, if any. Harvey, you and the lady need a ride home?"

The fire trucks left, and Harvey and Jennifer thanked the Rowlands.

"We'll bring Jennifer's car back for the evening service," Harvey told them. "The bomb squad should be finished with my vehicle by then." He put Jennifer into the front seat of Mike's Lincoln and got into the back.

"So, Ms. Wainthrop, I meet you at last," Mike said.

"Captain Browning."

"Your reputation has preceded you."

Jennifer blinked at him. "May I ask how?"

"Eddie Thibodeau," said Mike. "He informed me four days ago that you were 'drop-dead gorgeous.' Eddie usually exaggerates. I don't know how he slipped up that day."

Harvey expected Jennifer to blush and stammer, but she just said, "Eddie has been nothing but courteous to me."

"Oh, I'm sure. He can charm the antlers off a moose."

Mike could be charming himself. He was always gallant with the ladies, but Harvey didn't take it seriously. He knew it was only Mike's wife, Sharon, who counted. At the station, the men all knew Mike was crazy about her.

Jennifer directed him to her house, and Harvey got out and opened her car door. When she was out, he leaned down and stuck his head inside the car.

Mike said, "Harv, your first hour tomorrow is at my desk, and we'll go over the report on this thing."

"Got it."

"And check the lady's car now, please."

It was the first time Harvey had thought about Jennifer being targeted, except when she was with him. But someone wanted to hurt him, and she was vulnerable. He walked around Mike's car to Jennifer's Escort and got down under it. His pants were taking a real beating today.

"Everything looks okay." He stood up and brushed off his pants. Jennifer stood by the steps, watching.

Mike had his window down, now that Harvey was on his side of the car.

"All right, you check her car and yours before every entry. I'd hate to see that pretty little girl blown up because she associates with an old reprobate like you. Better teach her to check it herself when you're not here. She have your cell number?"

"Yes."

"She got a cell phone?"

"Yes."

"Watch yourself, Harvey." Mike glanced toward Jennifer and said, "What does she see in you, anyhow?" He backed out of the driveway.

Harvey smiled and shook his head as he went to Jennifer.

"Mike says I need to teach you to check your car, and he's right."

"All right. But you should change your clothes. Take my car."

• • •

Jennifer put on old pants and a sweatshirt and took her hair down and braided it. She tried to forget how frightened she was. Harvey was back in half an hour, wearing jeans and a plaid shirt.

"You need to do it before you open the car doors or anything," he said as they stood looking at her Escort. "And do it every time you're going to drive."

"That will be a treat in the parking lot at work."

He looked at her sharply. "You've got to do it, Jenny. This is important."

She nodded. "I will, until you tell me to stop."

"Take a blanket or something to lay down on the ground when you need to."

They got down beside the car, and he described what to look for and where to look.

"It might not be on the gas tank. It can be anywhere underneath, or under the seat inside." He pointed out all the most likely spots. "Do you have a flashlight? Always carry one in your purse. If it's at night, do the check with a light. Be thorough."

She nodded, fighting the fear brought on by the urgency in his voice. She would need extra time in the morning now. If she treated it as an exercise and didn't think about *why* she was doing it, she thought she could handle it.

Finally they went inside.

"Harvey, why are they doing this?"

"I wish I knew. Bomb cases are so rare in Maine. I've seen maybe eight in twenty years. Kids make them nowadays and explode them in their backyards, but still, we don't get many. There was Bobby Nason. He blew up his boss's store. And a couple of years ago we had a guy who threw a Molotov cocktail through a window. He was trying to torch his ex-wife's house." He shook his head. "Somebody's got it in for me."

Jennifer drew a shaky breath and tried not to follow that thought through.

It was almost supper time, and she put together a light meal.

"Are you still up for church tonight?" she asked him.

"I think so. How about you?"

"I'd like to go, if you still want to."

"My Explorer's still over there, anyway."

"Right. What did you think, overall?"

"I need to ruminate on it," Harvey said. "Mr. Rowland is pretty convincing, but I don't think you can pick and choose what you believe in the Bible. It's sort of all-or-nothing. I can't say yet whether I could accept it all."

"There's so much more to it than I realized." She shook her head. "I felt so ignorant this morning."

"Well, we'll just keep at it until we know, one way or the other."

"Right. Until we believe it or we don't." It

came to her that one of them might believe it, and the other might not. That was a bleak thought.

"I think reading the Bible will help," Harvey said.

She nodded. "Do we just read right through, or skip around?"

"I don't know. Do you want to read it together?"

"I'd like that, but if we only read it together, that would really limit us, wouldn't it?" she asked. "I might be able to read it on my lunch hour or something, but you wouldn't be there."

"Well, when we're together, we can read together. I'll leave this Bible the pastor gave me with you tonight."

"No, he gave it to you. I think you should have it."

"I'll get you one tomorrow," he promised.

"Thanks. I've got that new computer program almost ready for you." She had stayed up late several nights to work on it, but neither of them had mentioned it since the night of Donna-jean's arrest.

"Great. Would you want to come to the office and install it?"

"Sure. I could come tomorrow after work."

"I'll clear it with Mike."

She washed the dishes, and Harvey dried. She felt comfortable doing the mundane task with him. They sat down in the living room afterward, and she listened raptly as he read the first two chapters of Genesis aloud. She had never heard it before. It was like poetry, or a legend, or some other literary genre she couldn't classify, but it was beautiful. When he stopped reading, she sighed.

"Do you suppose it really happened that way?" she asked. "God just spoke, and things appeared?"

"Maybe. Why not? Does it make less sense than a huge explosion in space? But I'm not sure it makes any *more* sense, either."

She stretched her arms. "I guess it's time to get ready for church."

"Jenny, before we go, there's something I need to tell you."

Her pulse accelerated by about thirty beats a minute. "What is it?"

"Take it easy. I would have told you this morning, but I didn't want to ruin our day together, and then with everything that happened . . . well, I'm sorry, but I want you to hear it from me."

"You're scaring me, Harvey."

"I don't mean to. It's just . . . well, I might as well just say it. They found some remains up in Franklin County last night—"

Jennifer gulped. "Remains? You mean, a body?"

He nodded. "There's no identification yet. The M.E. took it to Augusta. But . . . it could be Nick Dunham."

She sat still. "Pretty awful."

"Yes. Well, no. I mean, if it is him, his wife will know, at least."

She nodded. "I don't know whether to hope it's him or not. Lisa can keep hoping, if it's someone else."

"That's pretty hard to live with, not knowing one way or the other."

"I guess you're right. I'd rather know for sure than wonder for years and years."

"It's probably on the news tonight. They may not be able to make a positive ID for a while, but people will wonder." He smiled. "So. Now that I've wrecked what's left of the day, we'd better get dressed."

Jennifer looked out the window at the car in the driveway. "I wish I knew . . ."

"What?"

She smiled ruefully. "The same old thing. I wish I knew about God. If I knew he was real, I could pray for Lisa Dunham. This has got to be hard for her, either way."

He went out to check the car again in his jeans, then took his church clothes in and changed in Donna-jean's empty room while Jennifer watched the car from the window. Then he went outside and sat on the steps while she put on dressy pants and found a notebook.

At the church, Harvey parked next to his Explorer, and they went in. They sat close to where they had that morning, and everything was more familiar. They sang more that evening, and she recognized one of the songs, "Amazing Grace." Singing with Harvey made the last of her tension slip away.

The pastor's text that night was in Ephesians, chapter six, on "The Whole Armor of God." It described the armor of a Roman soldier and related each part to the spiritual realm. The helmet was salvation, the breastplate was righteousness, or goodness, the pastor said. The sword represented the Bible. Jennifer's favorite was the shield of faith, which quenched fiery darts. A belt of truth and shoes of the gospel of peace completed the armor. Harvey and Jennifer both took notes.

When the service was over, Ruthann Bradley greeted Jennifer enthusiastically. "You came back! There's someone here I want you to meet." Beside her stood a young woman with shoulder-length dark hair, vibrant brown eyes, and a wide smile. "This is Rick's sister, Beth Bradley," said Ruthann. "She's staying with us."

Jennifer liked Beth immediately. The three of them chatted, and Rick walked around the women and talked with Harvey, bouncing Ethan up and down gently all the time. Clarissa hung between her mother and her aunt, sleepy and a little fussy.

Jennifer told the women she worked for a

computer company, and Beth said she taught kindergarten. Ruthann said, "I'm a stay-at-home Mom."

"And don't we envy you," Beth said. They all laughed.

"So, you're living with Ruthann and Rick?" Jennifer asked.

"Just until the end of the school year," Beth said. "It's getting crowded around there with the new baby."

"Our house is so tiny," Ruthann said. "Beth shares a bedroom with Clarissa. Ethan is sleeping in our room right now."

Jennifer heard Harvey tell Rick they would be back the next Sunday. On the way out, they again lingered to speak with the pastor.

"I'm sorry about what happened this afternoon," Harvey said as he shook Rowland's hand. "I'm sure that wasn't what you had planned for today."

"God is in control," said the pastor.

"It made for an exciting afternoon," Mrs. Rowland added.

"You were wonderful hosts," Jennifer said. "Thank you again."

Harvey nodded. "I enjoyed tonight's message. The armor of God is a great metaphor."

"I guess we saw something like that today," said the pastor. "I thought of it when the bomb squad arrived in their protective clothing."

"The department has something called riot gear," said Harvey. "We don't use it much. SWAT teams use similar stuff. There's a helmet and a bulletproof vest—"

"The breastplate," said the pastor.

"Yes, and an acrylic shield they would use for riot control. Of course," he smiled, "we don't use swords. The only thing I would use would be the vest, and then not very often. Maybe once a month."

"Why don't officers wear them all the time?" asked Mrs. Rowland. "Wouldn't it save lives?"

"The patrolmen wear them when they're on active duty, but the vests are hot, and not very comfortable. In our unit, we use them if we know we're going into a high-risk situation, but sometimes I sit all day at a computer. We don't wear them around the office."

"And I suppose cops don't get shot at in real life as often as they do on TV," Pastor Rowland said, "although there have been more incidents lately."

Jennifer didn't like to think about the number of times nationwide when uniformed cops had been targeted just because they were officers.

"I wanted to ask you," Harvey said to the pastor, "what kind of Bible should I buy? I looked online, and there are so many to choose from."

Mr. Rowland wrote down the name of a Christian bookstore and the type of study Bible he thought would help most. "You can order one online, but the people at this store are very helpful. And you can even get Bible apps on your phone."

"I should have thought of that," Jennifer said.

They went out into the twilight. The Rowlands called good night and walked to their house, and Harvey checked both their cars.

"I'll follow you home," he said.

"You don't have to. I'll be fine."

"No, I want to. I need to know you're safe."

He drove home behind her and took her up to the door and unlocked it. She recalled vaguely the feeling that loving a man like Harvey would be too stressful. But that was before this contentment had set in.

It was nearly dark, and a mosquito buzzed around them.

"Bug season's started," he said.

"Too bad."

"So, you're coming to my office to work on the computer tomorrow night."

"I'll be there around 5:15."

"Okay." He still stood there, looking as uncertain as she felt.

"Did you want to come in?" she asked. It still seemed slightly improper, especially after dark, but she was getting used to his presence, and the old uneasiness was gone.

He hesitated. "Better not." He put his arms around her and pulled her against him for just a second, then released her. "Good night."

Chapter 14

Harvey jogged around the softball diamond in the park while he waited for Eddie the next morning. He was glad he had worn a sweat-shirt. They did their usual Monday route of three miles. As they walked a little to catch their breath, Harvey told Eddie about the new bomb incident.

"So, it looks like you were definitely the target, Harv."

"Better keep checking your truck to be safe."

"No worries there. So, where did you and Jennifer go this weekend?"

"Fancy dinner and theater Saturday, church twice on Sunday, with the bomb squad sand-wiched between."

"Wow!"

"How about you and Nicci?"

"I took her for eats and dancing Friday night. She wants to go to Old Orchard Beach this summer, but I don't know."

"Why not?"

"She's okay in small doses, but I like a woman who can carry a conversation."

"I thought she was a physics major?"

Eddie grimaced. "I think she fabricated that to impress me."

Harvey nodded. "Sorry, buddy."

"You were right, as usual."

"Well, I never met a cocktail waitress who was a rocket scientist on the side."

"She might be fun at Old Orchard, though."

"That's the last place I'd want to go," Harvey said.

"Really? It's a fun date."

"Sure, if you like rides and junk food and trashy souvenirs."

"Gotta live a little, Harv."

"I do."

"Yeah?" Eddie grinned at him. "So when are we going to have that double date? Jennifer seemed agreeable."

"With you and Nicci? Never."

"I was thinking I'd ask somebody else."

"Who?"

Eddie shrugged. "There's somebody I've got my eye on."

"Yeah? So come on over to my place and eat breakfast and tell me about it."

"Do you have a table yet?"

"No, but we can eat Wheaties and bananas in the living room."

"Still sleeping on the floor?"

Harvey scowled. "So?"

Eddie shook his head. "I'm so hungry, I must be delirious. The thought actually entered my mind of asking you to move in with me."

"Forget it."

"Agreed. We'd hate each other inside a week. I don't know what came over me."

Ten minutes later they were slouched in Harvey's worn chairs drinking coffee and balancing their cereal bowls.

"So who's the girl you're thinking about?" Harvey asked. "I refuse to accept an engagement on Jennifer's behalf without knowing what we're getting into."

Eddie swallowed and gave him the Innocent French Boy stare. "You know her."

"That means nothing. I know every lowlife in the city. Oh, no, don't tell me. It's not Jennifer's so-called friend from Coastal Technology? Because I don't think I could stand to be within a mile of her for more than five minutes."

"No, I ruled her out, too. When I'm with a woman, I like to have a turn to talk."

"Whew. So, who is it?"

"Sarah Benoit."

Harvey set his mug down with a jolt. "Sarah? No, no, Eddie, not a good idea."

"Why not? She's pretty, she's smart, and she likes me." Eddie took a bite of Wheaties.

"Yeah, but a female cop? Don't start that, Eddie."

"Why not? She likes me."

"Women cops are hard, Eddie."

"Sarah's not hard."

"She's tough as nails."

Eddie scowled. "Are you ready to go to work?"

Mike gathered the men of the unit around his desk to receive their assignments for the day. "Harvey, you stay here to look at the bomb squad's report. Eddie can handle the paperwork from your last case and that habitual offender arraignment. Pete, Arnie, you see if you can track down Bobby Nason."

"Let me," Harvey said.

"No, you can't be objective about this. If Nason's in the city, Arnie and Pete can find him."

Harvey disagreed, but he didn't want to say so. "There's one thing that bothers me."

"Just one?" Mike said. "For a morose guy like you, that's phenomenal."

Harvey didn't respond.

"So what's the one thing?" Arnie asked.

"If Bobby Nason wanted to kill me, why did he wait so long? The first car bomb was planted three months after he got out of prison."

Mike took a pen from his shirt pocket and wrote something on the file folder on his desk. "You couldn't find anything that would tie it in with one of your current cases, could you?"

"No, I'm pretty sure it had nothing to do with the drug ring at the school, and I don't see anyplace else where it fits in. But here we've got another attempt."

"Somebody's got a long-standing grudge against you," Pete Bearse said.

"None of it makes sense to me." Harvey shrugged. "At first I thought maybe the bomb wasn't meant for me. Maybe someone had it in for Eddie."

"Yeah, some girl he forgot to call back," Pete said, and they all chuckled.

"Well, now there's no question who it was meant for," Mike said. "But keep checking your vehicles before you drive, you two."

When the others had left, Harvey sat across Mike's desk from him. The captain's tie was already askew, and he was chewing gum. He had the new bomb squad report and a copy of the one from the week before. They went over them meticulously.

"The two bombs had to be made by the same person," Harvey said.

"Agreed. Too coincidental otherwise."

"And I'm not sure I believe in coincidence anymore."

"One good fingerprint," Mike observed.

"Not Nason's."

"I'll have Arnie and Pete run the print."

"Please let me work on this, Mike."

The captain shook his head. "You know I can't. It's personal for you. Let Pete and Arnie look for Nason and any other potential suspects. You and Eddie need to keep a low profile until we get to the bottom of this. I'll put you on something totally unrelated."

"We know all Bobby's haunts," Harvey protested.

"Look, Harv, I've almost lost both of you guys in the past ten days. Forget it."

Harvey knew Mike was following standard procedure, but he still didn't like it.

Mike sighed and popped his gum. "I'm getting too old for this. I think I'll retire. Get a camp on Moosehead Lake or someplace. Sharon wants to get out of Portland and live in the woods."

"You should have been a game warden instead of a cop," Harvey said.

"Maybe. What were you doing at that church, anyway?"

"Going to church. What else?"

"I never knew you went to church."

"First time for everything."

"Do you believe in the trinity?" Mike asked.

"Trinity? Three Gods in one?" Mike was the last person Harvey expected a religious question from.

"Three people, one God, that's what Sharon says. She believes it. You know, the Father, the Son, and the Holy Spirit?"

"I don't know," Harvey said. "I'm just starting to learn about this God thing."

"Jennifer's religious?"

"No. Well, we're sort of studying it together."

"Huh." Mike chewed for a few seconds. "Well, Trask needs two extra men today. He's got a big investigation going on at some warehouse and needs guys to sort boxes or something. I'll send you and Eddie."

"Trask?"

"Yeah, I know." Mike shook his head. "He's a plodder."

"This is supposed to keep us alive? It will bore us to death."

At lunch time, he and Eddie managed to shake the new assignment for an hour. They got into Harvey's vehicle.

"There's a bookstore I need to visit on Forest Avenue," Harvey said. "That all right?"

"Can we drive through the Burger King first? I'm starved."

Harvey made the lunch stop, then drove over and parked in front of the Christian bookstore.

Eddie eyed the sign dubiously. "Harv, this isn't your kind of bookstore."

Harvey got out without saying anything. A hymn played on the speaker inside the store, and Bibles and religious books were prominently displayed. The glass case under the counter held cross pendants and dove pins. A large poster on the walls shouted, "Vacation Bible

School Materials." He pulled the piece of paper Pastor Rowland had given him out of his shirt pocket and handed it to the clerk.

"Do you have these Bibles?"

"Oh, yes, sir. That's a very nice study Bible." The clerk walked over to a display, picked one out, and opened the box on the counter for Harvey.

"Harv?"

He turned around. Eddie was right behind him, looking warily about the store.

"What?"

"Did you mean to come in here?"

Harvey turned back to the clerk. The man had lifted the Bible out of the box. Harvey took it and looked it over. Nice paper, shiny gilt edges, soft black leather cover. He flipped to the back and saw maps and appendices.

"How much?"

"Sixty-nine-ninety-five. We also have it in hard cover for $39.95."

Definitely leather for Jennifer. "Okay, I'll take two of these." Eddie stepped up beside him with bulging eyes.

"What colors would you like?" the clerk asked serenely.

Weren't all Bibles black? "What colors you got?"

"That one comes in black, white, brown, red, rose, or teal."

"Uh . . . one black, one rose, I guess."

The clerk got a second box from the shelf and held it up for Harvey's inspection. He nodded.

"Anything else, sir?"

"Uh, yeah." Eddie was right on his elbow. Harvey scowled at him. "Do you have a book called a concordance?" Pastor Rowland had mentioned that to him as well. He could find it online, but he liked his reference books in print.

"Yes. I'll get you one for this Bible version." The man walked to another shelf and came back with a hardcover book the size of a good dictionary. "Twenty-four-ninety-five."

Harvey got out his credit card.

On the sidewalk, Eddie couldn't hold it any longer.

"You dropped a hundred and fifty bucks on Bibles? I can't believe this!"

Harvey got into the Explorer.

"I coulda got you one for nothing," Eddie said. "There's an old one lying around my Mom's house. Nobody ever reads it. You could have it."

"These are special."

"But you're the guy who never buys anything new!"

Eddie ate his lunch and drank a milkshake while Harvey drove. He knew Trask would be looking for them soon, and he managed to down his burger at traffic light stops.

Eddie kept looking over at him as they headed

back toward the warehouse. Finally he said, "Harv, you didn't have to go to that church where they tried to bomb you. You could have come to my church."

Harvey looked at him. "Did you go to church yesterday?"

Eddie looked out the window. "That's not the point."

"Look, Ed, It's just a philosophical difference. Jennifer and I both come from Protestant backgrounds."

"What's wrong with the Catholic church?"

"I dunno. Maybe nothing."

"You don't have priests," Eddie said in an accusatory tone.

"You're right. So?"

"Priests are in the Bible."

Harvey pulled into the warehouse lot and parked. He grabbed the bookstore bag and took out the concordance and looked up the word *priest*.

"You're right. There's a page and a half of listings for the word *priest* here. Every one of them is for a different place that word is in the Bible."

Eddie looked impressed but still not won over. "So how come you Protestants don't have priests if they're in the Bible?"

"I don't know," Harvey said, "but I'll ask the pastor." A vague memory of Martin Luther came to mind. He decided he needed to get out some of his history books, too, and read about the Reformation again before he engaged in a lengthy debate with Eddie.

They spent the afternoon at Trask's beck and call. By four-thirty, Harvey had lifted so many boxes his back ached. Trask let them go back to the station to wrap things up for the day. Harvey didn't have any reports to write, so he got online and checked his stocks. His restaurant stock had split. The drug company was up ¾, and Coastal Technology was looking good. Should he invest in Jennifer and her productivity? He decided to wait. He looked at his watch. It was five o'clock, and Jennifer would arrive soon.

"Guess I'm going." Eddie sounded lonely. Harvey thought of making a basketball date for later, but he wasn't sure how long he would be with Jennifer.

"You got a ride?"

"Pete's dropping me off."

"Good night, Eddie." Harvey headed to the locker room, took out his electric razor, and started to shave.

"Well, well," said Mike as he came through the door. "Have to shave twice a day now, Harv? Just how thick are you two?"

"She's a lady," he replied.

"Well, if this computer program is as good as you think it's going to be, I may ask the lady to install it on my machine. Keep me posted." Mike took his jacket out and slammed his locker door. "How'd you and Eddie make out today?"

"Awful. Did Arnie and Pete find anything?"

"No."

"Put us back on the case, Mike."

"Not yet."

"I'm begging."

"I'll find you something else for tomorrow." Mike swung the jacket over his shoulder. "Harvey, I want you to think back. Is there something you did that would make somebody mad at you?"

Harvey shook his head. "Nothing a cop doesn't do every day. Maybe Pete's right, and Bobby Nason has held a grudge since I put him away."

Mike sighed. "We may never find that shrimp. He's got a brother up in Newport. Arnie's asked the department up there to shake the family tree. But discounting Nason, what else could it be?"

Harvey shut off the razor and blew the dust out.

"I don't know. Bobby's the only significant collar I know of who's been released lately."

"Something else, then. Something before the first car bomb. What did you do that week?"

"I'd have to check my reports. We had the school case, I know."

"Isn't that when they found Dunham's car in the river?"

"Yeah. I went back to the computer place, but nothing came of it. Jennifer and I had our first date that weekend." He shrugged. That was no help, but for some reason lately he'd been measuring time in relation to Jennifer.

"Write me a list," Mike said. "Put it on my desk in the morning. Everywhere you went, everything you did, on duty and off, for a week before that first bomb."

"Come on, Mike. My memory's not that good."

"It may be worth your life," Mike said. "Tell me you don't have something to live for now."

Chapter 15

Everyone at Coastal Technology expected Jennifer to work harder than usual. Mr. Owen was encouraging, but a little pushier than usual. The other partners were on edge. They all wanted her back on the special program, but they wanted the company's online security perfected first.

She was constructing a complicated protocol in the personnel section of their database when her desk phone rang. She sighed and grabbed the receiver.

"Jennifer, I'm glad I got you. Are you busy?"

"Yes, actually I am, Mom."

"Well, are you coming home this weekend?"

"I'm not sure."

"Your father has to go to Portland tomorrow on business. I thought I might ride along."

"Great. But I have to work."

"Oh, we'll go down after lunch, and he can do his business in the afternoon. Then we can meet you at your place, or would you rather have us come to your office? We'll take you out to dinner."

Jennifer sensed an unspoken motive. "Would you like to meet Harvey?"

"We'd love to. What a wonderful thought!"

“I’ll see if he can join us. Let’s meet at the office at five, okay?”

She skipped lunch and went through the afternoon on coffee and fruit from the snack bar. Over and over she tested the system, made a minor adjustment, and tested it again. At five o’clock, she was thankful to close her computer files. Her head ached a little, and she didn’t really feel like spending the evening doing more computer work, but she would see Harvey. That perked her up a little. She went back to the coffee station and took a bottle of juice from the compact refrigerator.

As she tipped it back to help her swallow two aspirin, Jane approached.

“Jennifer! Are you heading out?”

“Yes, I have an appointment.” Jennifer checked her watch. It wasn’t far to Middle Street, and she estimated five minutes would get her to the police station, unless traffic was a problem.

“A date? On a Monday?”

“Not exactly.” Jennifer took another swallow of juice and tossed the bottle in the recycling bin. “Are you seeing Brent tonight?”

Jane sighed. “No. He wants to go sailing this weekend, but I don’t know.”

“I thought you two were cozy.”

Jane shrugged. “I was really hoping that detective would call me. I gave him my home number.”

Jennifer wasn't surprised. Jane had mentioned Eddie several times, and she had decided from the first not to reveal that she knew the handsome detective. Jane would never leave her alone if she knew Jennifer was dating his best friend.

"Maybe he has a girlfriend."

Jane's red lips were pouty. "No, I don't think so. He looked really single to me."

Jennifer laughed. "What does a *really single* man look like?"

Jane shrugged. "I've just about given up on him. But there's someone else who's been paying attention to me lately."

"Really? Terrific. I hope it works out for you. I've got to run." Jennifer felt just a bit guilty as she strode toward the door, but she wasn't about to get into a drawn-out discussion of men. She hoped Jane wouldn't hurry outside after her and see her looking under her car. That would necessitate some sort of explanation, and she couldn't deal with more Jane right now.

The Priority Unit's office was usually empty at night. The men quit at five o'clock, unless they needed to continue an operation into the night. Downstairs, the regular units had shifts around the clock. Harvey went down and leaned on the front desk, shooting the breeze with the night sergeant, Brad Lyons, until Jennifer came in the front door carrying her leather portfolio. He took it from her and carried it upstairs.

"Sorry I'm late," she said.

"Are you tired? Maybe we should do this another time."

"No, that's okay, I'll just get right at it, if you don't mind."

She looked around when they entered the unit's office but made no comment. Harvey made another mental comparison with her working conditions at Coastal and figured she pitied him. He took her to his computer and let her sit in his chair. She brought up several programs in succession and checked things he never even knew were there.

"I think it will work," she said at last, "and it won't interfere with any other program on your network. But it will probably take me an hour or so."

"Okay."

"The program hierarchies are in online cloud storage. I'll download what you need to interface with what you've got."

"Can I get you anything?" he asked.

"Nope. Just peace and quiet." She took off her sweater and hung it over the back of the chair. "I almost forgot. My mother called this morning. My father has business in town tomorrow, and they'd like to take us to dinner. Can you go?"

"Yeah, I think so. I'd like to meet them."

"Great. They'll be at my office at five. Should we come over here?"

"Sounds okay."

He sat down in Eddie's chair and watched her work.

Her hair was wound tightly on the back of her head, held there somehow with pins he couldn't see. She wore a royal blue blouse. It was her color. No other woman should be allowed to wear it.

After about ten minutes, she swiveled around and looked at him. "Are you staring at me?"

"Guilty."

"Do you have to?" She seemed a little embarrassed. "It's hard for me to concentrate with somebody watching me."

"Right." He stood up. "Why don't I order some food in? You've got to be hungry."

"Well, I could look forward to an enormous Chinese dinner after."

"You got it. I'll just go downstairs for a while and let you work in peace."

He wandered down and leaned on the front desk again. Brad Lyons said, "Well, Harvey, who's the beautiful blonde who came in a while back?"

"Name's Jennifer. She's doing some computer work."

"Really?" Brad cocked his head.

"Yes, it's for the department."

"So there's nothing personal there?"

"If you mean, can you go up and hit on her, forget it." Brad was divorced three times and had a reputation for being perpetually on the prowl.

Harvey stuck his head into the communications room. The com room was busy, day and night. The three dispatchers wore headphones and constantly answered calls. No one to talk to there. He went back upstairs.

Jennifer looked up.

"How you doing?" he asked.

"About half done, I think. I didn't mean to drive you away."

"It's okay. I hate it when Eddie looks over my shoulder."

She smiled. "How's Eddie doing?"

"Well, he's a little confused right now. He doesn't understand why I'm so interested in God all of a sudden. He thinks you've bewitched me or something. Say, he asked me again about a double date. I don't know if you're really interested."

"Why not? It would be fun."

"Okay. Maybe we can set it up for this week-end."

Jennifer scrolled down on the computer screen. "Great. Just let me know. Now I need a few names you want flagged, so I can test it. You can add to them anytime, sort of like bookmarks."

"Okay, how about Bobby Nason?"

"Is that his real name?"

"Robert."

"So we'll enter both, because he might show up as either. Who else?"

"Paul Gordon. We arrested him a few days ago for embezzling. And put in your missing coworker, Nick Dunham."

"Okay. You can flag other items, too, not just names. Like types of crimes, if you think that would be helpful."

"You mentioned that. Can you add *car bomb?*"

She closed her eyes. "Sure."

He put his hand on her shoulder and stooped down close to her. "I'm sorry."

"No, it's okay. It would make me very happy if my program helped you catch him." She entered the item and completed a few more keystrokes. "That's enough for now. You can add the rest some other time. I'll be done in a minute."

He watched carefully, and the process seemed very simple. "How do you know how to do all this?"

She shrugged. "It's like the security programs I write. I've been doing so much of that lately, I haven't had time to develop anything new. It's almost all they let me do anymore."

"Well, they should have you revamp the security on their personnel records. They're tough, but they're accessible." He winked at her.

She laughed. "That's exactly what I've been doing."

He swallowed. "Really?"

"Yes. Someone's apparently been cracking into the company's databases. But don't let that worry you. You've reformed, remember?" She smiled.

Harvey said carefully, "That's your big, secret assignment? Keeping people like me out of your personnel records?"

"No, they took me off the special project to upgrade the security programs. I'll probably be back on that other job tomorrow. Unless someone goes after Coastal's records again."

Harvey's brain was whirling. Should he tell her he had accessed the company's files a second time, after his interview with Tom Henderson?

Jennifer smiled apologetically. "I need a few more minutes. Do you have something you can work on?"

"Sure."

He sat down at Eddie's computer and opened a new text file, thinking he might as well work on the report Mike had requested. He typed, "Friday, May 7: Car bomb. Lunch with Jennifer at Catassi's just prior to the bombing; morning at high school." What did he do the day before? Everything before Jennifer was a blur.

He pulled out his notebook and flipped back through it, but this one didn't go back far enough.

He went over to his desk. Jennifer's fingers were flying.

"Excuse me," he said. She flashed him a smile, and his heart flip-flopped. *People my age don't feel this way.* He opened the bottom desk drawer, took out the previous notebook he had used, and went back to Eddie's desk.

When he had compiled all he could remember from May first to the seventh with the aid of his notes, he printed it out and laid it on Mike's desk.

"I'm finished," Jennifer said. "Everything seems to be working."

He went over to look. "Great." He bent down to look at the screen, his hand on the back of her chair. "I'll test it for real tomorrow, when we get the state updates."

"You might need to flag a name that you know is in the update. Otherwise, it won't give you any alert unless one of these three names we've put in appears."

"Got it. I'll call you and let you know if it works. Are we ready to go eat?"

"Yes. I'm really hungry, and really tired."

"I won't keep you out late, then. Let's go get some food, then I'll take you home." He was tired, too, but wished he could sit down with her for a while and talk, and look at her without feeling guilty.

He grabbed her hand in the stairwell and gave it a squeeze. She held on, and he was smiling when they passed Brad Lyons at the desk.

He checked his Explorer, and they drove in it to Wing Fu's. She kept her word and ate more than he'd ever seen her eat. He checked under the vehicle again, and they went back to the station. He checked her car. This was getting old. Harvey followed her home. It was dark now, about nine o'clock, and he took his flashlight and the bag with the rose-colored Bible out of the Explorer. She was waiting by the steps.

"I know you're exhausted," he said, "but I have something for you. Can I step in for a minute?"

"Sure." She opened the door, and they went in and sat on the couch.

He took the Bible from the bag and handed it to her. She took it out of the box carefully and felt the leather, then put it up to her face and smelled it. She smiled. "New car smell."

"Do you like the color? Because they have other colors. I think they dye the leather."

"I like this. Thanks a lot."

"You take your phone with you wherever you go, right?" he asked.

She nodded and pulled it from a pocket.

"And you've got my number."

"On speed dial."

He grinned. "Call me anytime something seems not quite right, okay?"

"I will. Thank you, Harvey."

There were so many other things he wanted to say. The spiritual quest was tangled up in his growing love for her, and her safety had become critical to him. He wasn't sure how he could express all of what he felt, or if she was ready to hear it.

"Now you need to sleep," he told her.

They both went over to the door. He turned around and looked at her. Always a difficult moment. Should he, or shouldn't he? Once you kissed a woman, you couldn't take it back. Well, he told himself, there is a great deal to be said for anticipation.

"Sleep tight."

She nodded. "You, too."

He made himself open the door. He'd never agonized before over the perfect moment to kiss a girl. With Carrie, that hadn't been a problem. She'd taken charge on the first date.

But Jennifer was different. Very different. And he was meeting her parents tomorrow. Better to face her father with in impeccable record. He smiled and went out.

He made one last check under the SUV with his flashlight, climbed in, put his glasses on, and drove home. Sitting in the living room, he took his Bible out of the box and read for a long time. He started at the beginning of the book of John and read the text and the notes at the bottom. He kept on through the first six chapters, then pulled out his notebook and went over the sermon notes again. So much to think about. He put his feet up on the coffee table and looked at the ceiling. Aloud, he said, "God, if you're real, show me what this all means."

He fell asleep in the chair and woke up about midnight with a stiff neck. He staggered into the bedroom, took off most of his clothes, and lay down on his spot on the floor. *I need a bed,* he thought, *I really need a bed.*

Chapter 16

Jennifer got up early on Tuesday and read through the third chapter of Genesis. She recognized the story of the fall of man from *Paradise Lost* and read avidly. It took her a long time. There were more footnotes than text. Some of them were interesting, and some were confusing. There were so many references to other places in the Bible that she couldn't read them all.

One note particularly caught her interest. It said that in the New Testament it was clearly stated that the woman was deceived in the Garden of Eden, but the man wasn't, citing the verse I Timothy 2:14. It took her some time to find it, but, sure enough, it said, "And Adam was not deceived, but the woman was deceived and became a transgressor."

She went over to the bookcase where she kept literature books, pulled out an anthology of British literature, and opened to Milton. She found the spot, and read,

> She gave him of that fair enticing fruit
> With liberal hand. He scrupled not to eat
> Against his better knowledge, not deceived,
> But fondly overcome with female charm.

Would Harvey give up paradise for her? It was a romantic idea, but a frightening one. He was a police officer, and she knew he revered the law. How would he feel about God's laws? She hoped that if she did something horrible, he would walk away, not stay there and take the punishment with her. She put the literature book back on the shelf and went to work.

Harvey read some more from the book of John while he ate breakfast. Eddie arrived at seven-forty.

"Are you driving today?" Eddie asked.

"You'd better. I won't be riding home with you tonight. Jennifer's parents are coming, and we're going out to dinner with them."

"Meeting the parents! I *knew* this was serious."

Harvey didn't deny it. He took his Bible along and read while Eddie drove.

Mike handed them a surveillance job on a case of his own for the morning. They sat in Eddie's truck outside an apartment building, across the parking lot from the suspect's door, where they had a good view but weren't conspicuous. It was boring, but surveillance always was.

"Do you care if I read, Eddie?"

"No, go ahead. I'll watch."

Harvey opened to John chapter 9.

"What's it about?" Eddie asked.

"Jesus heals a blind man," Harvey said, reading the heading.

"Read it out loud."

He did. It was mostly about how upset the religious leaders were when Jesus healed the man.

When he reached the end of the chapter, Eddie said, "That's some story. Sounds like an investigation."

"Yup. The guy made them mad, and they hauled him in for interrogation."

"They even picked up his parents for questioning," said Eddie. "I liked it where they told them to buzz off and let the kid speak for himself."

"Yeah, he really told them off." Harvey looked at verse 30. "*Ye know not from where he is, and yet he hath opened mine eyes.* Pretty obvious to him that Jesus was God, but the leaders didn't see it. And they didn't like the kid trying to teach them theology."

"Tossed him out," Eddie said. "They coulda put him in the lockup." He was still watching the apartment building closely. Eddie had discipline when he needed it. "Do you think it's true?"

"I dunno. It says, *If this man were not of God, he could do nothing*. That at least is true, I guess. If Jesus wasn't God, he couldn't have healed him like that."

"But is the whole thing true?" Eddie frowned, still staring out the windshield.

"The whole Bible?"

"Yeah."

"I guess that's the question. That's where Jennifer and I are right now."

Harvey skimmed down through the chapter again and stopped at verse 31. "What about this? *Now we know that God heareth not sinners; but if any man be a worshipper of God, and doeth his will, him he heareth.*"

"God won't listen to sinners?" Eddie shook his head. "That's weird."

Harvey thought about that. He qualified as a sinner, he guessed. Or was sin just an idea somebody made up? He knew he'd done a lot of things that weren't the best, but who hadn't?

"Do you think there's such a thing as sin? Absolute right and wrong?"

"If there's not, then why are we cops?" Eddie asked.

"Okay, but does it matter to God? If there is a God."

"I believe in God," Eddie said.

"You do?"

"Well, sure. I was born a Catholic. You have to."

"So you believe the whole Bible is true, then."

"I dunno. I didn't know all this stuff was in

it." Eddie glanced at Harvey, then back at the building. "Hey, we got action."

Their target was walking to a car near the apartment house, carrying a gym bag. Eddie started the engine and put the truck in gear.

Things were a little better at work for Jennifer. The pressure was less intense, but she still didn't get to work on her own projects. Instead, she was back on the foreign account. John Macomber told her confidentially that he thought the software was going to help an Asian industrialist pirate American designs. Jennifer wasn't sure whether to take him seriously.

She went out to lunch with Jane, at the deli across the street, and while they were eating, Jennifer's phone rang.

"Excuse me, Jane." Jennifer took it out of her purse, feeling a twinge of guilt. There were rules of etiquette about phones in restaurants. "Hello?"

"Hey, gorgeous."

"Hey yourself." She couldn't help grinning.

"Eddie and I have been out all morning. I just got time to check the program, and it works like a charm."

"One of your flags came up?"

"Yes, Paul Gordon's got a new hearing scheduled."

"Good. Now you just have to add the names you want in there."

"How you doing?"

"Great. Jane and I are eating lunch." She smiled apologetically at Jane.

"I won't keep you. See you later, gorgeous."

When she put the phone away, Jane was watching her with interest. "So who's the guy?"

"Just somebody I met."

"Come on, he must be special. You're blushing."

Jennifer hated that. "His name is Harvey." She hoped Jane wouldn't put it together with the detective handling the Dunham investigation.

"Is this going to be serious?"

"I think it is. He's meeting my parents tonight."

After he called Jennifer, Harvey walked down the street to a menswear store. He really needed something to wear, and all of his suits needed cleaning. Mike had been after him for months to use more of his clothing allowance. Maybe it was time.

He and Eddie had picked up Mike's suspect that morning. Mike was very busy with the case, and the two detectives ran errands and pulled documents for him. It beat working for Trask, but they hadn't had a break, so Harvey felt a long lunch was justified.

He went back to the office carrying a new

gray sport jacket, darker pants, and a tie with a subdued design in blue, navy and silver, wondering if it was too fashionable for him. He didn't usually worry about his clothes.

He just had time to grab a sandwich at the diner. Mike kept him and Eddie busy. On his afternoon break, Harvey checked his stocks. The restaurant shares, 1,000 since they split, were rising. He totaled his market accounts, and the idea came to him unexpectedly that he could buy a house if he wanted to.

At quarter to five, he took his cell phone with him to the locker room and shaved and put on the new clothes. When he came out, the office had emptied, and Eddie was closing his computer.

"Pretty snappy," Eddie said, looking him up and down. "Conservative, but with panache."

"Think so?" Harvey still wasn't sure. "Is it parent-proof?"

"Take your badge off."

Harvey unclipped it and put it in his pocket.

"Less intimidating." Eddie grinned. "How could they not approve?"

Harvey walked restlessly to the windows by his desk and looked down at the traffic. He had his holster on under the jacket, and his handcuffs in their case on his belt, where they wouldn't show. He hoped he'd thought of everything that might offend her parents.

His phone rang. As he answered it, Eddie waved and walked out the door.

At ten minutes to five, Jennifer's personal phone rang.

"Hi, honey. We're outside," her mom said. Jennifer jumped up and hurried to meet them at the door.

"Hello!" She kissed them both. "I'll be done in just a minute."

"Want us to wait outside?" her father asked.

"No, you can come over here if you want. I just need to close up my program. Come meet Jane."

She took them to her work station and introduced them to her friend.

"So, you're meeting Harvey," Jane said knowingly.

"Yes, that's part of the plan," Marilyn Wainthrop said. "Do you know him?"

"Haven't had the privilege," Jane said, "but I get the feeling this guy is going to be around for a while."

Jennifer was annoyed to feel a flush spread over her face. She liked Jane, but discretion was not her friend's strength.

"Excuse me. I'll just call him and tell him we're coming." She took out her cell phone. "Hi. It's me. We're on the way over," she said self-consciously.

“I’ll meet you out front, gorgeous.” Her blush deepened.

As she tucked the phone into her pocket, her father said, “So, this is where the computer girl works. Not too shabby.” He looked around the large room and nodded with approval. Jennifer could tell he was proud of her.

She led them to the parking lot and stopped beside her car, suddenly realizing she had to do the bomb check.

“I’ll follow you,” her father was saying.

“Okay.” She stood staring at her Escort, not sure how to tell them.

“Shall I ride with you?” her mother asked.

“Fine. Uh, Mom, don’t open the door just yet.”

“Is it locked?” her mother asked.

“Yes, but—I have to do something.” She looked at her mother, then at her father.

“What is it, Jenn?” Her dad eyed her closely. “Did you forget something?”

“No, it’s just—I—I have to look under the car.”

“What?” Her father almost shouted.

“There was a little incident Sunday. The police advised me to check my car every time I drive.”

“What are you saying?” her mother gasped.

Jennifer laid a hand on her sleeve. “It’s nothing, Mom. Really. It’s just that someone I know had a bomb put on his car, so I’ve been told to check mine just to make sure everything's okay."

Without waiting for their reaction, she thrust her leather portfolio into her mother's hands and knelt on the tarmac.

"Jennifer, your good pants," Marilyn cried.

Other employees were coming out of the building, and John Macomber threw a curious glance at Jennifer as he passed them.

"Nobody else is looking for bombs," her father observed. "Do you want to tell us about this?"

"It's nothing, really, Dad. Just a fluke. Nobody got hurt."

"I suppose it was your friend Harvey who found the bomb under his car?"

"Well, yes. And his boss thinks we should both be careful for a while. Not just us. Harvey's partner, too." She went to the other side and looked, then unlocked the door for her mother. At the driver's door, she looked under the seat and the dashboard, then smiled at her father.

"All set," She hoped her tone was normal and confident. She got in and buckled and started the engine.

"Jennifer," her mother began, "how long has this been going on?"

"Just since Sunday. It's nothing to worry about, Mom. How did Daddy's meeting go?"

She kept the conversation on safe topics until

they got to the police station. Harvey was waiting for them on the sidewalk.

Harvey braced himself as Jennifer made the introductions. Her father shook his hand firmly and eyed him up and down. Mr. Wainthrop was Mike's age, but looked older. He weighed a little more, and his salt-and-pepper hair was cut short. Behind his wire-rimmed glasses, his eyes were a rich brown. Her mother was small, a woman who had been stunning thirty years ago and was still attractive. Her hair was still blonde, but a little faded, wavy, falling nearly shoulder-length. Harvey thought he could see Jennifer in her. Marilyn's eyes were the same serious gray. When Harvey smiled at her, she smiled back, and Harvey's hopes rose. This would work. It had to.

They exchanged pleasantries, and Mr. Wainthrop named the restaurant.

"You drive my car," Jennifer said to Harvey, and he took the wheel. Her parents got in their car, and Harvey waited for her father to pull into the street.

"They like you," Jennifer said.

"How can you tell?"

"Daddy does a quick appraisal, and it would be obvious if you didn't pass. Mom was very taken, I thought. By the way, I like the tie and the jacket. New?"

He touched his necktie. "Thanks. Yes. Eddie says I have panache."

She laughed, then sobered. "I had to tell them about the car bomb."

He glanced over, then signaled to follow her father on a turn. "How's that?"

"I had to do the car check when I left the office. Daddy had fits."

"Oh, boy. I didn't think of that."

"It's okay. I told them nobody got hurt and it was probably just a fluke. I didn't tell them about the first one."

"You know it wasn't random."

"Was that a lie? They were so worried."

He reached over and squeezed her hand.

At the restaurant, Harvey sat next to Jennifer. He hadn't been this nervous since he asked her for that first lunch date.

"How's business in Skowhegan, Mr. Wainthrop?" he asked.

"Not bad." Her father peered at the menu through the lower part of his glasses.

"Jennifer, you look a little peaked," said her mother. "Are you all right?"

"I'm fine. I'm a little tired, is all. We've been really busy at work."

The waitress came, and they ordered seafood all around.

Updates on Jennifer's siblings came next. Jeffrey, an EMT in Skowhegan, had applied for a job with the Portland Fire Department; Abby was putting in a lot of hours at the medical center in Waterville; Leeanne and the two younger boys had a couple of weeks of school left. Harvey let the talk flow around him until the food was served.

"So, Mr. Larson," said Jennifer's father, and Harvey came to attention. "How long have you been a police officer?"

"Eighteen years, sir."

"You're a plainclothesman?"

"Yes, sir. Detective in a special unit."

"What's special about it?"

Harvey checked for a moment on that one. "Well, sir, we handle cases that are urgent or have aberrations."

"You guys have some special capabilities, I assume?"

"Yes, sir." He didn't elaborate.

Mrs. Wainthrop smiled brightly. "Jennifer said you went to church Sunday."

"Yes, ma'am."

George became even sterner at the mention of Sunday. "Is Jennifer safe with you?"

"Sir?"

"This bomb situation. Is my daughter safe?"

Harvey swallowed. "Oh. Well, yes, sir, I think so. My boss had me teach her to check her vehicle for demolition devices as a precaution. We don't think there is any danger to her, but until the perpetrator is caught, we're just playing it safe." Under the table, Jennifer's hand found his.

Her father frowned.

"Daddy, I've been working on a new computer program that Harvey thinks the police department can use." Jennifer pulled out a sunny smile, but her voice rose in something like panic, and Harvey stroked her fingers in an effort to calm her.

Mrs. Wainthrop picked up her salad fork. "Now, Mr. Larson, you're not from Maine, are you?"

"No, ma'am, I was born in New Hampshire, but I've lived here almost twenty years."

Jennifer stared at her mother. "How long does it take to be a Mainer, Mom?"

"Now, dear, I wasn't being critical."

There came the inevitable moment when mother and daughter exited for the ladies' room. Harvey looked bleakly after Jennifer as she disappeared.

Her father wiped his mouth with his napkin. "All right, Larson, time to talk turkey."

"Sir?"

"Your intentions toward my daughter are . . ."

"Honorable."

"Hmm."

"Totally honorable."

"You're too old for her."

“Well sir, that’s debatable, and, with respect, I’d have to disagree.” Harvey wished he could take his jacket off, but then the holster would show, and that wasn’t good in a restaurant.

“Make your case.” Wainthrop’s dark eyes were uncompromising.

Harvey reminded himself that he wasn’t a kid and had no reason to be nervous.

“Well, for starters, I believe I could make her happy.”

“Hmm.”

“And I’m established in my career. I could support her and take care of her.”

“She didn’t encounter bombs before she met you.”

Harvey shifted in his chair. “Well, sir, that was an unforeseen event that we handled as best we could.”

“You see yourself as a family man?”

“Sir?”

“Are we talking marriage here?”

Harvey took a deep breath. “Well, maybe. I have to admit it’s crossed my mind, but, well, sir, I mean, I haven’t known her very long, and I haven’t even kissed her yet. We haven’t discussed marriage.”

“Hmm.”

Harvey played with his glass and sneaked a glance at the older man. He was very glad he’d restrained himself last night.

"Awfully late in life to start a family," Mr. Wainthrop said.

"Not too late, sir."

"You don't have two or three other families, do you, Larson?"

"Oh, no, sir."

"Never married?"

"Well, I was married once, sir, for eight years." Harvey hesitated. "My wife passed away."

"Widower," Wainthrop said.

Harvey let it pass. "No children."

Mr. Wainthrop nodded. "Sorry to be so direct, but Jennifer is our first daughter. I know she's a big girl, but she doesn't have her folks down here in the city to look after her. Now, I admit, I was quite concerned when she told me how old you were. Didn't know what to expect, but, well . . ." He sat forward and held out his hand. "Larson, I could like you."

They shook hands. "Thank you, sir. My name is Harvey."

"My name's George." He sat sideways with one arm across the back of his wife's empty chair and crossed his legs. "Ever go hunting, Harvey? You must be a pretty good shot."

"Mother," Jennifer said the second the ladies' room door closed, "You two have got to lighten up on him!"

"What do you mean?"

"You and Daddy are making him uncomfortable."

"I'm sorry. It wasn't intentional. We've been concerned, and we're just trying to get to know him."

"I told him that you'd love him. This is awful."

"Oh, Jennifer. What's so awful? We haven't insulted him or anything. He seems very nice. Nice smile, too. I can see why you're attracted to him."

"Can you?"

"Yes, honey. He's a good dresser, too."

Jennifer smiled a little. "I wish I'd brought him to Skowhegan first."

Mrs. Wainthrop nodded. "We would probably all have been more at ease then." She kissed her daughter on the cheek. "Jennifer, I know you're a sensible girl. Just take your time, dear. And if you decide to bring him into our family, we'll welcome him and love him like a son."

"Daddy, too? He's being pretty rough on Harvey."

"Your father wants to be sure he's responsible. You hear things. Police officers aren't known to have a good track record on their personal lives. And you are very dear to us."

"Mom, I think I love him."

Her mother smiled tenderly. "Does he love you?"

"I'm not sure. I know he cares. Sometimes,

when he looks at me . . ." Jennifer didn't know how to describe the look that made her melt.

Her mother nodded. "Aren't his eyes striking?"

By the time they got back to the table, her father and Harvey appeared to have made peace. George was telling a story about his moose hunt the year before, and Harvey was listening attentively. He looked up at Jennifer and smiled as she sat down.

Harvey got a cab on the street in front of the restaurant. He shook hands with her mother and father, then held Jennifer's hand for a second and said quietly, "Call me later," and got into the taxi. He was gone so suddenly that Jennifer felt let down.

Her parents went back to her house with her for a short visit.

"You come home and see us soon," her father said sternly. "You haven't been home in weeks."

"Bring Harvey," said her mom.

Her father nodded. "I'd like to show him the farm." He worked full time, but still farmed on a small scale. The family always had a big garden, and they kept a few animals on the twenty acres.

"You do like him, don't you?" Jennifer asked anxiously.

"We think he's wonderful," said her mother, settling on the couch.

"He'll do." That was praise enough from her father.

Her mother picked up a magazine from the coffee table. "You ought to get a new roommate. I'd feel easier about you living down here."

Her father nodded. "Don't like you coming home alone at night."

"I'm thinking about advertising," Jennifer admitted. "I just want to make sure I don't have any regrets this time."

Her parents left around nine o'clock, and she called Harvey.

"They're gone," she told him. "You lived through it."

"Barely. I thought for a while there your father was going to have me drawn and quartered. He thinks you're not safe with me."

"He was talking about the bomb, not you personally. You must have won him over. He told you the moose story."

Harvey chuckled. "It was a pretty good story. I like your dad."

"That means a lot to me."

"Well, he's a bit protective, but I can't say as I blame him. I'm concerned about your safety myself."

The tenderness in his voice thrilled her, and Jennifer wished he was there with her. "They want me to get a new roommate."

"Probably a good idea. But take your time."

"I intend to be very picky." She sighed. "I'd almost rather live alone, but they worry about me." The knowledge that she had naively let Donna-jean bring a drug dealer into the house still troubled her.

"Let it ride for a few days," he advised. "Things will look better then, and you might hear about someone who's more on your wavelength."

"I guess." She cast about for more cheerful topics. "So, have you and Eddie planned our double date yet?"

"No, but I guess we've got to, or he'll never quit pestering me about it."

"Eddie's fun."

"Yeah, as long as he brings along his own girl, and she's not an imbecile."

Jennifer wondered about that, but didn't pursue it. "What do you want to do Saturday?"

"I dunno. I ought to go to an auction or something and buy a table."

"A table?" It was out of the blue, and Jennifer sat up, trying to make sense of it.

"Yeah, I need one."

"What for?"

"To eat on," Harvey said. "Don't ask."

She could see that the surprises weren't over. A few days ago, she'd wanted to learn everything about him, but getting to know him was a complex task that encompassed thwarting crime, pondering ideas, and confronting painful memories. Maybe even buying furniture. But she still wanted to do it.

"We could drive out to the lighthouse at Portland Head," she suggested. "Isn't there a flea market out there somewhere?"

"I think you're right. There would be yard sales, anyway."

"You make the arrangements with Eddie, and I'll pack a lunch for four."

"Sounds good. Jenny, can I see you tomorrow?"

"Wednesday night? I don't know if I can keep up the pace, Harvey. I'm getting tired."

"I'm sorry. It wouldn't be a late night. I thought maybe we'd go over to the church."

"The prayer meeting is tomorrow night, isn't it?" She hadn't thought they would go. She and Harvey weren't in the praying mode yet, but there was a plaintive longing in his voice.

"I called the pastor tonight after I got home, and he invited us," he said.

"You called him?"

"Yeah, Eddie asked me a question yesterday about the Bible, and I couldn't give him an answer, so I called Pastor Rowland to see if he could help me."

"Did he?"

"Yes. See, Eddie asked me why we don't have priests. He's Catholic, and he was taking it personally, I think. The pastor told me why that is."

"Why?" She'd never thought much about it, but she was curious.

"Well, in the Old Testament they had priests to make sacrifices and stuff like that, but after Jesus came, they didn't need them anymore. They didn't need sacrifices, because Jesus was the ultimate sacrifice. So the priests were out of a job."

"That fits! Harvey, this morning I read Genesis 3, and there are notes where it tells how God planned way back in the Garden of Eden to send Jesus as the savior, and he killed animals to make clothes from their skins for Adam and Eve. That was the first sacrifice, but it was supposed to represent Jesus coming later to die for their sin. When I first read it, I thought the guy who wrote the notes was kind of reaching, but when you say that about not needing sacrifices and priests anymore, well, it's starting to make sense to me."

"Where was that part?" Harvey asked. "Genesis 3? I'll read it tonight."

She lay back on her blue pillow sham. "Harvey, this is great, to be studying the same thing and putting the pieces together."

"So, do you want to go to the prayer meeting? The pastor says we don't have to pray. There's Bible study, too."

"I guess so. I'd like to know how people who believe in God pray. Not the pastor, I mean. Just ordinary people."

"Thanks. I promise I'll get you home early."

She hung up, feeling more comfortable with him. More than anything, she wanted to be close to Harvey. They were making progress, but she still felt that exposing her innermost self to anyone would be harrowing. If Harvey was the one, it might be bearable.

She laid out her clothes for work and went to bed, drifting off as she mentally composed an ad for a new roommate.

Career woman seeks female roommate. Mature nonsmokers only need apply. Drug users will be arrested.

Chapter 17

When they met to run the next morning, Harvey told Eddie what the pastor had said about priests. Eddie was thoughtful, but not happy.

"Of course a preacher would say that," he said testily. "They hate Catholics."

"He doesn't," Harvey insisted.

"What about the Mass? Only a priest can do the Mass."

"Is the Mass in the Bible?" Harvey asked.

"I don't know." Eddie's brown eyes were troubled.

"I'll try to study it some more."

When they walked into the office, Mike called them over to his desk.

"The M.E.'s office just called. They've ID'd the body that was found Saturday. I'm sending Arnie and Pete out on another case, but you two get right on this."

"You mean it's our guy?" Eddie's eyes shone as if Mike had handed him keys to a new snowmobile.

"Nicholas Lee Dunham, age 32, last seen March 4 at the offices of Coastal Technology . . ." Mike handed the slip of paper he was scanning to Harvey. "Call Augusta and ask for Dr. Martin. He'll give you the details. They already sent somebody out to break it to the widow."

A dark-haired woman opened the door of Lisa Dunham's house to Harvey an hour later. She looked vaguely familiar, and Harvey tried to place her, quickly zipping through his mental catalogue of women connected to Coastal Technology.

"Hello. I'm Detective Larson, with the Portland P.D. Is Mrs. Dunham in?"

"Yes. Won't you come in? I'm Nick's sister, Jackie Wyman."

Harvey followed her into the kitchen, and Eddie stationed himself unobtrusively near the door.

Lisa Dunham sat at the table with a cup of tea before her. Her eyes were puffy and red-rimmed, and it looked as though she hadn't touched her tea, though her sister-in-law's mug was nearly empty. Harvey was glad Mrs. Wyman had been with her when the medical examiner's representative came.

He walked over to stand beside Lisa. "I'm very sorry, Mrs. Dunham. May I talk to you for a few minutes?"

She nodded, holding a tissue to her eyes.

"Would you like some tea or coffee?" Jackie Wyman asked, including Eddie in her glance.

"No, thank you," Harvey said, and Eddie shook his head.

Harvey sat down opposite Lisa and took out his notebook slowly, deliberately, to give her a moment to bring her emotions under control.

"Ma'am, now that we know for sure that your husband is deceased, we can go forward with the investigation. I'll work closely with the medical examiner's office. They've given me a full report, and we have lots of new information that should help us."

She nodded and drew a shaky breath. "The woman who was here this morning—her name was Hyde—was very nice. She told me—" She broke off with a gasp, and Harvey waited. Diane Hyde was good. He was glad they had sent her. Jackie stepped closer and rubbed Lisa's shoulders.

"I understand about the—the condition of my husband's body," Lisa whispered at last. She pulled tissue after tissue from the box, wiping her face repeatedly as the tears refused to stop flowing. "But she said they're pretty sure he was—killed—" She sobbed and turned toward Jackie.

Harvey was glad it was her sister-in-law hugging her and letting her cry all over her blouse. Eddie and Arnie, and even his old partner Chris, got into all sorts of predicaments by letting distraught women cry on their shoulders, and Harvey had determined years ago that he wouldn't let that happen. It wasn't that he didn't feel sympathy. He felt plenty. He just didn't like entanglements.

Lisa's sobs diminished. Jackie whispered, "It's okay, honey, it's okay."

Eddie wiped his eyes with the back of his hand and looked out the window.

"Mrs. Dunham," Harvey said gently. "The medical examiner told me this morning that your husband was shot three times. That's shocking, I know, but now we can look at the evidence they've got and try to determine who did this and why."

She nodded and took a deep breath. "It's so awful. I mean, if someone just wanted to rob him, why take him all the way up there, then drive his car back to—I just don't understand it."

"I don't either, yet, but I intend to find the answers to those questions."

She nodded, her tears spilling over again. "I've thought about all the questions you asked me before—did Nick have any enemies, and all that. I've thought about nothing else. But I still can't make any sense of it. At least now I know for sure he didn't—" She swallowed hard and reached for another tissue.

Harvey looked up at Nick's sister. Her eyes were brimming, too. "Where are the children, Mrs. Wyman?"

"They're at school."

Lisa said, "They were gone before Ms. Hyde got here. I—I was glad."

"The medical examiner's office called Lisa first, and she called me," Jackie said. "I got here while she was explaining things to Lisa. It was pretty gruesome."

Harvey nodded. "My partner and I will go to Coastal Technology, to speak to the partners there. After that we'll probably spend most of the day with the state police, compiling evidence from the scene."

"What can you do?" Lisa asked.

"Well, we know what caliber of weapon to look for now. That's one thing. There are other leads to follow." Harvey didn't really think it was time to reveal his plans for the investigation or more details that would haunt her dreams.

"What about Nick's phone?" Lisa asked.

"They haven't found it. I tend to think whoever killed him destroyed his company phone and his personal one when they disabled the car's GPS."

She nodded.

"I know this is very difficult for you," Harvey went on. "There will be publicity. You'll need to help the children get through this and decide what the family wants to do for a memorial, things like that. Is there anything I can do for you before I leave?" He looked from Lisa to Jackie.

"I've called my mother," Jackie said. "The family will get together here this evening. She touched Lisa's shoulder. "Would you mind if our pastor came over?"

"That's fine. Nick would want a service." Lisa pushed away from the table. "I'm going to lie down."

"I'll be in to check on you in a minute," Jackie said. When Lisa had left the room, she turned to Harvey. "Nick and Lisa didn't go to church much lately, but Nick grew up in our church, and he knew the pastor. My mother wants Pastor Rowland to do the service, and I think Nick would want that."

Harvey stared at her. "Pastor Rowland? Victory Baptist Church?"

Jackie's eyes widened in surprise. "Yes. Wait! You were there Sunday."

"Yes. I was visiting with a friend of mine." He hesitated. "She worked with your brother at Coastal."

"That's odd."

He nodded. "Very odd. But then, Pastor Rowland says there's no such thing as coincidence."

Jackie smiled. "God brings his people together when they need each other. Thank you, Detective Larson. I'm glad you're handling this."

"I'm really sorry about your brother—about Nick. Would you like me to call the pastor for you?"

"I'll take care of it. Just—please—find out who did this."

Harvey nodded, determined that he would.

The press got hold of it, and Harvey spent at least half his working time fending off reporters. He hoped they weren't bothering Lisa Dunham at home. He and Eddie had an intense session with the state trooper who had handled the recovery of the body, but they all knew the answers weren't in the remote patch of woods where the corpse had been dumped.

It was past one o'clock when they stopped at McDonald's on their way to Coastal Technology. Harvey called Mike as Eddie eased his pickup through the line to the drive-up window.

"We're on our way to the software company," Harvey said. "Any advice?"

"Our phones are ringing constantly," Mike replied. "You'll have to hold a press conference before the evening news."

Harvey groaned. "Can't you do that?"

"It's your case. Be back here by four, and I'll have the patrol sergeant set it up downstairs."

Eddie was at the speaker, and he glanced Harvey's way. "Big Mac?"

Harvey grimaced. "Chicken salad and milk."

"Say what?" Mike asked.

"Not you. Eddie. He expects me to eat fast food and then give a press conference."

"Sounds like ulcer material to me," Mike agreed. "Four o'clock sharp."

Harvey hung up and pulled out his wallet.

"I guess Jennifer will be surprised to see us," Eddie said as he handed Harvey his lunch and juggled the change and straws.

Harvey frowned. "I don't know as we ought to broadcast the fact that I'm seeing her socially. She told me her friend Jane is still drooling over you, and she doesn't want her to know she's met you outside the office."

"You'd think Jennifer would have better taste in friends." Eddie opened his sandwich and looked under the top layer of bun. "Jennifer is so quiet, but that Jane is a non-stop, walking, talking Computer Programmer Barbie."

"I think Jane is more or less a friend by default. They work near each other, and there aren't many other young, single women in the office. And Jenny finds it hard to reject people." He remembered her reluctance to confront Donna-jean.

"Maybe you should alert her that we're coming," Eddie said. "Then she can run interference with Jane for me."

Harvey laughed. "What, you can't take care of yourself?"

"That girl is so intense, she's scary."

The guard at the door of Coastal Technology checked their I.D. "Did you want to see Mr. Owen?"

"I'll find him." Harvey breezed past him and into the work room. His eyes sought Jennifer and found her. She saw him, too, but quickly looked away. He suppressed his smile and kept going toward the partners' offices.

Eddie kept pace until they neared the coffee island. Jane Morrow turned around with a mug of coffee in one hand.

"Oh, Detective Thibodeau! How nice to see you again."

Eddie smiled weakly. Harvey kept walking, but he could hear Eddie sputtering helplessly behind him. When he got into the hallway, he pulled out his cell phone and punched Jennifer's number.

"H-hello?"

"Hey, gorgeous. Eddie just got waylaid by your pal Jane. I don't suppose you could invent an errand for him? For some reason he can't cope with that one."

"Sure."

"Great. If it will help, tell him I asked for him to join me in Bart Owen's office. Or haul him off someplace else, I don't care."

"Got it."

She clicked off, and he smiled as he replaced the phone in his pocket and strode to Owen's door.

Owen rose as he entered. "Larson. Is there news?"

"Yes, sir. Perhaps you'd like to ask Mr. Rainey and Mr. Channing to join us."

Jennifer walked briskly toward the coffee station. Somehow Jane had cornered Eddie and was edging him toward the gourmet coffeemaker, giving him a rundown on an error one of their clerks had made that morning. Eddie was backing away from her nervously.

"So then we had to call the client and ask him if he'd give us an extra week to deliver the program," Jane said. "Would you like some coffee? We can sit over there on the sofa while you wait for your boss."

Eddie gulped. "He's not my—"

"You can have juice or soda if you'd rather." Jane laid her hand on his sleeve. "We keep all sorts of refreshments for visitors. You know, clients and salesmen."

Jennifer decided Eddie had stood enough. "Excuse me."

He turned gratefully toward her. Jennifer ignored his adoring brown eyes and said hesitantly, "Detective . . . Thibodeau?"

"Yes."

She thought his lips twitched, and she swallowed hard, determined not to laugh. "Your partner asked me to come get you."

"Thank you. Very much." As he turned toward Jane, his look of gratitude melted into contrition. "Excuse me, Ms. Morrow. Thanks for your—uh—hospitality."

Jennifer led him quickly down the hallway without looking back. As soon as they were out of sight and earshot of the workroom, Eddie asked, "Does Harvey really need me?"

She chuckled. "No. He buzzed me and said you needed extrication." She stopped before the open doorway to the conference room. "You can wait for him in here if you want."

"Jennifer, I owe you big time. How can I repay you?"

"No need. Although, there is something I've been wondering about." She hadn't considered confiding in Eddie, but he might be able to enlighten her on one little thing.

His dark eyebrows arched in anticipation.

"Well, you've known Harvey a long time." She stepped into the conference room, and Eddie followed.

"Five years. What is it?"

"This table thing."

"What table thing?"

"Harvey told me he needs a table."

Understanding broke on Eddie's face. "Does he ever."

"Could you explain that to me?"

Eddie gulped, then glanced toward the hall as if embarrassed. "Oh, no, I really shouldn't."

Jennifer considered that for a moment, then turned and shut the door. "Why not?"

"Well, Harv's kind of funny about personal stuff. It took him a long time to tell me about things like that."

"So, you think I should just wait until he tells me himself?"

Eddie said slowly, "Change is difficult for Harvey."

"Change?"

"You know, new car . . . new woman . . . new furniture."

She shook her head in confusion. "No, I don't know, Eddie. I'm not following you."

"Let me put it this way. It seems like every time I visit his apartment, he has less furniture than the time before."

"What do you mean?" Alarm seized her. "Is he burning his furniture or what?"

"No, nothing like that." Eddie stood silent for a moment, then leaned with one hand on the conference table. "Look, Jennifer, I like you, but I don't think I should be the one telling you this."

"I'm sorry, Eddie. I didn't mean to put you on

the spot. He mentioned getting a table when we go out this weekend, and I just hated to ask him about it. I guess if he wants me to know what it's about, he'll tell me. I just . . . I care, Eddie."

He sighed and straightened. "Okay, look. You know Harvey's wife left him, right?"

"Yes, he told me about it. Well, some."

"Did he tell you Carrie took most of the furniture with her?"

"No."

"Her parents gave them most of it as a wedding present. It was all this antique stuff, out of their attic in Boston. Dining room set, sofa, chairs, a secretary, a china closet. When Carrie left, she had a moving truck come and pack it off."

Jennifer thought about that. "That would explain a lot. But, Eddie, it's been years. Wouldn't you think he'd have bought new furniture before this?"

"I know. Like I said, change is difficult for this man."

"It's taken him this long to decide to get a table?"

"That about sums it up. He bought a new jacket yesterday."

"Yes, I noticed."

"Highly unusual. But it's a good thing. And it's because of you. Meeting your parents jolted him. It takes something major like that. And the night before Carrie's funeral—" Eddie stopped.

Jennifer waited, but he didn't say anything. He just shrugged uncomfortably.

"You're not going to tell me, are you?"

He squirmed a little. "Come on, Jennifer, he's my best friend. If he tells me something, I'm not supposed to blab."

She nodded. "It's okay."

"I gotta say, I think you're the best thing that ever happened to Harvey."

"Thank you. That's very flattering."

"It's true. Six months ago, if something depressing happened, we'd have gone out and got a twelve-pack and gotten plastered together. But now . . . He says that was another life. He doesn't want to drink anymore."

Jennifer stared at him. Her stomach seemed to be flipping, the way it did when an elevator went down too fast. "Harvey's had a drinking problem?"

"Oh, boy." Eddie gritted his teeth. "See, I told you, I'm not supposed to blab private stuff."

"Well, now that you've told me, how bad was it?" She'd been mildly surprised, but glad, that Harvey hadn't ordered alcohol when they went out, never imagining that things had been different in the past.

"Not that bad. It was just that once in a while, when he was down, I mean, *really* down, that was how he tried to deal with it. But not anymore. I asked him if he wanted to have a couple that night, and he acted like he couldn't believe he used to do that."

"That night being . . . the night before his wife's funeral?"

"Well . . . yeah."

"That was before we met."

"No—well, actually, we'd been here once, but it was before he took you to lunch that first time, you know, the day his car blew up and—" Eddie stopped again, a look of such compunction on his face that Jennifer understood better why all women wanted to mother Eddie or marry him. His dismay kept her temporarily from doing the math and wondering just what mental state Harvey was in when they met.

"It's all right."

"Harv's going to kill me."

"No."

"He spent months teaching me how to keep my mouth shut. I *never* tell his secrets to anyone."

"I believe you. And it's all right." Jennifer tiptoed carefully around the edge of the private, non-blabbable information. "So, when he was so depressed, was that because of . . . Carrie?"

"Pretty much," Eddie said. "Wondering if he could have done anything else to fix things with her. Not having any kids like he wanted, and figuring he was going to be alone for the rest of his life."

She nodded, remembering Harvey's face when

he'd looked at the Bradleys' baby. "Thanks, Eddie. I appreciate your loyalty to Harvey. You don't have to worry about the things you've told me."

Eddie smiled, and Jennifer realized that her first impression of Eddie had been deceptive. He was too good looking, all right, but he was sweet all the way through. She wondered how many girls were out there in Greater Portland with broken hearts because of that smile.

"Well, he's a great guy," Eddie said. "I told him ages ago he could sleep at my place, but he said he'd be okay on the—oops."

Jennifer stood very still. Harvey had told her that when he interrogated people, sometimes he just waited without asking them anything, and after a while they told him what he wanted to know. She was sure Eddie knew that trick, too, but he didn't seem immune to it.

"Okay, so he got rid of his bed. Look, don't tell him I told you, okay? Please?"

"His bed?"

"Yeah, it was like the one thing he and Carrie bought after they got married. After she died, Harvey said he couldn't sleep in it anymore. Oh, man, you can't tell him I told you."

"I won't tell him, Eddie. I care about him as much as you do."

"Possibly more?" His heart-breaker smile did its work again, and Jennifer knew that, in their mutual love of Harvey, she and Eddie were friends for life.

"I didn't realize change was so hard for him," she said softly.

"Well, it is, believe me. They tore down the old police garage years ago, and he's still got the key on his key ring. You see what I mean?"

She nodded.

"But he's finally worked up the nerve to start making a few changes. Like getting rid of the bed, and buying a table. And you."

"I wonder how he ever got up his courage to ask me out," she said.

"I don't know, but I'm glad he did."

Chapter 18

Eddie was waiting in the hallway when Harvey left the three partners. They said nothing as they walked through the work room and the lobby, but as soon as they were outside, Harvey said, "Where's Jenny?"

"She took her break. She didn't think she ought to see you now. If anyone else saw you together, especially Jane, they would know how highly she esteems you."

Harvey looked at him sideways. "Esteems, huh?"

"Well, that's not exactly what she said, but it means the same thing."

Harvey laughed. In spite of his somber errand, he felt light-hearted. "Let's get back to the station. Rainey forwarded me a copy of the program Nick Dunham was working on the day he disappeared."

"You think that will help us?"

"Who knows?"

The press conference was easier than Harvey had expected, although he always hated facing the cameras. When reporters fired questions at him one after the other, he couldn't help feeling incompetent. He ought to be the one asking the questions. And it was always important to represent the department well, but he didn't have time to think about that during the rapid examination.

Mike stood at the stairway door, watching as Harvey gave his carefully written statement to the reporters in the lobby of the police station.

"When did you actually know that Nicholas Dunham was dead?" the anchorman from Channel 13 asked.

"When the remains were found on Saturday, we wondered, of course, if it was Mr. Dunham, but we didn't give up hope that he was alive until the word came this morning from the medical examiner's office. Now that we know, it's a matter of bringing his killer to justice."

There were more questions, mostly ones he couldn't answer yet. He knew the reporters would cull the quotes and squeeze the ten-minute conference down to a sound bite or two. He'd probably look like a fumbling idiot. Finally he got an almost imperceptible nod from Mike, and shut off the barrage of questions.

"Thank you, that's it. Call me tomorrow for an update."

He headed for the stairs, and Mike punched in the security code that opened the door.

"Not bad," Mike said as they climbed the two flights.

"Thanks." Harvey went to his computer and checked the updates. A flag came up on the corner of the screen, and he opened the file.

"Hey, Mike!"

"What is it, Harv?"

"Bobby Nason. He's been seen in Newport."

"No kidding. Bobby's brother said Monday that he hadn't been around."

"Well, it's Wednesday, and I guess he has."

"Arnie!" Mike yelled.

Arnie was on the phone. He put one hand over the mouthpiece. "Just a minute, Mike. I got Newport on the phone. Nason's surfaced." He hung up and walked quickly to Mike's desk. "The chief of police in Newport said a neighbor called and told them Bobby Nason's been around his brother's place. They're going to LeRoy's house with a warrant. If they find Bobby, they'll hold him."

Mike sighed. "I guess we can't do any more. Let's call it a day."

Eddie dropped Harvey off at his apartment, and he snapped on the TV for the early news. "The body found in rural Wilton on Saturday has been identified as that of Nicholas Lee Dunham . . ." He decided he couldn't watch himself after all, and shut it off. He made a sandwich and sat down with the new DeLorme's Maine Atlas he'd bought, looking over the route to the lighthouse, then turned to the page that showed Skowhegan. He ought to take Jennifer up to visit her parents.

The ringing of his wall phone in the kitchen was unexpected. He used it so rarely that he'd almost had it taken out, but that was too much trouble. He got up and went to answer it.

"Harvey, it's Marilyn Wainthrop. We saw you on the news. We're so proud of you!"

"Well, hi," he said in surprise. "I didn't do much."

"But you will!"

Harvey ran a hand through his hair, unsure how to respond. "We have a lot of people working on the case."

"We were thrilled when we saw you! I wish we recorded it."

"Oh, well, you know, it was just part of the job."

"Harvey, will you bring Jennifer up here soon?"

"I'd like that, Mrs. Wainthrop."

"Marilyn."

"Marilyn. We're going to the lighthouse down here Saturday, but possibly next weekend?"

"We'd love to see you both. You're very special to her, Harvey."

There was a knock at the door.

"I'm sorry, Marilyn, I've got to run."

They signed off, and he opened the door to Rebecca Jenkins.

"Mr. Larson! We saw you on the news!"

He broke away as quickly as he could without being rude to his neighbor and drove to Jennifer's house.

When Jennifer opened her door to Harvey, she was struck by his obvious fatigue.

"You had a big day," she said.

"Oh, you heard."

"By telephone, television, and tell-a-Mom."

"She called me, too."

Jennifer grimaced. "I was afraid of that. I hope it wasn't too annoying."

"No, I guess I should be flattered that people are recognizing me as far north as Skowhegan."

They got into the Explorer, and he gave her the details.

"You looked good on TV," Jennifer said. A bit of the awe she had felt for him at first was back. She was just getting used to him being a top-notch detective, and now she had to assimilate the fact that he was a local celebrity. She wasn't sure how it would affect their relationship, other than cranking up her mother's admiration for Harvey.

"Thanks, kiddo. How did it go at Coastal after we left?"

"Mr. Channing gave the corporate speech. *This hour of sorrow . . . exemplary employee . . . compassion for the widow.*"

Harvey sent her a sidelong glance. “You’re not usually so cynical.”

Jennifer squinted her eyes shut and put her hands to her temples. “I’m sorry. I don’t mean to be. He just sounds so . . . insincere.”

Harvey turned in at the church parking lot. “If you’d seen Mrs. Dunham this morning . . .”

“You were the one who had to tell her? Harvey, I’m sorry.”

“The M.E.’s office told her, but she was pretty shaken when I saw her.”

“This is terrible for her.” The reality of Nick’s death hit Jennifer squarely. Lisa had lost the love of her life, the man she had pledged herself to, the father of her children. But learning for sure that Nick was dead had come almost as a relief to Jennifer and his other co-workers.

Partly, she knew, it was the attitude at Coastal that made her feel that way. The office gossip would stop now. No more, *Why would he run off and leave Lisa like that?* in the break room. No more, *How long will they let Lisa draw his salary?* She had heard those things, and the talk had made her feel ill. Between that and the elaborate covert software project, going to work had become abhorrent.

As Harvey guided the Explorer into a parking space, she twisted the end of her braid, fingering the covered elastic. Harvey shut off the engine and looked at her, but she couldn’t speak. Her tears were waiting to fall, and she couldn't blink them away.

He reached over and caught one gently with his thumb. "Jenny."

She pulled in a ragged breath. "I'm so selfish. When I said that about Mr. Channing, I wasn't thinking about Lisa at all."

"Sweetheart, it's okay." His tender whisper made her feel even more guilty.

"I hope she had someone to comfort her."

Harvey put his soft handkerchief into her hand. "Nick's sister was there. Have you ever met her?"

"I don't think so."

"She goes to church here. She was going to call Pastor Rowland, to see if he'll do the funeral service."

"Really? Nick Dunham's sister goes to this church?"

"Yes. Small world."

That made her feel better. People who knew how to pray were helping Lisa and the children through this.

They went in and sat near the back of the auditorium. The pastor led them in a hymn. Nick's sister wasn't there, but Pastor Rowland announced gravely that his body had been identified. The Wyman and Dunham families were at the top of the prayer list.

Jennifer sat subdued, clinging to Harvey's

hand. She didn't feel the euphoria she'd found here Sunday morning, but she still felt she hould be here, that there was something she needed in this place, if she could just recognize it.

The pastor spoke that night on the incarnation of Christ. Harvey took notes. Jennifer had brought her notebook, but she didn't open it. She silently soaked up the pastor's words, her hand tucked obstinately in the crook of Harvey's arm. Every few minutes he reached over and stroked her fingers, then went back to his notes. Jennifer fought tears and struggled to concentrate on the message.

Those who received Jesus became children of God, the text said. She felt more hopeful when she heard that. If she were God's child, she would truly belong here, and maybe she would understand what it was that united man and God. But right now it was too complicated. Her self-reproach became grief, and Lisa Dunham's pain became her pain.

The pastor asked for prayer requests and praise, and from all over the hall, people asked for prayer or told what God had done for them. All of these people believe it, Jennifer thought. They're not ignorant people. They're not wild-eyed fanatics. But they believe in God.

Rick Bradley came and took Harvey away to pray with a group of men. Ruthann and Beth joined Jennifer, and they sat together in the pew.

"I . . . I can't pray," Jennifer said.

Ruthann told her, "It's all right. You don't have to." She and Beth prayed, and hearing them was precious for Jennifer as they asked God's protection and peace for Nick's children and for Lisa. Jennifer wanted to be able to speak to God herself.

Beth's last request struck her in a different way: ". . . and, Lord, please help me to find a place to live soon."

When she said "amen," Jennifer lifted her head and looked at her.

"Beth, you're looking for a place to live? You said Sunday you were only with Rick and Ruthann temporarily, but I thought you meant you were just visiting."

Beth smiled. "They really don't have space for me. I need to make other arrangements."

"I don't know if you'd consider it, but I need a roommate." Jennifer gulped. She barely knew Beth, but it seemed right. She told her in whispers a little about the rental house.

"It sounds interesting," Beth said. "When can I see it?"

"How about tomorrow? I'll be home by five-thirty."

After the men returned and the pastor stood in front to close the prayer meeting, they settled the details of Beth's visit.

"Isn't that just like the Lord?" Ruthann said. "Beth prayed, and he had the answer sitting right beside her."

Beth smiled. "I guess we'll find out tomorrow."

"No obligation on your part," Jennifer said. "Just come see it and eat supper with me."

"Okay, I will."

Harvey stood in the aisle surrounded by parishioners who had seen him on the news. He was smiling and being polite, but his discomfort showed in the stiffness of his posture. Several men shook his hand and asked him questions about the case.

A middle-aged woman came over and spoke to him before they left. "I'm Nick Dunham's aunt, Margaret. Jackie told me today how kind you've been. Thank you."

Harvey was obviously struggling with the praise. "You're welcome. I really didn't do anything."

Margaret Dunham reached out and touched his shoulder. "Yes you did. You may not realize it, but you encouraged Jackie. The Lord used you."

"I'll do everything I can for your family, ma'am."

"I believe Nicholas is with God now." Margaret Dunham's voice broke, and she fumbled for a tissue.

Jennifer stared at her. Timidity almost held her back, but she made herself step forward. "Mrs. Dunham."

"Yes?"

"I worked with Nick. I'm very sorry."

"Thank you."

"Do you . . . may I ask you . . ." Jennifer shot a glance up at Harvey, and she felt his warm hand touch her back lightly. She felt bolder and looked back to Margaret Dunham. "You said Nick believed in God?"

Her face clouded. "Yes, I'm sure he did. He didn't come to church much the last couple of years, but as a young man, he was very faithful. I've talked with him about the Lord before, and I believe he's in heaven today."

Jennifer nodded. "Thank you." She wilted back against Harvey's side, and his arm tightened around her.

Mrs. Dunham left the church. The crush went on for a little while, but Harvey kept Jennifer at his side. Finally the crowd dispersed, and the pastor spoke to them.

"Harvey, I'm glad to see you both again tonight. Jackie Wyman told me you were at the house today."

"She did call you, then."

"Yes, I spent some time with the family. They want to hold a memorial service, but it will probably be next week."

Harvey nodded. “I don’t believe the body’s been released yet.”

“Nick used to be a member here.” The pastor shook his head. “After he got married, he drifted away. Got caught up in other things.”

“I knew him,” Jennifer said softly. “He was very likable.”

“Oh, yes. A nice young man. He let his priorities slip out of line.” Pastor Rowland nodded thoughtfully. “I hope that through this tragedy, Lisa will get back on track with the Lord. She and the children need that.”

Harvey drove in silence to Jennifer’s house and walked with her to the steps.

“Can we sit out here for a little while?” he asked. “If we go in, I’ll have to check the Explorer again.”

“Sure.”

It was warm, and they sat on the steps without speaking for a long moment as the dusk deepened.

Harvey swatted at a mosquito. “This afternoon I looked over the program Nick was working on before he died.”

“What was it?”

“Ho-hum stuff. An amortization thing for banks.”

Jennifer frowned. “That’s an old program. He finished that ages ago. Before Christmas, at least.”

"Are you sure?"

"Yes. Unless they had him update it for some reason."

"You don't say. Jack Rainey sent it to himself. Said he'd looked in Nick's files, and that was his last project."

Jennifer's eyes narrowed. "Harvey, I'm starting to hate my job."

He was quiet for a moment, then said softly, "So quit."

"I couldn't do that."

"Why not? They're not paying you that much."

"No. I know I could get more if I moved out of state, but I don't want to do that."

He put his arm around her shoulders, and she savored the security she felt when he touched her.

"Someone as talented as you can get another job any day of the week."

She sighed. "I don't think I even want to be a programmer anymore. When I got this job, I thought it was going to be so great. I used to love it, but it's no fun now."

"Give them your notice tomorrow."

"What if I couldn't get another job?" She hated revealing her lack of confidence. Leaning forward, she buried her face in her arms.

"Jenny. Sweet, sweet Jenny." He patted her shoulder.

She sobbed. "Nick was a Christian."

"Sounds like it."

"I never knew."

Harvey took a deep, slow breath. "That bothers you."

"Sort of. I wanted to know so desperately about God. He knew God, but he never said anything. I worked beside him for over a year."

"You think Christians should tell everyone what they believe?"

"Well, yes, don't you?"

"I don't know."

"You've been telling Eddie."

Harvey bit his bottom lip. "I wouldn't claim to be a Christian exactly."

"But even so, you've been telling him about it. You think it's important, don't you?"

"Yes. It's important."

She sighed. "I think I'll go and see Lisa Dunham."

"I think that would be good."

"I wasn't ready before, but now . . . I mean, Nick *was* my friend, even if we weren't close."

"Call her tomorrow."

"I will." She wiped her eyes, feeling a little braver.

"Jenny, I'm serious about your job. Don't stay at Coastal if you hate going in every day."

"It wasn't so bad before the big project."

"That foreign project?"

"Yes. Our part is almost finished. I'll be interfacing mine with John and Tessa's now. The translator was supposed to come today, but he didn't."

"Translator?"

"They're putting the on-screen stuff into another language." It was a common procedure with Coastal's commercial programs. "I thought it was for the military at first, but I guess it's not."

"What made you think that?" Harvey asked in frank surprise.

"I don't know. I guess because of all the security precautions, and maybe some of the language. But now I think it's an industrial thing for a foreign conglomerate." She smiled bitterly. "John Macomber says it will sabotage American industry."

Harvey drew back a little. "Does he know what he's talking about?"

"I doubt it. No more than I do." A mosquito landed on her knee, and she brushed it away. "The bosses are just being careful. They've had some programs pirated recently, and they're determined not to let it happen again. But they seem to be carrying it to the point of paranoia with this program."

"I think you should quit. The tension is too much for you."

"I'll be okay." She didn't want to leave Portland now. As long as Harvey was there to encourage her, she could put up with a lot at Coastal.

"But you ought to do something you love."

"Who gets paid for having fun?" she asked.

"Well, maybe not fun exactly, but something that gives you satisfaction and doesn't drain you."

"Is your job like that?"

"Some days. Some days it's pretty harrowing."

Kidnappings, murders, drug dealers. The Coastal partners' demands seemed inconsequential when she thought of the trauma Harvey dealt with daily. "Have you got any leads on the bomber yet?"

"Well, he was spotted at his brother's house in Newport. The police up there are looking for him."

She leaned her head against his shoulder, feeling quite daring. His arm tightened a little. "So are we going to the lighthouse Saturday? Did you talk to Eddie about it?"

"I did, and Eddie is bringing Sarah, one of our female cops. They'll meet us here at 9 a.m."

"Good. I need a normal, ordinary day with you."

"What about tomorrow? Can I see you tomorrow night?" His cheek brushed softly against her hair.

She smiled at his predictability. "Beth's coming to look at the house."

"That would be great, if she moved in with you."

"We don't know each other very well, but she seems so . . . wholesome. And she knows about God. I think she could help me."

"I think she'd help *us,* just being here," he said. "I wouldn't worry so much about you, and when I brought you home, I could go in the house and not feel awkward."

She lifted her head and looked at him. "Do you feel awkward in the house?"

He shrugged. "Sometimes. I'm just not . . . well, I want to do things right."

"Me, too."

She settled back against his shoulder. They sat in silence in the growing darkness.

"Harvey, what happens if we decide we don't believe in God after all?"

He shook his head. "I don't want to think about a world with no God."

"If we do believe, it will change a lot of things."

He was quiet for a minute, then he said, "It will change everything."

She whispered, "Have you thought about what happens if one of us believes and the other one . . ."

"No. I refuse to consider that." His voice was hoarse. He leaned close and kissed her temple, where the hair was pulled back into her braid. "No more what-ifs." He stood, extended a hand, and pulled her up. "Keep reading in the Bible, Jenny. I think we'll find our answers soon."

They were standing quite close together. He put both his hands on her shoulders. Jennifer's heart pounded. She wondered if he was going to kiss her. Harvey had taken things slowly so far, even cautiously, and she suspected he was trying to show himself trustworthy. She pulled in a ragged breath, telling herself she was ready.

He looked into her eyes for a long moment, then pulled her in against his chest. She let her hands sneak around his waist, below his shoulder holster. He held her there firmly, with his badge pressing into her cheek. *I'm going to have an imprint of Portland PD on my face,* she thought. He rested his chin on the top of her head for a couple of seconds, then stood back, and she felt cold.

"I'll call you tomorrow."

Chapter 19

Beth came soon after Jennifer got home from work, and she toured the house with growing approval. While Jennifer made supper for two, Beth set the table then sat down and told her about her kindergarten class at the public school. She was teaching a Sunday School class, too, for eight-to-ten-year-old girls.

"That's probably the class I should be in," Jennifer said. "I'm so ignorant about the Bible!"

"It must be hard, when you haven't been brought up with it," said Beth.

"You know, my parents are good people." Jennifer took a small meatloaf from the microwave. "In fact, they're wonderful people, and they don't drink or smoke. They've taught us kids to be moral and considerate. But they didn't seem to think religion was important."

"But you think it's important now."

"I do. Harvey and I started this thing as a sort of philosophical odyssey. We both wondered if God was real, and if you could *know* whether he was real."

"It's more than just knowing."

Jennifer stared at her. "That's what I've been thinking lately. It's not just an idea. If it's true, then it's . . . it's more concrete than that."

"It's a way of life. It's knowing Jesus Christ personally."

Jennifer nodded.

"So what do you think?" Beth asked.

"I'm leaning toward believing it. There's just so much I don't understand. And Harvey . . ."

"What?" Beth asked softly.

"I just . . . well, I hope we both end up believing the same thing." Jennifer set the pan on a trivet.

"You can't base your spiritual life on what another person thinks."

"I know. But if one of us believes and the other doesn't, then I'm not sure we can be together." She tried to imagine breaking up with Harvey. It was unthinkable. Her heart was bound closer to him now than it had ever been to anyone, and severing that bond would devastate her. She sat down soberly.

"Would you ask the blessing, please, Beth?"

As they ate, they talked about the house.

"I'm warning you, I've been terrible at picking roommates in the past," Jennifer said. "My last one got arrested for drugs. But I think you'd be easier to live with."

Beth laughed. "I promise, no drugs. Do you like classical music?"

"I love it! Tell me, quick. What do you really think of this place?"

"It's great. Oh, it's not the Ritz, but it's just what I need. Are you sure you'd want to room with me, Jennifer?"

"What's not to like?"

Beth sat back and looked at her. "I'm a Christian."

"Well, yeah. Do you not want to live with someone who doesn't believe in God?"

"I'll put you on notice right now, if I'm living with you, I'll be praying for you."

"That's bad?"

Beth smiled. "No. If you do believe, you'll be my sister in Christ. But I'm the kind of person who can't sit back and watch a sister make poor choices. I'd be sure to give my opinion."

Jennifer chuckled. "I have two sisters at home, so I know a little bit about that. But I was thinking you might help me, guide me in some spiritual things."

"Well, I've got a long way to go myself, but I'll help you any way I can."

"So, how soon can you move in?"

Harvey called after Beth had left.

"Hey, gorgeous." Jennifer was getting used to the upbeat greeting he could give over the phone, but not in person.

"I've got a new roommate."

"Terrific. Sounds like you're feeling better tonight."

"Much. Beth is going to her folks' in Freeport over the weekend, and she has parent-teacher conferences Monday, but she'll move in Tuesday after school. Rick and Ruthann will help her pack and move."

"Great! Need some more help?"

"Sure. We'll need all the muscle we can get. I'll probably make sandwiches with the Bradleys. You can join us for supper."

"Okay. Thanks. You'll like having Beth there."

"We've already agreed we're going to pray together in the morning, before we go to work. I'm really excited about her moving in."

John Macomber was responsible for a large portion of the special program, and Jennifer spent most of Friday working closely with him to mesh her security protocols with it. Time and again she ran into snags, and at last she went to John's desk feeling defeated.

"You'll have to give me access to the entire thing, yours and Tessa's, if we're going to make this work. Your part by itself looks good, but I didn't know you were using such a complicated framework. It's more extensive than the partners let on."

John shook his head. "You'll have to get their permission. I haven't even seen what Tessa's doing. She's got the core program, I guess."

"I thought you did."

"Nope. It's been like working in the dark, designing corridors leading to locked rooms full of . . . I don't know what."

"I don't see how we can deliver to the client, working like this. I've got to have everything. I may have to develop another whole layer to make sure everything's covered."

John cocked his head to one side. "Jennifer, if you could get permission from the bosses and get this thing finished, you'd make me a happy man. I'm sick of it."

"You and me both." She frowned. "All right, come with me."

"No way."

She stared at him. "You won't back me up on this?"

"Channing almost bit my head off yesterday when I asked to see Tessa's work."

Jennifer looked toward the hallway that led to the inner sanctum, then back at John. "Okay, I'll ask Mr. Owen. He's usually more agreeable than the other two."

"If you don't come back in ten minutes, I'll call the cops."

"That's not funny."

John's level gaze unsettled her. "You're right. It's not."

Jennifer's head whirled as she looked at him. "John, do you really think this program is something illegal? Because if you do—"

"Shh!" He looked around quickly, then leaned toward her. "Don't even say it. Whether it's classified or clandestine, or whatever, I don't know. Just get permission, and let's be done with it."

Jennifer went with trepidation to Owen's office. When she knocked, he called for her to come in, and she found to her dismay that Jack Rainey was in the room with him.

"Excuse me, Mr. Owen." She stepped forward and raised her chin. "Sir, I wanted to speak to you about the special program. I can't put it together the way things are. I really need to have all the components at once."

Rainey had turned his back to her and was jingling the change in his pocket as he stared out the window.

"Well, I don't know," Owen said slowly. "Jack, what do you think? Jennifer seems to be at a stalemate with the program."

Rainey whirled, fixing Owen with a steely glare. "You know we've agreed to keep it confidential."

"But if one person needs to see the whole picture in order to put it together right . . ." Owen looked expectantly at Jennifer.

"That's right," she said. "I can't complete the project this way, Mr. Rainey. I'm sorry. If you don't want me to have all the pieces, then someone else will have to do it."

"Oh, here, here," Owen said quickly. "We don't question your loyalty. It's just that this project is very sensitive, and our competitors would give their eye teeth for it. You understand."

"Of course." She looked down for a moment and came to a decision. She raised her chin once more. "Then I'm very sorry, but I can't do it. If you insist on keeping it so private, perhaps one of you gentlemen can assemble the components. I don't see how we can have it ready for the client otherwise."

A look volleyed between the two men, and Rainey gave a curt nod. "We'll contact the client and see what he thinks."

Owen smiled in relief. "Of course. If Mr. Massal will give his approval—"

"Bart," Rainey said sharply. "We'll let you know, Jennifer."

She nodded doubtfully and backed toward the door, more sure than ever that the program was fishy.

Harvey didn't say anything when Mike informed the unit they'd be putting in overtime that night. It came with the job. He'd hoped to see Jennifer but hadn't made any definite plans.

"You ready, Harv?" Eddie asked him in the locker room.

"Not quite. I want to call Jenny."

"Make it snappy. Mike's in a hurry."

He quickly punched in the number, and Jennifer answered almost immediately.

"Hey, I'm sorry, but I won't be able to come over tonight. Mike's got us on a breaking case, and we may be out late."

"I'm sorry, too. I wanted to talk to you about something."

"Can it wait? Things look clear for our trip to the lighthouse tomorrow."

Eddie stood in the locker room doorway. "Come on, Harv!"

"All right," Jennifer said. Her disappointment was perversely gratifying.

"I'll see you in the morning, gorgeous."

Harvey slept soundly that night on the floor, exhausted from his long day. As he'd feared, it had been late when they completed their assignment and finished up at the police station, but things went smoothly. Except for his fatigue, he felt good. He woke up without any lingering fragments of dreams.

He made himself a grocery list as he ate a sketchy breakfast of a bagel and coffee. *Milk, bananas, bread, Wheaties, detergent, yogurt, coffee*. There was time to do a load of laundry and run to the store before he went to Jennifer's.

He ran down to the basement with his dirty clothes, meeting Mrs. Jenkins on the stairs as he came up.

"Good morning, Mr. Larson."

He stopped and looked at her. "Mrs. Jenkins, I've lived above you for over fifteen years. Don't you think it's time you called me Harvey?"

She smiled. "Yes, and you should call me Rebecca."

"Well, Rebecca, may I carry your laundry downstairs for you?"

"You look like a man with places to go. I'm capable." She went on down to the utility room.

Harvey went out to his parking spot, looked under the Explorer, and drove to the grocery store. Banks of flowers and plants were displayed near the entrance. On impulse, he picked up a bunch of daffodils.

Back home, he unpacked his groceries and went down to the basement to throw his clothes in the dryer. Rebecca Jenkins sat in a rickety chair in the utility room, leafing through an old *Good Housekeeping*. Harvey set the dryer and looked at his watch.

"You going away this weekend, Harvey?"

"Just out to the lighthouse this morning. My pal Eddie and I have a double date."

She smiled. "That's good. You've found a nice girl?"

"Yes. She's wonderful."

Rebecca nodded in satisfaction. "You've been alone too long up there. You go on, and I'll take your laundry out."

"Oh, no, you don't need to." Harvey was a little flustered by her neighborliness.

"I mean it. I'll be here anyway. Pick it up when you get home."

He consulted his watch again. "Well, thank you very much, Rebecca." He went back upstairs and grabbed the flowers, his hat, and his gear. Outside, he looked underneath the Explorer again and stowed his gun, badge, and handcuffs in the glove compartment.

Jennifer let him in at a quarter to nine. She had on jeans and a short-sleeved mauve shirt, and her hair was in a ponytail that hung from the top of her head. He liked the Rapunzel Look, with one braid, better, but this was interesting. He held out the bouquet, and she took it with a brilliant smile. It was going to be a wonderful day, he could tell.

She led him through to the kitchen, where she had a box partly packed with food for their picnic.

"Can I help?"

"Nope. Just sit."

He watched her arrange the daffodils in a glass jar, then put fruit salad in a plastic container and make sandwiches.

"So how was work yesterday?" he asked.

"Could have been better." She ran water into a picnic jug with iced tea mix. "That's what I wanted to tell you on the phone."

"What?"

"Well, you know they've had me working on that special project for weeks."

"Uh-huh."

"They expect me to do things that are impossible."

"Like what?" He went over to stand beside her.

"They've had three of us working on it, but they never let any of us see the whole program. Each of us has a part of it, and we have to have several passwords to access the program." She stirred the contents of the jug. "I don't even have all the passwords for my part. Mr. Owen or Mr. Rainey has to enter one every day before I can start work."

She put ice cubes in the jug and refilled the tray with water. When she opened the freezer again, her ponytail brushed his arm, and he reached for it.

"So, anyway, I told them—"

He gave her hair a playful tug, and she jerked around suddenly. The ice tray clattered to the floor, splashing water all over them both, the floor, and the cupboard doors.

"I'm sorry," Harvey said. "Don't move. I'll get it." He put one hand out to keep her from stepping in the water, but the expression on her face stopped him where he was. "Jenny? Baby, I'm sorry. I didn't mean to startle you."

Slowly she put her hands up to her head,

pulled her ponytail over her shoulder, and stood clutching it. She said nothing, but stared at the ends of her hair.

"Are you okay?"

Her lips trembled. "Yeah. I just . . . I'm sorry."

Harvey was baffled. Surely he hadn't pulled her hair hard enough to hurt her.

"Jenny." He touched her hands lightly. "Come sit down."

She shook her head. "I'm all right." She sobbed, and he pulled her into his arms.

He held her tight against him. "Shh, it's okay. Come on. Don't step in the water." He eased toward the doorway and led her to the living room sofa. "Sit, gorgeous."

They sat down, and he watched her for a moment in silence.

"Tell me what I did. I don't want this to happen again."

"It's nothing."

"We've been there before. It's something."

She sighed and moved toward him. He put his arms around her, and she buried her face in his shoulder. "Okay. But it's stupid."

"No. No, it's not." He moved his right hand up to the top of her head and stroked back to the top of her ponytail, where the elastic caught her thick hair.

She pushed away from him and swallowed hard. "It's that."

He froze and looked cautiously into her flooded gray eyes. "It's . . . what?"

"My hair. He—it was—he just grabbed my braid and pulled me down by it and I couldn't get away."

Harvey sucked in a deep breath. "Are we talking about Joe College again?"

She nodded slowly.

Outrage screamed through him, but he tried not to let it show in his eyes. It must have, because she sobbed suddenly and hid her face in her hands.

"Jenny, sweetheart." Very tenderly, he pulled her toward him. "Baby, you should have told me."

"I'm sorry."

"No, no, don't be sorry. I just meant—maybe I could have done something about it."

"It was a long time ago." Her breath was a little gasp. "It's stupid to let it upset me now."

"No, it's not."

"I thought it was all right now." She whimpered and shivered a little.

He sighed and let out his breath, staring across at the *Starry Night*. "Jenny, we have counselors for . . . for rape victims."

She sat very still. "It wasn't—" She looked up at him and swallowed hard. "It was a near thing, but he didn't—I mean, somebody heard me scream, I guess. It was at a party, and . . .

he scared me pretty badly. He was really mad at me, and he hit me a few times."

Harvey waited until she looked fully into his eyes, and he was satisfied. He kissed her forehead. "You still might want to see someone."

"I told you, it's stupid. Every time something touches my hair, I panic. I should just cut it." She gave him a shaky smile. "I know I can trust you, but it was sort of a reflex when you grabbed my ponytail."

"You never reported him."

"No. I mean, isn't it hard enough to convict a rapist, let alone a near-rapist?"

He shrugged. "Assault can carry a stiff penalty. He did hurt you."

She rubbed her cheek as though it still hurt years later. "Yeah, but it was graduation week. My parents would have found out." She stood up. "Anyway, it's over. I never saw him again after that. I'm sorry I made such a fuss. I'd better go clean up the mess."

"I'll do it."

"Okay. I'll finish what I was doing."

They went back to the kitchen. Harvey hurriedly wiped up the water, then filled the ice tray and stuck it in the freezer. Jennifer covered the jug of iced tea, and he took the picnic things out to the Explorer. Eddie's truck pulled in beside it.

"Hey, Sarah, Eddie. You guys ride with us."

He opened the back of the Explorer and put the lunch in behind the back seat.

Jennifer came out of the house, and Harvey smiled at her. "Jenny, this is Sarah Benoit. Sarah, Jennifer Wainthrop."

"Hi," Jennifer said. "I'm really glad you could come."

"Thanks. It should be fun." Sarah looked trim and cool in khaki shorts and a sleeveless print blouse. It was the first time Harvey had seen her out of uniform, and he had to admit she was pretty.

They all piled into the Explorer, Jennifer in front beside Harvey, and Eddie and Sarah in back. They stopped at a dozen yard sales on the way to the lighthouse. Sarah bought an antique teapot with a Chinese design. "For my hope chest," she said to Jennifer. Harvey was mollified to see she had a feminine side.

At the fifth sale, he found a run-of-the-mill, round maple dining table with an extra leaf and two chairs for twenty dollars. He and Eddie took the legs off the table, and Harvey handed the owner the money.

"You can't beat that price," Eddie said as they put the pieces in the back of the vehicle. "I expect to eat breakfast with you in the morning and finally sit at a table."

Harvey and Jennifer homed in on used books at every sale. She accumulated quite a pile for a quarter apiece—a few mysteries, *Poetry of Robert Frost*, *Wildflowers of New England*, and a microwave cookbook. Harvey found a shop manual for his "new" SUV, and a cartridge reloading manual.

At one sale, Jennifer picked up a white china plate with cobalt blue flowers. It looked like the paint of the flowers had smudged and blurred. "Flow blue," Harvey said. "Do you like that?"

"You know antiques, too?" she turned it over and looked at the price tag then replaced it on the table, moving on to rummage through a box of small items.

The price for the plate was pretty good, Harvey thought. Much better than it would be in an antique shop. He picked it up and held an old *Popular Mechanics* over it until he could pay for it and smuggle it into the lunch box in the Explorer.

Eddie bought himself a belt, and an inlaid trinket box for Sarah. The four kept up a relaxed banter as they roamed from sale to sale. Eddie flirted outrageously with Sarah, so blatantly that even Sarah laughed at him. Harvey smiled often at Jennifer, and after a while the tension had left her shoulders, and she relaxed.

They got to the lighthouse at twelve-thirty. From a distance, the tall tower looked smooth and white, but as they got closer they could see that the surface of the 1790 structure was actually quite bumpy.

"Imagine building it all by hand," said Sarah.

Eddie leaned back and stared up at it. "I wouldn't want to be hauling rocks and lime up there."

"I wouldn't want to be up there at all," Harvey said. Just looking up at the light made him feel a little wobbly.

They carried their lunch onto the rocks near the shore. Sarah had pulled on a navy blue cardigan. It was cooler near the water, and the breeze stirred their hair. Harvey wished Jennifer's tresses hung free, but she seemed serene, and that made him glad.

She produced a bottle of sunscreen and made everybody use it, then snapped a picture with her phone of Eddie and Sarah sitting on the rocks, with the lighthouse keeper's house and the tower in the background. She asked Sarah to take one of her and Harvey. He pulled her in close for the picture, and Jennifer slipped her arm around his waist.

"We should do this every weekend," he said as Jennifer put her phone away.

"Sure, visit a different lighthouse every week, or one of the forts." She took the paper plates from the box and handed them to Sarah.

Everybody started listing off the sites they had been to, and arguing over which lighthouse was the most picturesque. Jennifer handed cups to Eddie so he could pour the iced tea. When she took out the sandwiches, she sat immobile for a second, staring into the box, then very gently reached down and lifted out the antique plate.

"Hey, Mémé Thibodeau has a platter like that!" Eddie said.

Jennifer looked over at Harvey and smiled, cradling the plate. He winked at her.

"We should go to Fort Preble next week," he said. "It's close, and they have cannon batteries from the Spanish-American War."

"Fort Knox is great," Eddie said. "My class went there for a field trip in fifth grade, and it was really cool. Long, dark hallways and dungeons and cannons."

Sarah argued for a cluster of lighthouses at Rockland, Owls Head, and Port Clyde that could be easily collected in one day.

Harvey watched Jennifer as they ate and talked. She seemed to enjoy Sarah's company. The two women were close in age, but Sarah was witty and gregarious, never at a loss for words. She gave Eddie as good as he dishe out. She was taller than Jennifer, and her hair and eyes were dark. Pretty, but not striking. It was only May, but already she was on the way to having a deep tan.

Jennifer was more serious, weighing everything that was said before reacting openly. In her sneakers and jeans, with the long blonde ponytail, she looked very young and defenseless, and Harvey felt he was taking on great responsibility in trying to make her feel secure. But he wanted to, more than anything.

"Do you enjoy working on computer programs all day?" Sarah asked.

"Not really." Jennifer made a face and looked quickly at Harvey. "I almost forgot. There was something I started to tell you."

"That's right. What was it, kiddo?" Immediately he wished he hadn't called her that.

"Well, see, they wanted John and me to put the special program together, to put my security part with his part, but I couldn't. It's complicated. The program, I mean. I guess I told you how they wouldn't let any of us see the whole thing. I started to tell you about the passwords and everything." She blushed and lowered her gaze.

He reached for her hand. "Yes, you were telling me this morning. I remember."

She looked up gratefully, then glanced toward Sarah. "Is it all right if I . . . I mean, I know Eddie's on the Dunham case with you, and Sarah's a policewoman, but . . ."

"It's fine. You can say anything."

She nodded. "Okay. Well, see, John has hinted several times that there's something odd about the program. Like it's for industrial spying or something. Yesterday he almost came out and said it's something illegal."

Harvey sat up straighter.

Eddie said, "This other guy, John, found something funny in the program?"

"I'm not sure. Maybe, like me, he just had a feeling things were odd. Like the terms it has to recognize." She looked at Eddie earnestly. "I told the bosses today I couldn't finish my work unless I had all the parts, but they make us put them in separate cloud storage, and they didn't want me to have them all. So I told them I was sorry, but I couldn't finish the project."

Harvey squeezed her hand, and she turned to face him. "What did they do?"

She shrugged. "It took a half-hour conference of all the partners, but Mr. Owen came out afterward and put the missing passwords in for me."

"So, you saw the whole program."

"Well, not in detail. It's huge, and I only had an hour or so left to work on it. And I had to shut everything down at five o'clock, of course. Harvey, I don't like it. I wanted to talk to John about it some more, but he acted like he didn't want to discuss it. But just before I closed it—" She broke off, her eyes wide.

"What, Jenny?" Harvey asked.

She turned to look at him. "I saw Nick's icon."

"What's that?" Eddie asked. "Like a picture?"

"It's something in the software that tells you who wrote the program," Harvey said.

Eddie laughed. "Oh. I thought for a second she saw Nick's ghost or something."

"You did not." Jennifer turned her smile on Eddie, and Harvey was sure that his partner was Jennifer's slave for life.

"So, what does it mean, that you saw Nick Dunham's icon in the program?" Sarah asked.

Jennifer sobered. "I thought about it a lot last night. The only conclusion I can make is that Nick worked on the program before he died."

They were all silent for a moment, then Eddie said, "Right before he died?"

"I don't know. But I do know that program Mr. Rainey gave Harvey is one Nick worked on months ago. And the day he disappeared, he told me he was working on something hush-hush."

Harvey nodded slowly. "You did tell me the first day we met that Nick was working on a special assignment."

"I don't know why I didn't realize it until now." Jennifer pulled a bag of cookies from the lunch box. "The partners told us it was a new contract. They made it sound like John, Tessa, and I were the first ones to work on it. In fact, they told us they had considered putting Nick on it, but since he'd disappeared and they couldn't wait any longer to start it, they were giving it to us."

"You started from scratch?" Harvey asked.

"Yes, on the security hierarchies. But after I saw Nick's mark today, I asked John what they gave him to start with. I didn't mention the icon, but he said they gave him a basic framework for the program with some of the initial work already done. And he thinks Tessa started out with something, too."

"And Nick Dunham wrote that first part of the program?"

"I think so. Maybe John thinks Mr. Rainey did, I'm not sure." She passed the cookies to Sarah.

"You think Jack Rainey could have begun the program?" Harvey asked.

She shrugged. "He's quite good. It's possible. But I definitely saw Nick's mark."

"Would John Macomber have recognized it?"

"I don't know."

"How do you know it was Nick's?" Eddie asked.

"A few months ago I had to go through one of his programs and find an error. He'd been troubleshooting it, but he couldn't find his own mistake, and he was getting really frustrated. Sometimes that happens. So I went to work and stripped it down line by line, and I found this meaningless group of characters. It wasn't a command. At first I thought that was the error. I pointed it out to Nick, and he said, *Oh, you found my mark.*"

"So ordinarily, he would keep it a secret?" Harvey asked slowly.

"Sure. For security. I mean, if everyone else knows your mark, it's meaningless. They can remove it. But under ordinary circumstances, no one would notice it. Only a true computer nerd would pick your program apart like that."

Harvey looked out over the shore, staring at the waves that broke on the rocks.

Chapter 20

When they got back to Jennifer's house, everyone unpacked their things from the Explorer in the driveway. Eddie and Sarah opted to eat supper at the Burger King. They extended an invitation, and Jennifer looked at Harvey. He shrugged, leaving it up to her. She thought he looked a little droopy, and decided he was ready for some down time, without the two chatterboxes. "Well, I've got a steak," she told him, a little surprised at herself.

"We're staying here, Buddy," he told Eddie decisively.

Eddie looked under his pickup, and Jennifer knew he was checking for bombs. She shivered a little and wondered how long they would keep doing it. It didn't seem to bother Sarah. She and Eddie climbed into the cab and left laughing.

Harvey followed Jennifer inside, and she once again felt self-conscious, wondering if she should have voted in favor of Burger King and company. She started supper and put away the picnic things. Harvey brought in her books and the plate and leaned against the counter, watching her as she moved about the kitchen.

"You shouldn't have bought me that plate," she said.

"Don't you like it?"

"I love it." She smiled. "Thank you. Did you have fun today?"

"It was good, considering my original vision of a double date with Eddie."

"Eddie's a good friend for you."

"Oh, yes, I'd do anything for him. But I don't want to double date with him all my life."

She chuckled and began setting the table.

"Are we going to church tomorrow?" Harvey asked.

"I hope so." She adjusted the fork at his plate.

He smiled. This is the way it's supposed to be, she thought as they sat down together. Her plain cooking wasn't fabulous, but he told her it was great and ate heartily.

When they had finished their meal, he said, "I suppose I'd better get going. Mrs. Jenkins has my laundry."

He stood up, and Jennifer did too.

"Harvey, wait."

He looked at her expectantly. She wanted to erase any awkwardness that lingered between them since her unexpected reaction that morning, but she couldn't make herself bring it up directly.

"What, Jenny?" He stepped closer.

"Would you feel differently about me if I cut my hair?"

He shrugged. "No. Nothing external like that is going to change the way I feel about you."

"Thanks. I needed to hear that."

He caught her hand and drew her closer. "It doesn't matter to me what you do with your hair. Grace Kelly, Rapunzel, Jeanie, or Pocahontas."

She frowned. "Who's Jeanie?"

"Jeanie in the bottle." He laughed. "It doesn't matter. You can frizz it like Einstein, or stick it out on coat hangers like Pippi Longstocking. I don't care. Get it?"

She nodded, smiling, and was very aware that the distance between them was closing. He pulled her nearer and slid his free arm around her. She rested her cheek against his shoulder, warm and solid, as he held her.

"So, are you going to cut it?" His whisper was hoarse.

She thought hard for a moment about what it would be like to have short hair. It would look different, feel different. She would gain at least two hours a week, from the time she now spent caring for it. Maybe the occasional moments of panic would end.

"You like it this way, don't you?"

"I love it this way." His held her against his chest, and she leaned against him, loving how warm and solid he was.

"What would you call it if I just left my hair loose?"

"I don't know. I'd have to see it to answer that one. Mona Lisa, maybe."

"Harvey, I think God is more important than anything else in our relationship."

He pulled away and looked down at her, his brow furrowed. "You may be right. Have you reached a conclusion?"

Jennifer pulled in a deep breath. She was almost afraid to discuss the results of their experiment. "I want to, but . . . I'm trying not to decide a certain way, just because I think that's what you think." She bit her lip as the anxiety surged. "I'm sorry. I want so much to just follow you, wherever you go on this."

He nodded and pulled her against him again, resting his chin on the top of her head. Jennifer felt she was stealing comfort and contentment she didn't deserve, as she stood with her head against his T-shirt, feeling him breathe.

"You have to believe for yourself," he said.

"I know," she choked, "but, Harvey, I'm afraid."

"You don't need to be."

"But what if—" she leaned back to where she could see his clear blue eyes. "What if I put all my trust in God, and then I find I've lost you?" She couldn't stop her tears from spilling over, and a look of pain and regret crossed his face.

He cradled her face in his hands and dashed the tears away with both thumbs. "Jenny, baby, this is the one time I'll tell you, don't trust me for this. Don't follow me. Don't believe in me."

"It's too hard."

He shook his head, and she saw that there were tears in his eyes, too. "Sweetheart, if you're just clinging to me, you'll be disappointed. I'm not infallible. I know that for certain."

Jennifer swallowed down a sob. "The God question is important to me. More important than I realized at first. But I don't know yet how important it is to you."

"And what if I told you I've decided I don't believe it?"

She jerked her head back, staring at him through her tears. The bitter disappointment inside her was sharp and painful.

"You mean that?"

His face was unreadable. "I'm just asking a hypothetical question."

"I guess . . . I'd need some more time to think about my own conclusion. Because . . . Harvey, I think a lot of your judgment. I rely on your opinions, and . . ." She shook her head helplessly.

He kissed her forehead softly. "Take all the time you need, Jenny. Just remember what I said. Don't trust me for this."

He went to the door and opened it. The temperature outside had dropped about ten degrees. Jennifer stood in the doorway with her arms folded around herself. She watched as he took his flashlight and looked underneath his Explorer, then opened the door cautiously and checked inside the passenger compartment. He looked back at the house and waved. Jennifer lifted her hand then turned and closed the door.

She sat tense and brooding beside him all through the morning service. Harvey regretted his iron stance on the issue, but couldn't help feeling he had done what was necessary. She needed to have her own faith.

Lisa Dunham brought the children to church that morning, and many people paused to speak to her after the service. She was gracious to Jennifer, and Harvey was thankful for that, knowing how splintery Jennifer's emotions were. He made a point of introducing her to Jackie Wyman, and when he turned around from greeting Rick Bradley, he saw Jennifer and Jackie standing between two pews, talking earnestly.

"Rick, would you pray for Jennifer and me today?"

"Of course."

Harvey felt very self-conscious, but Rick seemed to take it as a natural interchange. They stood talking for a few more minutes about jobs and baseball, until Jennifer came silently up beside him. He reached for her hand, and she clutched his.

He took her to lunch, then to the park near the bay, where they could walk along the shore. It was warm, and she left her jacket in his vehicle.

The sun gleamed on her hair. She had a new updo that day, braids intricately pinned on top. He appraised it carefully when they sat down on a bench together.

"What are you thinking?" she asked.

He couldn't answer that directly, couldn't tell her he'd been imagining pulling all the pins out of her hair and dumping them in the bay. The little braids mocked him, like the knots of mental anguish she was putting herself through.

He brought his hand up to rest lightly on the back of her neck. "They're having visiting hours for the Dunham family this afternoon at the funeral home. Do you want to go?"

She nodded. "Jackie told me. I'd like to. I wish I could do something for them, Harvey."

"You don't know it, but you have."

"Me?" Her gray eyes widened.

"We're going to catch Nick's killer, and you've helped."

"Good." Her expression was fierce, but he felt that she might dissolve into tears at any second. For a long time she was quiet, gazing out over the water. "Harvey, Nick's death has something to do with that program."

He took a deep breath. "Yes."

"And Mr. Rainey knows about it. At least, he gave you that other bank program, so you wouldn't find out what Nick was really working on. He has to know something."

"Mike and Eddie and I have talked about it."

"You have?" She swiveled on the bench to look at him directly. "When?"

"We put in a couple of hours last night."

"You got Mike out, after you left my house?"

"Yes. I decided I had to. He's very good at putting things in perspective."

"So, what did you all decide to do?"

Harvey caressed her shoulder gently. "We don't have enough information yet."

"But you can question Mr. Rainey again."

He hesitated. "We don't want to spook him, Jenny. He's probably not in this alone. But don't worry—we'll keep at it until we find something solid."

She blinked and turned away. For long minutes, the only sound was the waves beating the shore.

She gasped and brought one hand up to her lips, turning to stare at him. "I'm so stupid. It's Massal's program."

"What?"

"Massal. Mr. Owen said it Friday, when I asked for the other parts of the program."

Harvey felt a stir of excitement. He sat forward and pulled her around to face him. "Mr. Owen said what? Tell me exactly."

She frowned. "He said they would have to ask Massal if I could see the whole thing, and Mr. Rainey jumped on him, like he'd said too much."

“Who’s Massal?”

“The Arabic client. Jane and I have speculated about why he was there so much lately. She thought he was applying for a job at first. Lately I’d decided he was a consultant. But it’s his program. He’s the client.”

“And he’s Arabic.”

She shrugged. “Sorry. I know we shouldn’t profile, but I’m not really sure of his nationality. He has the Middle-Eastern look. I’ve never spoken to him.”

“Could you identify him?”

“Sure, if I saw him.”

“How about from a mug book?”

“With a thousand other Middle-Eastern men? I’m not sure. Jane might.”

“Jane Morrow?”

“She thinks he’s nice looking. But she thinks every man is nice looking.”

“She notices things about men, though.”

Jennifer chewed her bottom lip thoughtfully. “She doesn’t miss much in the office.”

Harvey pulled his notebook from his pocket. “Spell the name for me, gorgeous.”

“Massal? I never saw it written.”

“Okay, but you’re sure that’s the name.”

She shrugged. “We were calling him ‘the Arabic guy,’ but then I heard it somewhere.” Her face brightened. “Mr. Owen took a phone call when I was in there one day. I think it was Mr.

Channing on the other end. Yes, I'm sure. He said something like, 'All right, Ron. Massal's coming in this afternoon.' And then, after lunch, I saw the Arabic guy go in. So I figured it was him."

Harvey gritted his teeth. It was pretty thin. "That's it? Is there anything else you can think of?"

"Not until Friday. I just told you. Mr. Rainey said they would ask the client, and then Mr. Owen said if Massal gave his approval, they'd give me the rest of it."

"You're positive? This is important, sweetheart."

She nodded slowly. "There's no one else it could be. And he's been there a lot this past month. I saw him in the parking lot one day . . ." She broke off and looked at him with clear eyes. "He was with another man, younger than him. I'm sure it's him. He's the one who commissioned this nightmare of a program."

"Okay. I'll see if I can find out anything about him."

"It's Sunday," she said doubtfully. "You're not going to work now, are you?"

"No, I'm going to take you to the funeral home."

"Thank you."

He gathered her into his arms and pulled her close for a moment. If only they could stay on the bench in the bright sunlight forever, and forget about reality. But even as the thought came, he rejected it. The puzzle pieces were coming together, and an eagerness filled him.

He knew he would be up most of the night. The sun would be rising in Baghdad when he took Jennifer home this evening. There was plenty the Priority Unit could do. He was already cataloguing the federal and international agencies he would contact.

He left her on her doorstep at eight-thirty, without even a hint of going in, despite the longing inside him.

One glance up at the crescent moon reminded him of his most pressing duty.

"Jenny, I want to tell you something," he said after he had unlocked her door. "I know you're still struggling with things."

She nodded, and he felt the consuming ache that had been with him for days now. He stood with his hands on her shoulders, drinking in her sweet, forlorn features. "Sweetheart, we haven't spoken about it all day—believing or not believing."

"I know."

"We think so much alike, Jenny. Ask yourself, could we really not agree on something this important?"

A spark lit her woeful eyes, and he could see

that she was hovering, trying to fit that with his harsh disclaimer of the night before. *Dear God,* he found himself pleading inwardly, *Let her settle this. I don't know how much more we can stand.*

He backed away from her, and her shoulders drooped. His hopes plummeted. *If I held out my arms, she would come to me. And if I told her now . . .* It was tempting. Very tempting. He could end her agony in seconds. For the moment. But for the rest of her life? Someday she might be in Lisa Dunham's shoes. It wasn't unthinkable, with his job the way it was. And he needed to know that, if that happened, she would have someone stronger than him to hold her up.

He took his notebook from his pocket and scribbled "Psalm 91." *He is my refuge and my fortress, my God; in him will I trust . . .* She would find some comfort there. He tore out the sheet.

"I found this earlier, when I was reading."

Jennifer took it and squinted at it in the dusk, then nodded. Harvey hesitated, then put his hand to her cheek for an instant before she turned toward the house and he went down the steps.

He was about to get into his SUV when the house door crashed open and Jennifer ran out again, jumping down the three steps in one bound. She stumbled and regained her balance, and reached him as he looked beyond her to the house.

A shadow moved in the doorway, then disappeared inside.

Harvey grabbed her arm and pulled her behind the open door of the Explorer, then pulled his pistol.

"He's in there," she choked.

"You got your phone?"

"No. I dropped my purse."

Harvey fumbled for his and thrust it toward her. "911. Now. And stay here." He ran for the steps. At the doorway, he checked and faced the dark interior. His long training took over. Even as he braced himself to enter, he could hear a muffled sound and knew the intruder was escaping out the back. He brushed the switch by the door, flooding Jennifer's living room with light, and ran for the kitchen.

The back door was open, and he was outside in an instant, jumping from the back stoop in a fluid leap. A dark figure was fleeing across the small backyard. A five-foot fence separated Jennifer's yard from the neighbors'. Harvey had a chance.

"Hold it, police!"

The man jumped onto the board fence, but didn't clear it. He hung there, scrambling with his sneakers to gain the top. His hands were empty. Harvey ran over and pulled him off the fence.

"Put your hands on your head."

He stared at the young man. He'd been thinking so much about Massal, he'd been prepared for a foreigner and a struggle to the death. Instead he was holding at gunpoint a tall, thin young man with a blond ponytail and a feral, desperate look. Harvey stood him against the fence and patted him down, transferring a four-inch folded knife from the man's pocket to his own.

"What are you doing here, Billy?"

Surprise registered in the pale blue eyes, and Harvey smiled. He'd looked long and hard at Billy Cassidy's mug shot just days ago, and he had a good memory.

"Nothing."

"Come on, you know Donna-jean doesn't live here anymore. Put your hands behind your back." Harvey clipped the handcuffs on Billy's wrists and headed him around the corner of the house.

Jennifer watched from behind the door of the Explorer, breathing in ragged gasps and saying nothing. Almost at once, Harvey heard a distant siren wail.

"You were planning a little surprise for Donna-jean's roommate, weren't you?" Harvey asked.

"She asked for it."

Harvey shook his head and shook Billy a bit,

too. “You picked the wrong person to mess with.”

Billy sneered at him, but looked away quickly as Harvey glared back.

The squad car arrived, and Harvey gladly turned his prisoner over to Jimmy Cook and Nate Miller. When their backup arrived, the two of them entered the house for a thorough check.

Harvey went around his SUV and pulled Jennifer into his arms.

“You okay?”

She nodded and sucked in a breath, and he realized he was holding her so tightly she could hardly breathe. He loosened his grip a little, but she held on to him.

“You caught him.” Her laugh was a little hysterical.

“Yeah, I’m not quite decrepit yet.” He kissed her forehead. “I thought maybe Ali Baba and the forty thieves were in there.”

“No. Just Billy. I’m sorry.”

“Ha! Don’t kid yourself. That scum is dangerous.” He straightened and reached to take his phone from her hand, but she didn’t let go, so he bent slightly and began to peel her fingers off one by one.

“I’m sorry,” she said again, and she let go.

“It’s okay. I’m calling Mike.”

“What for?”

“To see if he and Sharon can put you up tonight.”

Her face was already white in the dim light, but she seemed even more distressed. "No, don't. I couldn't. Not your captain."

"Rick and Ruthann Bradley, then. Jenny, I'm not leaving you here alone tonight."

She swallowed hard. "All right, but the Bradleys don't have much space. Maybe—the Rowlands?"

He nodded. "Great. I'll have to get the number."

Jimmy Cook came down the steps.

"Stay here," Harvey said, and he walked toward Jimmy. "What did you find?"

"Nothing, but her stuff is strewn all over. He was looking for something."

"We did a thorough search when I had her roommate arrested."

"Must have missed something." Jimmy shrugged. "I heard the story about you blowing the whistle on the roommate. If she was tight with this guy, anything could surface."

"How bad is it in there?"

"It'll take a while to clean up."

Something brushed Harvey's sleeve, and he turned to find Jennifer beside him.

"Do you want to give us your statement now, ma'am?" Jimmy asked.

"He—he was in the living room when I went in. It was dark, and I didn't see him, but just as I shut the door, he said—" She stopped and looked at Harvey. "He said, *Where is it, Jennifer?* I didn't know who it was at first. I just opened the door again and ran."

"Do you know what it was he wanted?" Jimmy asked.

"No. But he and Donna-jean used to smoke pot in her room, I think, and she left some heroin in my freezer. Harvey was here when I found it."

"Yes, ma'am. I'll get a copy of the report. Billy Cassidy wasn't here that night, was he?"

"No, but he came and went a lot." She looked up at Harvey, and he reached for her hand. She'd been scared way back then, he knew.

"When your roommate was taken to the police station that night, what did you do with her things?" Jimmy asked.

"Her mother came for them a couple of days later. There were a few things left, and I boxed them up and sent them."

"Everything went to her mother's address?"

"Yes."

"Has your roommate contacted you since then?"

"No. Harvey said the judge told her not to." Jennifer's solemn eyes widened. "I found a CD a couple of days ago. It was in with my classical albums, but it was hard rock. I figured it was hers."

"What did you do with it?" Harvey asked.

"I mailed it yesterday to her mother's house."

Harvey nodded at Jimmy. "Have your sergeant

call the DA first thing, Jim. Get a warrant, then call the postmaster and pick up Mrs. Jacobs's mail in the morning."

"Will do."

Jennifer gave him Mrs. Jacobs's address, and Jimmy wrote it carefully in his notebook.

Harvey's fist clenched and unclenched. If Billy had waited ten seconds longer, he would have been gone, beyond hearing Jennifer scream. Beyond seeing her streak through the door and down the steps.

He reached out and wrapped her in his embrace again, not caring what Jimmy or the other cops thought. The timing was lucky. If she'd put the security chain on . . . if Billy had waited in her bedroom . . .

Providential, not lucky, he decided. A tremor went through him. *Thank you, God.*

"I'm taking you to the Rowlands' now," he said. "You can clean the house up tomorrow."

"You haven't called them."

"Come on, you get a few things together. I'll call them while you pack your toothbrush."

Chapter 21

Harvey and Eddie went to Harvey's apartment for breakfast after their three-mile run Monday morning. Harvey made a big production of serving Wheaties at the new kitchen table.

"This is almost like a real kitchen." Eddie poured a dollop of milk into his coffee. The dark circles beneath his huge brown eyes gave him a decadent air, making him almost wickedly attractive.

"So, what did you get on Billy Boy last night?" Harvey asked. He was sure his own fatigue just made him look old and tired.

"His car was parked down the street. You drove right past it when you took Jennifer home."

Harvey shook his head, mentally berating himself. "I'm losing my edge."

"Love can do that to you."

"It's not love, it's all these loose ends we have hanging. Dunham, the Coastal Technology partners, Bobby Nason, Massal. Billy totally blind-sided me."

"Out of the blue," Eddie agreed.

"So, where's Donna-jean? Did you check on her like I asked you to?"

"Her mother says she's visiting a friend in

Connecticut. She wasn't too happy about me calling her at 1 a.m."

"Would you be happy if your daughter was running with a dope dealer?" Harvey sighed. "I called the landlord. He's putting a new dead bolt on both doors at Jennifer's house this morning. I wish we could do more, but I don't know what, short of having her move."

"You said she's getting a new roommate. That ought to give her some peace of mind."

"I don't know." Harvey wondered if it was fair to ask Beth to take on Jennifer's mistake and the consequences. Billy Cassidy no doubt had a lot friends. Then there were the unexplained car bombs that were endangering Jennifer, Eddie, and anyone else connected to him.

Eddie picked up his cereal bowl and drank the milk. "So what did you and Mike turn up on the other business?"

"Massal is a likely suspect, all right. He's here on a Turkish passport. Supposedly he's a businessman, representing some technology interest in Istanbul. The State Department was a little cagey. So far we've got nothing concrete on him."

"You think they're watching him?"

"I don't know. I'm wondering if they'd lost track of him and don't want to admit it."

"Are we going in to Coastal again?"

“Not yet.” Harvey sipped his coffee.

“We ought to get a warrant for that program Jennifer talked about.”

“We don’t want to close in too soon.”

“Jennifer okay?”

“The pastor will look out for her.” Harvey glanced at his watch. “She’ll be at work in an hour.”

“She’s safe,” Eddie said. “We know where Billy Cassidy is.”

Harvey nodded, but the image of his car burning in front of the school was still in his mind. That had happened before Donna-jean’s arrest. “I’ll call her later.”

On the drive to the police station, he opened a different subject. “Are you going to see Sarah again?”

“Friday night.”

“Where you going?”

“I don’t know. Where would you take Jennifer?”

“Anywhere. But practically speaking, I’d suggest something a little sophisticated, for contrast. Let her see you in a suit.”

Eddie considered that. “Maybe so. Let’s go rattle Rainey’s cage, Harv.”

Harvey drew a slow, deep breath. “We can’t prove this secret computer program is anything out of the ordinary. Besides, Mike wants to touch base with his contact at the CIA first.”

• • •

Jennifer hated to call Harvey during working hours, afraid his phone would ring at a critical moment, but her instincts told her not to wait. He sounded normal and calm when he answered, and she was relieved.

"Harvey, please, can you meet me for lunch? I need to see you, but I can't be away from the office too long."

"Okay, gorgeous, how about that deli across from Coastal?"

"No!" She cringed as Jane walked past. She returned Jane's bright wave with a slight flip of her fingers.

"Too close to the spot in question?"

"Much."

"How about I get some sandwiches and meet you someplace?"

"Okay. You pick. I don't want to say much."

He named a drug store a block away, and she agreed.

"In the parking lot at 12:05," Harvey said.

"Yes."

Jennifer hung up and turned back to her keyboard, still agitated but determined to make the most of the intervening hour.

As promised, Harvey waited in his Explorer near the drugstore, with Eddie in the back seat. Harvey got out and opened the passenger door for her, then got in the other side.

"Hi, Jennifer. I hope you don't mind if I'm here," Eddie said, handing her a sandwich.

"No, that's fine, Eddie. How are you?"

He smiled. "Okay."

"You look tired."

"I was up kind of late." He smiled again, innocently. "Diet Pepsi for you."

"Thanks. You should take better care of yourself." He'd had a late date, she guessed, and she hoped he wasn't drinking. Eddie was becoming dear to her. She wondered if he'd taken Sarah out again, but she didn't ask. She turned instead toward Harvey.

"Are you all right?" he asked. The creases at the corners of his eyes were deep, and she knew suddenly that he and Eddie were on the edge of exhaustion.

"I'm fine. The Rowlands were wonderful."

He nodded. "Well, you don't have to worry about Billy for a while. He's not going anywhere."

"That's good to know." She hesitated and shot another glance at Eddie. "Did you guys sleep at all?"

Harvey smiled. "Enough. And a detective got the package you sent Mrs. Jacobs from the post office this morning."

"Guess what was in it." Eddie's eyes brimmed with suspense.

"A rock CD?" she hazarded.

Harvey smiled regretfully. “No, a CD containing a list of Billy Cassidy’s customers. He’d put it in the case to camouflage it.”

Jennifer stared at him. “He’s behind the curve in security. I’ve made a lot of trouble for you guys by being naïve, haven’t I?”

“Hey, it will give the vice detectives something to do this week,” Eddie said.

Harvey eyed Jennifer closely. “How were things at the office this morning?”

She took a deep breath. “Well, the translator came. It’s a young guy I saw once before. He was in the parking lot one day last week, talking to Massal.”

“You don’t say.”

“I do say. And you’ll never guess what languages the program is going into.”

“Esperanto?”

“No, it’s already in English and French; those are done in-house. And this guy is putting it into Arabic and Farsi.”

“Farsi? You aren’t serious.”

“Yes, I am.”

Eddie looked from Harvey to Jennifer and back. “What’s that?”

“One of the official languages of Iran,” Jennifer said. “English, French, Arabic, and Farsi. Those are the four.” She looked down for a moment, then met Harvey’s gaze again. “I don’t think I was supposed to know, but I was in Mr. Owen's office getting my instructions this morning. Mr. Channing brought the translator in and introduced him to Mr. Owen."

"Did you get his name?"

She frowned. "Hamad. First name . . . might be Rashid? I'm not positive. He looks like a kid. I knew Tessa had already put most of the onscreen stuff into French, but just as I was making my exit, I heard Channing say the young man was there to do the Farsi and Arabic translation. I was afraid if I stuck around any longer they'd be suspicious."

"Jenny, you've got to be careful," Harvey said.

"I know. But I thought you needed to know. You were saying last night you need to convince the government that this program is a real threat. I've looked at most of it this morning. It's pretty frightening."

Harvey frowned. "If they're putting the program in Farsi . . ."

"I'm sure now that it's military," she said. "At least, it has military applications. Tessa's programming is very detailed. I'm not an expert on national security, but that program is designed to allow access to other programs, and to recognize and deactivate protocols that have a definite military ring."

Harvey said slowly, "If they're selling Iran some kind of computer technology that will be detrimental to us militarily, it could be disastrous."

"Come on," Eddie said. "You really think they're writing spy programs at Coastal?"

"Well, stranger things have happened."

Jennifer nodded, not liking the thoughts she was having. "Before my day, there was a spy they arrested who had lived in Skowhegan. My dad used to talk about it."

"I remember. That was big stuff," Harvey said.

"The whole town was ashamed. But . . . Harvey, I'm working on that program! I'm making it so good nobody can crack it! If the wrong people get hold of it—"

"Let's not get all excited," he said. "We could be wrong. We wouldn't want to cause an international incident over nothing. Just keep your eyes and ears open. And don't take any chances."

"Okay." Jennifer unwrapped her sandwich slowly. "It occurred to me that I might be able to derail the program somehow."

"No. Too risky. If something didn't work right, they'd know you caused it."

She drew a shaky breath, glad he had said it. Just thinking of going back to Coastal frayed her nerves. "All right, but once we're finished with it, they'll send it electronically. We might not have time to act."

"That's true." Harvey didn't look happy.

"It's all right if I call you like I did this morning?" she asked. "Any time?"

"Any time." He watched her closely. "You're really stressed over this job, aren't you, baby?"

Her stomach flip-flopped. "Kind of."

"Look, you probably won't even want to think twice about this, but I heard the other day that there's a temporary position open at the station, in the records department. It's a maternity leave, so it's probably just for the summer, but it might give you a breathing spell if you really want to change careers."

"What would I be doing?" She couldn't believe she was asking.

"Extremely boring stuff, like filing and data entry. It would pay half what you're making, and they don't have air conditioning in the basement."

"There are a few perks, though," Eddie said.

"Like what?" Jennifer asked.

"Like us upstairs, and lunch every day with the Invincible Duo, if you want."

She chuckled, feeling calmer.

"Good," Harvey said. "You're not beyond laughing."

"Do you really think they'd hire me?"

"I don't know. They'll probably have a gazillion applicants, and you're grossly overqualified. But, if you want to take a shot at it, Mike would speak up for you."

"He would?"

"Yeah," Harvey said. "He's impressed with your computer work. I got the word on Bobby Nason the other day before the investigating officer did. And Mike thinks you're pretty sharp."

"Do you think I should apply?" The idea of leaving the familiarity and financial benefits of Coastal was scary, but working at the police station might offer her a different type of security.

"Do you want to?" Harvey asked. "That's all that matters."

"It's not all that matters to me," Jennifer said.

"Okay. What else matters to you about it?"

"Well, if I worked in the same building with you, and that became awkward for any reason . . ." She glanced toward Eddie, but he was studiously arranging the pickles in his sandwich.

Harvey didn't hesitate. "Come in on your lunch hour tomorrow. I'll talk to Mike in the morning. If the job looks too depressing, you can walk away."

Eddie said, "If you think it will help, I'll talk to Marge in Records."

"You have some pull with Marge in Records?" Jennifer asked, raising an eyebrow.

Harvey turned his eyes toward the ceiling. "Eddie has pull with every female in the department."

He drove her back to within sight of the Coastal building and stopped at the curb.

"We may work late again tonight, gorgeous."

Jennifer flushed, but Eddie was unbuckling his seat belt so he could get out and take her place in the front seat.

"You take care, Harvey," she whispered. "Don't they have rules about how much sleep you need if you're wearing a gun or something?"

"Don't worry. We'll get our rest. I have to cut out seeing you every night, is all."

Harvey gave Eddie an unaccustomed wake-up call on Tuesday. "Can we leave early this morning? I want to go to the big furniture store on Bay Street. It opens at seven."

"You're finally buying furniture?"

"I'm too old to keep sleeping on the floor. I get up all stiff in the morning."

"Okay, but you ought to go to the used furniture place first. It would be a lot cheaper."

"I know, but I've given this a lot of thought, and I've decided I want a bed nobody else has slept in."

At the furniture outlet, acres of bedroom sets confronted them. Harvey remembered why he hated shopping.

"How about the brass one?" Eddie said.

"Too gaudy."

They looked at modern, French Empire, and futons.

"Hey, here's one that looks like an antique, but it's new," said Eddie. "You like antiques."

The sleigh bed had gracefully curved head and foot boards. It was set up with a patchwork quilt covering the mattress and box spring.

"I could sleep in that." Harvey found a clerk and told him what he wanted, demanding same-day delivery. He had left a key to his apartment with Rebecca the night before, asking her to expect a truck.

"Bring the quilt, too. You got bookcases?" he asked the clerk.

"Yes, sir. This way."

Harvey quickly chose a couple of barrister's bookcases with glass doors and headed for the living room sets.

Eddie looked at his watch. "We need to get going. Besides, don't you think you should let Jennifer pick out the sofa?"

Harvey turned on him and growled, "What's Jennifer got to do with this?"

Eddie backed off with his hands raised. "Sorry. Too far?"

"Way too far."

As soon as they got to the office, Harvey told Mike about Jennifer's interest in the clerk's job.

"Why would she come work here for a pittance?" Mike asked.

"She hates her job. Besides, I'm thinking she may not have a job after we're finished with the Dunham case. Not that I've spelled that out to her."

Mike frowned, chewing his gum thoughtfully. "Well, it's only for baby leave, twelve weeks."

"I told her."

"Hey, the department could use a brain like hers. I'll write her a glowing letter this minute. Can I say I've known her a long time?"

Harvey laughed. "I don't think eight days constitutes a long friendship."

"Well, I can honestly say I've seen her work. How do you spell Wainthrop?"

She came at ten past noon. Harvey met her at the front door and walked her down to Records. Jennifer looked professional in black pants and a pale pink blouse, but not way overdressed for the modest workplace.

"Do you want me to wait, or would that make you nervous?" he asked.

"Why don't you just go eat?"

"Okay, I'll be at the diner down the street with Eddie. Come join us when you're done." He kissed her forehead. "Knock 'em dead."

She broke into a wide smile.

"You smile like that, and they won't be able to say no." Harvey was tempted to kiss her again, but she turned toward the door of Records and took a deep breath before opening it.

He kept one eye on Jennifer's car as he slowly ate a ham sandwich and drank coffee. When she finally came out, she walked swiftly toward him, and he went to meet her.

"How'd it go?" he asked.

"Good. The job's mine if I want it."

"Yes! Don't you want it?" He frowned at her lack of enthusiasm.

She looked up at him, squinting against the sun. "Harvey, are you absolutely sure you want me working here? Even for a short time?"

"Yes. It will be great." He couldn't understand her thinking he might object. Having her so close would be wonderful.

She smiled. "Okay, I'll take it. But I'd better call them from work and tell them, or I'll be late getting back."

He walked her to her car and handed her a paper bag.

"What's this?"

"Lunch. And you don't have to look under the car. Eddie and I have taken care of it."

"You sweetie."

He wished they were alone, not on the street in plain sight of the diner and the police station. "When do you start?"

"Two weeks from Monday. The mom plans to start her leave then. I'll give Coastal two weeks' notice."

"Give it this afternoon."

As he watched her drive away, Eddie came over from the diner. "Pete was just here. He said Arnie had news on the Nason brothers."

"Really? I thought Bobby and LeRoy both skipped Newport."

"They did. Nobody seems to be at the house, but the cops went back yesterday with a warrant and went in."

"Find anything?"

"Some black powder. Seems the brother shoots muzzle loaders, though. Could be nothing. They did get fingerprints. Took Leroy's off the can of powder. And guess whose off a glass and the telephone?"

"Brother Bob's?"

"Bingo."

Harvey nodded. "So, where are you and Sarah going for your big date Friday?"

"String quartet at the Wadsworth-Longfellow House," said Eddie.

"Classical music? You?"

"It was her idea."

"And you're happy with this?"

"If it makes her happy."

"Eddie, maybe you're growing up."

"Hey." Eddie nudged him and nodded toward the diner. Mike and his wife were approaching a free table on the sidewalk. Mike pulled out Sharon's chair and seated her. A waitress came out and took their order. Eddie ambled toward the table, and Harvey followed.

"Hey, guys," Mike called.

"Hello, Mrs. Browning," Eddie said shyly.

"Hi, Eddie. Hello, Harvey."

"I'm taking my wife out for a fancy lunch," said Mike. "BLTs and Moxie."

Sharon laughed. "I never get to see him anymore unless I come down here."

"Hey, Harv, I've got another question for you," Mike said. "Do people that die turn into angels? Sharon says it's not in the Bible."

Harvey was startled. Mike had never talked to him about religion until the car bomb incident at the church. "I don't know, but if it's not in the Bible, then I guess they don't."

"Good answer," said Sharon.

Mike laughed then turned sober. "There's a new report on the Nason brothers."

"Newer than what Pete just told me?" Eddie asked.

"See Arnie about it."

Eddie and Harvey went up to the office, and Arnie Fowler was to the point. "I got LeRoy Nason's fingerprints from Newport. That one print from the pipe bomb on your car—it's a match."

"Bobby's brother?" Harvey asked.

"That's right. Maybe he put the bomb on the car, and maybe he didn't, but he touched it. I put out an APB on both brothers, but they're slippery."

“This can’t be personal,” Harvey said. “I’ve never even seen LeRoy Nason.”

“Somebody’s bankrolling this job,” Arnie agreed.

Chapter 22

Harvey spent an hour going through computerized gun records. Nick Dunham had been killed with a nine-millimeter bullet, but no matches showed up in the system, and none of the partners at Coastal admitted to owning a handgun.

"They hired someone to shoot Nick," Eddie said.

Harvey stared at the monitor, thinking. "Is it possible the car bombs are connected to this case?"

Eddie shrugged. "I don't see how. We didn't even have a body back then."

"All right, but when we find the Nason brothers, we run any weapons they have on the IBIS system, against the bullets that killed Nick Dunham."

"Can't hurt."

"It's a long shot," Harvey admitted. "A nine-millimeter isn't Bobby Nason's style."

"Yeah, he likes a bigger boom." Eddie eyed the scar on his hand.

"Harvey, Eddie," Mike called, and they went quickly to the captain's desk. "I've got a CIA representative who'll see you at the federal building in twenty minutes. Seems the Pentagon had some leaks last fall. This Massal guy may be on the fringe of it."

Arnie and Pete came hurrying from the locker room wearing their Kevlar vests.

"Where you headed?" Eddie asked.

"Possible lead on the Nason brothers. We don't want to lose them again," Arnie said over his shoulder. He and Pete were out the door.

There was no word from them all afternoon. Harvey wasn't satisfied with the scant information he gained at the federal office building. They still didn't have enough evidence to go after Massal.

His thoughts kept straying to Jennifer as he worked at his desk. She was becoming dependent on him, and he wasn't sure that was good. She needed to be able to take care of herself.

He believed in God, and beyond that, he *knew* God now, although the acquaintance was newly formed. It had come to him gradually, a firm, unshakable certainty.

Jennifer needed that, too, regardless of what happened to him. He wanted more than anything to tell her he believed, but she had to understand that they were separate in their commitment. It was the only way they could become one. She was close to it, he was sure. He silently formed a prayer for wisdom, and was struck with amazement and humility that he was able to ask God for that.

"So, she's really taking the job in Records?" Eddie said.

Harvey realized he had stopped typing as he prayed, and was staring out the window, at the lawyer's office across Franklin Street.

"Yeah. Two weeks from Monday, she'll be downstairs cross-referencing our reports."

"Good deal," Eddie said.

Harvey looked at his watch. In two hours, he could go to her. As soon as he knew she had settled her own spiritual questions, he would tell her that he loved her.

The flag for Jennifer's program had appeared in the corner of his screen. When he clicked on it, an update from the State Police appeared.

"Eddie."

"What have you got?" Eddie asked.

"Donna-jean Jacobs was stopped in Kittery this morning. Drugs again."

"Send them your file on her," Eddie recommended. "She won't bail out so quick this time."

"Don't mention this to Jennifer."

At five o'clock, Harvey was heading to the locker room to shave when Mike yelled, "Eddie, Harvey, don't go!"

The captain was hanging up his phone as they turned toward his desk. "Arnie and Pete have tracked the Nasons to a motel. I told them to wait for us. Bobby's skipped off too many times, and I want to bring him in. Get your body armor.

I'll call downstairs and ask for more men." Harvey and Eddie ran to their lockers.

"Hope we get him this time." Eddie pulled his bulletproof vest over his shirt.

"I'd better call Jenny." Harvey took out his cell phone. Mike came in and swiftly put on his vest while Harvey made the call.

"Jenny, it's me. I know I promised to help move Beth in, but something's come up, and we have to work late tonight. I'm sorry. I'll come over as soon as I can."

"Okay," she said. "I'll be here."

He hesitated.

"Let's roll, Harvey," said Mike, heading out the door. Eddie followed him.

"Jenny, we'll talk later."

"Is everything all right?"

"Yes, but I have to go."

He ran after Mike and Eddie. Downstairs they added six more officers who had been leaving the day shift: Sarah Benoit, Cheryl Yeaton, Nate Miller, Jimmy Cook, and two more men. Jimmy and Nate, who had been at the school when Harvey's car was bombed, said they wouldn't miss this for anything.

"We'll surround the motel unit." Mike looked at Harvey and Eddie. "Ride with me." They piled into his car, and the others followed in two cruisers, with lights flashing, but no sirens.

When they arrived, they spotted Arnie and

Pete in the parking lot. The marked units parked down the street, and the officers waited for instructions out of view of the front motel rooms. Arnie briefed Mike quickly.

"Room 10, the third door from this end. They've been in there forty-five minutes. I figure they'll want supper soon."

"Pete, go ask the manager for the key," Mike said. "Arnie, tell four of the uniformed officers to go around behind the motel and be careful not to be seen from number 10's window. One door, one window to these units. We'll get them."

Sarah and her partner, Cheryl Yeaton, moved cautiously to where Mike stood, while the four patrolmen went to the back. Mike and the two women stationed themselves between vehicles, weapons drawn. Pete came across the parking lot, and Eddie and Harvey went with Arnie, approaching the door of Room 10. Eddie and Harvey flattened themselves, one on each side of the door, guns skyward. Arnie took the plastic key card from Pete and held it ready. He motioned Pete back and stepped to the side of the door, where Harvey was. Then he knocked firmly.

"Police! Open up," Arnie yelled.

Silence.

"You sure they're in there?" Eddie said softly.

They heard a faint sound, then a blast. Arnie

swore and shoved the key card into the lock, then pushed the door open hard. He went down on one knee, with his gun in both hands, and Harvey stepped quickly behind him, aiming into the room over his head.

Something hit Harvey hard in the chest, and he flew backward. He hit the edge of a concrete traffic barrier, and his breath whooshed out of him.

People shouted and gunfire erupted. He tried to roll over off the walkway, but it hurt too much, so he just covered his head with his left arm and tried to breathe.

The shooting subsided, and Sarah knelt beside him. "Harvey! Harvey, are you hit?"

He took his arm down, and that hurt, too. She was worried and kept glancing toward the motel.

"I don't know. It hurts like blazes."

Eddie crouched on his other side. "It's okay, Harv. We got them both."

"What happened?"

"They threw a pipe bomb out the back window."

"Anybody hurt?"

"Jimmy's got a pretty bad gash on his leg, and Ted Marston's got cuts and bruises, but nothing real bad. You okay?"

"It hurts."

"Where?"

"My back." He tried to sit up, but couldn't. He sank back, gasping, and Eddie opened the right side of his vest.

"I can't see any blood," Eddie said.

"I can't breathe."

Mike was there. "Harv, ambulance on the way. You okay, buddy?"

Eddie looked up, frowning. "He says it hurts, but I can't see anything."

"Probably bruising. Thank the Kevlar people. We'll get you to the hospital. Do you want me to call Jennifer?"

"She'll think it's worse than it is," Harvey groaned.

Sirens screamed in the background.

Arnie came from the motel room. "Mike, Bobby Nason's dead, and his brother's pretty bad."

"We need LeRoy," Mike said.

"It's an abdominal wound. We might lose him."

"Okay. Get Ted around here for the EMT's. They'll get Jimmy. Somebody with him?"

"Yeah, Cheryl. It's a nasty cut on his leg. I think there's shrapnel in it."

The sirens were ear-splitting.

"Call the medical examiner for Bobby," Mike yelled at Arnie.

When the ambulances cut their sirens, Harvey heard Mike say, "Take the prisoner first. One of my men will ride with him. Then get this guy—"

he gestured at Harvey, "and there's another man with a torn-up leg out back, and that guy over there has lacerations."

One team came to where Harvey was, and Sarah and Eddie stood back.

The EMTs threw questions at Harvey, and he tried to answer as they took his pulse and blood pressure.

Finally Mike came over again. "Can't you move this guy to Maine Medical? He can't breathe! He's gotta have cracked ribs at the least."

They put Harvey on a rolling stretcher, and he almost lost consciousness, the pain was so bad. Pulling air into his lungs was excruciating.

"Eddie, ride with him," Mike said. "I'll go tell Jennifer."

Sarah said, "I'll follow you in, Eddie."

Harvey was glad Eddie rode with him. It was reassuring to have him near his head, with his hand on Harvey's left shoulder. Eddie's badge hung down on a cord outside his vest, swinging as the ambulance navigated the turns and uneven pavement.

"You're gonna be okay, Harv," Eddie said.

"Thanks, buddy. If I'm not—"

"You will be."

Harvey nodded, but persisted. It was too important to leave unsaid. "If I'm not, you tell Jenny—" He winced.

"That you love her?"

"No. Well, besides that. Tell her it's true."

"What?"

"She'll know." He quit trying to keep his equilibrium and closed his eyes. A sudden stab of pain jolted him. "Yow! What are we doing?"

"IV line," said the EMT, inserting plastic tubing where the needle had penetrated the skin on the back of his right hand. "Just fluids."

The siren was muffled, but still obnoxious. Harvey looked up and saw that Eddie had pulled the crucifix he wore on a chain from inside his shirt, and his left hand clutched it. His right hand came down on Harvey's shoulder again.

Jennifer was disappointed when Harvey called, saying he would be late. He'd been working late a lot, but this seemed different, and she couldn't shake an uneasy feeling. She tried not to worry, but it kept gnawing at the edge of her thoughts as she changed into jeans and a sweat-shirt.

She had counted on seeing him. Underlying her calm facade was the need for his reassurance that she'd done the right thing. She'd actually quit her job. Mr. Owen had begged her to reconsider, but she'd told him with a tight smile that she would not stay. She had been offered another position. She didn't tell anyone it was in an airless office in the basement of the police station, typing old reports into their computer system. And after the maternity leave was over, what? How would she support herself then?

Somehow she had to find the stamina she'd need to call her parents and tell them. And she'd have to compile a résumé if she hoped to get a real job later. Yes, she definitely needed a shot of confidence from Harvey.

Beth and Ruthann drove up in Beth's car, with the babies in their car seats in the back. The trunk was full of boxes and suitcases. Rick followed in his mini-wagon, with a mattress crammed into the back. They took Ethan and Clarissa inside and started moving Beth's things in while Rick put the bed frame together.

It was nearly seven when they sat down to eat off paper plates.

"Where's Harvey tonight?" Rick asked.

"He was going to come, but he called me at five and said he had to stay late," Jennifer replied. "Would you ask the blessing, Rick?"

"Sure."

She added, "Could you also pray for Harvey? I'm just a little concerned about him and his partner tonight."

"Oh?"

"Well, this late assignment. It could be a drug raid or something. I just don't know."

They bowed their heads. Rick thanked God

for the food and for Beth's new living quarters and asked him to protect Harvey and the other officers on the job. Jennifer wished she could pray herself, but hearing Rick's petition made her feel a little better.

After they ate, Clarissa drooped on her mother's shoulder, half asleep. Rick and Ruthann began gathering up their belongings.

"Call if you find anything I forgot, and I'll pick it up tomorrow," Beth said, as Rick adjusted the babies' car seats.

"All right. You two enjoy your first night as roomies." Ruthann handed Beth a box of microwave popcorn, then kissed her and Jennifer on the cheek and settled into the front seat.

When they had left, Beth and Jennifer cleaned up the kitchen.

"Harvey said he'd call," Jennifer said as she wiped off the table. "We're supposed to go up to my parents' this weekend, but we haven't really settled the details."

"He'll call," Beth assured her.

"I think I'll get in the shower. Do you mind?"

"No, go ahead," Beth said. "Leave your phone out here. If he calls, I'll tell you. I just need to make my bed up."

Jennifer showered and washed her hair, then put on her terry cloth housecoat. She pulled out her hairdryer and started methodically drying her long hair. She was glad she hadn't cut it on impulse.

A knock came on the bathroom door. She shut off the hairdryer.

"Jennifer, there's a man here to see you."

She looked down at her bathrobe, and thought, *No way!*

She opened the door a crack. "I can't see Harvey like this. He'll have to wait while I get dressed."

"It's not Harvey," Beth whispered, clearly baffled.

Jennifer returned her look blankly, then shuddered as she remembered Billy Cassidy's unplanned visit. She stepped out into the short hallway and tiptoed to the corner and peeked around it. Mike Browning stood near her computer, looking at the Van Gogh print. Jennifer had a sinking feeling in her stomach, but she stepped into the room.

"Captain Browning?"

"Ms. Wainthrop," he smiled graciously, ignoring her wet hair and housecoat. "I'm sorry to bother you tonight, but Harvey's had a little mishap."

She froze where she was.

"He'll be all right, I think, but they took him to Maine Medical," Mike said.

Jennifer felt lightheaded. It was what she hadn't dared to think about.

Beth was beside her, her hand on her arm.

"Jennifer, sit down." She guided Jennifer to the computer desk, and she sat down with a thump, holding her bathrobe together tightly.

She looked up at Mike. "What's wrong with him?"

Mike's face was lined with concern. "Well, he took a shot on his bulletproof vest. Usually not too serious. Bruises and such. No bleeding. But we sent him over to be checked out. I can take you to the hospital if you like."

"Yes. Thank you. I'll have to get dressed."

She rushed into her bedroom and dropped the housecoat on the floor. Dressing rapidly in black slacks and a red cotton pullover, she fought back the panic that badgered her. She snatched her purse off the dresser and dashed back to the living room.

"Beth, I don't know when I'll be back."

"It's all right," Beth said. "I'll be praying."

In the car, Mike told her calmly how they had gone after the bomb makers. "We didn't want it to end this way, but they *will* resist."

Jennifer fumbled in her purse for a tissue. She realized she hadn't taken time to do anything with her hair, and it hung, slightly damp, over her shoulders. Mike sounded as if he were slightly annoyed with the Nason brothers. How could he be so calm, when several of his men had been injured?

She felt an overwhelming urge to pray, but she couldn't. God wouldn't hear those who didn't believe in him.

All at once, she knew she could. She believed God was real, whether Harvey did or not, that Jesus was God and had paid her debt with his life. She didn't have to wait any longer to speak to God. Silently, she began to beg him to spare Harvey's life.

When she opened her eyes, they had stopped at a traffic light, and Mike was eyeing her closely. "Miss Wainthrop, you and Harvey have been going to church. Do you believe in God?"

"Yes," she said, surprised at the conviction in her tone.

"I don't," he said frankly, "but my wife does. But I've been thinking, if there's a God, isn't it strange that he lets bad things happen to good people like Harvey?"

Jennifer swallowed, wondering how to respond. "There aren't any guarantees, but God is there, even when the worst happens."

She had talked for a long time about that very subject with Mrs. Rowland on Sunday night, after Harvey had left her at the parsonage. Jennifer could see now that God had been with her, had protected her when she encountered Billy Cassidy, and he would be with Harvey now. And no matter what happened at the hospital, God would give her the strength she needed so badly.

"Well, now, I believe in justice," Mike said. "How come the cops don't always win, and the crooks don't always end up in jail? God lets some people go to heaven and sends others to hell, for no reason I can see. Doesn't seem fair to me."

"It's *not* fair," Jennifer agreed. "We're all sinners. If it were fair, we'd all go to hell."

Mike drove in silence for a minute, then nodded. "See, now, that I can understand."

Chapter 23

At the hospital, they stripped Harvey down to his shorts and put all his things in a bag. By the time they had him down to his boxers, he was nearly unconscious from the pain in his chest and back. Then they did all the things the EMT's had done to him, all over again.

Eddie answered the questions for him, giving them Harvey's name, age, and address, and describing how he had been injured. Harvey just lay there and tried to hold it all together.

The ER doctor came in and looked him over, and Harvey gasped a request for his own doctor, Carl Turner. The nurse said she thought Dr. Turner was in the hospital, and they could have him paged.

Twenty minutes later, Carl came breezing in.

"Harvey Larson," he said reproachfully. "You're due for a checkup, old man. What are you doing in here tonight?" The ER doctor handed Carl a clipboard, and he scrutinized it for several seconds.

"Okay, let me look at you." Carl pulled the sheet down. "Contusions there," he murmured, poking Harvey's chest where it hurt. "Anything else?"

"My back."

Carl took hold of his hip and shoulder and started to roll him onto his side. Harvey yelled as the pain stabbed him, so Carl stopped, and felt along the back of his rib cage.

"You get shot in front or behind?"

"Front," said Eddie, "but it threw him, and he landed on a concrete parking barrier."

"That would do it." Carl touched Harvey in a place that made him want to suck air in, but it hurt too much to do that, so he just flinched and tried not to move at all.

"Okay, let's get a chest x-ray, then we'll talk." Carl walked out. Two technicians came in to take Harvey to the imaging department. Eddie left him as they went past the waiting room where Sarah had stayed.

Getting positioned for the x-rays was torture. Harvey wasn't a complainer, but he wished they had given him some ibuprofen first. When they took him back through the hall, he caught a glimpse of Mike. Jennifer was beside him, her eyes wide in her white face, her hair loose and full. He wanted badly to see her, but at the same time hated to have her see him so helpless.

Eddie brought her into the emergency room in the wake of the stretcher. One of the technicians smiled at Harvey. "Looks like your wife's here."

Jennifer had been crying, he could see, but

she pulled out a wobbly smile as she slowly approached the bed.

"Hey, I'm not dead." He tried to smile.

She stepped up and touched his hand, where the IV protruded. Two tears spilled over and tumbled down her cheeks. Eddie brought a stool over, and she sat.

"Are you okay?" she asked. "What happened?"

It was too hard to smile. "Feels like a mule kicked me. Guess I found out one of the duo was vincible."

Her lips twitched. "So, you got shot."

Eddie said, "Technically not. He took it on his vest."

"Thank God you wore the vest," Jennifer said fervently.

Harvey looked past her at Eddie. "You should take Sarah home."

Eddie shook his head. "It's okay."

"Go!" Harvey said hoarsely.

Eddie nodded deferentially and looked at Jennifer. "He's going to be all right. Really." He looked at Harvey.

"Go."

Eddie went away.

Harvey sighed and closed his eyes. Jennifer was still there, and he made the effort to open his eyes again and focus on her. Her hair was a flowing sheet of gold as she leaned toward him. She smiled tremulously, and he was able to grasp two of her fingers and give them a little squeeze.

Carl Turner came back, jaunty as ever. He had been Harvey's doctor for ten years, since the city had contracted with the HMO. He wasn't much older than Harvey, and they had developed a perverse sort of friendship.

"One fractured rib and a small pneumothorax," Carl said cheerfully.

"Which is?" asked Harvey.

"The rib nicked the lung, and it's about ten percent collapsed."

"A collapsed lung?" Jennifer stared at Carl in dismay.

Carl looked at her, then looked again.

"Can't be Mrs. Larson. I'd have known." He turned to Harvey expectantly.

"Jennifer," Harvey said. It was too painful to make a lengthy introduction.

Carl held out his hand to her. "I'm Carl Turner, Harvey's doctor. I'm pleased to meet you. Harvey's got part of a lung down, and a broken rib. He should be fine in a few days, but I think we'll keep him here overnight for observation. If things are stable in the morning, I'll release him." He bent over Harvey. "Hurts a lot, doesn't it?"

"Yup."

"We'll put some pain killer in your IV and tape your ribs up. Can't really do much else.

It'll be okay, but you'll be sore for a while." He turned to Jennifer. "Maybe you'd step into the waiting room and tell the captain. We'll send Harvey up to ICU on the third floor in a few minutes. You can see him up there."

Jennifer went, and Carl set to work, doing the tape job himself.

Mike Browning and a uniformed officer stood in the crowded waiting area. Mike held the plastic bag containing Harvey's clothes and gear. He introduced Jennifer to Nate Miller. "His partner Jimmy got his leg torn up," Mike said. "How's Harvey doing?"

"His lung is partly collapsed, and one rib is broken." Jennifer was unable to keep a slight quiver out of her voice.

"Sounds serious," Mike said with a scowl.

"They're putting him in the intensive care unit tonight, but the doctor says he can go home tomorrow. He seems to be in a lot of pain." Jennifer glanced around. "Did Eddie and Sarah leave?"

"Yeah, Eddie said he'll be back later and take you home."

"I guess I'll get going, Captain," said Nate. "They're keeping Jimmy a couple of days, but his wife's up there now. I'll come in and see him tomorrow."

"What about Ted?" asked Mike.

"They fixed him up, and he went home." Nate said good night and left.

"How about a cup of coffee?" Mike asked.

Jennifer didn't really want to go farther from Harvey, but there didn't seem to be a point in standing where they were. They walked down a hallway to the coffee shop. It was nearly deserted. Mike paid for their coffee, and they sat across from each other at a square table.

"This bomb thing is over now, Ms. Wainthrop," Mike said.

"You're sure the men you caught were the ones who tried to kill Harvey?"

"I'm sure. One of them left fingerprints on the bomb we got off Harvey's SUV. They threw a similar pipe bomb out the motel window when we knocked on their door. Two of my men got hurt by that one. It makes me mad, I'll tell you."

"Did they say why they did it? To Harvey, I mean?"

"We hope LeRoy Nason will tell us that, if and when he regains consciousness. If he can tell us who hired him and his brother to do the job, I will be very happy."

"So I don't have to check under my car anymore?"

"I don't think it's necessary." Mike drained his coffee cup. "So. Are you coming to work for the P.D.?"

"Yes, thank you, Captain." She could smile

then. "I appreciate the recommendation you gave me. I think it carried a lot of weight."

Upstairs in ICU, the nurses moved Harvey into a regular hospital bed. It didn't hurt quite so much since Carl had taped him up and the medication was beginning to take effect, but he wished they would just leave him alone and quit moving him.

One nurse bent over to check the data on his wristband against the chart. Her photo ID hung on a chain around her neck. "Sherri," he read. The picture looked just like her: short, dark hair, lively brown eyes, glasses, and a ready smile. She was nearly his age, he guessed, but she was wearing braces.

"I'll be taking care of you tonight," she said, like a waitress would. She checked his IV, then she and another nurse hooked him up to a fancy monitor. They stuck six electrodes on different parts of his chest with a special paste, between the bands of adhesive tape. The wires from them came together in a pigtail that fed into a cord that went to the monitor. Then they clipped a thing like a clothespin on the index finger of his left hand. A cord went from it to the monitor, too. They would have put a johnny on him, but he protested violently. Carl came in, told the nurses to leave him alone, and checked the monitor himself.

"I can't sleep with all this stuff on me." Harvey was finding it easier to talk, and he was feeling grouchy.

"Sure you can." Carl made a note on his clipboard.

"What are we looking at?" Harvey asked.

Carl touched the monitor screen with its three lines of data. "This is your heart rate." He pointed to the top row, where it said 74 on the right. "The middle one is respiration rate. Twenty-six is a little high, but your pneumothorax accounts for that. The bottom one is blood oxygen. That's what the finger clip measures. Ninety-five and fluctuating. That's not so good, hence your presence in ICU. This thing will automatically take your blood pressure every half hour, so the nurses don't have to bother you too much."

"Oh, the machine bothers me for them, in case they forget."

"Right. They've got a screen out at the desk that gives them all of this information, but they'll pop in on you once in a while to check your condition."

"Oh, joy."

"Don't complain. You're getting the best care. And if these numbers are better in the morning, you're out of here. Say, where did you find the gorgeous blonde?"

"Jennifer? At a software company. You heard

about the guy who disappeared? She worked with him."

"She's very ornamental."

"She's very sweet, too."

"Yeah?" Carl scribbled on the clipboard. "Is it serious?"

"Could be."

"Bring her over to see Margaret and me."

"You guys are never home."

"We can be. Call my office when you feel up to it, and we'll arrange something. Really. I think Margaret would like to meet her."

Mike and Jennifer appeared in the doorway. Mike stepped up to the bed, but Jennifer hung back a little, taking in the array of equipment connected to him and the flashing, humming monitor.

"So, is he all set for the night?" Mike asked, setting down the bag of Harvey's gear.

"Yes, I think he's as comfortable as possible, under the circumstances," Carl said.

"Okay, Harv, I'm going to check and see if they think LeRoy will make it, then I'm heading out. Just take it easy and rest up. You're off for the rest of the week, at least."

"Thanks, Mike."

"Thank you, Captain," Jennifer said as he turned toward the door.

"Anytime."

Carl said to Jennifer, "You can stay as late as

you want. The nurses will probably make a fuss at ten o'clock, but Harvey's a special patient of mine."

Harvey laughed and winced. Jennifer looked very serious.

"I'll be in on my rounds in the morning, sometime between nine and ten," Carl said. "I'll see you then, Harvey. Good night, Jennifer."

"Thanks, Carl," Harvey said.

"No problem."

Jennifer still stood by the bed. Harvey patted the mattress with his IV hand.

"It would hurt you if I sat there." She pulled a chair over close to the bed and sat.

"You're too far away." The bed was in the high position. She stood up and looked at the buttons on the inside of the bed rail, then pushed one that moved the whole bed down.

"Better," he said. "Put my head up." She did, until he was sitting most of the way up. Now they were almost on a level. She sat there, looking at him, a bit glassy-eyed. He was afraid she was going to cry again, and he wasn't sure he could handle that. He had the feeling he would drift off to oblivion soon, thanks to the pain killers, and there were things that urgently needed resolution first. Anticipation has its limitations, he decided.

"Come here, gorgeous."

She smiled a little and leaned forward.

"Closer. I want to kiss you."

She sat still for a second, just long enough that he wondered if he'd said the wrong thing.

"Harvey, I—I need to tell you something."

"What is it, gorgeous?"

She swallowed and leaned closer, stroking his wrist gently. "I've decided." She looked at him quickly, from beneath her lashes. "On the way over here, I realized that I believe it's all true, and I—I could pray for you then. And I'm not sorry. I just—" She gulped. "I'll be relying on God now, whatever comes."

He closed his eyes for an instant, with a prayer of gratitude that was less verbal than a wave of feeling. When he opened them, she was a little out of focus because of his tears.

"Come here."

She stood and bent toward him, holding her shimmering hair back with one hand. She closed her eyes as her lips brushed his so softly he barely felt their warmth. He tightened his grip on her arm and kept her there until she opened her eyes. She was so close, and her look was so tender, that he couldn't frame words. She put her hand to his cheek and kissed him again, sweetly, and her hair fell all around him, like curtains shutting out the world.

His breathing seemed more regular and comfortable, but he looked vulnerable in the bed, and he lay watching her from beneath his drooping eyelids. Jennifer wondered if she should have kissed him when he asked her to, at least until she knew what he thought about her newfound belief.

The tears welled in her eyes again as the strain of all that had happened that evening seemed to break. She sat down in the chair and put her hands on the bed rail, and her head on her hands. It frustrated her that she couldn't keep from crying. That wasn't what he needed from her now.

He reached up very slowly and stroked her hair. When she could control her sobbing, she sat up and got a box of tissues off the night table.

"Sorry." She stepped into the tiny bathroom with the tissue box, blew her nose, and washed her hands. Then she looked in the mirror. Her puffy, red eyes disfigured her face. She ran cold water and splashed a little on her cheeks, then took one of the hospital towels that she probably wasn't supposed to touch, and used it. Still red and puffy, but inevitable. She went back, carrying the tissue box, and sat down.

"Sorry." She tried to look composed, smiled the best she could, and said, businesslike, "So, you feeling better?"

"Some." They looked at each other. He wiggled his fingers a little, and she reached for his hand.

"I love you, you know," he said.

She started crying again, thinking, *This is so awful. I should be laughing, not crying.*

He caught the ends of her hair, where it fell over the bed rail, and let them slide through his fingers.

Jennifer smiled. "I didn't have time to fix it when Mike came. Sorry."

"Don't ever be sorry. It's fantastic."

She laughed. "Mona Lisa?"

"No, that's not glorious enough." She closed her eyes, but she didn't move away from his caress. He stroked the locks he could reach. "The Jennifer Look, I guess."

She smiled.

His blue, blue eyes were riveted on her face. "I believe it, too. You know that, don't you?"

She nodded slowly. "I hoped."

"I do. I wanted to talk it over with you, but I was afraid I'd mess things up somehow, if you weren't ready to decide."

She took a deep breath. She'd been terrified of learning the truth, but at the same time she'd known she could bear it now. "*He who dwelleth in the secret place of the Most High shall abide under the shadow of the Almighty*. I couldn't believe you would give me that passage to read if you weren't dwelling there yourself."

He nodded just a little, and set his teeth,

closing his eyes briefly. Jennifer touched his temple and lightly traced the fine lines back from his eye to his hairline. "You hurt a lot, don't you?"

"Some."

She smiled. "You don't have to be tough for me. I cried buckets when Mike told me. I was so scared, but I kept thinking of that psalm. *Thou shalt not be afraid for the terror by night, nor for the arrow that flieth by day*. I knew the Lord was going to bring us through this, even if—well, even if it was—really bad."

There was a soft knock at the open door, and Pastor Rowland came in.

"Harvey," he said, his eyes lighting up with pleasure. "I'm glad to see you looking so well. I was afraid you might be unconscious."

He approached the bed, and Harvey said, "Pastor, how did you know?"

"Beth Bradley called me. I hope it's all right. I know it's late."

"I'm glad you came."

Jennifer blinked back her tears as she greeted him, and Mr. Rowland went to the other side of the bed and sat down, asking for the particulars on his injury. Jennifer sat quietly, but now and then a tear rolled down her cheek, and she was emptying the box of tissues rapidly.

"I should call Beth," she said. There were signs everywhere prohibiting the use of cell phones in the ICU, so she used the phone on the night table. She told Beth that Harvey was doing well, and that she'd be home late, when Eddie came for her. When she hung up, she asked Harvey if there was anyone else she should call.

"Maybe my sisters," he said, then, "No, let's wait. I can call them from home tomorrow. They don't need to get all worked up tonight. It's not that big a deal."

"I'd better call my folks in the morning, too," she said. "If they hear about it on the news, Mom will be wild."

"I've been praying for you two all week," said Pastor Rowland.

"You mean because of the bomb?" Harvey asked.

"No—well, partly that. I've certainly prayed for your safety. But mostly, I've been praying for your salvation, that God would show you how much you need him."

"The helmet of salvation," Harvey said.

"Yes. The breastplate saved your life today, but you still need the helmet, Harvey."

Harvey smiled. "Pastor, we're a jump ahead of you. Jennifer and I were just discussing how we've trusted in Christ." He looked at the pastor gravely. "A few days ago, I came to the conclusion that God has to be real. He's out there, I'm sure of it. And I couldn't put off the decision any longer."

Pastor Rowland smiled. “That’s good news.”

Harvey nodded. “I believe it. The whole thing. Jesus has to be God, and he has to be the one who pays for our sins. Nothing else makes sense.” He looked quickly at Jennifer. “Jenny was just telling me she reached the same conclusion tonight. Our quest is over.” He reached for her hand.

The pastor cleared his throat. “I’m so very happy to hear you say that. May I go over a few scriptures with you?”

Harvey nodded, but he kept his eyes on Jennifer. The pastor went through a lot of the same things they had talked about the week before.

“So, Harvey, you understand all this and believe it?” the pastor said at last.

“Yes, I do.”

“And Jennifer?”

“Yes.”

She felt suddenly that it was like a wedding, and they were taking a vow to each other and God. She squeezed Harvey’s hand and didn’t try to stop the tears when the pastor prayed.

Pastor Rowland left a little after ten o’clock, and Harvey and Jennifer sat there for fifteen minutes, mostly looking at each other and smiling, waiting for Eddie to come back. Finally Harvey said, “I do love you, Jenny. I meant that.”

She took a deep breath. What she felt for him was deeper, more powerful than any emotion she had ever known. For the rest of her life, she wanted to do everything she could to help him and make him happy.

She looked at his hand, holding hers tight, and whispered, "I love you, too."

"Come up here." His eyes were very, very serious. She stood, and he pulled her down gently. She nearly lost her balance, trying not to touch his chest and hurt him, or dislodge the electrodes. He kissed her lingeringly, and her joy ran riot.

A piercing noise came from the monitor on the far side of the bed. Jennifer jumped upright and looked at it, then back at Harvey.

"What's going on?"

"I don't know. I'm still not dead."

Sherri the nurse came bustling in, and went right to the monitor and turned the sound off.

"Let's see here," she said, scrutinizing the three bands of data. "What are you up to? You set the alarm off. You okay?" She looked sharply at Harvey through her glasses.

He shrugged. "Yeah."

"Well, if your heart rate goes up quickly, or your blood oxygen goes down too fast, the alarm goes off. You got that?"

"Okay." Harvey looked a little guilty.

"So come up for air!" She laughed and left the room.

• • •

When Eddie came back, Harvey had him locate his key ring and asked him to take his clothes and gear home and to bring him clean clothes in the morning.

"Just jeans and a T-shirt," he said, but Jennifer corrected him.

"You'd better have a button-up shirt. You might not be able to get your arms up over your head."

"I'll get the bed set up," Eddie said.

"What bed?" asked Jennifer.

Eddie looked at Harvey, abashed. "Uh, Harvey bought a new bed."

Jennifer looked at Harvey, remembering her promise to Eddie. She wasn't supposed to let on that he had blabbed certain things. She smiled. "Don't tell me you've been sleeping on the couch?"

Eddie started to say something, and Harvey scowled at him. Suddenly, Jennifer knew that Harvey didn't have a couch, either.

"I just didn't like the old bed," he said. "I gave it to my neighbor and bought a new one this morning, but it's not set up yet."

"I'll see if I can get Mr. Jenkins or somebody else in the neighborhood to help me," said Eddie.

"Oh, my razor's in my locker." Harvey was barely keeping his eyes open.

"I'll get it in the morning," Eddie said. "Good night."

Harvey didn't respond. Eddie looked at Jennifer. "I'll wait in the hall." He went out, carrying the bag of clothes.

Jennifer leaned over him. "Sleep well, Harvey."

"I think I will," he said groggily.

"Are you hurting? Do you want me to tell the nurse?"

"No." He moved his hand a little and winced. She bent toward him, and he gently grasped a hank of her hair. "Good night, gorgeous. I'll miss you."

She smiled and held her hand against his whiskery cheek. "I'll miss you, too." She didn't kiss him again. His heart rate was slow and even, and she tiptoed out.

Chapter 24

Harvey awakened when a new nurse came in at six o'clock and checked all the medical equipment and made notes on his chart. He couldn't go back to sleep. He kept thinking about the shoot-out, and how it might have gone differently. The image of Jennifer crystallized, her anxious eyes the turbulent gray of Casco Bay in a storm. He sent up a swift prayer of thanks, and asked God to give him the thing dearest to his heart.

Jennifer and Beth walked in at eight-forty-five. Jennifer was wearing jeans and a blue shirt. Her hair was down again. Harvey hoped he beamed strongly enough to convey his approval.

"Hey, gorgeous!"

Her smile dazzled him. "Good morning!"

"Hi, Beth." Harvey pushed the button to raise the head of the bed.

Beth took in the heavy stubble on his face, the cords and electrodes, and the monitor that hummed serenely.

"You look awful."

He smiled and said to Jennifer, "You've got a mouthy roommate."

"Be nice," Jennifer warned him. "She took a personal day off from school to help us."

Eddie came to the door carrying a duffel bag, and Jennifer introduced him to Beth.

"They may throw us out," Beth said. She arranged chairs for herself and Jennifer. "They're pretty strict about visitors in ICU, aren't they?"

Harvey shrugged. "Carl hasn't come in yet. I can't wait to get out of here."

"You sound better." Jennifer sat down close to him.

"I'm sore, but I feel a lot better." To prove it, he reached out and caught her hand and held it. He couldn't suppress his smile, and she smiled back.

Beth carried the conversation, telling about moving into the house with Jennifer the night before and Mike's arrival with news of Harvey's injury. Finally Carl stuck his head in.

"What's this, a party?" He walked over to the monitor. "How you doing this morning, Harvey?"

"A lot better. I'm still plenty sore, but at least I'm breathing."

Carl turned and smiled charmingly at Beth and Jennifer. "I'll ask these lovely ladies to please move the party across the hall to the family waiting room. We'll make a quick examination, and if all goes well, the patient will be going home."

As Jennifer, Beth, and Eddie walked into the hall, a nurse came in and pulled the bed curtains and stood next to Carl. He poked and prodded

Harvey, but not too hard, and listened quite a while to his right lung.

"Okay, I'm going to have you sit up on the side of the bed, so I can listen to your back."

He put the head of the bed up more, until Harvey was sitting almost upright. "Now, swing your legs over the side and see if you can sit up on your own."

Agony, but Harvey was determined to pass Carl's test and go home. Carl put the stethoscope to his back, below his right shoulder blade. "Breathe as deeply as you can." After several seconds, Carl probed the taped area with gentle fingers. Harvey tried not to flinch.

"Okay." Carl scribbled on the chart, then looked at the nurse. "Let's get the IV out and take the monitor off. Harvey, I'm sending you home in the tender care of Ms. Wainthrop. Take ibuprofen for the pain, and I'm giving you a prescription for Vicodin at night. Take it easy for a few days. If there's any sharp pain in the lung area, call me."

The nurse reached for the IV needle and yanked it out.

"Yow!"

"Sorry." She produced gauze and a Band-Aid from somewhere. "Put a little pressure on that, please."

"You got something against cops?" Harvey asked.

"I love cops." She pulled the electrodes off his chest, and Carl switched the monitor off.

"Don't try to walk alone today, Harvey."

"Can I get dressed?"

"You'd better. You can't go home like that."

"Ha, ha."

"From whom would you like assistance?" he asked, "Your efficient nurse, Kimberley, the stunning Ms. Wainthrop, or—"

"Just send my pal Eddie back in here," Harvey grumbled.

"Will do." Carl handed him the prescription form and held out his hand. "Make an appointment with me for two weeks from now, and when you call we'll set up dinner with you and Goldilocks."

Harvey shook his hand, and Carl and the nurse left. Eddie came back and helped him get into clean jeans and a short-sleeved khaki shirt. He was stiff, and putting his arms into the sleeves hurt. He was glad Jennifer had nixed the T-shirt. He sat down, and Eddie put his socks and shoes on for him. Then he had to go through the excruciating pain of standing up again. Finally, he was dressed.

"I was going to shave, but I don't know if I can."

"Grow your beard for a couple of days," Eddie counseled.

Harvey didn't like the sound of that, now that

he and Jennifer had made lip contact, but he didn't say anything. Eddie went across the hall for Beth and Jennifer. The three of them gathered up Harvey's things, and the nurse brought a wheelchair. Harvey felt silly getting into it, but he didn't want to try walking down miles of hallways.

As they pushed him out of ICU, Eddie nodded toward another room.

"LeRoy Nason's in there. Doesn't look real good, but he's hanging on."

Jennifer brought her car to the hospital entrance, and Eddie helped him get in.

At the apartment building, Eddie practically hauled him up the stairs, one at a time, and pain grabbed Harvey with every effort. Two thirds of the way up, he said, "If I ever get up there, I'm never coming down."

"You should have come to my place," said Eddie.

"What good would that do? You live on the third floor."

"Yeah, but we have an elevator."

"Which is broken," Harvey said.

"No, they fixed it."

"After five years? Now you tell me." He looked up at the landing. "We're closer to the top than the bottom."

"We can do it," Eddie said.

He gave Jennifer Harvey's keys, and had her

and Beth go ahead. Jennifer unlocked the door, and Harvey thought, *Here we go. She's going to see the beast's lair.*

Jennifer and Beth waited for them in the hall. Eddie and Harvey limped into the kitchen. Harvey looked around. There was a tablecloth on his new table, and a healthy houseplant in the center. The counter and sink were spotless. He looked at Eddie.

"Mrs. J.," he said softly. "I told her Jennifer might come here today."

Harvey nodded.

The living room could have looked better. Harvey wished he'd had time to pick out a sofa. There were the three chairs, the ugly coffee table, and his computer setup, plus the board bookshelves and the two new barrister's bookcases. Eddie or Rebecca had put his recent book acquisitions in the new shelves, so there were no piles on the floor. On the coffee table were another plant and that day's *Press Herald*. He wished he had some art on the walls. There used to be a sampler Grandma Lewis had made, and a Matisse print, but they had gone with Carrie.

Jennifer and Beth trailed along behind them, taking it in.

"I knew you'd have lots of bookshelves," Jennifer said when she entered the living room. "Where do you want your razor?"

"Uh, in the bathroom, I guess. Just leave it on the sink." The bathroom shouldn't be *too* bad. He looked at Eddie, just in case.

"She cleaned everything," Eddie assured him.

Harvey stood in the bedroom doorway a moment. The sleigh bed was made up with sheets and the new log cabin quilt. He glanced at the dresser. Eddie had set all his gear on top: badge and gun, wallet, phone, handcuffs, and notebook. Harvey stifled the impulse to go over and rearrange them.

"Sit," said Eddie.

Harvey gingerly lowered himself to the edge of the bed. Eddie knelt and took his shoes off. Jennifer and Beth peeked through the doorway.

"What a beautiful bed," said Beth. "Is it an antique?"

Eddie caught his eye and winked.

"No," Harvey said, "it's a reproduction."

"Okay," said Eddie, "can you swing your feet up and lie down?"

"I think I want a shower."

"Better rest a while, Harv."

"Okay."

"Do you want your clothes off?"

"No. And you don't all have to stay. I'll be fine."

Jennifer came into the room and stood over him, looking at him with serious, gray eyes. "I'd like to stay a while. You're not supposed to try to get up by yourself. You'll need help."

Eddie took the prescription form from the dresser. "I'm going to go get your pills, then I'll come back, Harv. If you want to take a shower, I'll help you then."

"That's good, Eddie." He lay back, realizing how tired he was.

Eddie left, and Beth came to the bedroom doorway. "Harvey, your neighbor downstairs says she's sending chicken soup up for lunch. She wants to know how many people are eating here."

"Well, if Eddie comes back, four, I guess. Are you staying?"

"If you guys want me."

"I think—" Jennifer hesitated. "I want to stay, but I'd feel kind of funny being here alone with you. I mean—we don't want to give people the wrong impression."

Harvey said, "Beth, do you have any experience as a chaperone?"

She smiled. "Can I have free rein in the kitchen?"

"Anything you want."

"Great." She disappeared.

Jennifer went around the bed and sat down on the extreme edge.

"Is this okay?" she asked.

"No. Come closer."

"Not without my duenna."

"I can barely move."

"You're okay," she said. "But you should be asleep."

Harvey took a deep breath and winced. "Did you call your parents?"

"Yes, and they are very concerned about you. Do you still want to go up this weekend, if you feel better?"

"Sure."

"Great. I told Mom we might. I'll call her again tomorrow if it looks like a go." She punched up the pillow on her side of the bed and leaned against it, sitting up against the headboard. "This is a nice bed."

Harvey smiled. "You know what I'd really like you to do for me?"

"What?" Suspicion tinged her voice.

"Go to the store where I got this and pick out a sofa for me. They've got hundreds of them, and it's overwhelming."

"What do you like?"

"I never thought about it. No flowers."

"Something masculine looking?"

"Not necessarily. Something that will look good for a long time and be comfortable to stretch out on, I guess. Whatever looks good to you."

"I'll go with you when you're on your feet."

"Okay." He thought of a small embarrassment that might occur. "Don't tell Eddie, though."

"Why not?"

"Mmm, he'd just think I was nuts."

"Nuts to buy furniture?"

"No, it's just something I said to him yesterday. Forget it. He'd understand." He looked at her, sitting there so serenely. They had made a lot of progress in the trust department. "I love you, Jenny."

She smiled.

"Now come over here. I'll be good."

She shook her head, but she was still smiling.

He sighed. "So, you gave your notice at Coastal?"

"I did."

"And?"

"They seemed a little upset, but it's in my contract."

"Did they want you to stay longer?"

"I think so. Mr. Owen called me in later and offered me a raise."

"Wow."

"I turned him down graciously."

"What did you tell them today?"

"That I needed a day off. It's the first time I've ever missed work, but personal days are in my contract, too." Her eyes clouded. "Mr. Owen was really pretty nice when I gave him my resignation, but Mr. Rainey wasn't happy."

“Of course not. You’re their best designer.”
“Maybe. I think they just want me there to keep making security traps, not to design new programs.”
“I wish I could see that secret program.”
“I thought maybe I could copy it all to a terabyte flash drive and bring it to you, but now I don’t know if even that much memory would hold it.”
“It’s too risky.”
She nodded. “You’re right. They’d be able to tell if it was downloaded to another computer or device. They’ve been super vigilant since we’ve had security breaches.” She raised her chin, her gray eyes solemn. “Harvey, I thought of a way you could see the program. Mike, too, if he wants to. You could even show it to that man you met from the CIA.”
“Really?” He tried to turn toward her, but it was too painful, and he lay back on the pillow. “How?”
“You could get online on your computer here, or at the police station, and go into Coastal’s framework during business hours. If we agreed on a time, I could be at work there, looking at the program. I can show you a trick that will let you access what I’m working on.”
Harvey stared at her keenly. “This is actually possible?”
“Yes. It’s the partners’ nightmare that someone will do that.”

"I've wondered. It would be dangerous for you, though."

"Or for you. They'd see the tracer afterward."

"Similar to a tracer on a phone call?"

"Yes."

Harvey swallowed. "You mentioned the security breaches before, but I didn't realize they could follow it back. How specific is it?"

"They're pretty good."

"And you put tracers in all your security protocol?"

"Yes, we do on everything at Coastal."

Harvey's brain was overloading. "So . . ." He looked over at her. "What about on the personnel records? Do they have tracers?"

"Of course. Everything. It's nothing new."

"So they knew it was me who hacked into your personnel file?"

Jennifer breathed in sharply. "The background check you did on me."

"May sixth, the day I asked you to lunch. Did they know it was me?"

She considered for a moment. "They never told me, if they did. I didn't see it myself. Tom Henderson would be the one to report it. But they had me go in a few days later and strengthen the security. There had been another breach. Some hacker—" She broke off, staring at him.

Harvey closed his eyes. "I looked at Tom Henderson's personnel file and e-mail that

Friday night, after you told me what he'd said to Jane. I went and questioned him, and something didn't seem right. He asked my name, and all of a sudden he got real cocky. Would he have known that first breach came from the police station?"

"Well, yes, of course."

"Not me personally? Because I questioned him the day after I did the background check, and just hours after my car blew up."

She flopped back on the pillow. "If they tried, they could pinpoint the computer it came from."

"It was my computer, the same one you put the flagging program on. After I questioned Henderson, I went back to the station and broke into his records at Coastal. After that, they made you tighten security. And someone put another bomb on my new Explorer."

She rolled over on her stomach and looked hard at him, resting her chin on her hands, elbows on the bed. Her hair collapsed around her on the quilt. "You think Tom Henderson hired the Nasons to kill you?"

"Not Henderson. He's just the messenger. He told the bosses I'd looked at their files the day after Nick Dunham's car was found. I am such an idiot."

"No."

"Yes. I knew about tracers. I just didn't think they'd be so specific and so pervasive."

"It's a software company," she said gently.

"Yeah." He shook his head. *Idiot.*

"So, you think Mr. Owen, Mr. Rainey, and Mr. Channing wanted to kill you?"

"Maybe. Someone at Coastal, anyway, if they thought I was really after their secret program, or that I suspected they'd killed Nick Dunham."

"But the only thing you got the first time was the main menu on company records, then personnel, then my file, right?"

He tried to remember. "That's right. Your contract, too. And then Tom's personnel file and his e-mail." He lay staring up at his bedroom ceiling, going over it in his mind. How could he have been stupid enough not to realize they would know? He looked at her. "You're saying I could actually download that program?"

"Well, they keep all the programs on their cloud account, which we minions can't access without their assistance. When they get ready to send a program to the client, they used to transfer it to CD's. Now most of them are sent electronically, unless it's a program that will be sold commercially in stores."

He frowned. "If I did access it, they'd know I did it, and they'd guess that you let me. I wouldn't let you take the risk."

"I do think they're keeping an eye on me," she said. "Especially since I told them I'm quitting. And it's no secret that the cop who's bothering them has been buying me flowers and squiring me all over town . . ."

"Way too dangerous," Harvey said.

She nodded. "I'm supposedly finished with the special project. I shouldn't have had it yesterday, really. If I asked for it again, they might think it was a little too-too."

Yes, Harvey thought, *and if they caught you, you'd end up like Nick.*

She was quiet for a minute, and he reached over and touched her hand. "I love you. No matter what."

"Do you really think my bosses are spies?"

"No. Right now, I think they're greedy capitalists who saw a chance to make a bundle by selling sensitive material to a foreign state."

"And you also think they had Nick killed."

He sighed. "I don't know what other explanation there could be. You saw the evidence that Nick was working on that program. If they suspected he knew too much about it . . . well, like I said, it would be too dangerous for you to start poking around that program again. Are you planning to go to work tomorrow?"

"Yes. I have to finish out my two weeks."

He nodded. "Just stay away from that program, okay, gorgeous? I'm in no condition to kick down doors and rescue maidens in distress."

She laughed, and just hearing it lifted his spirits.

"You'd better have a nap now," she said.

"I think I'd better update Mike on all this."

She went to the dresser for his phone. He started to reach for it, but a pain caught him.

"You do it," he said.

He inched over a little, wincing, so she'd have enough room to sit on the edge of the bed near him. She selected Mike's number, then held the phone up to his ear. Mike answered.

"Hi, Mike. It's Harvey."

"Doc Turner let you go home?"

"Yeah. Listen, Jennifer just gave me some information that could be related to the case we're wrapping up. Could you possibly come over to my place today?"

"I could be there by two."

"Sounds good."

Jennifer hung up for him and took the phone back to the dresser. She sat down close to him again, and he resisted the temptation to play with her hair.

"Harvey, is this something we can pray about?"

Inside him, something that had been out of joint for a long time fell into place. This was a preview of what life would be like with Jennifer. He hoped he lived a long time, and that he would be allowed to spend it close to her.

"Absolutely," he breathed.

A few minutes later, Beth knocked on the door jamb and looked in. "Lunch is served. Do you want it in here, Harvey, or do you want to try to come to the kitchen?"

"I think I need to get up and move around a little." With Jennifer's help, he was able to sit up. Standing was the worst. Beth brought a straight chair in for him to hold on to, and he clenched his teeth and stood up. He went slowly to the kitchen, with his left arm across Jennifer's shoulders. Before sitting down, he sneaked a kiss just in front of her ear, when Beth's back was turned.

Eddie showed up just after Beth asked the blessing, and she jumped up and set another place for him. They had Mrs. Jenkins' homemade soup, and Beth had managed to find the ingredients for biscuits.

"You need groceries, Harvey," she told him.

"We could go to the store," Jennifer said.

"Yeah, that's good. Eddie's going to help me get a shower."

After lunch, the two women left, and Harvey brought Eddie up to speed on the Dunham case.

He didn't stay in the shower long, because he was afraid the adhesive would start to peel, but it felt good, and he washed off the residue of paste where the electrodes had been. When he got out, Eddie helped him dress and gave him a dose of ibuprofen.

"Get some rest while you can," Eddie said. He

opened the bed, and Harvey crumpled into it. Eddie left him with just the sheet over his legs, and went into the living room. Harvey heard the newspaper rustling for a while, then fell asleep.

Chapter 25

Mike sat backward on the straight chair, with his arms crossed on the back of it. He listened closely as Harvey, lying back on his pillow, outlined the concerns he had about Coastal Technology. Jennifer was still a little in awe of the captain, and she sat next to Eddie, on the far side of the bed.

Harvey asked, "So, what do you think of a software company that makes programs so secret their employees don't know what they do, and so secure I can't crack into them?"

"Pentagon contract," said Mike.

"That's what Jennifer thought, until they brought a fellow in to translate the instructions into Arabic and Farsi."

Mike whistled. "Could be big. And the data we've been getting on this Massal character you asked about doesn't make me sleep any better. Tell me more about the company, Ms. Wainthrop."

"Please call me Jennifer. Coastal Technology is about ten years old. I've been there more than two years. Almost three. There are about two dozen employees. I think two of the partners, Rainey and Channing, were friends who decided to go into business together. Mr. Owen is older.

I wouldn't be surprised if they brought him in for a more stable image, or to spot them some capital."

"Local boys?"

"I'm not sure. Mr. Channing has a New York connection, I think."

"What kind of software do they produce?"

"They generate sophisticated programs for a small company. We've done a lot of industrial and retailing programs, several for municipal infrastructure, and at least a couple of military jobs. One I worked on was a buoy tracking system for the Coast Guard."

"And your responsibility is . . . ?"

"I started out developing programs, but lately they've had me doing security for all the programs that other people create. They've kind of forced me to specialize in security programming. I'm starting to hate it, especially since that's what we think made them try to kill Harvey."

Mike said, "You lost me. You think they're the ones who hired Nason?"

She looked at Harvey, and he said contritely, "It's my fault, I guess. I made a mistake when I first met Jennifer."

"What kind of mistake?" Mike asked, with a *What now?* expression on his face.

Harvey sighed and looked at the wall, then back at Mike. "I used my computer at work to check Jennifer out. I just wanted to find out if she was as terrific as she seemed."

"Harv, the Priority Unit is not a dating service."

Harvey looked penitent, and Jennifer longed to reassure him, but the time didn't seem right, with his stern boss glaring at him.

"I know. I'm sorry, Mike. I've already apologized to Jennifer. The point is, stupid as it was, I did it. I looked at her credit record and some other stuff, including her personnel record at Coastal."

"When did this take place?"

"May sixth, the day after they found Nick Dunham's car. Remember, I told you I was doing a background check that afternoon? Well, Jennifer was the subject."

"And you had to break their security codes to do that."

"Yes. They weren't nearly as complicated as the ones they put on their clients' programs. It took me a little while, but I got in and accessed her file. I didn't think about the program having a tracer, which was extremely careless of me."

"A tracer? Like on a phone line?"

Jennifer spoke up. "The tracer is standard on security systems. It follows the breach back to the point of origin. The new one on the secret program we were talking about would even trace an attempted breach, successful or not."

"I don't understand how that's possible," said Mike.

"It works sort of like caller ID."

"And I should have known that," Harvey said. "I probably *did* know it, I just ignored it because I wanted my own way. I thought I was smarter than they were. Well, we all know now that I'm not."

Mike stood and began to pace. "Let me get this straight. Harvey, you went to investigate the disappearance of Nick Dunham and met Jennifer. A few weeks later, you tapped into her company's files. They traced it back to you. It made them nervous that the PD was looking at their files, so they hired an ex-con to get rid of you. While Bobby was busy blowing up your car, they put Jennifer to work making their security more secure."

Eddie and Jennifer were quiet. Harvey said, "Does it make sense?"

"Maybe. *If* the partners had guilty consciences, and *if* they thought we were onto them." Mike walked over to the window and looked out. "Is there anything concrete that we can check on, to see if this cockamamie theory has any merit?"

"Jennifer's seen the whole program now She's sure it will give the client military capabilities."

"How so?"

Jennifer hesitated. "It seemed to me that this

program would let them access other files, say Pentagon files. Parts of it had to do with military operations, covert exercises, and materiel stockpiling. There was a lot more. I didn't dare copy any of it, and I was a little out of my field."

"Jennifer and I discussed it," Harvey said. "If she had copied any part of that program or sent me pieces of it, the bosses would know immediately."

Mike stood frowning and leaning on the windowsill.

"There's the kid," Harvey said. "Hamad, the translator. Jennifer gave me his name Monday, but I couldn't find anything on him, and I haven't heard back from the State Department yet."

"Well, I can check with them."

"Get on my computer in the office," Harvey said. "I checked his name first thing to see if he matched any lists of terrorists, diplomatic personnel, or convicted felons, but nothing turned up that I could identify with him. It's a fairly common name, and it would help if we had his first name. Jennifer thought it might be Rashid, but I haven't gotten any solid hits on that for the particular guy."

He struggled to sit up, gave up, and sank back with a groan. "I also put out a request for information on him with all the national and international law enforcement databases."

"You have that much clout?" Jennifer asked in surprise.

"Yes, I can exchange data with several government agencies."

Mike said, "We've spent a lot of time building up Harvey's credentials in the computer field. It's paid off, but not on an international thing like this."

Jennifer said slowly, "Maybe Jane Morrow knows Hamad's first name. She does some of the translating in the office—German and Italian—and she seems to keep tabs on every man who comes through the door. It's possible she's met Hamad. I'll ask her tomorrow."

"Do you trust her?" Mike asked.

Jennifer hesitated.

"She talks too much," Eddie said.

"I think I could make it sound innocent, especially if I get her talking about guys first." Jennifer looked to Harvey for approval.

"Be discreet."

She nodded.

"No sense arousing suspicions at this point," Mike said.

"Take me to the office," said Harvey. "I need to get back on this thing now."

Mike shook his head. "You're wiped out."

"Don't you think we should move on this?" Harvey insisted.

"I'll contact the State Department and the CIA.

I'll also drop by the hospital and see if LeRoy Nason can talk. You're not coming back to work until Dr. Turner gives the word."

Harvey let him win that round, and Mike stood up.

"Eddie, you coming in tomorrow?"

"Yeah. I just wanted to make sure Harvey was all right today."

"That's fine. We'll talk later."

Jennifer walked to the door with Mike. Before he went out, he looked at her keenly. "You take good care of Harvey. He's my best detective."

She nodded.

"Harvey's the last man I would have expected to be checking out a girl on city time." Mike smiled. "I'm just glad you didn't stuff him in the reject bin when you found out."

"I'm sorry, Captain." She knew her face was scarlet.

Mike nodded. "Well, Harvey needed a stabilizing influence in his life. Maybe you're it. You and God, I guess."

She swallowed, groping for a response.

"So why *did* God let Harvey get shot?" he asked.

She looked at him quickly, but Mike was serious. "He let the Nason brothers get shot, too."

"Hmm. Right."

"I don't know *why,* but I think it's all part of

something bigger, something we can't see. I can trust God for that."

Mike nodded pensively. "My wife would say that." He winked at her. "Now, if I could just find a nice young lady to take Eddie in hand!" He went out.

Beth had put away the groceries and baked brownies. They went back to Harvey's room with a tray of brownies and milk for four. Eddie and Harvey were arguing over whether Harvey should be alone that night, and finally it was settled that Eddie would sleep there. He would go to his mother's for supper and come back by seven o'clock. Beth and Jennifer would stay until he returned.

"Do you want to go to prayer meeting tonight?" Beth asked Jennifer.

"I'd like to." Jennifer looked at Harvey.

"Take notes for me, gorgeous." He sounded groggy.

"Sure."

Beth said, "We'll wait until Eddie gets back. It won't matter if we walk in a few minutes late."

"You don't have to baby-sit me," Harvey said fretfully.

Jennifer thought maybe her presence all day was too much of a good thing for him. "Do you want us to leave now?"

"Not really."

She smiled. "Then don't complain."

Beth produced her Sunday School material, and Jennifer sat on Harvey's bed cutting out flannel graph figures for her, while Beth settled in the living room to study the lesson book. Harvey seemed to drift off for a while, then Jennifer caught him watching her.

She leaned over and rubbed his cheek. "Are you going to grow a beard?"

"Nah," he said sleepily.

"It would look good on you."

"Think so?"

She studied his face, considering. "Well, maybe not."

He smiled. The corners of his eyes crinkled up. "I'll try to shave when Eddie comes back."

"I can help you."

"No," he sighed, "that would be dangerous."

She stooped lower and kissed the corner of his eye softly. Before he could react, she stood up and carried the scraps of flocked paper to the wastebasket. Turning, she said, "I want a picture of you in that bulletproof vest."

He gave her the look she had tried to describe to her mother. "Come back here."

"No." Although she was tempted. "You're the one who's dangerous."

"Me? I'm an invalid."

"Ri-ight."

He made a face. "Okay, then, can you get my Bible?" She got it and sat in the chair Mike had vacated. Harvey asked her to read to him from Genesis. He lay back and closed his eyes, and Beth came in after a while, bringing another chair. Jennifer read through the ark and the flood and the tower of Babel.

"He's asleep," Beth whispered when Jennifer paused at the end of the chapter. She stood up and pulled the sheet up a little, to Harvey's chest. "He's cute when he's sleeping."

Jennifer laughed. "Thanks for giving up your whole day for us."

"No problem."

When Eddie came back, Jennifer woke Harvey.

"Do you want to get up?" she asked him.

"If you're leaving, I do."

"So you can shave?"

"No, because you won't kiss me on the bed." He struggled to his feet and reached for her. She went into his arms. "Don't squeeze."

He flinched as she touched him, so she slid her hands up around his neck and let him hold her.

Eddie was so good to him that Harvey felt guilty for all the times he had yelled at him. He slept in a sleeping bag on Harvey's living room floor and helped him dress and shower and shave, and all the other things Harvey took for granted when he didn't hurt.

Jennifer came by the apartment in the morning,

before work. To Harvey's chagrin, he was still prone and hurting badly. She stayed a few minutes and left for Coastal, leaving him with a book on historic codes and ciphers.

Eddie went to work and apparently told Mike that Harvey was complaining. Mike's response was to call Carl Turner and beg him to make a house call.

Carl came late in the afternoon and listened to Harvey's lungs, then poked dispassionately at his muscles.

"Stiff?"

"More like excruciating agony."

"You shouldn't be here alone."

"Eddie will be here in an hour. I made him go to work, but he came over on his lunch hour and fed me."

Carl shook his head. "Well, You've got to get up and move. A hot shower might help. This is no way for our city's finest to be treated in his hour of need. Where's Goldilocks?"

"Working."

"Oh, right, computer stuff. You'd better marry her and take her out of the work force."

Harvey scowled. "You're telling me this? Your wife is a doctor."

"That's *why* I'm telling you this. Tell me you don't dream of coming home every night to a hot meal and a little cuddling, not necessarily in that order."

“What, Margaret’s quit cooking?” Harvey laughed.

“She’s always out nights, delivering babies. She’s seeing too many patients.”

“And this gives you license to put my life in order.”

“Just a little friendly advice.”

Harvey said nothing. He couldn’t argue too far, or he’d have to admit he did have dreams like that. Jennifer waiting at the door at the end of a trying day.

“Taking your meds?” Carl asked, putting his stethoscope to Harvey’s chest.

“Ever been shot? Ibuprofen doesn’t touch it.”

“Well, do you want to be lucid and in pain when Eddie gets here, or comfortable and unconscious?”

“I’ll tough it out,” Harvey said. “Jennifer’s going to be along, too.”

“Right. Lucid it is. Let’s get you in the shower.”

“I need to go to work tomorrow.”

“In your dreams. Give it over the weekend. Monday’s a holiday. I’ll tell Mike Browning you’re not allowed within ten blocks of the police station before Tuesday.”

Chapter 26

On Friday, Eddie was at Harvey's apartment when Jennifer got there after work.

"No ride to Skowhegan tomorrow," Eddie said sternly. "Doctor's orders. By Monday you should be up to it."

Harvey scowled. He still felt drained, but he didn't want to admit it.

"I've already told my folks we're postponing the trip until Monday," Jennifer said. "Stop fretting. I brought you something." From her purse she produced a hand-held computer game. "Cops and robbers. It seemed appropriate somehow."

Harvey smiled, but laid it on the quilt.

Eddie left to pick up a pizza, and Jennifer sat down in the chair and held Harvey's hand.

"You're getting better."

He sighed deeply. "How was work?"

"All right. Tessa called in sick, but it was probably her daughter who was actually sick. I did ask Jane about the translator."

"Anything come of it?"

"No, he's too juvenile for her to notice, I guess. But she did say something disturbing." Jennifer's gray eyes clouded. "She has a date tonight, and it's not Brent."

"So?"

"She usually can't tell me enough about her love life, but she's really clammed up this time."

"You think she's going out with someone you know? Someone from the office?"

"I'm not sure. I'm almost afraid she's getting involved with a married man or something."

"What were the partners up to today?"

"Not one of them spoke to me. Mr. Owen was on the road, and I saw a group of prospective clients go in after lunch. Mr. Channing showed them out an hour later. Mr. Rainey wasn't very visible today."

"This whole investigation is fizzling," Harvey complained. "I need to get on it."

"No, you don't," Jennifer returned heatedly. "You heard Eddie. Mike's working out the details with the federal agents. You need to rest and stay out of it."

Harvey sighed. Being powerless was totally demoralizing. "I don't see why we can't go to your folks' tomorrow."

Jennifer smiled. "Just take it easy. They'll still be there Monday. If you're good over the weekend, we'll have a great day together."

Harvey did his best to avoid looking petulant. "Can we at least go to Nick Dunham's memorial service tomorrow?"

Jennifer frowned. "I was hoping you'd forget about that."

"I haven't. Have you?"

"I was going to bring some cookies and tuck you in for a nap, then go to the service."

"I want to go."

"We'll see."

"How about we drop by the police station after the service? I'll use the elevator."

"Forget it."

Eddie agreed to drive Harvey to the church Sunday morning. Harvey was looking forward to it. He'd seen the wisdom of skipping the memorial service, and Jennifer had gone alone. Her description of Lisa Dunham and her fatherless children had only renewed his resolve to find Nick's killer. He'd been restless ever since and slept only when Eddie insisted he take his narcotic.

His ribs weren't quite as sore as they'd been the day before, and going down the stairs wasn't so bad.

Jennifer and Beth were waiting outside the church. They both looked great, and Beth was wearing one of Jennifer's skirts. Jennifer had on a blouse Harvey didn't recognize, but he thought might be Beth's. The roommate match was a success.

Eddie carried Harvey's Bible and walked with him to where the girls stood.

"Eddie, you look sharp! Are you coming

to church with us?" Beth asked, as Harvey clasped Jennifer's hand and gave her a private smile.

Eddie seemed embarrassed and kicked a rock with his toe. "No, I was going over to Mass. I haven't been for a while."

Ten steps led up to the front door of the church, and Harvey started up, then swayed back down off the first step, feeling a sharp tug in the muscles of his back. Jennifer stopped mid-stride and looked at him anxiously. He put one hand up carefully to her shoulder. Immediately Eddie was on the other side.

"Let me help you, Harv."

"Okay, but let's think about this. There's a ramp on the side of the building." Eddie went around with him to the handicapped access ramp, and Jennifer and Beth followed. With his arm around Eddie's shoulders, Harvey walked slowly up the ramp. They came into the auditorium from the side, and Eddie settled him in a pew about halfway back.

"Thanks, Eddie. I think I'll be okay now."

Beth headed for her Sunday School class, and Jennifer settled on the other side of Harvey. Eddie hovered in the side aisle.

"Maybe I should stay with you."

"I'm fine," Harvey said. "Beth's brother will help me if I need it." He looked around and saw Ruthann and Rick installing themselves farther back, on the other side. Ruthann and Jennifer exchanged waves.

"I think I should stay," Eddie said firmly.

Harvey looked up at him and realized he didn't want to be sent away. He felt a surge of tenderness for Eddie. Jennifer moved over, and Harvey hitched himself over carefully, so Eddie could sit beside him on the aisle.

Eddie sat nervously through Sunday School, alternately looking around and staring straight ahead, eyeing the side door anxiously once or twice, but he sat through the next installment on the book of Colossians.

Dick Williams read the scripture in chapter two, and when he reached verse six, *As ye have, therefore, received Christ Jesus the Lord, so walk ye in him,* Jennifer's hand nestled into Harvey's. He sat contented, trying not to think about the pain that still came with each breath.

Between Sunday School and church there was a break. Harvey looked over at Eddie speculatively. "You can still get over to the late Mass if you want to."

Eddie looked at his watch. "Nah."

"Okay, but I think I need to stand up for a couple of minutes."

"Pretty stiff?"

"Yeah."

Eddie stood and gave him his arm. Harvey

heaved himself to his feet and flexed his muscles a little, grimacing. Beth came and sat beside Jennifer, and the two of them started talking quietly.

"No candles," Eddie observed, nodding toward the pulpit. Harvey tried to imagine how different the church was from Eddie's. He remembered how uncomfortable he'd been two weeks before, when he and Jennifer had first walked through the door.

Pastor Rowland came up the side aisle, greeting people along the way. Harvey introduced him to Eddie, and he was sure the pastor knew Eddie was the one who had asked him about priests, but he didn't say anything about it.

"Pleased to meet you, Mr. Thibodeau," Pastor Rowland said, shaking Eddie's hand, then he turned to Harvey. "You're looking well. I'm so glad." Harvey forgot to warn him, and the pastor's handshake jarred his ribs.

Mr. Rowland stayed only a moment, then went up to the platform. Everybody sat down, and the hum of conversation gradually subsided. Small beads of sweat gleamed on Eddie's forehead.

"You okay?" Harvey asked.

Eddie glanced sideways at him. "Do you kneel? You might not be able to get up."

"We don't usually."

Somehow Eddie made it through the pastor's

message on God's mercy. Afterward Beth left in her car, and Harvey got carefully into Jennifer's. Mike had promised to drop in after lunch.

Harvey sat idle at his kitchen table while Jennifer and Eddie set out a light lunch. Cottage cheese, fruit salad, rolls and butter. They talked a little, and it was nice, Harvey thought, having two of his favorite people sitting at a table with him in his kitchen.

Jennifer got up to put a cup of coffee in the microwave for him.

"Do you think it counts that I went there?" Eddie asked.

"Counts?" Harvey wasn't sure what he meant.

"Is it a sin? For a Catholic to go to a Protestant church, I mean?"

"Oh, Eddie," Harvey said.

Jennifer turned and looked at him over Eddie's head. Her face was all compassion.

"It's never a sin to hear God's word, Eddie," she said. "The place doesn't really matter."

"But I know I'm not supposed to go there," Eddie persisted. "The priest wouldn't like it."

Harvey said, "God is what matters, and the Bible. If a church teaches you what the Bible says, then it's okay to go there."

Eddie still looked troubled as he took his coffee from Jennifer and stirred sugar into it. "You don't confess, do you?"

"Yes, we do," Harvey said. "We can confess anytime, just by talking to God."

"Really? He lets you?"

"Yes, Eddie, anytime." Harvey thought Jennifer was going to cry.

Mike knocked on the door just then, and Harvey tucked the conversation away, but he thought he and Eddie would get it out again later, in the truck, or when they ran, or at the diner.

Jennifer got coffee for Mike, and they all ate apple pie that Mrs. Jenkins had sent up.

"Well," Mike said, when he pushed his plate back, "I've got a little news. LeRoy Nason is still in ICU, but I got his story this morning. He says he never met the people who hired Bobby, never even knew who they were. Bobby went up to his place when the city got too hot for him after the first bomb. But he wanted to come back here and finish the job, because the client wouldn't pay him unless he got the hacker."

"The hacker?" Harvey pounced on it.

"That's right. LeRoy said Bobby was hired to take out a computer hacker. That would be you, I guess. He said Bobby got a make on your car and followed you. When Eddie drove the car to Bretons' and left you at the school, he followed the car. I guess he'd hung back so you wouldn't spot him and didn't realize it wasn't you in the car. He saw his opportunity while Eddie talked to Mrs. Breton and made his move." He turned to Eddie. "You are some lucky guy."

"Not lucky," said Jennifer. "God protected Eddie."

Eddie turned adoring eyes on Jennifer.

"If you say so," said Mike. "Anyway, Bobby brought LeRoy back with him to help him watch you around the clock, Harvey. They arrived in Portland on Saturday. Your new vehicle threw him off at first. Sunday morning they followed you to the church and planted the bomb. Bobby wired it to the ignition with a five-minute delay."

"Weren't they afraid of being seen?" Jennifer asked.

"It wouldn't take Bobby a minute, and the parking lot was full of cars, but everybody was inside. When there was no explosion, he realized he'd goofed again. The people who hired him were mad, and he and LeRoy decided to lie low for a while."

Harvey shook his head. "And all because I did the background check. I put so many people in danger."

Jennifer touched the sleeve of his jacket.

Mike looked at her. "And that brings us to your part in all this, young lady."

She returned his gaze gravely. She had a vulnerable look, and Harvey covered her hand with his.

"I ran the names you gave me," Mike said.

"Took a while. A fellow in the CIA worked on it last night. This Hamad is here on a student visa. He's from Tehran, and he's fluent in English, Arabic, and Farsi."

"What about Massal?" Harvey asked.

"They've linked him to a right-wing extremist group in Iran. He has a Turkish passport, though, and hangs around Washington a lot. He had an invitation to a dinner at the Iranian embassy May first. The CIA would love to get some dirt on him."

"Does he have diplomatic immunity?" Harvey asked.

"Don't think so."

"So, what do we do?" asked Eddie.

"Well," said Mike, "tomorrow's a holiday. I assume Coastal Technology will be closed, and even Washington likes their holidays."

Jennifer nodded. "I'm off tomorrow."

"And I think we should all take a day off," Mike said. "I'm supposed to get photos of Massal and Hamad from Washington, so Jennifer can identify them. On Tuesday, she can go back to work."

Harvey bridled at that. "Mike, is that a good idea? Jennifer could be in danger."

Mike shrugged. "She worked last week."

"I know, and I didn't like it then, either. If they've been after me all this time, they know I have a connection with Jennifer."

"We don't want to spook them. I told you, business as usual until everything is in place."

"So when do the feds come in?" Harvey asked.

"Well, we don't really have much," said Mike. "If we can prove this Massal at Coastal is the one the CIA is looking for, they'll be very interested. Short of that, they consider it a local thing, and they don't want to get involved. We don't want to yell for help and end up with egg on our faces if this mystery software turns out to be something that teaches Iranian toddlers to count to ten in four languages."

"We know it's more than that," Harvey said, "And we know Bobby Nason was hired to kill me."

"Well, we have LeRoy's secondhand word that the target was a computer hacker. But he never said it was a cop, and he claims he can't identify Bobby's employer. There's no proof he was hired by Coastal. The fact that you accessed their computer files is circumstantial." Mike shrugged.

Jennifer said, "But Nick Dunham—"

"Yes. Nick Dunham." Mike frowned. "When this is over, could you show the CIA's computer guru Nick Dunham's icon in the software? Assuming we wind up with a copy of it."

She nodded.

"And you could also show it to them in other programs Dunham designed?"

"I'm sure I could."

Mike nodded. "Could be enough to show motive. But we still have no particulars on who actually pulled the trigger."

Jennifer shuddered. "I'll do anything I can to help, Captain."

Mike smiled. "Just go about your everyday routine until the cavalry shows up. Keep things looking peaceful." He looked at Harvey. "You folks got plans for tomorrow?"

Harvey glanced at Jennifer. "We were going to drive up to Skowhegan."

"Do it. Call me when you get back. If there's anything new, I'll get together with you then." Mike looked around at the three of them. "Don't say one word about this to anybody," he cautioned, looking at Jennifer, then Eddie, then Harvey. "Not your roommate, not your mother, not your priest."

They all nodded solemnly.

Eddie met Jennifer at the door of Harvey's apartment Monday morning. It promised to be a warm day, and she wore cut-offs and a blue India gauze top, and her hair was plaited in a long braid.

"He wants to drive," Eddie said. "Don't let him."

"Don't worry, I won't."

Harvey came into the kitchen. "Hi, Jennifer." She thought he looked a little grouchy.

"Good morning. We're taking my car, and I'm driving."

"No, I want to take the Explorer."

"Absolutely not. You'd pop your rib."

They volleyed back and forth until Harvey agreed to let Jennifer drive the Explorer. It seemed the best compromise she could get, so she agreed.

Harvey wore jeans and sneakers and a dark green T-shirt, and carried a chambray work shirt to throw on over it. Eddie helped him solicitously down the stairs and into the Explorer, running back up again for his glasses. Mrs. Jenkins came out and handed him a box of cookies through the window, and at last they got away.

Jennifer took her time driving the short distance to the highway ramp, getting used to the feel of the controls. They breezed up the interstate, and she stopped for gas when they got to Skowhegan. Then she cruised around a little, showing him a few of the sights, first her high school and the state police barracks. She drove over the bridges, past the fire station where her brother worked, and down the crazy one-way street downtown, past the city police station and out Route 2 to the Great Eddy in the Kennebec River, then back up to the towering Indian statue.

They went on out to the farm, where her

parents and Travis and Randy waited for them. Leeanne and Abby came pounding down the stairs to hug Jennifer and meet Harvey. They would have hugged him, too, but Jennifer told everybody Harvey had a "no hugging" rule that day because of his ribs. He raised his eyebrows at her, but she couldn't interpret it.

"Jeff's on duty at the fire station, but he'll be here for lunch," Marilyn said. They all walked very slowly around the garden and into the barn to see Leeanne's baby goats. Then Harvey was ready to sit for a while.

"So you got the bombers," George Wainthrop said. Harvey had to tell the story of the shoot-out, and he told it well, but it made Jennifer a little queasy, hearing some of the details for the first time.

Travis and Randy pumped him for more gory cop stories, but Harvey looked at Jennifer and said, "Maybe something less violent. How about parlor games?"

"Parlor games?" Travis hooted, "You are *old!*"

Harvey smiled, and Jennifer knew he had chosen the anachronistic term for effect.

"Trivial Pursuit?" suggested Abby.

He glanced toward Jennifer. She shrugged, leaving it up to him. He looked at Randy and Travis. "Men versus women?"

"Yeah!"

"Oh-oh," Jennifer told Abby and Leeanne, "Harvey has a phenomenal memory."

"He'll know all the old movies and history," Abby teased.

After a spirited game, George started cooking chicken on the barbecue. Marilyn, Abby, and Leeanne carried vast amounts of food to the picnic table. Jennifer started to get up and help, but her mother said, "No, dear, you stay with Harvey."

Harvey wanted to get up and stretch, so she let him lean on her shoulder. They walked slowly out to where George tended the grill. The men started talking guns, and Harvey still leaned on Jennifer enough that she didn't dare remove her support.

Jeff drove in for lunch, peeled off his uniform shirt, and tossed it in his truck, so he wouldn't get barbecue sauce all over it. He and Harvey hit it off immediately. Jeff was twenty-eight, but he and Harvey found they had a lot in common. They both liked to shoot and reload and had an interest in aviation. Jeff told Harvey he had an interview and practical test scheduled for the second week in June with the Portland Fire Department.

"Come stay with me," Harvey said.

"You serious?" asked Jeff. "I was going to ask Jennifer."

"I have a roommate now," she reminded him.

"You can sleep on my couch," said Harvey, and Jennifer knew they were going to the furniture store soon. He told Jeff he was now on a first name basis with at least two Portland EMT's, and he made the ambulance ride with Eddie sound funny.

Marilyn called them for lunch, and everybody gathered. George's grilled chicken was some of the best Harvey had ever eaten, and Marilyn's potato salad would rival the best from any restaurant. Harvey wished he wasn't in pain, so that he could be a better guest, but he enjoyed the family dynamic tremendously.

Jeff went back to work after the meal, promising to call Harvey by the weekend for final arrangements. Jennifer helped her mother clean up the lunch things while her younger brothers and sisters played badminton. Harvey and George were left, companionable, on the porch.

"Abby's been out with an intern," Marilyn said fretfully as she washed up the silverware and serving dishes.

"Is he nice?" asked Jennifer.

"I'm not sure yet. I've only met him once."

"Well, did he make you feel uneasy?"

"He seemed a little slick, somehow," Marilyn said. "He's from Connecticut."

"There are nice people in Connecticut."

"Oh, I know, but he's not like Harvey."

Jennifer put her arms around her. "I love you, Mom."

Marilyn returned her embrace. "You two seem very happy together."

"We are."

"Did you go to church again yesterday?"

"Yes, we went in the morning. My new roommate, Beth, and Harvey's partner, Eddie, went with us." Jennifer told her a little about them, and Marilyn seemed pleased that her daughter was making nice friends in Portland at last.

Jennifer went to where Harvey and her father sat in lawn chairs, watching the badminton game. Harvey's eyes smiled first, then his lips, and he reached for her hand.

"Hey, gorgeous!" She thought her father's eyebrows twitched a little.

"Are you tired?" she asked Harvey.

"A little bit."

"Sack out in the hammock," George said.

Harvey did, and Jennifer went up to the attic to sort through some boxes full of her old books. She packed one box that she wanted to take back to Portland. About four o'clock, she went back out to the yard. Harvey still lay in the hammock, but he opened his eyes when she approached.

"I think we'd better head south," Jennifer told him.

"Already?" asked her father.

She looked at Harvey's face and tried hard to see what he wanted.

"I guess we should," he said, struggling to sit up. Jennifer reached out and braced him. "I've got to check in with my boss tonight."

"Didn't they give you sick leave?" George asked.

"Yes, sir, but I think I'll be ready to go back to work tomorrow." He stood up carefully, using Jennifer for leverage.

Everybody came around to say last things, and Jennifer sent Travis to the attic for her box of books. George brought Harvey a baseball cap with his company's logo on it. Leeanne begged Jennifer to let her come down for a while during the summer, and everyone called goodbye at once as they drove out of the yard.

It was suddenly very quiet. Jennifer looked over at Harvey. He was smiling contentedly.

Chapter 27

A nearly perfect day, Harvey thought. Jennifer's family had become his family, and her parents treated him like an old friend. He only wished he had felt better. He didn't argue about who was going to drive home. When they arrived at his apartment about six o'clock, he called Mike.

"I've got photos of Massal and the kid," Mike said. "Should I drive over now?"

"Sure, Jenny can take a look."

Harvey called Eddie next, and he said he'd come, too, and Jennifer called Beth, just to tell her they were back.

Jennifer suggested that Harvey lie down until Mike got there. He was on the verge of sleep when she brought his phone to him.

"It's your sister," she said. He thought she looked a little apprehensive as he took the phone. She turned and left the room.

"Harvey, this is Gina." She was closest to his age. He felt guilty that he hadn't called her in weeks.

"Hi, Gina. What's up?"

"I just heard that Carrie died last month. You . . . you knew, didn't you?"

"Yeah. Sorry, I should have told you. They didn't notify me 'til the last minute, and I wasn't exactly thinking straight."

"It doesn't matter. Did you go down for the funeral?"

"Yeah, I did."

"Was it totally gruesome?"

"Kind of."

"I'm really sorry. I hope it's closure for you."

"I think so."

"So how are you doing?"

"Not terrific, actually. I've got a cracked rib."

"Oh, what happened?"

"We had a little shoot-out last week. No big deal. I had my vest on."

"Harvey!" Gina cried, and he knew she knew he was downplaying the incident. "You got shot on your flak vest?"

"Yes, but I'm okay, really."

"They x-rayed you?"

"Yeah, I spent Tuesday night at Maine Medical, but it's nothing."

After she'd fussed a little and he had assured her he was healing, she said, "Hey, a woman answered your phone."

"Yes, that's Jennifer."

"Who is she?"

Who was she, as far as his sister was concerned? He hesitated a little too long. Gina said, "You're dating at last?"

"Gina, I'm in love."

"Finally!"

"You'll really like her."

"Does she make you happy?"

"Happier than I thought I'd ever be again."

"I love her already," said Gina.

When Mike and Eddie arrived, Mike opened a file and laid out six photos of men whose faces bore the signs of a Middle-Eastern heritage on the edge of the bed in a lineup.

"Definitely this one," Jennifer said immediately, touching one. Her anxiety rose, just from looking at the thin face and bushy eyebrows.

"You're sure?"

"Positive. He's Massal, the one I think is the buyer for the software." She looked at the others carefully. "This could be Hamad. I'm sorry, I'm not a hundred percent sure. I've only seen him a couple of times."

"That's okay," said Mike.

"What do we do?" she asked.

"Will they be at Coastal tomorrow?"

"I don't know. I kind of expect Hamad to be. The translation wasn't finished Friday. It's a big program."

"I'll call my man in Washington tonight and tell him we've got a positive ID on Massal. You go to work as usual in the morning. Act natural, and if all goes well, the CIA will pay a visit to Coastal Technology."

"What if they don't?" Harvey asked.

Mike frowned. "Plan B, I guess."

"Which is?"

"I don't know yet."

Harvey frowned. "I don't like it. Why can't she just call in sick?"

Mike shook his head. "No, they might be suspicious of Jennifer already. Remember she's played around with their pet project and given her notice, and she took a day off last week. If she doesn't show up for work again, they might realize what's up."

"Then put Eddie and me on surveillance outside Coastal," Harvey pleaded. "I want her to be safe."

Jennifer reached for his hand. She felt stronger, just knowing he wanted to protect her.

Mike scratched his chin, frowning. "No, Harv. I don't think so."

"Why not?"

"A., they might spot you. They all know what you look like. B., you'd probably waste an entire day sitting there. The CIA man is supposed to work with the Pentagon on this, but you know government agencies. It takes them a while to get their act together."

"Jennifer might need help," Eddie said.

Mike turned to Jennifer. "Do everything as usual, young lady. If you think something's out of whack at Coastal, you call us."

She nodded and tried to picture herself going in to work as a special agent. She wanted to be as dependable as one of Mike's policewomen on an undercover assignment. She could do it in a play, but this was too real. People she knew were suddenly recast as criminals.

"Unfortunately, these things happen," Mike said. "We've had industrial espionage in Portland before. It's just a step away from military spying. Your bosses saw a quick buck in selling some sort of military access to a hostile nation."

"Do you really think Jennifer will be safe in there tomorrow?" Eddie asked.

Mike said carefully, "I don't think we have a choice."

"I don't want her in there," Harvey said.

Mike sighed. "The way I see it, we've got to make it look normal, not scare them off before the feds are ready to act."

They argued for another ten minutes, but they came back to Mike's logic every time.

"I'll be fine," Jennifer told Harvey, squeezing his hand.

Mike stood up. "All right, I'm heading out. I'll call my CIA contact right away."

"You'd better get going, too, Ed," Harvey said. "Come pick me up at seven-fifteen in the morning and take me to the office. I'll be fine tonight."

"It's getting dark," Eddie said. "I don't want Jennifer to go down to her car alone, and you shouldn't go down those stairs and up again tonight, Harv."

"All right, but I've got something to say to Jenny. Give us a minute."

Eddie followed Mike to the kitchen. Harvey stood up slowly with a grimace and took Jennifer into his arms. She held him gingerly, knowing he was still in a lot of pain.

"I don't want anything to happen to you, Jenny. I don't want to scare you, but I'm scared myself."

"I'll be all right." But inside she had reservations.

"Let's pray." They clung to each other, eyes closed, and Harvey asked God to keep her safe. She didn't want to leave him that night. She had an inner strength now, but she would still be vulnerable when she walked into Coastal Technology alone.

Her hands rested softly on his back, where she could feel the adhesive tape through his shirt. His tender kiss became more intense, almost fierce, and after a few seconds, she pushed away from him gently, but firmly.

She put one hand up to his cheek. "Harvey, God is in control, not us." He closed his eyes and nodded.

Jack Rainey paced back and forth in his den, shooting uneasy glances at the thin young man who stood near the doorway.

"This is taking way too long."

"I told you, he's never alone." The young man pulled a pack of cigarettes from his shirt pocket.

"Don't smoke in here."

He scowled, but replaced the pack. "His cop buddy is with him all the time, or that blonde girl, and the old lady downstairs is like a watch-dog. I tried going to his apartment last night, but the French cop apparently lives there. This morning I went back, and the place was empty. I stuck around for hours, but no one showed."

"It's a holiday," Rainey said vaguely, toying with the cord to the window blind. Too bad Bobby Nason only bounced a bullet off Larson's vest. It would have been perfect if the detective had been killed while trying to capture Nason.

Rainey realized he had his back to the man, and turned around quickly, darting a glance toward him. "Did you go back this evening?"

"Yeah. The place is full of people."

"He's having a party?"

The man shrugged.

Rainey thought for a moment. "This job has to be done right away. If you can't get him alone, get him whenever you can. If his friend is with him, too bad. He probably plans to go back to work tomorrow. I suggest you be there when he leaves his building."

The young man winced. "I don't know. They're part of that hotshot police unit."

"Let me put it this way," Rainey said coldly. "You want the rest of your money? Do it. Within the next twenty-four hours. Preferably before you show your face tomorrow at Coastal."

The young man frowned and turned on his heel.

Rainey paced for a few more seconds, then went to the window and raised the blind. He watched the car pull out, then sat in his recliner and speed-dialed a phone number.

"Ron. Our man was just here. He's had some trouble getting at Larson."

"Don't tell me that cop is still breathing."

Rainey winced. "Seems his buddy's always with him. They're like well-armed Siamese twins."

Channing swore. "We're moving the material soon, Jack. Larson has got to be out of the way. Maybe Jennifer Wainthrop, too."

"No, we can't. That's too many people connected to the business. The cop we can make look random, but since Dunham . . ."

"She knows," Channing said. "We never should have let her have the whole thing."

"She had to have it."

"So she said."

Rainey took a deep, slow breath. "I'll check over the logs and see how much time she spent on it after we gave her access. But . . . I just don't see how we could do it, Ron. Are you prepared to move your family out of the country at short notice?"

There was silence for a moment, then Channing said softly, "Tell him to do his job, Jack. Larson will ruin us. And if needed, we have a good system in place here to take care of the other. Only this time, the car goes in the Atlantic, and the body stays with it. They can speculate for years, but they'll never be sure."

Jennifer was glad Beth was at the house with her, but it was hard not to tell her the details of the situation. Beth didn't ask, but Jennifer could tell she knew things were brewing at Coastal. After they prayed together Tuesday morning, Beth left for school.

"I'll keep praying for you today," she said as she went out the door.

Jennifer dressed carefully in gray pants, white blouse and black shoes, then braided her hair and coiled the braid tight on top of her head. She looked in the mirror and thought, *Harvey would hate this look.* She took it down and went for the plain braid, hanging down behind. She looked again. Her face was pale, and her eyes were too big. She got her purse and put her phone in her jacket pocket.

The phone rang as she was about to walk out the door.

"Hey, gorgeous! All set?"

"Yes. Where are you?"

"At home. Eddie and I are just heading out for

the office. I wanted to tell you again that I love you."

Jennifer took a deep breath. "I love you. It's going to be okay."

When she reached the office, Jane greeted her with, "Hi, Jenn! Did you and your honey go out this weekend?"

Jennifer did her best to smile and act carefree. "Yes, we went up to my parents' in Skowhegan yesterday." What would Jane say if she told her that her 'honey' had been shot last week and spent a night in the hospital, and was now making a gallant effort to protect her from international spies?

"So how was your weekend?" she asked.

Jane smiled and looked away. "Good. Really good."

Jennifer raised her eyebrows. "You're not seeing Brent anymore, are you?"

"Brent's history. His idea, not mine, but that's okay. I'm seeing someone else, and it may be important."

"Important? Jane, is this guy . . ." Jennifer stopped. She wasn't really sure she wanted to know.

Jane's brown eyes clouded. "Don't worry. He's . . . he's great."

Jennifer frowned. "Does he have a name?"

As she'd feared, Jane hesitated.

Jennifer stepped closer and whispered fiercely,

"Just don't tell me it's Mr. Rainey. Jane, I care about you."

Jane's stunned stare told her she was off the mark, and she was glad.

"No, it's not . . . who you said," Jane faltered, glancing about quickly. "It's . . . well, do you remember Aiden Schweitzer?"

"Brent's clumsy friend? Sure. What about him?"

Jane said nothing.

As the light dawned, Jennifer drew a sharp breath. "You're dating Aiden now?"

Jane turned away, tossing her dark hair. "I knew you'd hate it. That's why I didn't tell you. You think he's a boring klutz."

"I never said that. Okay, maybe I did, but . . . Jane, if you like him—"

"I do." Jane faced her with a fierce, protective set to her jaw.

"That's . . . great."

Jane sniffed. "Are you just saying that? Because I really do like him."

"So, that's why you didn't tell me about him . . ."

"Because you turned your nose up at him."

"I'm sorry. Are we still friends?"

Jane smiled. "Of course. Want to eat lunch together?"

"The feds have got to be interested, now that Jennifer's ID'd Massal," Harvey said as they left his apartment.

Eddie paced his steps down the stairway so Harvey could keep up. "Guess you'll be glad to have her working at the police station."

"I sure will. I don't know what she'll do after the temporary job ends. I think she wants a complete change."

"Change is good."

"You got any ideas?" Harvey asked.

"I think she should be a housewife."

Harvey tried unsuccessfully to glare as they reached the street door.

"Too far?" Eddie asked.

He shook his head. "Not too far."

Harvey pushed the door open and stepped outside the building. *Bang!* The edge of the door splintered next to his head. Harvey hit the pavement behind the rear tire of Eddie's pickup, and Eddie ducked back inside.

A wisp of movement between the cars parked parallel to the street caught Harvey's eye. He glanced back at the apartment building. Eddie had flattened himself beside the door frame, and his Beretta poked cautiously around the jamb.

"Harvey?" a thin voice quavered.

Harvey looked quickly and saw Eddie turning. "Stay inside, Mrs. J."

Eddie could deal with her, Harvey decided. He lay down to look between the wheels of the pickup.

Rebecca's voice came clear in the abnormal

silence. "What's going on? It sounded like a gunshot."

"It was. Call the cops," Eddie said.

"You boys *are* cops."

"More cops, Mrs. J. And keep inside."

Harvey eased his phone from his pocket and dialed the patrol sergeant's emergency line. "We've got a shooter on Arden Street. Send every unit you can to my house, Terry."

"You okay?" the sergeant asked.

"So far, but this guy's got me and Eddie pinned down, and there are civilians close by. I don't like doing this without Kevlar."

He hung up and punched Eddie's number.

"Yeah, Harv?" Eddie said softly in his ear.

"He's down the street a couple of cars. I can see his feet."

"Keep your head down."

"10-4. Is Mrs. J. out of sight?"

"That's affirmative."

"I called for backup. Should we wait?" Harvey asked.

"He might just fade away."

"Do we care?"

"Aw, Harv, we gotta get this guy."

Harvey sighed. "Discretion, Eddie."

"What?"

"The better part of valor."

"Whatever. I think he's moving."

Eddie burst from the doorway, firing rapidly.

Chapter 28

An hour after Jennifer got to work, Massal came in. After one swift glance, she avoided looking directly at him. In her peripheral vision, she saw him walk through the workroom and head down the hall toward the private offices.

She hadn't received any orders that morning, so she pulled up the neglected hospital program she'd begun months earlier and looked it over, refreshing her memory. Maybe she could finish it in her remaining few days with the company.

Half an hour later, Mr. Rainey came and stood by her desk.

The other partners dressed a little less formally, but Rainey always wore tailored suits and designer shirts with distinctive ties. In fact, his ties were often the talk of the office. His suit was gray today, with a white shirt and a red tie with a silver geometric motif, conservative for him. French cuffs must be back in, Jennifer thought, noting his monogrammed silver cufflinks. She was always a little intimidated when he was in the room.

"Jennifer, I'd like to see you for a moment in my office." He turned and walked away.

Her heart raced, and her breath came too fast. She stood up slowly and put her hand in her pocket, touching her phone briefly, for comfort. She told herself to be calm, that he was just going to give her work orders for the day. She walked slowly down the hall to his office door.

He stood with his back to her, looking out the window that faced the parking lot.

"You've had the confidential program out since you finished with it," he said with no preliminaries.

"I guess I did, on Friday." Jennifer strove for a light, normal tone while she struggled against anxiety. "I hope you're satisfied with it. I wanted to check it one last time, just for my own satisfaction."

"You think it will meet the client's rather lofty standard for security?"

She overcame her nerves, keeping the quiver from her voice. "It's definitely the most sophisticated security we've ever made. If we tightened it any more, the user would find it too cumbersome."

He turned toward her abruptly. "Have you had any contact with the police department recently?"

"The police department?" Fear stabbed her as she tried to think what to say. She couldn't lie in her new-found faith. Surely if she trusted God, He would protect her. "I was questioned after Nick Dunham disappeared. And my old roommate was arrested on a drug charge. I was there."

Rainey's piercing eyes looked directly into hers for once. "This detective handling the Dunham case. Have you seen him outside the office?"

Jennifer swallowed. "Yes."

He gazed at her then sat down at his desk and picked up a sheaf of papers clipped together and looked at them. She stood feeling awkward, wondering what he knew.

"Did this Detective Larson ask you to compromise the security of this company?"

"No, absolutely not."

He looked at the papers again. "But you are seeing him socially."

"Yes."

He looked full into her face.

"And your reason for leaving us is . . . ?"

"I told you, sir. I've been offered another job."

"More money?" His penetrating eyes made her shiver.

"No, that is—I—I thought it would be less stressful." She was floundering. She knew he had no right to ask her what the other job was paying, but she was too afraid to stand up to him. The tremor was there in her voice now.

He laid the papers down. "What are you working on today?"

"I pulled up that hospital program I started earlier, but if you want me to do something else, I can—"

"No, that's fine." He gave a dismissive wave, so she nodded and went back to her desk, thankful to leave his presence.

Jane watched her with wide eyes when she returned to her desk. Jennifer quickly opened the hospital program and immersed herself in it. When she went to the ladies' room just before lunch, Jane followed her.

"Jennifer," Jane hissed, closing the restroom door behind her.

"What?"

"Are you in trouble?"

She smiled and said, as innocuously as she could, "I hope not. Why?"

"There's a rumor," Jane said.

"What kind of rumor?"

"That Rainey called you on the carpet this morning."

"Nonsense. He just wanted to ask me about the security on one of the programs."

Jane looked down, then back at Jennifer. "Tom said he raked you over the coals about something you did."

"And if that were true, how would Tom know?"

Jane blinked. "Good point."

"This office gossip is sickening," Jennifer said.

The door pushed open, and Tessa Comeau came in. Jane and Jennifer said bright hellos, and busied themselves with combs and lip gloss.

"So, are you ready to go eat?" Jane asked, meeting Jennifer's eyes in the mirror.

"Sure. Where are we going?"

"Pizza Hut?"

"Too fattening."

"As if you have to worry," Jane said. "All right, the Chinese place."

"I like the Lotus," Jennifer said. "Let's go."

"Care if I join you?" Tessa asked.

"That's great," said Jane, shooting Jennifer a sidelong glance.

"Oh, there's one thing I have to do first." Tessa ran a brush through her dark curls. "How about if I meet you there? Order me a shrimp egg roll and some fried rice. I'll be right there."

Jane shrugged.

"Sure," said Jennifer.

She and Jane went out to the workroom. Massal was just walking out the door, carrying his briefcase.

"You boys always manage to find a little excitement." Mike stood on the sidewalk in front of the apartment building, watching as the medical examiner bent over the body of the gunman.

"I can only take so much bed rest," Harvey said.

"Well, he's the same kid Jennifer told us about, Hamad. First name Mohammed. He's a student at the university. Has a few priors. Assault, criminal threatening." Mike put a stick of gum in his mouth. "I'm having his apartment searched, and Pete's getting his phone records."

Mrs. Jenkins peeked out the doorway. "Harvey?"

He turned toward her. "Yeah, Rebecca? You okay?"

"I'm fine. I thought maybe you got shot again."

"No, I'm good," Harvey said.

Eddie grinned. "Me too, Mrs. J. And you did just right. Thanks for taking orders so well."

She nodded, glanced at Mike, and disappeared in the direction of her apartment.

"You two better come to the station and type up your statements," Mike said. "I want thorough reports on this one. Eddie, you know you'll have a review."

"Sure."

"What about Coastal Technology?" Harvey asked. "While we're filling out paperwork, they could be selling out the country."

Mike set his jaw. "We'll get them."

At the restaurant, Jane and Jennifer put in their orders and sipped tea. "So, how do your parents like Harvey?" Jane asked.

"They like him a lot."

"What's he like?"

"Well . . ." She stalled, wondering if keeping

the relationship from Jane mattered any more. Jane seemed so transparent and harmless. Or was she being naïve again? Until Nick Dunham's murder was solved, she'd be foolish to trust anyone at Coastal. "He's really nice, and he's smart and funny. He's a little older than me."

"Isn't he a computer buff?" Jane asked.

"Why do you say that?"

"Last time on the phone, you said something to him about software—adding names to a program or something."

Jennifer tried to remember what she and Harvey had talked about. "I guess that was something he was doing at work." She eyed Jane, wondering if she'd already confided too much to her.

The waitress brought their food, and while she arranged it, Tessa breezed in. "Jane, Mr. Channing wants you to go right back to the office."

"What?" Jane's didn't mask her incredulity.

"He's got potential clients for the utility program coming in at one, and he wants you to help him with the presentation."

"Oh, for Pete's sake, why couldn't he tell me this an hour ago?"

"Debra went home sick." Tessa slid into the booth next to Jennifer. "She was supposed to do it. You did a lot of work on that program, didn't you? I guess Mr. Channing figures you're familiar with it. He caught me just as I was leaving and asked if I knew where you were."

"Great. I don't even get to eat lunch."

"Eat, Jane," Jennifer said. "Five minutes won't make much difference."

Tessa looked from one to the other. "Fine. Do what you want. Tell him you didn't get the message in time. Personally, I'm hungry." She picked up her egg roll.

Jane sighed. "I suppose I have to go. Jennifer, sorry to mention it, but you drove."

"Here, take my car," Tessa said, holding out her key ring. "It's right out front."

"Thanks." Mournfully, Jane looked at Jennifer. "Would you mind having them put my meal in a carton?"

Tessa moved to the other side of the booth, and Jennifer began to eat. Tessa was watching her. "So, how are things going with the boyfriend?"

Jennifer chewed while she formed her answer. "Fine."

"Are you two serious?"

"Well, maybe." Jennifer smiled. "How's Courtney?"

"Good. She's good. Her father hasn't paid me any child support for two years, but she's a great kid."

Jennifer nodded and cast about mentally for another topic, but Tessa's daughter seemed safer than work. "How old is she now?"

"Just turned three."

They kept up a piecemeal conversation as they ate, but Tessa didn't seem inclined to linger. She broke open her fortune cookie, looked at it and laughed. "That figures."

"What?" Jennifer asked.

"*Happiness is an elusive treasure.* Isn't that the truth? What does yours say?"

Jennifer broke the brittle cookie and picked out the slip of paper. *"Faith will sustain you."*

Tessa's eyebrows arched. "Those aren't fortunes."

"I guess that's the oriental way." Jennifer shrugged, but inwardly she felt they were very appropriate. They paid for their meal and walked out to Jennifer's car. She placed Jane's carton of food carefully on the floor behind her seat.

"So, do you have faith, Tessa?" she dared to ask as she backed out of the parking space.

"No. Do you have happiness?"

"Well . . . yes, I'd say so." Jennifer pulled up at the exit to the parking lot, looking left toward the oncoming traffic. "It's so hard to get out of here."

"Turn right," said Tessa.

"And then turn around down below? It would probably be easier." Jennifer changed the turn signal to right, then cranked the steering wheel toward Tessa. A glance toward her passenger made her freeze.

In her right hand, Tessa held a pistol, low below the level of the car window.

"Just turn right," she said placidly.

Jennifer's lips trembled. She pressed them hard together and swallowed with difficulty.

"Tessa?" It came out as a plaintive squeak.

"It's clear. Drive," Tessa said harshly, looking beyond her toward the traffic.

Jennifer inched the car slowly down the block, trying to keep her hands steady on the wheel. "Where are we going?" she managed to whisper.

"I'll let you know. Go straight at this light."

Dear God, help me, Jennifer prayed silently. *This is what happened to Nick. Please don't let me die.*

The words of the psalm Harvey had given her the week before came back to her. She had read the chapter over and over, exulting in the grandeur of its promises. *I will say of the Lord, He is my refuge and my fortress, my God; in him will I trust.*

Slowly peace settled over her, and her prayer changed. *Whatever you want for me today is all right with me. But please don't let Harvey despair. If you want to take me to heaven, let him know he's not alone again.*

"Why are you doing this?" she asked aloud, amazed that her voice was steady and strong now.

Tessa gave a short, mirthless laugh. "You have no idea what it's like, do you? Being a single mother, having to do everything yourself. Being responsible for every breath your child takes."

Jennifer was startled. "What does this have to do with Courtney?"

"Everything. I'm doing this for my daughter."

Jennifer shook her head. "I don't understand."

"Financial independence, Jennifer. When I get out of this car, I'll have earned enough to take Courtney away and start over. No more day care. No more going to work every morning and leaving her screaming with a bunch of strangers. Somebody else heard her say her first word. Do you know how much that hurts? I had a nanny for a while, but it got too expensive. But you know what? She was calling the nanny Mama."

"Tessa, there are ways to work through your problems."

"You bet there are." Tessa raised the gun a bit. "Get into the left lane and get ready to turn."

Harvey pushed his computer to capacity while Eddie filled out reports.

"Harv, we may have something," Mike called across the room.

Harvey swiveled his chair to face him.

"Pete's found out Massal and Hamad are both booked on a plane to New York tonight."

Pete Bearse stood beside Mike's desk. "Massal is going on to Paris and Tehran," he said.

Harvey sat still for a moment. “Tonight.”

“Right.”

“That program is being sent out today.”

“For sure,” Mike said. “If the CIA wants the software, they’ll have to move fast. I’m calling them now. And Pete, alert airport security, just in case he gets by us.”

“Maybe we should get over to Coastal,” Eddie said. “They could be sending the program over the internet right now.”

Mike reached for his phone. “I’ve sent Arnie to the courthouse for the warrants. He should be back any second.”

“Let’s go, Eddie. Get your vest.” Harvey started for the locker room.

“No, wait,” Mike said in a tone that brooked no argument. “You two can’t go storming in there alone. You’ll tip them off, and half the suspects will get away. Just give me ten minutes to set it up, Harvey. I figure we need at least ten men.”

“But every minute we delay makes it more likely they’ll get away.”

“Come on, Harv,” said Eddie. “We’ll go get a sandwich at the diner, and Mike will be ready when we get back.”

“That’s good,” Mike said, and turned back to his phone.

Harvey sighed and glanced at his watch. It was a quarter to one. As he and Eddie trudged down the stairs, he pulled out his cell phone and punched Jennifer's code. Eddie said nothing.

Harvey listened as the phone rang once, twice. It might take her a moment if she had it in her purse. There was a click and then a sharp, "Give me that." He stopped on the stairs in surprise, but now he heard nothing.

"What?" Eddie asked, turning to look back at him from the landing.

"Something strange." He pushed Jennifer's number again. This time the phone rang repeatedly, but no one answered. Harvey scowled.

"You got Jane Morrow or John Macomber in your phone contacts?"

"Probably." Eddie took his phone out and scrolled down the screen. "There."

He handed Harvey the phone, and Harvey tapped on John's name.

"Hello?"

"Is Jennifer Wainthrop there, please?"

"Uh, no, I'm sorry. She's at lunch. Do you have her number?"

"Yeah. Do you happen to know where she's eating today?"

"No, sorry."

"Thanks."

Harvey hung up and looked bleakly at Eddie. "Jenny didn't answer her cell phone. Macomber says she's out to lunch."

"Probably nothing," said Eddie.

"I heard another person say 'Give me that.' I'm going over there."

Pick up the shield of faith, Jennifer told herself. Although the depth of her danger weighed on her mind, she was conscious of signs of God's faithfulness. Even her fortune cookie had given her a reminder.

As she slowed for another traffic light, the clicking of the door locks startled her.

"What—?"

The rear passenger door opened as she spoke, and she was aware of another person sliding smoothly into the back seat. Jennifer caught her breath and stared into the rearview mirror.

The man handed Tessa an envelope. She glanced inside it, then shoved it and her pistol into her purse.

"So long, Jennifer." Tessa opened her door and hopped out of the car.

"Drive."

Jennifer took a shaky breath.

"Your light is green. Drive," said Massal.

Chapter 29

Harvey's fingers shook as he fastened the Velcro closure on his Kevlar vest. It was too soon to be going into high risk again.

"I'm coming with you," Mike said from the doorway. He crossed to his locker. "Lights, no siren. Terry's sending six units of backup."

The guard at Coastal Technology looked startled when Mike showed his credentials.

"Let's not call anyone," Mike said sternly as the man reached to call inside. He left Eddie outside to make sure the guard didn't forewarn anyone in the offices and to deploy the other men.

Harvey strode into the work room. Jennifer's work station was vacant, and so was Jane Morrow's. He looked slowly around the room. About a third of the chairs were empty. He glanced at his watch. Ten after one. He walked briskly between the desks, sensing Mike on his heels.

He stopped by one of the recliners. "You're Macomber?"

The man looked up in surprise. "Yes."

"I'm detective Larson."

"Sure. I remember. Did you call me?"

"Yes. Did Jennifer Wainthrop return?"

"I haven't seen her." John Macomber stared at him.

"How about Jane Morrow?"

"In the conference room with—no, there she is now." He nodded toward the end of the room, and Harvey saw Jane come in from the hallway and go quickly toward the coffee station.

"Thanks." He hurried after Jane.

"Miss Morrow!"

Jane jumped and whirled around, nearly dropping the coffee pot.

"Oh! You scared me."

"I'm Detective Harvey Larson."

She nodded. "Yes, I—Harvey? Oh." Her brow furrowed.

"Do you know where Ms. Wainthrop is?"

"Well, I left her about an hour ago, having lunch at a Chinese restaurant."

Harvey felt the first inkling that he may have overreacted. "You ate lunch together?"

"She ate. I didn't. I was called back to the office. She should have been back by now with my doggie bag." Jane frowned at her watch. "Oh, well, guess I'll have to make do with coffee with the clients."

"Wait." Harvey put out his hand to detain her. "Jennifer's overdue from lunch?"

"Only a few minutes. But still . . ." Jane's dark eyes were troubled. "It's not like her. She's very conscientious."

"I know."

"You know?"

"I know."

"You're Harvey."

"Yes."

Jane nodded. "I thought you were just some computer guy. I mean, that Jennifer's boyfriend was just . . . Oh, man." Jane's face crumpled. "Why doesn't your partner like me?"

Mike cleared his throat.

"Jane, this is important," Harvey said quickly. "Were you with Jennifer when she got a call on her phone?"

"No."

"Was she alone when you left her?"

"No, she was with Tessa."

Harvey's apprehension returned, greater than ever. He glanced at Mike. "Tessa Comeau also worked on the special project."

Mike nodded.

Jane was clearly alarmed now. "You think something happened to Jennifer and Tessa?"

"The restaurant?"

"The Lotus."

"Do you have the phone number?" Harvey asked.

"At my desk. Do you know where my desk is? I—I really need to get back to the conference room. Mr. Channing will be upset if I don't."

"He's in there now?"

"Yes, with potential customers."

Mike, meanwhile was working his phone rapidly. "Got the number, Harv. I'll call the restaurant." He stepped away.

"Where are Rainey and Owen?" Harvey asked.

"Mr. Owen's gone to Boston, and Mr. Rainey's here. Somewhere," Jane said. "In his office, I guess."

Harvey nodded. "Please don't tell the partners we're here."

"O . . . kay."

He let her go. Mike beckoned to him, near the front door, and Harvey went to him. Mike faced him soberly.

"Harvey, I'm sorry. Jennifer and the woman who was with her left The Lotus at least half an hour ago."

"But it's only five minutes from here."

"Yes. I put out an APB on Jennifer's car."

Harvey looked at him, not wanting to understand, but his brain insisted on clicking through the possibilities.

"Thanks, Mike."

"Maybe you should sit down."

"I'm fine."

"All right, the boys will be here any second with the warrants."

Harvey nodded. "I suggest we make sure Rainey and Channing don't slip out the back door in the meantime."

"And we'll be able to lay our hands on the special software?"

"Jennifer thinks she might be able to get into at least her part of it, but we're not sure about the full thing. I'm hoping I can find something in one of the partners' offices that will help."

The door opened, and Eddie came in. "We're all set. I've got six men around the perimeter and four for in here."

Mike nodded. "Extreme caution, Eddie." His phone whirred, and Mike flipped it open.

"Browning." Mike's eyes flicked to Harvey. "Okay. Got it. Thanks." He put the phone in his pocket, frowning with regret. "Harvey, I'm sorry."

"What is it?"

"Jennifer's car has been involved in an accident on Brighton Avenue. The 1200 block. Go. We've got things covered here."

The ambulance pulled away as Harvey arrived. Three black and white city patrol cars were lined up to one side with their blue lights flashing. Harvey double-parked his Explorer and hurried past the patrolman directing traffic. He recognized the officer who stood next to the first marked car.

"Detective Larson," he said, waving his badge. "What happened?"

The uniformed officer blinked at him. "Hey,

Larson. One car. Side-swiped that utility pole pretty hard. They took the guy to Maine Medical."

"Guy?"

"Yeah."

"Wasn't there a woman in the car?"

"Yeah, she was driving. She's shook up, but she'll be okay."

"Where is she?"

The officer nodded toward the next car. Harvey walked toward it, half afraid he would find Tessa Comeau there.

Jennifer looked very small, sitting in the squad car. Her face was streaked with tears. Harvey opened the door, and she caught her breath and stared up at him.

"Hey, gorgeous."

Very slowly, she lifted her arms.

"Are you okay?" He pulled her to her feet and put his arms around her. She clung to him with all the tenacity he could have hoped for.

"I hit the telephone pole," she whispered, burrowing her face into his collar. "They think I'm a dumb blonde."

"You're not."

She gulped. "He wasn't wearing his seat belt, and I was. I figured it was worth a shot."

"It was perfect."

"I think Massal's hurt bad, Harvey. And Jane's rice is all over the place."

He smiled and patted her shoulders. “It’s okay, baby. It’s okay.”

Still she didn’t loosen her hold around his neck. He turned around and leaned against the squad car, holding her. One of the patrolmen came toward them, but stopped a few paces away.

“Where’s Tessa?” Harvey asked.

Jennifer pushed away and looked up at him, her big gray eyes rimmed in red. “I don’t know. She got out when Massal got in. You know about Tessa?”

“I’m putting it together.”

“She threw my phone out the window. That was you, wasn’t it?”

“Yeah, that was me. Couldn’t stand to go a whole shift without talking to you.”

She pulled in a ragged breath, and he hauled her in close again. Deep, wrenching sobs started low in her chest and wracked through her.

Harvey held her, stroking her head and shoulders. “It’s okay.”

“God was with me,” she choked.

“Yes, God was with you.”

Beth and Harvey babied her that night. After the shock wore off, Jennifer discovered that her nose hurt and her cheeks felt as though she was sunburned. The airbag had left its mark. She couldn’t think about food without feeling nauseous, and Beth made a pot of peppermint tea in their kitchen. Beth pampered Harvey, too, and fed him supper, not letting him do anything to help.

"You're still healing," she insisted.

Mike called and talked to Harvey for a long time, then Harvey sat on the couch with his arms around Jennifer and told her the CIA was very happy with her and the Portland P.D. Priority Unit. He had called the Boston Police Department, and they had detained Bart Owen, who was so shocked by what they told him that he cooperated.

With Owen's help and passwords Jennifer and John revealed, the CIA's best computer man had cracked the secret program, and they were turning it over to the Pentagon.

"Owen says they hadn't sent it out yet," Harvey said. "The last bit of translation wasn't finished, and—and their translator couldn't do it today."

"So the client didn't get it," Jennifer whispered.

"No. No one else got the whole program. The CIA isn't done analyzing it—that will take a while. But they think the program would have let the Iranians access our most confidential military files."

"What happened at Coastal after you left?" she asked.

"Mike and Eddie rounded up the partners and

Tom Henderson. We'll be looking closely at all the employees."

"And Mr. Owen was arrested in Boston?"

"Yes. They don't think he was in on Dunham's murder."

"No? I'm glad. He was nice to me."

Harvey nodded. "Mike's thinking all three partners went into the deal with Massal, but when Nick learned what they were doing, Rainey and Channing made the decision to have him killed. They're claiming Massal insisted."

Jennifer sobbed, and he held her closer.

When she was calm again, he wiped the tears gently from her cheeks and said, "Jane told them Tessa wouldn't leave town without her daughter, and she was right. They picked Tessa up at the day care when she went for the little girl."

"She wasn't the one who shot Nick," Jennifer said with certainty.

"No, she was just the decoy. But they were paying her well to be convincing."

"I didn't suspect a thing."

Harvey shrugged. "The up side is that you don't have to go back to work there again. Coastal Technology is dissolved, and a court will decide what's going to happen to the company's assets."

"So what do I do now?"

"Just rest until your new job starts." He stroked

her hair as her head came down gently on his shoulder. "You know, I almost bought stock in Coastal last week."

"What about Hamad, the translator?" Jennifer asked. "Is he going to be charged, too?"

Harvey looked over at the Van Gogh print. "He, uh—" He looked down into her persistent gray eyes. "He's dead."

She took a deep breath, but she didn't ask him what happened. Instead, she whispered, "They were going to kill you. Massal said in the car that they sent someone to shoot you today. He told me you were probably already dead."

"I'm not." He held her head against his shoulder.

Beth came in from the kitchen and shook her head at the sight of them.

"You both need some recovery time, Harvey. You'd better go home and get some sleep. I'll get Jennifer to bed."

"Guess you're right." He tipped Jennifer's face up and kissed her tenderly.

She sniffed. "I'm sorry I fell apart."

"Jenny, Jenny. You were terrific."

Harvey drove with Jennifer up to Rockland in his Explorer that Saturday. Jennifer had been home to Skowhegan for two days, and her mother and sisters had fussed over her and made her rest. Harvey had worked with the CIA unit all week, helping them check other programs they found in Coastal's vault, looking for other illegal operations, and acting as liaison for the Portland P.D. Every day the press wanted more information on the spy case.

They walked out to the lighthouse on the breakwater. Harvey kept Jennifer's hand in his as they stepped over the cracks between the uneven granite blocks. It was a long walk out the causeway, nearly a mile, and when they got to the lighthouse they were ready to sit for a while. Beyond the house that supported the square beacon tower, they claimed a big rock part way down the drop toward the water.

Other people were standing and sitting on the rocks, looking out over the harbor. Harvey sat with his arm around Jennifer for a long time, facing out to sea.

A schooner put out from Rockland, and it came quite close to the lighthouse. Tourists who had paid handsomely for the cruise worked the rigging, and the sails went up as the ship passed. They watched in silence as it moved past the breakwater and out toward the bay. Seagulls landed on the rocks below them and picked at the seaweed.

"How could I not have known they were making spy programs?" Jennifer asked at last. "I feel so stupid."

"Most of the programs were legit."

"I should have—"

"Stop, Jenny. That building was full of smart people, and you were one of the few to pick up on it. Don't make it your fault. It isn't." He squeezed her a little, and got just a twinge from his sore ribs.

They sat a few minutes more. Jennifer asked a woman they didn't know to take a picture of them. "To show Eddie and Sarah," she said. The woman was happy to click the photo on Jennifer's phone. They were adding to the catalog of happy memories. Harvey liked that.

When they started the long walk back, the wind came up, whipping Jennifer's hair all over. Harvey took a picture of her on the causeway, with boats in the background and her hair swirling. Then he kissed her, and she protested because it was a public place, but not too much.

On the seaward side of the breakwater, gentle waves began to wash over the tumbled granite slabs that dashed them into foam, and the spray splashed up toward them.

They stopped for lobsters at a shorefront restaurant, then headed home, down Route 1. Harvey spotted a used book shop, and the Explorer seemed to turn in at the drive of its own accord.

Classical music was playing when they walked in. "What is that?" Harvey asked, jerking his head toward the speaker over the counter.

"Handel's *Water Music*," said Jennifer.

The bookstore was perfect, all short hallways and little rooms by topic, and shelves from floor to ceiling packed with used books, thousands upon thousands. The store was bigger than it had looked from outside, with alcoves and crannies and dead ends everywhere. Larger rooms led into one another.

Harvey got sidetracked in Aviation, and Jennifer wandered on down the aisle. He saw her disappear into History. He went looking for her and stopped a few minutes in Criminal Justice, which filled a nook about the size of a phone booth. It took him a while to find her. He went through Biography and Cookbooks and into Fiction. Then it was genre fiction, and he meandered through Westerns, Sci-Fi, and Suspense. He had thought he would find her there.

She was way back in Romance, which surprised him, with a paperback in her hand. He was sure there was nobody within three crannies, so he put his arm around her and kissed her cheek. She looked up at him and smiled. "Hi!"

"It's so romantic in here. Whatcha reading?"

"Elizabeth Cadell." She held up the book and he read the title, *The Toy Sword.*

"I don't know this author."

"You'd like her. She's an older author. A lot of her books have mysteries in them."

He kissed her again, finding her lips this time. Elizabeth Cadell fell to the floor with a thump.

"Harvey, you can't do that in a bookstore," she said softly.

"But Romance is all around us."

She cuddled down against his chest, and he held her.

"Jennifer, I love you. Will you marry me?"

She sighed.

The music coming softly over a speaker changed to Pachelbel's *Canon in D*. That he recognized.

"I love that piece," said Jennifer.

"Come down the aisle to it."

"If you want."

His arms tightened. "Is that a yes?"

"Yes."

He kissed her again, thoroughly this time, amid the floor-to-ceiling Romance. She pushed him away. "You can't do—"

"Yes, I can. Marry me soon."

"How soon?"

"Tomorrow."

She laughed. "Can't. It's too soon."

"Next week, then."

"Can't."

"Why not?"

"It wouldn't be fair to my family."

"They can be there."

"Yes, but I'm the first child getting married. We have to have the church, and engraved invitations, and my sisters in formal gowns, and you and Eddie in tuxedoes."

"We do?"

"Definitely." She snuggled in again.

"Okay. Two weeks."

She laughed again.

"How soon, minimum?" Harvey asked.

"Six months."

"One month," he countered.

"Three."

He kissed her.

"One month," he said.

"Two."

"One." He kissed her again, both his hands in her hair.

"Six weeks, and that's my limit," she said, close to his ear.

"Six weeks, then."

Footsteps approached the doorway of the Romance room. He stooped to pick up the book she had dropped.

"Come on," he said. "You promised me you'd help pick out a sofa."

Discussion questions for *The Priority Unit*

1. Harvey is firm about keeping his personal life separate from his professional duties, but that's hard when he meets Jennifer. Eddie, on the other hand, blurs the lines. What can these two learn from each other?

2. Why does Tim call Harvey, when the rest of the Lewis family would be just as happy if he didn't know about the funeral?

3. Carrie's grandmother plays a small but pivotal role in Harvey's faith journey. How does God use this sweet elderly woman to draw him closer?

4. Harvey's supposed to be the one with a past, but Jennifer made a bad choice in college and had to break off a romantic relationship gone bad. Now she wants to forget it, but it will come back later to be dealt with. What could she have done in this book to avoid a future confrontation between Harvey and "College Joe"?

5. Harvey is uneasy working with female officers. He doesn't hate women, he says.

He just doesn't like to see them frisking suspects and shooting at criminals. Is Harvey hopelessly old-fashioned, or does he have a point? How can he step into the modern age on this front? What encouragement could Jennifer give him?

6. Mike is both a boss and a friend. What good things do you see in his relationship with Harvey?

7. Mike says frankly that his wife believes the Bible, but he doesn't. He tells Jennifer, "I believe in Justice." What would you say to Mike?

8. Eddie's French-Canadian background and family have a profound influence on him. How is Eddie different because of it? What concessions does he make to his roots?

9. Jennifer says women all want to mother Eddie or marry him. How does this personality get Eddie in trouble? How does it save him?

10. Would you accept a proposal in a bookstore? Harvey negotiates the engagement period down from six months to six weeks. Is Jennifer wise to drop her final offer so low?

About the Author

Susan Page Davis is the author of more than seventy published novels. She's a two-time winner of the Inspirational Readers' Choice Award, and also a winner of the Carol Award and two Will Rogers Medallions, and a finalist in the WILLA Literary Awards and the More Than Magic Contest. A Maine native, she lived for a while in Oregon and now lives in Kentucky. Visit her website at: www.susanpagedavis.com, where you can sign up for her occasional newsletter and read a short story on her romance page. If you liked this book, please consider writing a review and posting it on Amazon, Barnes & Noble, Goodreads, or the venue of your choice.

Find Susan at:
Website: www.susanpagedavis.com
Twitter: @SusanPageDavis
Facebook: https://www.Facebook.com/susanpagedavisauthor

Center Point Large Print
600 Brooks Road / PO Box 1
Thorndike, ME 04986-0001 USA

(207) 568-3717

US & Canada:
1 800 929-9108
www.centerpointlargeprint.com